Until She Comes Home

Also by Lori Roy

Bent Road

Until She Comes Home

LORI ROY

DUTTON

DUTTON
Published by the Penguin Group
Penguin Group (USA) Inc., 375 Hudson Street,
New York, New York 10014, USA

USA | Canada | UK | Ireland | Australia | New Zealand | India | South Africa | China

Penguin Books Ltd, Registered Offices: 80 Strand, London WC2R 0RL, England
For more information about the Penguin Group visit penguin.com.

Published by Dutton, a member of Penguin Group (USA) Inc.

First printing, June 2013
10 9 8 7 6 5 4 3 2 1

REGISTERED TRADEMARK—MARCA REGISTRADA

LIBRARY OF CONGRESS CATALOGING-IN-PUBLICATION DATA
Roy, Lori.
  Until she comes home / Lori Roy.
    p. cm.
  ISBN 978-0-525-95396-8 (hardcover)
  I. Title.
  PS3618.O89265U58 2013
  813'.6—dc23
  2012031919

Printed in the United States of America
Set in Fairfield LT Std
Designed by Alissa Amell

PUBLISHER'S NOTE
This book is a work of fiction. Names, characters, places, and incidents either are the product of the
author's imagination or are used fictitiously, and any resemblance to actual persons, living or dead,
business establishments, events, or locales is entirely coincidental.

Because once was not enough. . . .
To
Bill, Andrew, and Savanna

Until She Comes Home

CHAPTER ONE

M alina Herze stares down on her dining-room table, her lovely dining-room table, and clutches a red-handled hammer to her chest. Her best linen, line dried and ironed this morning, still bears the round stains left by two water glasses. They sat on the table for almost four hours before Malina poured the tepid water down the drain. A highball glass still sits alongside her husband's place setting, the ice melted and the drink inside ruined. On paydays, Mr. Herze likes a scotch and Vernors. That's today. Payday. Every Wednesday of every week—the day he brings home the sweet, musky smell Malina has washed from his shirts for exactly one year.

That must be why, at this late hour, Malina's driveway stands empty. It's been one year. An anniversary, of sorts. There's no reason Mr. Herze should stray. Malina's waistband is looser than the last time she wore this skirt, hangs lower on her sharp hipbones. She's not one ounce heavier than she was twenty-five years ago when she and Mr. Herze wed. He was almost thirty then; she, seventeen. He liked her the way she was—thin and slight. Don't go changing on me, he had said. And she hasn't. She weighs not one ounce more. No reason for Mr. Herze to stray. No good reason.

Walking from the dining room to the foyer, her white heels most probably denting the linoleum, Malina drops the hammer in her brown leather handbag, the largest of all her handbags. The tool, taken from the pegboard over Mr. Herze's workbench, is rather heavy given its size. If called upon to defend herself with it, she may well have to use both hands. The women, Mr. Herze's girl most certainly among them, come on payday when the men are sure to have money. They stand in the broken-out windows of the warehouse next door to the factory where all the men work. Most say the women are colored. Even now, Malina can imagine the smell of Mr. Herze's girl as if it has come so many times into her home that it has seeped into the walls and the upholstery and the flocked drapes hanging in her living room.

In the hall mirror, Malina smooths her hair, reapplies a red lipstick suited for evening, wipes a black smudge from under one eye, and, lastly, pulls on her driving gloves. Once outside, she glances up and down Alder Avenue. Perhaps none of the neighbors have noticed the empty spot in her driveway where Mr. Herze's car should be parked. Every night, he arrives home at 5:45 sharp. Every night, save this one, so of course, the neighbors have noticed. Even now, a few curtains ruffle where they're peeking out to see if her husband has yet arrived home, and directly across the street that ridiculous Jerry Lawson goes so far as to wave at Malina. Clad in no more than an undershirt and boxers, the man stands at the end of his driveway, where he's watching over that wife of his as she strolls their baby down the street and back. Nearly a month ago, Betty Lawson marched into her house, a new baby swaddled in her arms though she had never carried one in her belly. Adopted, all the neighbors had whispered. Before she suffers any further embarrassment, Malina hurries across her brittle lawn, slips into her car, and slowly, because the glare of the streetlights does so trouble her, drives toward Willingham Avenue.

Every morning, Malina and the other ladies board the bus and travel to Willingham Avenue to do their daily shopping. From the deli or the bakery or the cleaners, the ladies can look to the end of Willingham, where it dead-ends into Chamberlin Avenue in a T-junction, and see the factory where their men make a living. While dashing about, bags slung over their arms, the ladies can also see the warehouse where the colored women gather on paydays, but the ladies are afraid of what they might see there and so they cling to their wares and take only fleeting glances.

Malina rolls to a stop in front of Mr. Ambrozy's deli and turns off the ignition. At night, under a glare that isn't so troublesome because most of the streetlights don't work in this section of the city, the shops have lost their foothold and seem to hover, loosely rooted, above the dark street. Next to the car, the easel where Mr. Ambrozy writes his daily specials still stands in the middle of the sidewalk. He never erased today's specials—thick-cut chops and flank steak—and the white chalk letters are smeared as if someone drew a finger across them. Double-checking that the doors are locked, Malina rests her head against the seat, closes her eyes, and begins to count. At her last appointment, Dr. Cannon insisted this would relax her and that she need only practice the technique.

When she reaches twenty, her heartbeat has not slowed and the tightness in her throat has not softened. If she tells Dr. Cannon of this failure, he'll say that she need only practice more often and that the failing is hers.

As expected, Mr. Herze's car is parked in the lot next to the factory where he spends his days. While the other men labor with the tool-and-die machinery, Mr. Herze acts as their boss. The simple rust-colored brick building is surrounded by a chain-link fence that sags in some spots and is rusted through in others. The factory is hanging on, just barely, Mr. Herze sometimes says. Staring at the lone car looking more like a shadow than an automobile, Malina has no idea what she is to do now that she has found her husband. She'd had plenty of time to formulate a plan as she sat alone at her dining-room table for several hours, a supper growing cold and dry in her kitchen, the empty spot in her driveway shouting out to the neighbors, but she squandered the time with anger. It's quite likely, in the hours, days, weeks, or months to come, she'll remember this as her first mistake.

A dozen or so times over the years, Mr. Herze has forgotten his lunch and Malina has delivered it to him. She has always used the side door just off the parking lot when visiting Mr. Herze on those days. This is the door that opens. A person—a small, dark person—appears in the doorway. She stumbles because the door is so heavy. Malina has done the same several times. A woman, or perhaps she is still a girl. Little more than a child. Long, thin legs. Narrow hips. She wears tapered blue slacks that hug her ankles and a white blouse and is no taller than Malina, both of them childlike in size. Of course she would be small. Petite, even. Just like Malina.

4

Standing partly in the shadows thrown by the building and partly in the glow of the closest streetlight, the girl rights herself and tugs at the tail of her blouse. This person, this small, dark person, doesn't glance about as if feeling guilty, and neither does she look behind as if wondering who might have followed her. Instead, she turns sharply to her left and, taking strides that appear quite long, not because she is tall but because she is slender and lean and certain of her movement, she vanishes into the shadows that hug the side of the factory. Malina reaches for the ignition, tries to throw the car into drive before she has started the engine, and fumbles with the parking brake, but she drops her hands to her lap when the girl reappears.

She moves with the same sense of purpose, or perhaps she moves with the confidence that comes from having done a thing several times before. Her back is straight and her chin is cocked high, almost as if she is proud. The girl, the small, dark girl, pushes a baby carriage. Malina falls back against the seat. The girl crosses through the parking lot, turns onto the sidewalk, and walks toward the Detroit River.

Of all things—a baby carriage.

Grabbing the leather bag from the seat next to her, Malina throws open the car door. The air here is cooler than on Alder Avenue and tinted with the smell of dead fish and damp, rotting garbage. It's the river. During her days spent shopping on Willingham, she forgets that the river runs nearby. She should get back into her car, start up the engine, drive home, and return to her upholstered seat at the dining-room table. The veal and creamed cucumbers will be ruined by now, but she could serve them anyway because

Mr. Herze does so hate waste. She knows from all her married years that if she is to walk down this street, she is putting herself in the path of a danger not even her hammer will be able to fend off. But there is a carriage, a baby carriage. She'll be quick about it. One glimpse is all she needs. What harm could such a small person do her? Any one of the ladies would do the same.

The girl is past the factory and half a block ahead of Malina. The high-pitched squeal, rhythmic and slowly fading, must come from the carriage's metal wheels. Reaching the sidewalk and falling into the girl's wake, Malina stops, can't help herself, because the scent lingers—the same sweet, musky smell Malina had pulled from her hamper on every payday of every week for exactly one year. Up ahead, just past the factory, the girl turns right and is gone. Malina hugs her handbag so the hammer doesn't knock about and follows.

Malina has never ventured this far south, has never had cause. When she reaches the spot where the girl disappeared, she stops. The familiar shops are behind her now; ahead, an unfamiliar street that eventually empties into the Detroit River. Keeping her feet on the sidewalk, she tips forward and looks down the dark alley that runs along the factory's southern edge. She squints, leans farther. Still no sign of the girl. Here again, she should turn around. If not for that empty driveway, an embarrassment like none other except perhaps a baby carriage, she would run back to her car, head down, hoping not to be recognized and, despite the terrible glare, drive as quickly as she could back to the house. So many years of carefully grooming herself to behave just-so. Supper at six, breakfast at seven, shirts hung only on wooden hangers, collars lightly starched, newspaper untouched until Mr. Herze has his turn at it. The list goes on. When she was younger, she wrote down these things and checked off each reminder with a freshly sharpened pencil. After so many years, she should no longer need reminders.

One deep breath propels her. She steps from the sidewalk into the alley. A cool draft sweeps past. The sound of the squeaky wheels has faded. There is the quiet slapping of the river water and then a woman's voice breaks through the night air and then another answers her. They are muted, as if coming from behind a closed door. There must be another building at the end of the alley, perhaps where the girl lives. So many of them do that now—live in abandoned buildings as if they haven't anywhere else to go.

There is the squeal again. Warped metal wheels, wobbling, struggling in the alley's soft, dry dirt. A carriage. Obviously a baby inside. A caramel-colored baby. Mr. Herze is soft and white, pasty white, with hair that was once blond but now is a thinning ridge that runs ear to ear leaving the top of his head bare. The girl, however, as far as Malina could tell, is dark brown. The baby would be a soft, warm color, somewhere between their two shades. Malina takes a backward step, lets her arms hang at her sides.

Mr. Herze's baby?

She thinks again of the smudged easel. Like the muffled voices, the easel is a reminder that people are here, somewhere nearby. She slides one foot in front of the other, forcing herself into the alley. Dust will be gathering on her shoes. When she gets back home, she must remember to clean them with a damp cloth. Unsnapping the kiss-clasp on her brown leather bag, she pulls out the hammer and wraps both hands around the red handle.

A few more steps and Malina has walked beyond the reach of the streetlights. The only remaining light comes from a window in the factory's second story. It's little more than a yellow pane that does nothing to brighten her path. It's Mr. Herze's office. It must be. Holding the hammer as if it were the handle of a frying pan, she follows the girl's path. The air continues to cool. It dries the damp spot on the back of her neck where her thick hair meets her lace collar. The steady pulse of the river follows her, growing no louder, no softer. She must see inside that carriage, has a right to see inside that carriage.

"And who the hell you think you be?"

Squeezing the hammer in both hands, Malina lifts it overhead and swings it toward the voice. The heavy forked head sails through the empty air, missing its target and yanking her off balance. She stumbles, drops her only weapon.

The woman who stands in front of Malina is plump. She has round, black cheeks and her eyes must be brown, although there isn't enough light to know for sure. She stands Malina's height but is much wider. It is not the girl. Malina leans toward the dark figure, squints to make certain. If she wanted, she could stretch out one hand and touch the woman's face. To avoid the temptation, Malina crosses her arms. This one is not like a child at all, but like a woman. A round, rotund woman. Her stubby legs are planted wide and her back is straight. She leads with her chin as she bends forward, puckers her lips, and stares at Malina.

"Damn," the woman shouts. Her breath is sweet, like a half-eaten peppermint.

From the end of the alley, another voice calls out. "What you all doing down there?"

Malina inches away. Her white cotton blouse clings to her back and her hair has most certainly wilted. The round woman stares. Her black cheeks and thick upper lip glisten.

"I know who you are," the woman says, smiling, perhaps even laughing at Malina. "Bet you're wondering what's inside that carriage."

Malina shakes her head, takes a few more backward steps, spins around, and hurries down the alley.

"Hey," the woman shouts. "Where you going? You forgot your damn hammer."

CHAPTER TWO

Julia Wagner sits at the back of the room. Somehow, this is always where she finds herself. It could be because her wiry red hair is impossible to tame. No matter how much she teases, pins, or sprays, she can never fashion the sculpted styles the other ladies wear. Her best hope is to corral it into a ponytail, as she has done for today's luncheon. Perhaps she curses too much. On diet day, she definitely smokes too much. Or it could be because she is rounder than the other ladies. Her clothes have a way of fitting too tightly in all the wrong places. Or all the right places, according to her husband. Good Kentucky stock, her mother always says, often when reattaching one of Julia's buttons. But the truth is, none of these force her to the rear of the room. She finds her way there because things like this—the monthly gathering of the Ladies of the St. Alban's Charitable Ventures Committee—are altogether more tolerable if she keeps her distance.

And if Julia is generally at the back of the room, Malina Herze is generally—or more accurately, always—at the front. This is where she stands today. As chair of the committee's annual bake sale and clothing drive, Malina should be handing out sign-up sheets and issuing instructions as to how, when, and where to deliver donations for the thrift store. Instead, she is doling out stern warnings to the dozen ladies scattered about the living room of their hostess, Grace Richardson. Grace is Julia's best friend, only true friend really. This is another reason Julia sits at the back of the room. She is the friend who will stir the beans while Grace attends to her guests or answer the door should a latecomer arrive. But soon after Malina informed everyone that the woman found near the factory was most definitely dead, Grace excused herself to the kitchen, where she'll stir her own beans, answer her own door, and won't be in need of Julia's help.

Snubbing out her second cigarette, Julia tugs at the blouse that dips a bit low for a luncheon and exhales a louder-than-intended sigh. A few of the ladies frown at her. They want to hear what Malina has to say. Her husband is in charge down at the factory and so she knows more than most. The woman was found yesterday morning in the alley that borders the factory and is within casting distance of the shops on Willingham Avenue. She was most definitely colored and most definitely deceased. Someone bashed her in the side of the head, so it wasn't an accident. No chance of that.

Over and over, Malina issues these warnings, and as ten minutes stretch into thirty and she has nothing new to tell, the ladies tire of her. They begin to whisper to one another, some sharing stories of what their husbands have told them, others fretting over why their husbands have told them nothing. They stand to talk across one another and switch seats to hear something new, and as they move and shift and sit and stand, they stir up perspiration and the room grows hotter and the scent of their perfume and hairspray and body lotion and styling gel grows stronger and stronger. Sucking a lungful of smoke from her cigarette, Julia considers excusing herself to see to the twins. Every summer, her nieces visit for two weeks, and they arrived a few days ago. They're home alone, poor things. They're probably desperate for a bite of lunch. That would be a plausible excuse.

Even given the unseemly circumstances surrounding today's meeting, Julia is more comfortable at Grace's house than she ever is at her own. Whenever the two get together for coffee, it's almost always at Grace's house. When they play cards, it's at Grace's kitchen table. When their husbands watch a game, it's in Grace's living room. When they barbecue steaks, it's in Grace's backyard. The two houses stand on the same side of Alder Avenue and are separated by two blocks. From the outside, one house is the exact replica of the other, but inside, they have their distinctions. Grace has a tiled kitchen; Julia, linoleum. Grace's walls are freshly painted. Julia's are not. The linens are ironed at Grace's house. They are wrinkled at Julia's. Grace is pregnant. Julia is not.

The sound of breaking glass is the thing that finally silences the room and gives Julia her excuse. It also sets Betty Lawson's baby to crying. She has been out in the kitchen, where it was supposed to be quiet so she could sleep undisturbed.

"Let me," Julia says, leaping from her seat. She drops her half-smoked cigarette in the remains of her iced tea and raises a hand so Betty Lawson will keep her seat on the sofa. "I'll see to her."

A few of the ladies tilt their heads and press a hand over their hearts as if to say how sweet. A few others raise their brows as if to warn Betty against trusting Julia with her baby. Crying or not, this little one, the first born on Alder in three years, is a reminder to Julia and every other lady that Julia no longer has a child of her own.

In the kitchen, the baby is still crying, and on the floor near the sink lies a broken jar, partially held together by its paper label. White globs of mayonnaise are splattered across the tile and the bottom of the refrigerator.

"Soapy hands," Grace says, rocking the carriage to calm the baby inside.

For the occasion of hosting today's luncheon, Grace has swept her blond hair into a French roll. She wears an apron stained with barbecue sauce, and a few loose hairs dangle about her face, and yet she is the elegant one. Julia, who labored all morning on her hair and twice ironed the blouse she bought at Hudson's for just this event, is the rumpled one.

"Do you mind?" Grace nods off toward the back door. "It'll be Elizabeth."

Julia sidesteps the broken jar, picking up the larger pieces along the way and dropping them in the trash can under the sink. It's not the sound of a crying baby that draws up the memories of Julia's own little one. It's the smell. Julia bought the same lotion for Mary-anne. Back then, Mr. Olsen kept it on the second aisle of his drug-store, top shelf, pink bottle. Probably still does. Sliding between the refrigerator and Grace's dinette, Julia hears it—a quiet tapping.

Elizabeth Symanski stands on the other side of the screened door. Every day, she comes to Grace's house for lunch, and as is Eliz-abeth's normal posture, her head sags, her shoulders are stooped, and her arms dangle at her sides. Her long blond hair, dull and frayed on the ends, makes her look much older than her twenty-one or so years. As Elizabeth walks into the kitchen, the hem of her lavender dress brushes against Julia's shins. Elizabeth normally wears yellow on Fridays. The colors help her remember the days. Red for Mondays. Blue for Tuesdays. White for Wednesdays. Before Elizabeth's mother passed away, a year ago this spring, she dressed Elizabeth every morning. In her final days, Ewa Symanski's bony fingers struggled to thread the buttons and knot the bows, and she worried aloud who would tend to her daughter when she was gone. Now Mr. Symanski must struggle with the same. Even though Elizabeth is old enough to be called a young woman, twenty-one or twenty-two, she is unable to dress herself.

Because she is wearing one of her finer dresses, Elizabeth also wears her black shoes, her Sunday best, and as she walks heel-toe, heel-toe, they click across the tile floor. *Click, click, click*, until she reaches the dinette, where she sits. By the time Elizabeth has settled into her seat, the baby has stopped crying. Normally Julia might remind Elizabeth to keep her voice down so as to not wake the baby again, but there's no reason to hush Elizabeth. She rarely speaks, and when she does, she asks after her mother, Ewa. Mr. Symanski always says to humor Elizabeth, because what's the harm? Tell her Ewa will be along shortly and that Elizabeth should mind herself until then.

Backing away from the quiet carriage, Grace slips around the table and reaches for the telephone. Letting the receiver hang over her shoulder, she dials with one hand and, with the other, fingers the loose threads left by a button missing from the back of

Elizabeth's dress. By tomorrow, Grace will have picked up the dress from Mr. Symanski and reattached a new button. She waits for the phone to ring once, her usual signal to Mr. Symanski that Elizabeth has arrived safely, and then hangs up and flops into a chair at the kitchen table.

"Did you know half the members wouldn't come here today?" Grace waves a hand around her kitchen. "All this food will go to waste. They didn't want to park their cars on this street, that's what they said. As if it's not safe here anymore."

Though no one actually thinks the prostitutes have made their way to Alder Avenue, other coloreds have. Three families have moved into the Filmore Apartments on the west end of Alder, and isn't that proof enough trouble can't be far behind? Just last night, the paper was filled with news of another plant closing. This is what should worry the ladies. So many factories already stand empty—rotting shells surrounded by boarded-up restaurants and taverns. The green glow, so much like a fog, that once clung to the city's rooftops has begun to lift. Murray, Packard, Studebaker. All of them closed. This is what should worry the ladies.

"Never mind them," Julia says, wiping up the last of the mayonnaise spill. "So you and James will have leftovers for the next six weeks."

"Have you read today's paper?" Grace asks.

Turning her back on the baby carriage, Julia steps up to the stove and inhales the steam rising from the baked beans. The brown sugar and catsup that bubbles up does little to mask the smell of the pink lotion.

"No, and I don't intend to," she says, dragging a finger through

15

the simmering beans and sticking it in her mouth. "Needs more brown sugar."

Even over the stove, the sweet smell of a new baby fills the kitchen. It's the white powder, too. Julia was always careful not to use too much on Maryanne.

"But aren't you curious? Don't you wonder who might be involved?" Grace flicks her eyes in the direction of the living room as if one of the ladies' husbands is the possible offender.

"No, I don't. I don't have the slightest damned interest, and neither should you. It's all but blown over already. Bill says the police are gone. Hardly even bothered with any questions. Brown sugar?"

Grace points to an overhead cupboard. "What more did Malina tell everyone?" Grace says, touching Elizabeth's fingertips so she'll stop tapping her foot. Though Elizabeth never has much to say, she has a habit of tapping her right foot. In her nicer shoes, it makes a clicking sound that might disturb the baby.

"She's doing nothing but frightening everybody, getting them all worked up. She keeps asking if anyone knows what the dead woman looked like. Was she portly? Was she slender? Why would she ask such a thing? I swear that woman couldn't find her behind with a compass and a candle. Did you know she's thinking of having a bomb shelter dug in their backyard?"

Grace slips a rubber band off what must be today's newspaper and spreads it across the table. "There has to be something in the news, don't you think? It's been two days. Who was she? Where did she come from? Don't you wonder?"

"James will tell you what you need to know," Julia says, drawing a spoon through the beans in a lazy figure eight. "You shouldn't worry about it."

"But he tells me nothing."

"Only because he adores you."

"Bill adores you," Grace says, turning to the next page, "and he's told you every horrid detail."

"No husband adores his wife like your husband adores you."

It's the smooth blond hair and clear skin that plague Grace. She's slender, when not pregnant, but not skinny. Her ankles are delicate, her neckline sharp, and her blue eyes startle people when they first look into them. *Angelic*, that's the word to describe Grace, and no husband wants to pollute his angelic wife with news about a dead prostitute.

"Besides," Julia says, tapping another quarter cup of brown sugar into the beans, "you know I'll tell you everything I hear."

"But I shouldn't have to get the news from you. I worry there might be another reason James isn't telling me things. Last night, I came right out and asked him about it."

"Asked him what?"

"If he had ever seen them."

"And?"

"He said he never has."

"There you go. Nothing to worry about."

"Do I dare believe him? Malina says those women stand top-less. How could he not look?"

Julia pulls the paper away from Grace, folds it over, and jams it into the trash. "So what if they look? It's what men do. Be thankful James doesn't want to burden you with it."

17

In the front room, the voices have grown louder. One of the ladies speculates on what the weapon might have been. A bat, perhaps, or a crowbar. Aren't people always using crowbars for such things?

"Malina told me the shops on Willingham will close on paydays now," Grace says, fishing the newspaper out of the trash and returning to the table. "Did she tell you the same?"

"Along with all her other gibberish, yes," Julia says, shaking her head when she catches herself staring at the carriage.

Grace irons out the wrinkles Julia caused when she shoved the paper into the garbage. Again, she pats Elizabeth's hand, a reminder to still her feet. "Do you mind?" she says. "Would you see Elizabeth home? I'd rather she not hear all the talk going on in there, and I really should see to the rest of lunch."

"You don't want help setting the table? Wrapping up all these leftovers?"

"You should get home to the girls," Grace says, and turns to the next page. "They'll be getting hungry."

Grace, like Julia, will know this baby is the first on the street since Maryanne, and she's giving Julia an excuse to escape, at least for today. In the early weeks after Maryanne died, Grace was the only one brave enough and stubborn enough to walk into Julia's home. She came every day, even when Julia slammed doors and screamed at her to leave well enough alone. Grace kept the blood flowing, kept the house from collapsing. Even more than Julia's own husband, Grace saved her.

"You'll ring Mr. Symanski again?" Julia says, holding the door open for Elizabeth and wondering if it will always be like this. Will

Grace forever try to intercept the memories of Julia's daughter, and how successful can she be once her own baby is born? "You'll let him know Elizabeth is on her way?"

Grace taps the tip of her thumb to her tongue, flips to the next page in the newspaper, and nods. "There has to be something in here, don't you think?"

And then Julia realizes. Grace is happily married. Her husband does adore her. She has no worries about James. She doesn't wonder who that woman was or who killed her or whose husband might be the guilty party. Those discussions were for Julia's benefit, a means to distract her from the baby in the corner, and they almost worked.

Outside the house, Julia and Elizabeth walk together to the end of Grace's driveway and from there, Julia watches Elizabeth make her way home. North of Alder, a round of fireworks explodes. For the past week, the air has been laced with the smell of them— sulfur, maybe charcoal. They're another reminder, other than this heat, that July is fast approaching. The ladies' voices and the sounds of silverware clattering against Grace's best wedding china drift out of the living room's open windows. Betty Lawson's baby is crying again. A block and a half away, Elizabeth has neared her house. Reaching out with one hand, she trails her fingers along the top rail of the iron fence that hems in her front yard. She's been taught hers is the house with the iron fence. When Elizabeth stops at her gate, Julia turns toward home.

CHAPTER THREE

Most of the ladies shop on Willingham Avenue every day. They stop first at Mr. Ambrozy's deli. Their freezers frost over and ruin his hand-stuffed kielbasa, so they prefer to buy it fresh, daily. Things never keep as well at home, never taste as fresh as they do straight from Mr. Ambrozy. Every weekday morning, the ladies board the south-bound bus. They come with recipe cards tucked inside their handbags, some of them liking to share, others not. Strolling through Mr. Ambrozy's aisles, they carry shopping baskets and pick through his sweet and mild sauerkraut and hand-stuffed sausages—among the best in all of Detroit. But they don't come to Willingham Avenue only for the deli. At his shop on the corner of Woodward and Willingham, Mr. Wilson irons the sharpest pleats and stitches an invisible hem like none other. On the opposite side of Willingham, beyond the drugstore and a vacant fenced-in lot, Nowack's Bakery sells the freshest bread and pierogi fine enough for the ladies to say they rolled and boiled it themselves. It's a secret the ladies say is best kept quiet.

At the kitchen table, her feet propped on the chair opposite her, one ankle crossed over the other and relieved for some peace after a long afternoon with the ladies, Grace studies Mother's pierogi recipe and feels quite certain she has forgotten or possibly misplaced something. Before her passing, Ewa Symanski always made the pierogi for the bake sale. St. Alban's has a good many widowers, and some would wait all year for Ewa's pierogi because they no longer had wives of their own to roll and boil the pierogi. In the wake of Ewa's death, Grace will take over and finally have a specialty like all the other ladies. First thing Monday morning, to avoid the sugar-cookie fiasco of last year, she'll visit Mrs. Nowack at the bakery for some advice. No one makes better pierogi than Mrs. Nowack.

"You shouldn't trouble yourself, Mother," Grace says, running her fingers over the crisp card that Mother wrote out when she arrived shortly after the last lady left. Mother sighed to have to write it down yet again. "I'm sure you'll want to get home soon."

On the floor near Grace's feet, Mother, on hands and knees, is scrubbing the tile. Her apron slips off one slender shoulder and her thinning silver hair glitters in the late afternoon sun. "You keep a clean house and tend to your husband," Mother says, "or some other woman will."

It must be all the talk about the prostitutes and the dead woman that has Grace feeling out of sorts. Mother heard it too, though from where Grace isn't sure, but when she arrived to help tidy up after the luncheon, Mother knew.

Outside the kitchen window, the back alley is quiet. From a few doors down comes the whirl of a reel mower, the hiss of someone hosing off his driveway, a neighbor's clothesline creaking as the lady of the house takes in her sheets and towels. The children in the neighborhood are teenagers or altogether grown and off on their own, so there are no sounds of laughing or running, no children leaping the hedges between houses or throwing rocks in the alley. The late-afternoon air has finally cooled and a breeze blows through the kitchen, in through the open window, out through the screen in the back door. The sweet smell of fireworks blows through every so often. The sharp, cool air should make Grace feel better, and yet something in the house isn't quite right. She tries not to watch the clock. No need to worry about James today. It's not payday.

At the sound of tires rolling over loose gravel, Grace checks the clock over the stove—5:30. The car slows as it nears the garage in back of the house. The engine idles and goes silent. James, home from work. Right on time. Always right on time. Again, Grace promises herself to stop watching the clock. James has given her no cause to worry, and she doesn't, not really. A car door opens and closes, but there is no sign of James at the back stairs. Grace glances down at Mother, who raises a brow as if James has gotten himself into no good in the distance between the garage and the house. James has given Mother no cause to worry either, other than his being a man. When the back door finally swings open, James steps inside, drawing in a gust of the cool air that, for a moment, makes Grace set aside her worries over something forgotten.

With his eyes only on Grace, James crosses the kitchen in three long strides. The smell of grease and oil, the smell of a day at the factory, fills the small room and masks the rich scent of fried onions and the tuna casserole baking in the oven. Taking no notice of the wet floor or Mother, who is still crouched near the sink, James stretches one arm out to the side, his hand cupped as if holding something, and wraps the other around Grace. He pulls her close and kisses the top of her head. His empty hand slides over her shoulder, down her arm, and rests on the baby.

During the day, the oil and steam of the factory dampen James's clothes and body, and dust sticks to the thick, black hair on his arms, making his skin like gritty sandpaper. He will sometimes apologize for being so rough and coarse, and Grace will touch the hair on his chest or run a hand over his wrist and up his forearm so he'll know she likes the feel of him. He's the man she always hoped for, broad enough to fill a doorway, tall enough to look down on most around him, bristly enough that her skin, by contrast, will always feel smooth and young to him. What surprises her still is that he's also a playful man. He'll tease her over a ruined roast, chase her with the hose when she is trying to pull weeds from her flowerbeds, or press an ear to her growing stomach as if he can hear the baby inside. Touching the shadow on his lower jaw that has grown since morning, she kisses the rough cheek and frowns at his cupped hand. Shards of green glass sparkle in his palm. He jostles them as if they were a pair of dice.

Two blocks down, where Julia lives in the same style three-bedroom, two-story redbrick house with a porch off the front door and a detached garage out back, she finds broken glass in the alley almost every day. Usually green, sometimes brown. She says that over the past few months the glass has become as regular as leaves in autumn. It's a sign of their changing neighborhood, one no one talks about. Grace nods in Mother's direction so James won't say anything he'd rather not. He greets Mother, drops the glass in the trash basket, letting the shards tumble from his hand one by one, and excuses himself to bathe before supper.

After a quiet meal, Mother gathers her purse and gloves. She'd just as soon not be caught in this neighborhood after dark, she says, and while James sees Mother to her car, Grace runs water to wash the dishes. Something begins to tug at her again. It might be the thought of those women on Willingham, but they are still a bus ride away, a safe distance from Grace's life here on Alder. Or perhaps it's the green glass. She has always assumed it was left there by the colored men who cut through the alley on their way to Woodward Avenue. She hears them during the day when James is at work and late at night when he is asleep and she is awake, nursing an aching back. The men always pass at the same time. They have a schedule. It must be the buses that drive their routine.

"You've missed a spot," Grace says, nudging James who has returned to help her with the dishes. Soapy water drips from her rubber gloves.

"It's time I do some checking, Gracie," James says, setting the dish aside.

"Checking?"

"Not waiting until things get even worse. Time I get someone in here to tell me what this house is worth."

"It's just a few bottles," Grace says. "A little broken glass." But she knows it isn't.

"I'll find someone who can sell this place for us," James says. "Someone who can get us a fair price."

"But what about our friends? I'd hate to leave Julia. And Mother is so close."

"Should be able to find something farther north with the money we make." James wraps his arms around Grace's round belly. His fingers are warm through her thin cotton blouse. "High time we face facts. Things are starting to add up in a way I don't care for. No good to be the last ones standing."

Wearing a pair of her nicer heels, Grace is the perfect height to rest against the broadest part of James. His white undershirt is soft against her cheek and smells lightly of bleach. She wants to ask if he, like the ladies who wouldn't come to her luncheon, is worried the dead woman on Willingham means something to them. "I have brownies," Grace says instead, because she's not sure she wants to hear his answer. "Feel like dessert?"

James rolls his rough cheek against the soft spot at the base of her neck. She leans into him and lays her head aside so he can more easily kiss her there.

"And ice cream," she says, closing her eyes and inhaling the spicy cologne he slapped on after he washed up. "I'll bet I have some in the freezer."

And then that nagging feeling, that certainty she had forgotten something or misplaced something, rises up. She drops her chin to her chest and shakes her head.

"Oh, James. Today is Elizabeth's birthday. She wore the lavender dress. Not the yellow. Because it's her birthday. The ice cream, I bought it for her. How could I forget?"

While Grace plates a dozen leftover brownies and grabs a gallon of ice cream from the freezer, James pulls the car into the driveway. It's a short enough walk, but by the time they come home, it'll be dark, so James insists on the car.

When Mr. Symanski answers the door, his silver hair, usually smoothed straight back, hangs across his wrinkled brow. His white-collared shirt is untucked, his tie has pulled loose at the knot, and his pants are rumpled at the knees. He has shrunk in the year since Ewa died, the kind of withering that happens when a man loses his wife.

"I'm sorry to disturb you so late," Grace says. "But I realized, after all the ladies left . . ."

She leans around Mr. Symanski so she can see into the living room, where Elizabeth usually sits in the evenings. She likes the brown wingback that used to be her mother's. Ewa called it her fireside chair. It stands empty.

"I realized that today is Elizabeth's birthday," Grace says.

Mr. Symanski looks first at James and then at Grace. "I was sleeping." He tugs on the pants hanging loosely at his waist. "I think I was sleeping."

Like Grace did, Mr. Symanski leans to get a better look, as if Elizabeth is standing behind James.

"She is being with you?" Mr. Symanski says.

James steps forward. "Charles, it's James and Grace. Are you all right?"

"Elizabeth, she is with you, yes?"

"No," Grace says. "No, she isn't. She came home. Hours ago. She left me hours ago. We came to wish her happy birthday."

Mr. Symanski looks into the house to where Elizabeth would

usually sit, her head lowered, not noticing someone at the door. The living room is dark. One of Ewa's crocheted blankets lies across the sofa where Mr. Symanski was probably napping. No smell of anything baking in the oven. No radio. No voices.

"Elizabeth is being with you?"

James begins the search in the backyard. He starts in the garage, where it stays cool even on the hottest days, and checks behind the weeping forsythia that grows along the back porch. And while James searches outside, Grace helps Mr. Symanski to a seat in the kitchen and then hurries through the house, both hands supporting her heavy stomach. She opens every door, leans into each stale room, calls out Elizabeth's name. She checks every closet, waves away the smell of mothballs that reminds her of Ewa. In the bedrooms, she checks under the beds, brushing aside the cobwebs that cling to her forehead and coughing at the dust kicked up when she throws back the patchwork quilts and lifts the lace bed skirts. She calls the neighbors, one on each side. They call more neighbors, and they, still more. The husbands set aside their newspapers and shut down their televisions. Ladies leave the dishes not yet washed and the laundry not yet folded. From upstairs, from down the hall, from in the cellar, Grace calls out for Mr. Symanski to stay put. Don't worry. You know how she sometimes wanders. We'll find her. We'll find her in no time.

In the Symanskis' front yard, James gathers the neighbors, and on the back of an envelope, he sketches Alder Avenue and Marietta one block to the south and Tuttle one block to the north. He draws six boxes, dividing up the area, assigns one man to each and tells them, "Get together as much help as you can. She's small, you know. Check every porch, every garage. Behind bushes. Inside cars. She might be scared. Might want to hide."

The men separate themselves into groups and some run north, while others run south. One group lingers and Orin Schofield gathers them across the street from the Filmore Apartments. Orin lives two houses down from Grace and James on the opposite side of the alley. He lost his wife three years ago. Grace takes him a roast with carrots and new potatoes the first and third Sunday of every month, always the same thing because it's one of the few dishes she can count on to turn out well for her, and while she cleans his kitchen, he talks about moving south to live with his daughter.

"I'd bet good money someone in there can tell you the girl's whereabouts," Orin shouts, pointing toward the Filmore. The top of his balding head is red though the sun has fallen low in the sky. If she could, Grace would tell him to take himself inside and sit in front of the fan. Your heart, she would tell him. The strain is no good for your heart. Continuing to shout, Orin shuffles up and down the sidewalk, dragging his tan suede shoes. Blue trousers pool at his ankles. As he walks, he leans on a three-foot-long scrap of wood as if it were a cane. James helped Orin replace the joists on his back porch last summer. The wood must be a leftover. Lifting the wood and stabbing it toward the apartments, Orin shouts again, "Good money says that's the place to look."

The men point to each side of the simple two-story brick apartment building, seemingly most worried about the shrubs and overgrown grass that run along the west side. Around back, they'll find a thick stand of poplars hugging a narrow stream that runs east to west. The sun has set but the sky still glows with the last of its light. They'll want to get a good look before darkness settles in. For the past year, these neighbors have been talking, some louder than others. More than being afraid of the coloreds living in the apartments, they are afraid of one buying and moving into a house, because that would be a lasting change and their lives would never be good again, never be the same. They have to stick together. If one falls, they all fall. That's what the loudest neighbors say. Pointing this way and that, the men, a half dozen at least, split into two groups and flank the apartment building, disappearing around back for a time, reappearing in front.

"What'd you find?" Orin shouts, waving one fist in the air.

The men hold up their hands. Nothing. Most of the apartment windows are dark. The doors remain closed. No one from the Filmore comes out.

"You've got to go on in there." It's Orin again. "Nothing's going to stop you."

And then the police arrive, two black-and-white cars, two officers in each. They tell the men to stay clear of the Filmore.

"No one is allowed in there," an officer says.

Leaving the group of six to linger on the curb, Orin Schofield still shouting and wielding his plank of wood, James escorts the officers into Mr. Symanski's house. They sit around the kitchen table, and it takes him and Grace some time to explain about Elizabeth.

"No, she's not a child," Grace says. "A woman. Twenty-one years old. No, twenty-two today. But she's like a child. She's lost all the same. I saw her last. She left my house. Walked home. It's such a short trip. That's the last I know."

The police insist Mr. Symanski stay at the house and not join the other men. James agrees.

"She'll need a friendly face when we bring her home," James says.

"Yes," Grace says, resting a hand on Mr. Symanski's shoulder. "James will see to it. He'll see Elizabeth home."

But really James must worry about Mr. Symanski's heart. He won't let Grace join the search either.

"See to him," James says, nodding at Mr. Symanski. "Put on some coffee. Answer the phone. And keep yourself in the house."

So while James goes outside to show the officers his map, Grace hunts for the coffee. She dumps the old grounds in a can she finds under the sink, rinses and fills the pot, brews a fresh batch. In the refrigerator, she finds a loaf of bread, cheese, and the sliced roast beef she delivered this past Wednesday. Like Orin Schofield, Mr. Symanski always gets the same dish. Spreading extra butter on the sandwich, she cuts it in half and slides it toward him.

"How long since you last ate?" she asks.

Mr. Symanski looks at the small white refrigerator as if it might give him the answer. "I am not knowing," he says, then picks up one half of the sandwich but doesn't take a bite.

Not worried that coffee will keep Mr. Symanski awake tonight, Grace pours him a cup. No one will sleep until Elizabeth is home. She adds cream and two sugars because that's the way James takes it, and presses one of Mr. Symanski's hands between both of hers. Perhaps Mr. Symanski would prefer bourbon, but James said coffee.

"Please," she says. "You really should eat."

As more people arrive to help in the search, Grace points them toward the police cars parked outside the house. One officer stands there, talking into a small radio. Grace calls after each neighbor, reminding him to check behind the bushes and in every garage because that's what James said to do, and she jots down the name of every person who joins the search.

The neighbors continue to look well past dark. They carry flashlights and kerosene lanterns. Children from nearby streets swat at mosquitoes, and the ladies run home to flip on porch lights and kitchen lights, everything to light up the street for Elizabeth. Teenagers shuffle up and down Alder, the bright orange tips of their cigarettes glowing in the dark. In the kitchen, Grace scrubs the counter with baking soda while Mr. Symanski and two officers talk across the table. One officer has dark hair that curls on the ends, one strand cupping the top of his left ear. His name is Officer Warinski. The other officer, whose name is Thompson, has straight brown hair that was probably once blond, and he slouches as if he has always been the tallest. Both wear heavy, dark shoes that will leave scuff marks.

The curly-haired officer, Officer Warinski, points at Grace and then at the table. After Grace has taken a seat, the officer asks if Elizabeth would have had a plan and if anything is missing from the house that the girl might have sold for money. Hunched over the table, propped up by his elbows, his face resting in his hands, Mr. Symanski shakes his head.

"Elizabeth doesn't know how to use money," Grace says. "She doesn't know what it is."

Together, the officers, Grace, and Mr. Symanski walk to Elizabeth's room. Again, the curly-haired Warinski does the talking. He asks if anything is missing. Officer Thompson holds a yellow pencil and a small pad of lined paper. Officer Warinski wonders aloud if Elizabeth had been planning a trip and asks Grace and Mr. Symanski for the names and telephone numbers of Elizabeth's friends.

"She hasn't any," Grace says. "Only me. Me and a few of the other neighbor ladies. She's like a child, frail, not well. You must understand that."

Back in the kitchen, the taller officer bobs his head in the direction of the coffeepot, signaling he would like a cup. Both officers and Mr. Symanski return to their seats at the table. Officer Warinski brushes aside the curl that again grabs on to the top of his ear. He stretches his hands into the air, cups his head, and tilts his chair, balancing on the two hind legs. His skin is smooth like a boy's.

"One more time," he says to Grace. "You last saw her when?"

Placing an empty cup in front of each officer and pouring until both are full, Grace glances at Mr. Symanski. He stares down into his own empty cup, his hands wrapped around it as if warming himself. Grace pushes the sugar bowl and creamer across the table toward the officers.

"She comes every day for lunch," Grace says. "Like always, she came. It gives Mr. Symanski time to catch up on chores or to nap. I rang him when she arrived and later sent her away because of all the talk."

"The talk?"

"Talk of the woman found dead on Willingham Avenue. Most

of our husbands, they work down there. Elizabeth left me at about one thirty. I rang Mr. Symanski again. One ring on the telephone to let him know she was on her way."

Across the table, Mr. Symanski's silver hair has fallen across his forehead and into his eyes.

"But I got busy," Grace says. "I think he never rang back. I'm supposed to listen for him to ring back so I know she made it home."

The curly-haired Warinski asks twice about the telephone rings that Grace and Mr. Symanski exchange. Grace explains that in the year since Ewa died, Grace and Mr. Symanski have taken to trading rings to signal Elizabeth's safe arrival. She wanders too far sometimes, twice walking past Grace's house, going as far as Woodward before she was spotted. The officer squints at Grace. He doesn't understand.

"Elizabeth wanders. Those rings, it's how we know she's safe. We ring when she leaves or when she arrives. The other rings back to signal she made it safe and sound."

"And did you ring Mrs. Richardson?" the officer asks Mr. Symanski. Before Mr. Symanski can answer, the officer says to Grace, "Did he ring to signal that the girl was on her way for lunch? Did he ring that she made it home? Did he ever ring?"

Grace shakes her head. She's certain she phoned Mr. Symanski after Julia and Elizabeth left the house. She must be certain. She let it ring once just as she always does, but did he ring her back? Did he ever ring her at all? Did he know Elizabeth had come? Did he know she left his house?

"I don't know," Grace finally says, rubbing one palm to the

bridge of her nose. "I don't remember. But I rang when she arrived and when she left. I know I did. I'm certain of it."

The taller officer slouches even when seated. He reaches across the table and taps his pencil in front of Mr. Symanski. "Sir?"

"I can't remember things," Mr. Symanski says. "It is being so shameful I can't remember. I was sleeping. Sometimes I am sleeping too long."

"So," Officer Warinski says. He leans forward, the chair's front legs hitting the linoleum with a thud. "Elizabeth made her own way home when she left your house?"

Grace starts to say yes but stops. She mirrors the officer's movement, slides forward on her chair and presses her hands flat on the tabletop.

"No," she says. "No, she didn't. I asked Julia Wagner to see Elizabeth home. She didn't stay for lunch. The twins, Julia's nieces, are here. She had to get home to them. Julia saw Elizabeth last."

Officer Thompson stands and says he will go speak to Mrs. Wagner. Grace is relieved, happy that this thing she has remembered will amount to something good. Julia will be able to tell them what happened. She'll be able to help.

When the officers have left the house, Grace helps Mr. Symanski into the living room. He sits in Ewa's chair. Grace sits on the tweed sofa, where she is close enough to reach out and pat his knee.

"Today is being Elizabeth's birthday, you know," Mr. Symanski says.

Grace nods to make him think she remembered even though she hadn't. She hadn't remembered because she'd been thinking about pierogi and those women on Willingham and how best to distract Julia from memories of her daughter. The lavender dress should have reminded Grace sooner. Mr. Symanski sinks into the chair that is too large for him and rests his cheek on one of the cushions as if it were Ewa's shoulder.

"I'm sure she'll be home soon," Grace says, placing a hand on Mr. Symanski's knee. It's like a small wooden knob under her fingers. "You know James. He'll take care of this."

James always knows what to do, how to fix things, how to make things right. When the car sputters, he knows which tool to use and what needs to be tightened or replaced. When the water heater stops warming, he tinkers until it works. When the television shows only static, he knows just how to turn the antennae. When, after five years, Grace still wasn't pregnant, he insisted no wife of his would have such worries. He scolded her when she cried over it, promised to stay no matter how many years passed, and eventually he put an end to that problem too and gave Grace a baby.

"He'll have Elizabeth home in no time," Grace says. "I have brownies for her. And I know how she loves the ice cream. She'll be home before you know it."

Mr. Symanski takes a sip from his coffee. "I'm feeling she won't," he says, staring at a blank wall. "I'm feeling very badly she won't ever come home."

CHAPTER FOUR

It's well past bedtime for Izzy and Arie, short for Isabelle and Arabelle, when they tiptoe down Aunt Julia's stairs. Both of them wear nightgowns yellowed at the seams where Grandma used too much bleach. They stare straight ahead as they pass through the entry so they won't be tempted to glance at the telephone. Mrs. Witherspoon, Grandma's neighbor, promised to call if their cat turned up. Patches is her name. She ran away from Grandma's house two weeks ago. Grandma said it's what cats do when the weather turns warm and not to worry. Now that Elizabeth Symanski is missing, the girls shouldn't be concerning themselves with a cat, but they didn't know Elizabeth all that well, and they'd had Patches for almost a year. One thing's for sure, though. Staring at a phone won't make it ring. Once in the living room, where Aunt Julia says they can all wait together until Elizabeth comes home, the girls sit. Their bare calves hang over the side of the loveseat, and their feet dangle, nearly touching the floor, but not quite. Next year, they'll reach.

Every summer since before they can remember, the girls have looked forward to visiting Aunt Julia and Uncle Bill. Back home, where the twins live the rest of the year with Grandma, they are almost never allowed out of the yard, especially when the weather warms up. It's the polio, Grandma always says. No sense tempting fate. Now, here they are, cooped up just like at Grandma's. Every other summer, Friday night at Aunt Julia's meant an evening at Sanders. That's the real reason the girls packed their store-bought dresses. They would sit, the girls, Uncle Bill, and Aunt Julia, at the Sanders counter, and as Uncle Bill ordered from the man wearing an apron and small white hat, Aunt Julia would scold the girls for twirling on the round stools. Then they'd all eat hot-fudge sundaes from fluted glass dishes.

Outside Aunt Julia's front window, streams of yellow thrown from flashlights drift back and forth across the lawn. Dry grass crackles under heavy boots, and as broad-shouldered shadows glide past the windows, voices call out to Elizabeth. Mostly men's voices, deep and scratchy. Some are close, next door or down the street. Others are muffled, as if coming from a block or two away. The quieter voices are harder to listen to. They mean the men have traveled farther and farther away, thinking Elizabeth has done the same. The quieter voices come from someplace dark, where all the porch lights aren't shining and the front doors don't stand wide open. The quieter voices mean maybe Elizabeth won't be found as quickly as Aunt Julia thought. The twins, and Aunt Julia, too, are waiting for silence, because silence will mean the men, whether near or far, have stopped shouting and Elizabeth has been found. Silence will be a good thing.

"What will Elizabeth do?" Izzy says, turning her back on the telephone so she won't be tempted to think about Patches or warm, bittersweet chocolate. Her stomach clenches and reminds her they skipped supper. Another great thing about Aunt Julia's house is the food. She cooks as well as Grandma, maybe better, and never insists on clean plates and always makes enough for seconds. Food isn't such a chore at Aunt Julia's house. "When it's time for bed," Izzy says, "what will she do?"

Izzy's damp red hair hangs in strands over her shoulders, the ends frayed where she didn't bother to comb through them after her bath. Grandma is always shouting—Izzy, get busy. Izzy, get busy brushing your hair. Izzy, get busy making your bed. Izzy, get busy. Arie's hair is nearly dry because she is better about scrubbing it with a towel. No one ever shouts at Arie to get busy.

"What do you mean, sugar?" Aunt Julia says.

"What will Elizabeth do without a bed to sleep in?" Arie says before Izzy can answer for herself.

Izzy stares hard at Arie and shakes her head. Grandma doesn't like it when they do things like finish each other's sentences and thoughts. She says it feels like something the good Lord didn't intend. Scooting to the edge of the sofa so she doesn't have to look Izzy in the eye, Arie begins rubbing the ends of her fingers, one after the other, no doubt wishing she held Grandma's rosary in her hands so she could rub its smooth, ivory-colored beads instead of her own fingertips. But the rosary is upstairs, hanging from Arie's headboard, where she has kept it since they arrived.

"I believe Elizabeth will sleep in her own bed tonight," Aunt Julia says. She stands, tugging at her slim skirt where it buckles on her hips, and walks over to the front door. "I was with her just this afternoon at Mrs. Richardson's. She'll be happy as can be to see you two." Pushing open the screen door, Aunt Julia leans out and looks up and down the street. "I bet she'd be pleased to help you find that cat of yours. Just as soon as she's home, we'll all go together. We'll take out the sedan, drive over to Grandma's, and have a look around."

Outside, a few doors slam shut and, soon after, engines fire up, rumble, and fade as the cars roll down the street. The bushes along the west side of the house rustle. The men are kicking them or swatting at them with yardsticks. They must think Elizabeth is hiding there. Aunt Julia rubs her thin reddish eyebrows, inhales a deep breath, spins around on one heel, and returns to her seat at the larger sofa. Deep voices continue to call out to Elizabeth. "Come on home," they shout. "Supper's on the table." Following Aunt Julia's example, the girls rest their hands in their laps, cross their ankles, and sit with a straight back.

As the twins stare out the front window, Aunt Julia trying to smile each time they glance her way, they realize the neighborhood is quiet. The voices have stopped calling. The girls close their eyes and each takes a breath, together at the same time because that's how it works between them. They don't want to hear another man shout out that supper is waiting or that Papa is home and misses his Elizabeth. After a few more moments of silence, the twins open their eyes, look at each other and then at Aunt Julia. Arie squirms to the edge of the loveseat, stands, and leaps into the center of the room. She claps her hands together and draws them to her chest. Aunt Julia smiles, shows her teeth. She hears the silence too. All three turn when a heavy foot hits the front porch. Aunt Julia jumps from the sofa.

Uncle Bill's head is the first thing to poke through the open screen door. He's wearing his black Tigers cap, the same one he pulls on every night as soon as he gets home from work. His hair is almost as dark as that hat. He crosses into the house, his black steel-toed work boots clumping on the wooden floor, and as he passes Arie, still standing in the center of the room, he scoops her up with one arm, cradles her to his side, and together they drop down on the large sofa opposite Izzy. Aunt Julia closes her eyes and exhales a long breath. Taking steps that make no noise at all, she follows Uncle Bill and sits next to him. Uncle Bill wraps his other arm around Aunt Julia, settling back into the sofa's deep, square cushions, dragging her with him. She laughs and slaps at his chest, but not slaps that would hurt. Then she leans into him, lets her head rest on his shoulder, and seems to forget for a moment that the twins are in the room.

"I'm so relieved," Aunt Julia says, sinking into Uncle Bill's side.

Grandma says the girls are the spitting image of their mother, but Izzy and Arie don't know their mother. Grandma says take a gander at your aunt Julia. That's close enough. Izzy resists a peek at her own flat chest. There is no chance Aunt Julia ever looked like Izzy and Arie and no chance Izzy and Arie will ever grow to look like Aunt Julia.

Stretching an arm around Uncle Bill's waist, Aunt Julia hooks a finger through one of his belt loops. "Where was she?"

Uncle Bill kisses the top of Arie's head and winks at Izzy across the room. It's not too late, yet. Maybe there will still be time for a drive downtown and chocolate sundaes. When Uncle Bill doesn't answer, Aunt Julia unhooks her finger, slides to the edge of the sofa, and shifts in her seat so she can face him square-on.

"You found her, didn't you?" Aunt Julia's voice becomes thick and slow. Her Southern roots have a way of breaking ground whenever she gets especially worked up. "That's why you're home, right? You found Elizabeth."

Arie pokes Uncle Bill and points at the cap he still wears even though he's inside. Uncle Bill gives her the same wink he gave Izzy and snaps the bill of his cap between two fingers. It flips off his head, spins end over end, and lands in his lap.

"Not yet," he says, pinching the tip of Arie's chin.

"What do you mean, not yet?" Aunt Julia stands and stares down on Uncle Bill. "It's pitch-black out there. She has to be home."

Uncle Bill pats the cushion next to him, and when Aunt Julia sits again, he pats her knee. "We've stirred up a hornets' nest, girls," he says, rubbing his rough face against Arie's cheek. He's done that to Izzy before so she knows why Arie tucks her chin and giggles. Izzy touches a hand to her own cheek because she can almost feel it too. "You're going to have to stay close to home for a while."

"Grandma says hornets will leave us well enough alone if we leave them well enough alone," Izzy says.

"Not that kind of hornets, kiddo."

"What is it, Bill?" Aunt Julia says.

"A lot of angry words being tossed around down at the Filmore. Best the girls stay close to home until Elizabeth is found."

The Filmore Apartments are the reason Grandma almost didn't let Izzy and Arie come to Aunt Julia's this year. Coloreds live there, and Grandma said it's only a matter of time now. If people are throwing around angry words, that must mean they think the coloreds have been stirring up trouble and maybe they stirred up trouble for Elizabeth. Maybe she didn't wander off like Aunt Julia thinks she did.

"What about our cat?" Izzy says. The words pop out before she can stop them. It's easier to think about a lost cat than a lost person. "If we can't leave the house, we can't very well find her. Isn't that right? You're saying we can't look for Patches."

"It'll only be for a short time," Uncle Bill says. "You can put out food on the back porch. Milk, maybe. Cats like milk. Try to tempt her home."

Izzy stands and takes a few steps toward Aunt Julia and Uncle Bill. "Couple days won't hurt, I guess," she says, but before she can finish, Uncle Bill wraps one long arm around her waist and scoops her up too.

"But no leaving the house without Aunt Julia's permission," he says, rubbing his day-old beard against Izzy's cheek like he did Arie's. "Understood?"

Like Arie, Izzy tucks her chin and laughs.

Together, the twins say, "Understood."

"So you'll go back now?" Aunt Julia says. "You'll go and help the others." She stands again and smooths her skirt. Every part of Aunt Julia is plentiful and round. She is forever reattaching buttons and stitching up stressed seams. "You should get going. The girls and I will be fine."

Uncle Bill squeezes the twins close and talks over Izzy's head.

"There's one more thing, Julia. It's the police. There's a fellow outside, an officer. He'd like to talk to you."

"To me?"

Uncle Bill nods. "I'll come with you. You girls are fine here for a few minutes, aren't you?"

"No," Aunt Julia says. She waves a hand at the three of them and smiles but doesn't show her teeth this time. "I'm happy to talk with him. You all stay put."

———

The man standing on Julia's front porch wears a blue hat, a dark shirt, and a tie. A police officer's uniform. He removes his hat, squints into the overhead light. "Ma'am."

"I have children in here," Julia says, meaning she doesn't want the girls to hear what this man might say.

The officer backs away, a signal for Julia to join him. Once they have moved off the porch, the officer's eyes drop to Julia's chest and loiter. She pulls closed the lightweight cardigan she slipped on at sunset, crosses her arms, and scratches at a small grease stain on her sleeve.

Outside the house, the shadows that had floated past the living-room windows have transformed into real people stooping to search under parked cars, wading through bushes that grow between houses, crawling under porches. A few flashlights settle on Julia before sweeping on past. The shouts have started up again and the air no longer smells of sweet sulfur. Everyone has put away the fireworks for the night.

"There's news?" Julia asks, wrapping her arms more tightly around her waist.

The officer introduces himself. Officer Thompson. Julia wants to run a finger up his back like she does to the girls when they forget their manners and slouch. The officer has been at the Symanski house. He asks if Julia knows the Symanski girl and she says of course. They are waiting, she and the twins, for news Elizabeth is safe. The girls are too young to be out and are afraid to be left alone, so they are waiting at home, together.

"And you saw her today?" Officer Thompson asks. His light brown hair is matted to his forehead where his hat rested. "You saw . . ." He flips through a small pad of paper. "Elizabeth Symanski?"

"Earlier in the day," Julia says. "Around lunchtime. Much before any of this."

"And what can you tell me of that meeting?"

The officer stares down at his pad and only looks up when Julia is too long in answering. "You recall having seen her?"

"You make it sound so formal. I walked her home, is all. It was one thirty or so. Lunchtime at Grace Richardson's house. Much before any of this."

"You saw her to her door?"

Julia squints into a set of headlights rolling past. "I suppose I should say I watched her walk home."

"You watched?" the officer asks. "And what is it you saw?"

"From the sidewalk, I watched her. She reached her gate, the iron gate outside her house. And then her door. I saw her make her way inside."

The officer motions for Julia to follow him. She glances back at her house before joining the officer at the end of the driveway. Once there, he places both hands on Julia's shoulders and turns her to face the west end of the street. Then he moves behind her, leans forward until his chest bumps against the back of her head, stretches out his right arm and points down Alder Avenue.

"Like this?" he asks. "From the end of a drive like this you watched Elizabeth make her way home?"

"Yes," she says, inching away from the officer. "But I stood on Grace's driveway. Much closer to the Symanskis'."

"Eight houses," Officer Thompson says. When Julia tries to twist away, he grips her by both shoulders again and forces her to continue to look toward the Symanskis' house. "I counted eight houses between the Richardsons' and the Symanskis'."

With one extended finger, the officer counts out eight houses. His arm brushes against the side of Julia's head. She takes one step away, but the officer draws her back with a hand to her shoulder. Again, he points.

"I wonder," he says, "are you quite certain you saw her enter the house? From a distance such as this, even in good light? Is that possible, do you think?"

"The iron gate," Julia says. "She ran her fingers along the iron gate. I saw that. She reached her gate."

And now Julia knows. She was the last to see Elizabeth Symanski.

"Elizabeth's been gone all day?" Julia says. "All this time? Has no one else seen her?"

"You're quite sure she opened the gate?" the officer says, not answering Julia's questions.

"It was a difficult day," Julia says.

"She pushed it open?" the officer asks again, now standing at Julia's side. "You're quite certain? Walked through it and then up her sidewalk?"

"There was news," Julia says, silently counting out eight houses. In the light of day, she'd have seen much better. "The ladies were all talking. And the twins. They've only recently arrived. I had much to think about. She's done this before, you know. Elizabeth has strayed before. Surely someone else saw her after I did. One of the other ladies. One of the neighbors. She's wandered off. That's all."

She can't tell this man that instead of concerning herself with Elizabeth's well-being, Julia had been worried about the dead woman on Willingham and the prostitutes who come to the factory over the lunch hour. She can't tell him that Bill has been a good husband for the last two years and still she worries like all the ladies worry. She can't explain to him how Betty Lawson's baby cried and forced Julia from Grace's house. How those cries made Julia ache and want to double over from the pain of it but instead she dipped a finger in the baked beans and called for more brown sugar. She can't tell him that three years ago her own baby died and her husband won't father another, that he won't even touch her, not in that way. The officer wouldn't understand that Julia had to leave Grace Richardson's house before lunch was served because the fear of never having another baby had suffocated her and now she is so very sorry she didn't watch Elizabeth closely enough. Avoiding the officer's eyes, Julia says none of these things.

"I saw her," she says. "Elizabeth was home. I'm sure she was home. Surely someone else has seen her. Surely I wasn't the last."

———

Malina steps away from the window when Julia and a police officer walk down Julia's driveway toward the street. She leans against the wall, where no one will be able to see her, and continues flipping through the newspaper. Twice she's read through it and has yet to find anything about the dead woman on Willingham. If only a reporter would have commented on the woman's stature. Was she slender and petite or on the stout, portly side? This is all Malina needs to know.

If it weren't for all the people shouting out to Elizabeth Symanski, Malina might open a window or two to cool down the house. While her skirt's wide, six-yard sweep is perfectly suited to emphasize her narrow waist, it's a curse in the heat. It's only her imagination that those voices are getting closer. The men aren't circling her house, closing in because they suddenly realize Mr. Herze is not among them. If anyone asks why Malina's driveway is once again empty at long past suppertime, she'll tell them Mr. Herze is busy dealing with that nastiness down on Willingham. Someone must coordinate with the police and see to it the matter of that dead woman is solved. This is what she'll tell them, but only if someone asks.

"Good evening."

Malina closes the newspaper, crumples it as she draws it to her chest, and swings around. Mr. Herze stands in the doorway, his briefcase in one hand, his hat in the other.

"You've startled me," Malina says. She folds the newspaper in thirds. "I didn't expect you home so early. I rather thought the police would be keeping you busy."

Under the soft glow thrown by the porch light, the fringe of white hair around Mr. Herze's head glistens with perspiration. This unusual heat, even when it breaks in the evenings, is difficult for him to manage. He glances at the newspaper Malina still holds in one hand and then at Malina.

"It's yesterday's," she says. "Today's is there." She points at the entryway table. "Right there, waiting for you." Malina won't search today's paper for news of the dead woman until Mr. Herze has gone to bed, or better yet, not until he has left for work tomorrow.

"You must be famished," Malina says. "The table is set. I'll have supper on in no time."

"What's going on out there?" Mr. Herze says, kissing the cheek Malina offers him and then leaning through the open door.

Across the street, the officer and Julia still stand at the end of her driveway. Malina lures Mr. Herze into the house with a nod of her head and closes the door. He pulls a kerchief from his front pocket, pats his upper lip and forehead, and glances about the house as if wondering why it's so hot. His white shirt has wilted since this morning, and it clings to his soft middle.

"It's nothing," Malina says. "A lot of fuss over nothing."

This is how it should always be—Malina waiting at the dining-room table, supper in the oven, the ice bucket full. She should never find herself rushing through the back door, stuffing one of her nicer dresses in the closet, ruining a perfectly good pair of utility nylons because she couldn't take the time to slip them off with care, and crawling into bed without removing her makeup or pinning the hair at her temples. After leaving Willingham Avenue, her hammer abandoned in the alley, this is what she had done. As it turned out, she needn't have been in such a hurry. Mr. Herze followed a full thirty minutes later. The hair at the nape of his neck had been slightly damp and he smelled of fresh soap. His shirt, however, smelled of the girl. No matter that he always washed up afterward, only Malina could rid those shirts of the stench. This evening, he appears dry throughout and smells only of cigarettes smoked in a closed office, warmed-over coffee, and the faded remnants of cologne sprayed on first thing this morning. No trace of his girl.

"What do you mean, nothing?" Mr. Herze says. "Why are there people running about with flashlights? And why are there police on the street?"

Malina sets Mr. Herze's briefcase in the front closet and hangs his hat on the hook inside the closet door.

"I imagine it has to do with Elizabeth Symanski," Malina says.

"What of her?"

Malina smooths Mr. Herze's thinning hair, rests one cheek on his shirt, the limp cotton moist against her skin, and inhales through her nose. Still no evidence of the girl.

"Elizabeth?" Mr. Herze says again, nudging Malina to continue. "What's become of the girl?"

"Apparently, she's wandered off," Malina says, pulling away. Tomorrow, she'll fish this shirt from the hamper and smell it again.

"And they are searching for her?" Mr. Herze says, crossing in front of Malina to look out the dining-room window. "Have there been many men searching?"

"Yes, I suppose there have been."

Without another word, Mr. Herze lumbers up the stairs, taking them two at a time. A few minutes later, he returns, wearing brown trousers and the white undershirt he normally wears when fussing about in his garage. His chest pumps and his face glistens.

"Have you taken to driving at night again?" Mr. Herze's face, except for the sheen on top of his head, disappears in the dark entry. His white shirt glows.

Malina inhales, holds the air in her chest, and slowly, so Mr. Herze will not see it or feel it or hear it, she exhales. "Certainly not. Why on earth would I do such a thing?"

Mr. Herze trails his fingers over Malina's wrist, past her elbow, and wraps them around her upper arm. He knows she doesn't care for sleeveless blouses, doesn't like for others to see the loose skin that hangs there, and so this particular area will never show. His fingers dig into the slender bone.

"It's difficult for you still to see after dusk?"

Malina smiles, controls each breath so it flows smoothly. "The reflections are intolerable."

Still holding Malina by her arm, her fingertips tingling from lack of blood, Mr. Herze opens the door. He stands in the threshold, not quite inside, not quite out.

"So, you're home then? Every night?" he asks, and slides his hand up to Malina's shoulder, where he burrows his thumb under her delicate collarbone.

The proper name is the clavicle. She knows because Mr. Herze once broke one of hers. He presses his face close and studies her eyes. He's inspecting her for signs she's taken one of her pills. She stares back, doesn't let her eyes stray, holds her lids wide while reminding herself to blink so he'll know she hasn't. Dr. Cannon says if she does her counting and gets plenty of fresh air, she'll have no need of them.

"You're certain you've not taken to driving after dark?"

Malina drifts closer to Mr. Herze so anyone passing will think she is nuzzling her husband.

"Why would you ask such a silly thing? I have so much to do with my evenings. I can't remember the last time I started an engine after sunset."

And before she can stop herself, Malina has lied to her husband.

CHAPTER FIVE

It's been one full day since Elizabeth disappeared. Grace stands at the kitchen window, both hands resting on her hard, round stomach, and looks onto the dark alley, hoping Elizabeth will shuffle out from behind the garage, her arms stiff at her sides, her head lowered. But there is no one. The night air is cool and motionless. Inside, the oven clicks and heats the house, filling it with the smell of apple-banana muffins. Grace gathers her hair on top of her head, twists it, pins it in place, and turns her face toward the small fan Mother placed in the open window. The fan rotates from side to side, drawing in the outside air, cooling Grace's face and neck.

The neighborhood is quiet because after a full twenty-four hours, no one expects to find Elizabeth on Alder Avenue. The search has moved north and south, east and west. After the first night, James brought home maps of the city, and like he did on the back of an envelope, he drew boxes, numbered them, and wrote men's names inside each. When Saturday morning broke, everyone piled in their cars and congregated at the church. James separated the men and told them where to go. All day, they searched. They walked along Woodward Avenue, stopping in every shop, store, or restaurant to ask if anyone had seen Elizabeth. They knocked on doors, asked neighbors to unlock sheds, and pressed their faces to the windows of parked cars. For now, no one is talking about who killed that woman on Willingham or if men will lose jobs for taking up with colored prostitutes. All is forgotten until Elizabeth comes home.

Grace spent the day at the church with the other ladies while the men searched. The ladies gathered in the basement and kept the coffee brewing and plenty of hot food at the ready. But at five o'clock, James took Grace home because her ankles and fingers had swelled and she was kneading her back with her fists. "No more," he had said as he pulled into their driveway and left the car to idle. "You'll stay home from now on, for the good of the baby." He loves Grace, wants only to protect her and the baby they have dreamed of for five years. It's all Grace has ever wanted—a man and a child to love. Now she has both. Maybe it's too much. Maybe it's more joy than one woman should have and that's why this bad thing has come into their lives. "You and your mother stay with the phone," James had said before leaving Grace and returning to the search. "Call the hospitals again. You never know." And then he had held Grace's face in his two hands, made her meet his eyes with hers, and said, "You have to stop blaming yourself. You know how she wanders. Don't worry. I'll find her."

It's well after dark when the ticking from the small timer over the stove begins to slow. It stops altogether and dings. Mother pulls a tray of muffins from the oven and sets them on the table.

She'll take them to the church in the morning. If Elizabeth is found tonight, and surely she will be, the muffins freeze well, so there's no harm in making as many as they can manage.

"They're dry," Mother says, tapping the top of each muffin. "Told you those bananas weren't ripe enough." Her silver hair is pulled back as it always is for baking and she wears a loose gray duster. "I'll have a new batch in the oven in no time."

"Don't throw them out," Grace says. "We'll need as many as we can bake."

But even as Grace says it, Mother dumps the silver tray and a dozen muffins tumble into the trash can sitting near the back door.

"Put yourself to use," Mother says, poking her fork at the over-flowing garbage and then at the screen door. "Go on and take that out before it draws bugs."

Grace gathers the trash can and pushes open the door. At her last appointment, Dr. Hirsh said her joints would start to loosen soon to make room for the baby. He warned her to take care she didn't stumble into a nasty fall. The baby is growing heavier every day. She is especially heavy late in the afternoon and into the evening, so with her free hand Grace holds the metal railing and carefully makes her way down the three concrete stairs, testing each with her toe before stepping down with her full weight.

Any moment, news will come that Elizabeth has been found. Life will resume. Mother will return to her own house east of Woodward. James will fix the leak in the hot-water faucet upstairs, tighten the banister, trim the back bushes, so things will be just right before the baby arrives. Grace will wash all the diapers, blankets, and clothes the neighbor ladies have passed on. She will fold them, each one carefully, all the while talking to her baby girl, telling her about her new room; her strong, handsome daddy; the patch of green grass in the backyard where she will hopefully play next spring in the shade of the maple tree. Though James is rooting for a boy, because every husband does, Grace knows she is carrying a little girl, has known it from the first flutter, and once James sees the tiny face, he will love his baby girl as he loves his wife.

Outside, all up and down Alder, the houses, though empty because everyone has joined the search, are lighted up in hopes Elizabeth will find her way home. Rounding the back of the house, Grace listens for the deep voices she sometimes hears late at night. As she nears the garage, the light from the kitchen throwing a dim glow into the alley, she sees their glass. There's more every day. Tomorrow, Grace will pick it all up and not tell James. She jerks her head left, thinking that was the sound of gravel being crushed by a heavy foot, and then right, thinking something or someone has rattled a doorknob.

Bracing the trash can against one hip, Grace backs toward the garage. The porch lights throw odd shadows, some long and thin that stretch across the ground, others round and broad that crouch at the alley's edge. Only when she notices the Williamsons' house does she exhale and realize she had been holding her breath. A light shines in Mrs. Williamson's kitchen window and in an upstairs bedroom, where Mr. Williamson listens to his ball games. Not everyone has gone to the church. Some of the older folks have stayed behind. Those are probably the sounds of Mrs. Williamson fussing about in her cabinets or washing the supper dishes. On such a lovely evening, she would have left her windows open and noise does have a peculiar way of traveling among the tightly knit houses. But there is that sound again—tiny bits of gravel crushed under a heavy foot.

———

At the church, the ladies have had all day to realize that Julia folds a sloppy linen and dishes out servings that are too large. By day's end, they are weary of cleaning up after her and so put her in charge of the coffee. The search will soon end for the night, and when the men return, they'll want something hot and fresh. The job is really quite important, the ladies say. You are the best cook among us, no question about that, and you brought so much food. More than your share. Let us take care of the serving. So while Julia sees to the coffee by readying two percolators, fetching the cream, and scrounging up silver tongs to accompany the box of sugar cubes, the rest of the ladies tend to a table crowded with covered casserole dishes and foil-wrapped trays. Mr. Symanski is the only man among them. He sits on a wooden chair near the kitchen, his back rigid, his feet resting on the ground.

At the bottom of the narrow stairwell leading into the basement, the first of the men appears. They were instructed to quit by ten o'clock. The police insisted. No one wants those men roaming the streets any later and giving the police more to contend with. After last night's search, everyone agreed there was no sense looking on Alder anymore. The men, at least two to a car, were to roll through the nearby streets and call out for Elizabeth. She doesn't like to be left alone and she doesn't like the dark so she'll stay near the houses with brightly lit porches. Call out that Ewa wants her to come home. She'll believe it even though Ewa is dead.

After the first man appears, another follows and then another. Under the white lights, their skin looks gray. The ladies hurry toward the men, arms extended, and usher them to the food. The first night of the search, which went on until morning, the men had looked tired, their eyes red from squinting in the darkness, but they had all agreed daylight would bring more success. Tonight, as more men duck under the low-hanging threshold and congregate at the food table, the overhead lights throwing heavy shadows on their faces, their backs are rounded and they shake their heads from side to side. Their hope has faded.

The men stand in small groups that grow as more searchers file down the stairs and, slowly, some of the ladies abandon their serving duties and join the men. A few of the ladies suggest the bake sale be postponed, but Malina Herze says it's too early to consider such a thing and reminds the ladies to keep those donations to the thrift store coming. Each time a new man walks down the stairs, every head turns as if the searchers and their wives are expecting some news. Arthur Jacobson, who lives well north of Alder now but still comes to Sunday services at St. Alban's, is one of the last to walk into the basement. With hat in hand, he gestures toward the narrow windows that open out onto the parking lot above.

James Richardson and a few other men stand in the parking lot with two police officers. A streetlight shines, its yellow glow penning in the group. Even from this distance, Julia can see that James is tiring. His head hangs and he kneads his forehead with the palm of one hand. He doesn't only have the search to cause him worry, but he must also worry after Grace and their baby. As one of the officers reaches out to show something to the group, James and the others lean in. After a few moments, they stand back, almost in tandem, and shake their heads.

A few more words are exchanged and the group breaks up, the officers walking to their patrol car while James and the other men drift toward the church entrance. The group inside the basement breaks up too. Julia returns to her coffee, where she busies herself by straightening and counting the cups and saucers. Twenty-three won't be enough. The room where they usually hold wedding receptions and celebrations of first communion is almost full. Resting her fingertips on the table's edge, Julia says hello to Harry Bigsby, the only man to come for coffee. She slides a cup and saucer toward him and offers him cream.

"May I get you a plate, Harry?" she says, taking his corduroy cap and brushing lint from its brim before handing it back.

"Doesn't look good," he says, shaking off Julia's offer. He dips his head in thanks and walks toward the center of the room.

James Richardson is the next to walk down the stairs. He removes his hat, pushes his fingers through his dark hair, and shakes his head. "Seems we're done for the night," he says.

Julia pulls her sweater closed. It's her loosest cardigan and yet it's too tight.

"Any of you ladies familiar with Elizabeth's belongings?" James asks. "Familiar enough you might recognize a shoe?"

The room is silent, but unlike Julia, the others aren't surprised. They shake their heads because this must be the news they were waiting for, the sign things would not end well for Elizabeth. Be-hind James and the other men who had been talking with the of-ficers, Bill ducks under the threshold and stands, hat dangling from one hand. He nods in Julia's direction to reassure her the twins are fine. After spending most of the morning with Julia, the girls had begged to go back home and promised to lock the doors and win-dows and pull closed the drapes. Bill, in turn, promised to check on them when he was out.

"Julia?" James says, searching the room until his eyes settle on her. "You think you would know Elizabeth's things?" He is asking because everyone knows Julia was the last to see Elizabeth.

"I'm afraid not, James," she says. "I suppose Grace best knows Elizabeth." All around the room, people are staring at Julia. Some lower their eyes. Others look at her with wilted lids. "Or Charles. Won't you know, Charles?"

"Found a shoe," James says. "A few of the fellows did. They found it near Chamberlin and Willingham. Near the river. From what I saw, it's white. Soft-soled. Small, that's for sure. Not too beat-up. Doesn't appear it's been there long. Could belong to any-one, though. Just a shoe. But they say Elizabeth knew that street. Say she used to shop there with Ewa. Think she could have found her way down there and maybe it's her shoe."

Someone has handed Mr. Symanski a drink. He doesn't look up from the sweaty glass he clutches between two hands. Before Ewa died, Elizabeth rode the bus with her mother. She learned to pick out tomatoes that weren't too soft and bananas that were bright yellow and firm.

"Ask Grace, she'll know," Julia says again, hoping she repeats it because it's true and not because she wants to remind people Grace saw Elizabeth that afternoon too.

"Police'll see to it," James says, pulls on his hat and disappears up the staircase that will lead him back to the parking lot and home to Grace.

Julia crosses the room, rests one hand on the back of Mr. Symanski's chair, and squats at his side. "I'm so sorry, Charles," she says, and manages a smile. "It doesn't have to mean something bad. We have plenty of reason for hope." She squeezes his arm, which is much thinner than she would have expected. "Let me get you a bite to eat. Something sweet to keep your strength up? I brought my rhubarb pie. No one beats my rhubarb pie. You know that's true enough."

"Everyone is doing much for my Elizabeth. They are caring very much for her, yes?"

"I saw her last," Julia says, tugging again at her boxy cardigan.

"The police are telling me this." Mr. Symanski brushes one hand across Julia's hair and smiles as if Ewa's hair must have once been red too, and he is remembering it fondly. "But there is being no need for what you are trying to say."

"I should have watched her more closely."

"You are always being good to my Elizabeth." Beads of water from the cool glass drip onto his blue trousers. "These others are being unkind to you, yes? They are blaming you?"

"They're troubled, is all," Julia says. "We're all troubled."

While the men continue to eat their fried chicken and thick slices of Bundt cake, the ladies begin to pack up their dishes. They dash this way and that, their skirts fluttering about their calves, their heels in basic black and tan clicking across the gray-and-white speckled tile. Dishes and glassware knock against each other; spoons tap the rims of coffee cups. The ladies iron out their used sheets of aluminum foil, fold them, save them for another day. Perhaps tomorrow, when they gather again. Everyone is worrying Elizabeth may have drowned in the river. As sad as it is to consider, that's what they are thinking. And because they fade away when Julia passes among them, it's also clear they are wondering how Julia will ever live with what she has done. After all that Julia has already been through, how ever will she manage the strain?

CHAPTER SIX

W hile the adults spent the day at the church, Arie and Izzy
stayed inside like they promised. Mostly they stayed in
their room and looked out the window onto Alder Avenue, hoping
to see something, anything. Down on Woodward, the hum of traffic built as the day wore on, and the faster the traffic soared by and
the more cars that piled up, the louder the hum became and the
more Arie and Izzy felt themselves left behind. When, after an
entire afternoon, they saw nothing down on Alder except a few
cars and one stray dog, they gave up on the window and plugged in
their record player. Sitting like a small black suitcase on the end of
Izzy's bed, it had been waiting for the girls when they first arrived
at Aunt Julia's house. A gift for both of them. Propped up next to
the small case had been a Tune Tote carrier filled with 45s. All
afternoon, Arie spun those records, always especially careful when
she lifted the needle at the end of a song so as to not scratch the
vinyl. She wanted the music to last. Not that she really cared much
for the records. None of her favorites were inside the pink carrying

case anyway. It was mostly full of Peggy Lee and Frank Sinatra. What Arie did care about was making Izzy happy again so she didn't do anything to cross Uncle Bill and Aunt Julia.

Song after song, Arie rolled the small knob on the record player, making the music louder and louder so Izzy would dance and spin and stop thinking about Elizabeth and their lost cat. Izzy had been sulking ever since Uncle Bill made them cross their hearts and swear to stay inside and not go searching. But listening to records, no matter how loudly, did not make Izzy forget and they did not make her happy, and what Arie feared all day finally happened after Uncle Bill checked in for the last time. He said he and Aunt Julia would be back home in an hour or so and that Izzy and Arie should behave until then. Even before Uncle Bill was out the door, Arie knew Izzy had a plan.

"Who'll ever know?" Izzy says. "It's dark now. No one'll see us and we'll be back long before Uncle Bill and Aunt Julia come home. We'll look for Elizabeth, but we might find Patches, too. Happens all the time. Animals follow their people all the way across the country, so why not to the other side of Woodward? Street's so quiet, we just might find them both."

Arie agrees only when Izzy threatens to go with or without her. Together, they slip on their sneakers in case they have to do some running and decide to leave the house through the kitchen door. Less noticeable than the front. Arie goes first and Izzy follows, letting the screen slap shut. Arie scolds her with a shake of her head, but before she can follow up with a reminder to be quiet, Izzy yanks her down the stairs. They run across the backyard, brightly lit because Aunt Julia made sure both the front and back porch lights were switched on and that both bulbs were fresh. She didn't want one burning out when they were most needed. They run until they reach the shadows thrown by Uncle Bill's garage, Izzy dragging Arie all the way, and once there, they flatten themselves against the rough siding. Both breathe deeply. Their chests pound up and down, not so much from the long run, because it wasn't so long, but because sneaking outside and running into the dark and listening for any sound at all on the empty street and hearing not one thing are all scary enough to make every breath hard to find.

"I'm not going on the street," Arie whispers, one hand pressed to her chest to slow her heart. "Someone's sure to see us out there."

The garage scratches their bare shoulders and arms. They should have thought to put on long sleeves. The air is always cooler when the sun sets, so they should have known. Arie shivers, partly because of the cold but mostly because of the dark.

"Then I'll search the street by myself." Izzy talks a little too loudly, as if trying to fool herself and Arie into believing there is nothing to fear. "You check the alley," she says, and begins to slide her feet, one after the other, toward the far end of the garage. "Nobody'll see you back there. Be sure you kick all the bushes. We'll meet here in fifteen minutes."

Arie waves at Izzy to come back. She wants to ask what will happen if she kicks a bush and accidentally kicks Elizabeth or their cat or something else entirely. But before Arie can ask, Izzy has disappeared around the side of Aunt Julia's house. Another question Arie should have asked is how are they to know when fifteen minutes is up. Neither of them wears a watch, so how are they to know? One thing she is certain of—she won't be kicking anything. She'll walk to the end of the next block and back again. That's not so far, and when she returns long before Izzy, Arie will lie and say she only just got back too.

Stepping into the alley, Arie immediately drifts toward the middle. Even though the edges are more brightly lit, something or someone could hide along the edges. The center feels safer, like whatever might be hiding would have to jump out at her, giving her time to run for home. She continues walking, letting her eyes roll from left to right and, every few yards, checks behind her. It used to be, on a night like this, Arie would watch the dark sky for hours, hoping for a glimpse of that Russian rocket. She imagined it would look like a bolt of lightning, shooting from one end of the sky to the other. She stopped watching and stopped hoping the dog inside was alive when her teacher said the ship had fallen back to Earth. She forgets sometimes, on a night like tonight when the sky is especially dark, and still looks up, hoping to see that bright light.

When she reaches the Obermires' house, she stops walking. They don't have a garage, and Arie can see between the houses all the way to the street. No sign of Izzy. She takes a few more steps, keeping her eyes on the space between the houses as long as she can. She's going to watch the street until she can't see it anymore and then she's going to run as fast as she can all the way to the end of the next block. It doesn't matter how tired she gets or how much her feet burn or her lungs ache. She won't stop running until she's standing back at Uncle Bill's garage. Buckling up her fists, she dips her head, takes three long strides, and stops.

He must have stepped out of the shadows hanging over the Richardsons' garage and into the center of the alley because Arie would have seen him if he'd been there all along. He's only a house and a half away. She would have seen him. She backs up a few feet and stops again when he lifts a hand. He holds it out like a stop sign and leans as if he's talking to someone inside the garage. He straightens. He's a solid shadow with arms and legs. He waves a hand like he's swatting away a bug. He means for her to slip over to the side of the alley. He means for her to hide. He leans again, straightens again, and this time, touches a finger to his lips to silence her.

Grandma would call this prairie grass. No one must mow back here. Mrs. Schofield died and Mr. Schofield doesn't care about the overgrown grass. Arie parts the tall stalks and pushes her way through, wishing again she'd changed into slacks and long sleeves. She slides down the side of the garage and squats there. Her breath is too loud. It rushes down into her lungs and back up again. She cups one hand over her mouth and wraps the other around her knees. The garage digs into the knobs of her backbone.

The man who was a shadow stands at the Richardsons' garage. Mrs. Richardson is Aunt Julia's best friend. Her blond hair is almost white and always smooth no matter what the weather is like, and in a few months, she's going to have a baby. Izzy and Arie both agree: if they could look like someone, anyone, they would look like Mrs. Richardson. The man leans into the garage again, tilts his head in Arie's direction, and when he straightens, two more men walk out. One of them is the same size as the man who waved Arie away, and the third is taller—taller even than Uncle Bill.

When the men have taken a few steps in Arie's direction, she tucks her head and hides her eyes. Air races through her body, much too loudly, so loudly they'll hear her. Count to twenty. Count to twenty and they'll be gone. But the counting makes her dizzy. She holds her breath. Gravel crunches and tiny rocks bounce across the hard dirt path as they're kicked about. The footsteps stop. Arie lifts her eyes. The group stands a few feet beyond her hiding place. One of them, the largest, stoops and picks up something from the ground near his feet. The other two walk on down the alley while the largest rears back and throws. Glass shatters and the three men take off running.

Izzy will be back soon. After fifteen minutes, she'll come back and she'll press herself against Uncle Bill's garage where they started out, where she'll be hidden from the men. Arie tries to count again, but her hot breath and the garage digging into her back and the stalks poking and scratching her arms make her want to cry and she can't count when she's crying. Somewhere close by, a door opens and heavy boots hit a wooden porch. Arie cups both hands over her mouth.

At the far end of the alley, where it meets up with Woodward, the men run around the corner. They're gone. Arie unfolds her legs, rubs her hands over the scratches on her arms, and lifts one foot and then the next up and over the tall grass. Inside the Richardsons' garage, something bangs about, not loudly, but quietly, as if someone is trying not to bang about at all. There is a thin, soft groan. Someone standing. Arie backs away from Mrs. Richardson's garage, swings around, and runs for home.

———

Most on the block are not yet home from the church. Malina would have normally stayed until the last dish was washed and packed and the tables folded and stowed in the storage closet, but when Mr. Herze said he'd be making a final run through a neighborhood north of Alder and that one of the men would drop him at the house, Malina had said she'd be happy to drive the car home. She had taken the keys, smiled, and only then noticed how closely Mr. Herze watched her.

"You're not concerned about the glare?" he had asked.

"How can I be concerned with my own fears when our poor Elizabeth has yet to be found?"

Mr. Herze had stared down on her for so long that the ladies standing nearby drifted away. When finally he left with the other men, Malina excused herself, trusting the rest of the ladies to do the cleaning.

She drops her keys and the large brown handbag on the entry table. The house is dark. Leaning to peek outside, she sees one of those twins running up the street toward Julia Wagner's house. It's the first Malina has seen of either one of them this summer. She leans out the door, looking for the other one and thinking she might scold them for running about at this inappropriate hour, but she hasn't time for such matters.

Checking the street one last time and seeing no sign of Mr. Herze, Malina closes the door and opens her handbag. It was a terrible embarrassment to be carrying this monstrosity at the church, being out-of-season as it is, but she had needed the large bag again if she was going to tend to the things that needed tending. Now she'll hurry up about it before Mr. Herze comes home. From the bottom of the handbag, she pulls out the hammer she purchased from Simpson's Hardware earlier in the day to replace the one she dropped down on Willingham.

Making her way across the driveway and toward Mr. Herze's garage, Malina holds the hammer with both hands, and as she walks she tests the weight and feel of it. Much like the other hammer, as best she can remember. At the sound of a car engine, she stops and listens, but the engine continues on past her house and fades as the car drives down Alder. Not Mr. Herze. If she had the time, Malina would count to twenty to try to slow her heart and quiet the tension that has settled in her neck and shoulders. The nerves have traveled as far as her stomach tonight, and she might need to chew a sliver of ginger root before slipping into bed. Dr. Cannon says there's always time for a few deep breaths, but he's wrong. There's never time for counting and breathing when a lady is truly in need.

Inside the garage, Malina tiptoes through the boxes and bags scattered about the floor, all of them donations for the thrift store that the other ladies have dropped off with her to be sorted and delivered, and once she reaches the center of the room, she stretches overhead and tugs on a small chain. She squints in the sudden brightness. The breeze that followed her through the door stirs up the single bulb that dangles from the ceiling and light rolls around the small room, aggravating her already-queasy stomach. The thin silver chain swings from side to side and eventually hangs motionless.

There is always a certain smell in the garage, like sawdust, though Mr. Herze rarely runs a saw, particularly in the summer.

He prefers to tackle his projects in the autumn and early spring. But some odors are like that—always sticking to things and making a nuisance of themselves no matter how many weeks or months have passed.

In Malina's hand, this new hammer's wooden handle is smooth. She can't remember if the other one, the one she dropped in that dark alley, was also smooth. And wasn't the other handle red? But the hardware store hadn't had a red-handled hammer. Only this brown-handled one. It isn't as if she regularly touches Mr. Herze's tools, but she is quite certain the head of the hammer she carried down the factory's alley was forked on one side. She is quite certain of that. How much more could matter about a hammer?

Edging toward the wooden slab that Mr. Herze uses as a work surface for his gluing and sanding, Malina reaches out with both hands and gently lays the new hammer in two metal hooks hanging from a pegboard. The board is a result of careless neighbors. So many times Mr. Herze has loaned out a tool only to find it missing when he later discovered a need for it. By that time, he often forgot to whom he had loaned the tool. Now, with one glance at the black outlines on his pegboard, he can know which tool is not in its proper place and he no longer forgets. The rest of his equipment—fishing rods, a shotgun handed down from his father, a black pistol, filet knives, and an ax or two are locked up in a cabinet alongside the pegboard because Mr. Herze must worry the neighbors will make off with those things too. Oddly, not as many neighbors ask to borrow tools anymore.

The night she took the hammer and dropped it in her handbag, she had briefly, only for a moment, considered unlocking the cabinet and taking the black pistol for her protection. A gun, however, would require a certain degree of skill, and she didn't begin to know about bullets and triggers and such. Mr. Herze once mentioned he kept the weapon loaded. In an emergency, a man wouldn't want to be fooling around with boxes of ammunition that might spill or, worse yet, be misplaced. But Malina had no way of knowing for sure if it was loaded or not, so she had settled on the hammer.

Tilting her head first to the right and then to the left, Malina reaches out with one finger and adjusts the hammer upward a quarter inch until it slips inside the black outline. Even with this adjustment, the head of the new hammer is much smaller than the head of the hammer she lost, and the outline no longer fits.

If it weren't for Mr. Herze's sudden questions about her nightly driving habits, Malina wouldn't have concerned herself so with the hammer she lost in that alley. But eventually, Mr. Herze will make his way into the garage and will notice his missing hammer with only a glance. First, he will ask Malina if she has seen the tool. Next, he'll stomp from neighbor to neighbor, accusing them along the way. He does so hate it when people borrow his things. Eventually, he'll think it odd his hammer disappeared so mysteriously, and he'll give thought to something he might otherwise dismiss.

If someone has told Mr. Herze that Malina was driving that night, perhaps the same person will tell him she carried with her a red-handled hammer. It would do no good for Mr. Herze to learn Malina was at the factory. He has never tolerated a wife who asked questions or poked about in his business. Malina learned this in the early years. And for all the years that followed, she's remembered. If only she had gone back for the hammer or, better yet, if only she hadn't worried so about an empty driveway and a ruined supper. If only she had gone back, there would be no proof. If only she had gone back, she would have no need for red-handled or brown-handled hammers or any type of hammer. If only she had gone back, Mr. Herze would never know for certain she had been on Willingham. He'd never know for certain she lied.

————

At the garage, Grace had set aside the garbage can and reached down to grab the heavy wooden door's handle. Taking out the garbage had definitely been a sign the evening was drawing to a close. James would come home soon enough and they would go to sleep for the second night knowing Elizabeth was not yet home. With both hands wrapped firmly around the small metal handle, Grace gave a good yank, slipped her hands under the door's bottom edge, and shoved it overhead. It was harder for her now that the baby had grown so large.

Inside, the garage was dark. James's car was parked in its usual spot. Howard Wallace drove him to the church, or was it Al Thompson? James had his maps to study and his notes to make. The others wanted him thinking and planning, not driving. Two silver garbage cans stood next to the car in their usual spot. She dropped a tissue over the handle of the first trash can so as to not soil her fingers. That can was full, so she dropped the silver lid, and as she lifted the second, a tissue still protecting her from the grimy handle, a hand slapped over her face.

The hand was bare, hard, and cold. The large palm and thick

fingers covered her nose and mouth, cutting off her air. She threw her head from side to side, forward and back. A body, wide and tall, forced her, stumbling, tripping, deeper inside the garage. Her lungs burned. She reached for the hand, scratching at it, tearing at it, and then someone standing in front of her grabbed her wrists.

"Shhhh, now," a deep voice whispered. His breath warmed her cheeks and eyes. The words rattled as if they burned the man's throat.

The one behind slid his hand over her mouth. She sucked air through her nose. Their scent was sour. The man who stood in front had a small beard on the tip of his chin. He was tall, taller even than James. The man drew three fingers over the beard, drawing them to a point. He set a green bottle on the trunk of James's car. Green glass like Julia finds behind her house, like James and Grace find behind their house. He looked at Grace's belly. Smiled, laughed maybe. Holding her by the wrists, he swung them from side to side like they were children singing on a playground.

"Good girls are quiet," he said.

The one behind took her arms, crushed her wrists in one hand, and covered her mouth again with the other. He pulled her arms back, grinding his body against hers. Her shoulders burned.

The smiling one in front touched his chin, pet the small tuft growing there. A third said, "Jesus Christ," and turned his face away because Grace's stomach rose up at them as she arched her back. The one behind scrubbed his cheek against hers, like gritty sandpaper. One hand touched her stomach and then another. One slipped under the hem of the blouse that floated over her baby. She tasted his stale breath. The hand pulled on the elastic panel that

73

stretched more every week. The hand was cool and wet on her skin. It lay there, not moving.

"Jesus damn." This man couldn't watch. He had tired eyes. He blinked slowly, shook his head, and disappeared.

The one behind yanked her head until she was staring into the dark rafters. Overhead, shadows folded in on themselves. That same hand slid off her mouth, pulled down over her throat, and pinched tightly so that for another moment she couldn't inhale. It was a warning of what he could do, and then he reached through the neckline of her blouse. Mother hand-stitched the lace there. When the hand couldn't fit, it pulled at the seam, tearing it open, tearing the lace. Jagged nails snagged her blouse. Rough, callused fingers touched her skin. Her breasts were heavier than before, heavier every day, and Mother said that meant the baby would come early. She said Grace would need to bind herself after the birth because her breasts would fill with milk and they wouldn't have need for it.

Falling backward, Grace's arms flew up and she landed on her tailbone. Two hands pushed her to the ground, pinned her wrists. The darkness settled in around her. From somewhere above her, she heard their voices. Two of them. One talked of the newspaper and wondered if they would write about Grace. Would anyone care to print an article that told of what happened to her? Would the police ever come? Would they act as if it never took place? They knew that colored woman on Willingham. At the very least, knew of her, the dead woman no one talked about since Elizabeth disappeared. The dead woman who was never written about in the newspaper. The dead woman whom the police dismissed with a few questions over coffee and cigarettes. These men, this man, knew about her, and this was what he'd do to set things right.

One of them pressed Grace's face away, forcing her cheek into the ground. She stared into the side of one of James's tires. The green bottle fell off the car, shattered on the garage floor. One entered her. This was what became of Elizabeth. The breathing came from behind her, above her, all around her. This was what Elizabeth last heard. He was on top of Grace, his hands planted on either side, thick cords and dark wiry hair running up his forearms. This was what Elizabeth last saw. Grace stared at the black tread. James had once shown her how to stick a penny in a tire and check that the tread was safe. She had laughed because she never did learn to drive. When they sell this house and move away because no one wants to be the last to get out, James says he'll try again to teach her.

"Jesus damn," one said from somewhere far away.

This was what happened to Elizabeth. They must have started with her and this was how they'd set things right.

And then it is quiet.

CHAPTER SEVEN

Inside the empty garage, Grace's skin cools. The men are gone. Somewhere down the street, glass breaks. Then silence. She inhales, exhales—only the sound of her own breath. Next to James's car, green glass sparkles where the moonlight hits it. His car doesn't have the sharp angles or sparkling chrome of some of the newer models. Its back end is rounded; its nose, short and blunt. Rolling onto her side, she pulls up her knees as high as her belly will allow and gathers the front of her blouse. Mother's lace hangs in shredded pieces. Grace places her other hand on her baby. The doctor said she would drop in another month or so and begin to position herself for birth.

Piecing her blouse together, Grace pushes herself off the ground. The kitchen trash can lies on its side. The dry muffins are scattered across the dirt floor. A few have rolled under James's car. A few more have been trampled, mashed into the ground. Clutching Mother's ruined lace in one hand, Grace uses the other to pick up the muffins, even the few that are no more than crumbs, and empties the trash in the second silver garbage can.

Outside the garage, the alley is empty and dark as if the men were never there. Beyond the house, the lights from the street make her blink. She closes her eyes, breathes in through her nose and out through her mouth. Sulfur hangs in the air. She heard them earlier in the evening, fireworks crackling a few blocks over. They start earlier every year, kids and their firecrackers. Every July 4, she and James board the *Ste. Claire* at the foot of Woodward and travel down the Detroit River. It's where they first met. This summer, because of the baby, James says they might need to skip a year.

She was ten that Fourth of July; James, eighteen. He says he remembers her, even as a child. That's romance, and not reason, talking. Grace had stood among the adults and other fidgeting children, the wooden gangplank underfoot, and for a time, thought only of the cold river water below. Those are her first memories of the *Ste. Claire*—the tingle in her stomach when her feet hit the hollow wooden planks, the fear of plunging into the cold water below, and the sharp, sweet smell of sulfur. The ship's horn soon followed, a deep blast. Mother said, because she said the same every year, that it was a sorrowful sound and this was no time for sorrow.

Because she was ten, Grace was too old to run ahead of her parents. In years past, she would leave Mother's side and weave in and out of the other passengers to reach the front of the line. Being one of the first on the ship meant the brass railing leading to the upper deck would be untouched, unblemished, and the mahogany woodwork would shine. But it was high time Grace behave like a lady, and being a lady meant she wouldn't be one of the first aboard. All the hands of the passengers who came before her would ruin that perfect shine. The year she was ten, she stood in line, hopping from one foot to the other, one gloved hand tucked inside Mother's, already sorry for what she would see when she stepped aboard.

The ladies, all ages, who waited alongside Grace stood a little taller that year, as if preparing for something. Mother said the whole country was bracing itself and had good reason to shore up its footing. Grace didn't know what that meant or why the country needed a sound foothold, but the spirit of those ladies with their full sleeves and cinched waists and hair that hung loosely over one eye and down their backs lifted her up. She walked with her shoulders back and her head high and wished her dress weren't one sewn for a child.

The men who boarded the *Ste. Claire*, that year and every other year, wore suits because when the sun set, a band would play on the upper deck. As the engines churned and the music throbbed, the gentlemen would wrap their arms around the ladies' tiny bound waists and spin them across a dance floor polished with cornmeal. This was where Grace first saw James, his right hand cradling the small of a young woman's back and his left hand wrapped around hers. Their feet floated across the glossy floor, and with each spin, he pulled her closer. He was tall, taller than every girl wearing her best heels, and his shoulders were broad and full and one dark curl fell across his forehead, tossed out of place by the spinning and twirling.

As he danced, James had laughed easily with the girl he held in his arms, perhaps too easily. He laughed as if she were a sister, and each time he did, the girl's frown deepened. Grace noticed him because of the easy laugh. She always covered her mouth when she laughed. But he laid his head back and opened his mouth wide, not afraid of who might hear or who might see. She felt certain he would be a kind man, and this kindness is what she would most remember in the years to come. In the end, the girl with a hemline that floated scarcely beneath her knees and yellow hair that glowed under the overhead lights crossed her arms over her chest and flipped that yellow hair when she stomped away to find another partner. Grace had been happy to watch her go.

From somewhere north of Alder, more fireworks crackle. One shoe is gone, so she walks toward the house with an awkward gait. Step, pause. Step, pause. At the back door, she makes her way carefully up the stairs because she holds the trash can in one hand and her tattered blouse in the other. She has no free hand to hold the railing. Careful, now, the doctor had said. You don't want to take a nasty fall.

In the kitchen, the fan still sweeps from side to side, wobbling on its stand. The oven timer beeps in a steady rhythm. Clutching her blouse in two fists, Grace sits at the table, both feet flat on the floor. She stares straight ahead at the clock over the stove. She waits to feel the familiar rumbling that means her baby girl is stretching and rolling. The fan sprays gusts of air that blow loose bits of hair across her face.

"Good Lord in heaven," Mother says, wiping her hands on a towel as she walks into the kitchen.

Mother has already wrapped a scarf around her hair and removed her makeup for bed. She still wears her gray duster but has changed into her felt slippers. With all that's going on, she'll spend the night. James insisted.

"See to those muffins before they burn," Mother says.

And then she sees Grace.

Walking around the table, her duster's full skirt fluttering about her, Mother keeps her distance. She picks up the trash can Grace set inside the door and puts it under the sink. She silences the timer and pulls the muffins from the oven.

"Mother?"

"Come with me, child," Mother says, holding Grace's forearm with one hand and cupping her elbow with the other.

They walk up the stairs and into the bathroom. Grace undresses because Mother tells her to and waits while Mother runs the hot water. Soon, the tub is full and Mother leads Grace to it, holds her by the arm as she lifts one foot and then the other over the edge. Grace lowers herself, pressing one hand to the tiled wall and keeping a strong hold of Mother's arm with the other. The warm water chokes her. She coughs into a closed fist, feels as if she might vomit. Mother rests a hand on Grace's shoulder until the nausea passes and then hands her a bar of soap.

"Go on and clean yourself," Mother says.

Grace's arms float at her sides, her belly rising up between them. Mother wraps Grace's fingers around the soap and begins to pull the gold pins from her hair. One at a time, Mother drops them on the side of the tub. A few slip over the rounded edge and fall silently to the floor where they catch in the beige bathmat. When every pin is out, Mother brushes Grace's hair until it is smooth and pins it up again using the same pins.

"I feel the baby," Mother says, resting one hand on Grace's stomach, where it rises out of the warm water. The one spot that is cool. "She's moving fine. Kicking. Do you see? Kicking hard and strong."

Grace slides both hands over her belly. It's hard like a shell, and after a moment of stillness, the baby shifts. Relief is the thing that makes her cry. When she first married James, the other husbands winked and slapped him on the back. Need only brush up against one this young. You'll have yourself a son in no time. But it didn't happen. For so many years, it didn't happen. Grace prayed every night for a baby, lit candles at St. Alban's, slept with a scrap of red ribbon under her pillow. She wanted a baby beyond all else, not only for herself but also for James. It will happen, James said when she cried. It will happen.

Mother helps Grace into her white cotton nightgown and into her bedroom and into her bed. She pulls up the sheet to Grace's chin and folds back the top blanket. This is what Mother did when Grace was a child. In the window, the white sheers flutter. A breeze brushes across Grace's face.

"I'll tell him you're feeling poorly, that you have a fever. I'll tell him to sleep on the sofa."

Grace rolls on her side and lays a hand on the baby. Another nudge from inside. "Elizabeth?" she asks.

Mother tilts her head. "Nothing. I've heard nothing."

Grace wants to ask Mother if anyone searched the Symanskis' garage even though she knows they did. She knows James looked there and others, too.

"The twins," she says, pushing herself into a sitting position with one hand while keeping the other on the baby. "Julia left them at home tonight. She said they were old enough. She thinks they're safe."

"I'll see to them," Mother says, waving at Grace to lie back and then pulling the curtains closed, cutting off the breeze. "You stay. Rest. Hardly a mark on you. You'll be well in the morning."

A flick. The door closes. The room goes dark. The air is still. In the bathroom, the water drains from the tub and Mother shuffles about, probably collecting Grace's clothes. She'll throw them away, won't bother to mend them.

The door opens again and light from the hallway spills into the room. Grace's eyelids flutter.

"Did you see the color of him?" Mother asks.

Grace nods or perhaps she only blinks.

"No man wants to know this about his wife," Mother says. "He can't live with it. Do yourself this favor. No man wants to know."

Surely this is what became of Elizabeth Symanski. Surely this is what she suffered.

The door closes again, and the room falls dark.

———

For tonight, the search is over. Outside Julia's dining-room window, the block is mostly quiet except for the steady buzz of insects, cicadas though it's early for them to be out. One by one, bedroom lights switch off up and down Alder Avenue, though every porch light still shines. Nearby, a baby cries. That will be Betty Lawson's little one, her cries carrying through the open window in her nursery. Upstairs, Bill and the twins sleep. Nothing should wake them.

No more slamming doors, no more cars rolling down the street. The pie plates have been washed and dried. The unused rhubarb has been wrapped in aluminum foil and stored in the refrigerator. Julia promised the twins a pie of their own tomorrow. She'll have to get up early to roll out the crust before she goes back to the church. The twins will be able to do the rest.

Through the dining-room window, Julia watches for Betty Lawson. After the last feeding before bedtime, Betty will tuck the baby in her carriage and stroll her down Alder. Betty says it's the only way to get the little one to sleep. Every night since the baby came to live with Betty and Jerry, Julia has watched Betty make this trip. Only once has Julia joined her. "The baby so favors you," Julia had said to Betty as they walked that night. She meant her comment to be kind, as if to say, without really saying it, that Betty and Jerry Lawson adopted the perfect child, one who would be mistaken for their own. "She really takes after Jerry's mother," Betty had said.

Each night since, Julia has watched Betty and the baby from her window, a wilted article about the Willows tucked in her front pocket. Julia cut the story from the newspaper almost a year ago, and she keeps it in the top drawer of the entry table. The Willows is a home for unwed mothers. Only good girls from nice homes. Every train in the country leads eventually to Kansas City and the Willows. This is most assuredly where Betty and Jerry went to adopt their perfectly matched child. Julia hadn't wanted to consider it. Why would a couple once successful consider adoption? But maybe it's a better way. Betty Lawson is definitely happy. Even though she won't admit she and her husband adopted their new baby, she is still happy. Her hair is flat these days and she regularly forgets to comb out her pin curls since the baby came to live with them, but her eyes are softer. It's the look of relief.

As Julia has watched Betty and her baby night after night, she has tried to force herself out the door again to ask Betty about the Willows. For three years, Bill has barely touched Julia, hardly seems sorry for it anymore. There may not be another baby if not for another way. I won't tell a soul, Julia would say to Betty Lawson. But as each night came and went, Julia stood at her window, unable to force herself out the door, and suffered an ache in her chest that wouldn't dissolve until morning when she woke to find Bill, and now the twins, sitting at the kitchen table, wondering what was for breakfast. Maybe, if Julia and Bill were to adopt they wouldn't be afraid a baby born to other parents would die. A boy this time. Dark like Bill because a son should favor his father. His skin would have an olive tint, ever so slight, and he would have Julia's blue eyes. This one would live.

"You're not going, are you?"

Julia lets the drape fall closed. "What are you doing awake?" she whispers so as to not wake the others.

Late at night or early in the morning, it's difficult to tell Izzy and Arie apart. Both will have brushed out their hair and scrubbed their faces. In these silent hours, both will be quiet, tender. This is always the way for Arie. Not for Izzy.

The girl standing the top of the stairs clutches the banister with both hands. "You promised Uncle Bill."

Arie.

"You're right," Julia says. "And never let it be said I broke a promise."

Hiking her slender skirt over her knees, Julia runs up the stairs two at a time, meaning to chase Arie back to bed, but she doesn't turn and run in her usual way. She doesn't dip her head and cup a hand over her mouth to muffle the laugh that might wake the others. Instead, she lets go of the banister and wraps her arms around Julia's waist.

Definitely Arie.

"What's this sour face all about?" Julia unwraps Arie's arms to get a good look at her. "What's wrong, sugar?"

The house is dark except for a light that shines from inside the girls' room. Arie's fair eyelashes glitter in the soft glow, and she blinks slowly as if forcing herself to stay awake.

"Let's get you tucked in," Julia says.

Inside the girls' room, Izzy sits up in bed, her eyes wide. One lamp flickers at her bedside.

"Told her to stay put," Izzy says, swinging her legs over the edge of the mattress so her feet dangle to the floor.

Julia walks Arie to her bed and pulls back the covers, but rather than crawling in, Arie steps up to the window and looks down on the street below.

"I just don't know, Aunt Julia," Izzy says. "She's been acting this way all night."

"Is something troubling her?" Julia says, speaking to Izzy but watching Arie stand at the window, her face and hands pressed to the mesh screen. A breeze kicks up and tousles her hair, but she doesn't move away or wrap her arms around herself even though the air is cool.

Izzy pops out of bed. "How would I know? I didn't do anything. I think she's afraid of getting snatched like Elizabeth."

Julia rolls her head around until her eyes meet Izzy's. "No one snatched Elizabeth. That's a terrible thing to say."

Izzy crosses her arms and stares at Julia for a moment before letting her gaze float off to the side.

"Aunt Julia," Arie says, her face still pressed to the window screen. "I don't see Mr. Lawson." She waves a hand to get Julia's attention. "Go get Uncle Bill. Go get him and tell him to stop Mrs. Lawson."

Julia walks up behind Arie. On the street below, Betty Lawson, pushing her carriage, has neared Julia's house.

"What do you mean, sugar?" Julia says. "Stop her from doing what?"

"Mr. Lawson, he's not there. He's not watching from the driveway."

Julia leans around Arie to get a better view out the window, but Arie pushes her away.

"Get Uncle Bill," she says. "Get him now. Tell him to stop Mrs. Lawson."

"You need to calm down. Get yourself in bed, and I'll go see to her."

Arie dashes past Julia.

"Arie," Julia says. "Don't wake Uncle Bill. I'll go. I'll see to it she gets home."

Arie stops at the door, one hand on the knob. "No," she says. "I don't want you to. Uncle Bill has to go. Uncle Bill."

"What's wrong with you, Arie?" Izzy says, dropping on her bed, bouncing once and coming to rest against her headboard.

Arie leans into the hallway. "Uncle Bill," she shouts. "Uncle Bill. Uncle Bill."

Julia rushes across the room. "Arie, hush. What on earth has ruffled your feathers?"

Pulling away from Julia, Arie jumps into the hallway. "Uncle Bill, hurry. Uncle Bill."

Bill appears in the threshold leading to his and Julia's bedroom. He stretches his eyes open and struggles to thread a second arm through his shirt.

"Go, Uncle Bill. Hurry." Arie lunges for Bill and pushes him toward the stairs. "Go get Mrs. Lawson. Go stop her."

Bill looks at Julia over Arie's head and Julia lifts both hands in the air, palms up, to signal she doesn't know what to tell him.

When Bill reaches the bottom of the stairway, Arie runs back into the bedroom. Julia follows and together they watch out the window. One story down, Bill appears on the sidewalk. As he walks toward the street, he buttons his shirt and looks up and down Alder. At the end of the sidewalk, he lifts a hand and says something, though from the second-story window, they can't hear.

"There," Julia says, pointing toward the street. "See there. Do you see? That's Mr. Lawson. He's right where he always is, keeping an eye. See that? He's in his undershirt and shorts." Julia starts to laugh but Arie's eyes shine like she's about ready to cry. "Mrs. Lawson is safe, Arie. Safe and sound. She's on her way home already."

Arie dips her head until she can see Mr. Lawson and doesn't move until Betty and the baby have returned to their own driveway.

"Is everything all right now?" Julia says. "Ready for bed?"

Instead of bouncing onto her mattress like her sister, Arie slides under the sheets and lies stiffly while Julia pulls up the covers and tucks them in around her.

"You'll sleep well?" Julia says, smoothing Arie's hair off her face and kissing each cheek. At Izzy's bed, Julia does the same. Bill appears in the doorway, leans there but says nothing. "I have early rhubarb in the refrigerator. Pink and sweet. You girls can mix up your pie tomorrow. Something fun to do while Uncle Bill and I are at the church." Looking down on Izzy, she says, "There has to be something you're not telling me. Did you two behave today?"

"I didn't do anything," Izzy says, folding her arms and kicking off her sheets and covers. "It's not my fault she's completely bats."

"You sure do favor your mama when you talk like that," Julia says, and then is sorry for it.

Izzy rolls away at the mention of Sara, Julia's sister. All the girls know of their mother is what they see when they look at Julia.

Julia switches off the lamp and, outside the girls' door, cuts out the hallway light. She pulls the door halfway closed and says, "Remember, pie in the morning."

"Aunt Julia," Arie says. It's Arie because Izzy won't speak to Julia until morning, not after the mention of Sara.

"Yes, sugar."

Arie pulls loose of the tightly tucked covers and pushes herself into a sitting position, not intending to sleep for a long time. "Elizabeth is never going to come home."

———

Arie waits until Aunt Julia has pulled the door closed, but not all the way closed because the girls like a slice of light from the hallway to shine into the room, and she waits some more until Izzy has rolled away and yanked the top sheet over her shoulder. When

Izzy's breathing changes from short puffs of air she exhales because she's angry with Aunt Julia into long, slow breaths that mean she is asleep, Arie slips one finger under the rosary hung from her headboard and drapes it across her lap.

Grandma has always said the rosary is made of mother-of-pearl beads and that's why it's something special. But then Izzy will say mother-of-pearl beads don't splinter and chip and that rosary is no more special than any other. Every night back home at Grandma's house, Arie runs her fingers over the smooth beads, usually while holding them under the sheet she has tented with two bent knees. Even though she tries to hide her praying from Izzy, Izzy always knows.

When she was younger, Arie would pray for Mama to come home and sometimes still does. Then there was the Russian dog. Arie prayed only five prayers a night for her and never told Izzy or anyone else because praying for a Russian, even if she was a dog, was probably a sinful thing to do. Izzy says Arie doesn't do it right anyway. She is supposed to recite Our Father and Hail Mary and follow a path around the beads. This is why Arie hides them and waits until Izzy is asleep. Tonight, as she slips her fingers from the first round, cool bead to the next, she thinks she'll say twenty prayers for Elizabeth. Or maybe twenty isn't enough. Maybe she'll pray all night until morning comes and somewhere along the way, she'll say a prayer for Mrs. Richardson, too.

CHAPTER EIGHT

I t came down directly from the bishop. A special dispensation, he called it. No Mass on this Sunday morning. Every parishioner was excused. The search for Elizabeth was far more important and wouldn't the good Lord agree. Malina was certain He would.

This morning, Malina has flyers for the men to nail on lampposts and tape in store windows. Mr. Herze had one of the girls in his office make them on a machine at work—a perfect, crisp stack of one hundred flyers, one exactly like the next. A marvel, really, and a blessing in a situation such as this. With the stack tucked securely under one arm, Malina kicks open the kitchen door, the pan of butternut rolls she carries still warm. At the car, she sets the rolls and flyers on the backseat, tucks under her skirt, and stoops to her flowers.

The snapdragons have sprouted early this year. The red, yellow, and pink blossoms draw a colorful border that extends along the front of her property and follows the walkway to her front porch. She reaches into the towering plants and yanks out a dandelion, inspects the threadlike roots, sniffs them, and tosses the weed aside. Another strange smell, but this time, it has polluted her flowers. This is her third visit to the car, and with every trip, the smell grows more robust, as if gaining strength as the day heats up. Whatever the source, it's not the roots of a dandelion.

All along Alder Avenue, wives click up and down their sidewalks because, although there is no Mass today, it's Sunday and they feel obliged to wear their leather heels, slender skirts, and white gloves. They carry trays of fried chicken and meatloaves baked early this morning. Others carry desserts, finger foods the men can easily grab. Something sweet and frosted to lift their spirits. Directly across the street, a burst of laughter erupts and those two young girls tumble out of Julia Wagner's front door. Oversize gardening gloves dangle from their hands. Their wiry arms and legs are bare. Once on the porch, where they must remember the block is praying for Elizabeth Symanski's safe return, the twins silence themselves, walk down the stairs to the front yard, kneel on the sidewalk that leads to the street, and begin to pull weeds.

It's been the same since the twins were three years old. Early every summer, Bill Wagner pulls in the drive in time for supper and two girls crawl out of his backseat. When they were younger, they would wear sweet plaid dresses with puffed sleeves and Peter Pan collars. Wearing a full bib apron, Julia would greet them and kiss each on top of her head. But this year, instead of lace-trimmed dresses worn thin at the seams, the girls wear matching navy shorts and blue-and-white striped blouses. Malina didn't get a good look at the one she saw last night because it was too dark, but this morning, it's apparent they've grown up in the past year. They've let their red hair grow well beyond their shoulders and their cheeks have thinned out. It's also apparent their skin is a darker shade. Obviously they are allowed to play outside unattended for hours each day. Their legs, too, are changed. They are longer, thinner. Their hips, straight and narrow. Their arms, slender, even frail. They could almost be mistaken for young women.

If not for the color of their hair, they could almost be mistaken for Malina.

At the sound of her own front door opening, Malina pushes back on her knees. Mr. Herze's hard-soled shoes hit the wooden porch. The screen door slaps shut. Staring across the street, most probably at those two girls, Mr. Herze mops his forehead with a white kerchief. He is already suffering though the day has yet to heat up. Malina greets him with a wave and lifts a forearm to wipe the perspiration from her top lip, but stops short of touching herself because that smell has grown stronger. It's urine. She's smelling urine.

"I'm making a mushroom soufflé this evening," she says, staring down at her bare hands. Someone has urinated on her flowers. "I hope you'll be able to make it home for supper. These long days will take their toll."

Without bothering to lock the front door, Mr. Herze marches across the porch and stomps down the stairs and toward the street. "Not in my yard, Jerry Lawson," he shouts.

Malina stands, holding her arms out to her sides so as not to touch herself with soiled hands, and looks for what has drawn Mr. Herze's attention. It's Jerry Lawson, coming at them from across the street. He wears blue-and-white broadcloth boxers and a

V-neck cotton undershirt. At the curb, Mr. Herze stops, stretches his shoulders back, which causes his large stomach to jut out, and lifts a flattened palm toward Jerry, who is fast approaching.

"Don't you come any closer," Mr. Herze says.

Jerry stops in the middle of the street. His lower jaw is gray with a heavy shadow. His undershirt is untucked; his boxers, rumpled. He wears only stockings on his feet. Across the street, the twins have disappeared inside. Jerry reaches out to Mr. Herze, not to shake hands, but as if he wants to brace himself on Mr. Herze's arm.

"What is a man if he doesn't have a job?" Jerry says.

Mr. Herze yanks Jerry toward him until they are standing close enough to whisper. Mr. Herze does most of the talking, though Malina can't hear what is being said. He points toward the Lawsons' home and shakes his head a few times.

"Wait," Jerry shouts when Mr. Herze begins to walk away.

Mr. Herze stops, exhales, and circles back.

Jerry points at Malina, directly at Malina, and takes one step toward her.

"She knows," he says. "Mrs. Herze knows."

Malina slides next to the car, putting it between her and Jerry. "What on earth are you talking about?"

"You saw me," Jerry says.

Mr. Herze jams a hand in the center of Jerry's chest, preventing him from moving any closer to Malina.

"Tell him," Jerry says. "Tell him you saw me from your car. I waved at you and you waved back."

Malina leans into the sedan, not at all worried her yellow dress will pick up dust or grime. "What is all this about, Warren?" she says. "What ever has gotten into him?" She glances at the neighbors on either side, wondering who might hear. Most have already left for the church.

Mr. Herze drops the hand from Jerry's chest and turns to Malina.

"I know you saw me," Jerry says, stepping up beside Mr. Herze. "That Wednesday night. It was nearly eleven o'clock. I was here, in my very own driveway. You were driving that car."

Mr. Herze stretches one arm across Jerry's path but he keeps his eyes on Malina. "Malina?" he says.

"Yes," Jerry says. "You remember. Betty was walking Cynthia. Pushing her in the stroller. I was nowhere near Willingham. Nowhere near that woman. Tell him, Mrs. Herze."

"I'm afraid you're mistaken, Mr. Lawson," Malina says. This is why the counting and breathing don't work. There's never time. Shielding her eyes from the scantily clad Jerry Lawson, she says to Mr. Herze, "I don't drive at night. And certainly not at that ridiculous hour. Tell him, Warren. Tell him how the glare bothers me so. I don't know what this is all about, but I most assuredly have no comment on the matter."

"You were driving that car," Jerry says, pointing at the pale green sedan parked in front of Mr. Herze's car, and again he tries to press forward, but he can't get at Malina because Mr. Herze blocks the path with a stiff arm. "That car right there. You drove to the corner and turned down Woodward."

Malina knows from many years of experience to keep her eyes on Mr. Herze. She knows not to let them drift to one side or the other. It's how he knows she's lying. "I'm sorry I can't help you," she says. "You're mistaken, I'm afraid."

Mr. Herze grips the front of Jerry's rumpled undershirt, pulls him close, and speaks in a whisper. Jerry says nothing else, certainly nothing Malina can hear. Mostly he shakes his head. Signaling the conversation is over, Mr. Herze drops Jerry's shirt, tucks in the front of his own shirt where his belly has pulled it loose of his trousers, and walks back to the house. Reminding herself to smile, Malina opens the passenger-side door, smooths under her skirt, and sinks into the front seat. She closes her eyes and rests her arms on her lap, her palms open, not touching anything. Outside, Mr. Herze walks back to the front porch, locks and pulls twice on the door, and joins Malina in the car.

"Warren," Malina says, blinking because keeping good eye contact is more difficult when Mr. Herze is sitting this close. "Have you fired Jerry Lawson?"

It's the question any wife would ask under normal circumstances.

"Him and three others."

"Has it to do with those women on Willingham?" Malina reaches across the bench seat and rests one hand on Mr. Herze's thigh. It's the thing any wife would do. "Has it to do with the dead woman?"

"The police will see to it," Mr. Herze says. "It's of no concern to you." With both hands on the steering wheel, he stares straight ahead at the back end of Malina's car. "Is there truth to what he says?" His knuckles and the backs of his large hands are white from clutching the steering wheel. "Were you driving that night?"

"Why would I ever be out at such a late hour?"

Mr. Herze lets go of the steering wheel with one hand, pulls the lever to put the car into reverse, throws his arm over the seat back, and looks out the rear window. Malina looks too. The twins have reappeared on the porch and Bill Wagner stands between them.

"You're quite certain," Mr. Herze says, waving at Bill and the twins through his open window as the back of the car swings around and the front points down Alder Avenue.

Perhaps Malina should have told Mr. Herze the truth when he first asked. Yes, she was driving and she did see that ridiculous Jerry Lawson. And then a lie. It had been her night to deliver supper to the shut-ins and she'd forgotten. Yes, it was awfully late to be serving supper, but because she had felt so guilty for overlooking her responsibility, she took the food anyway. That's the reason she drove down Alder that night. She wasn't checking up on him or looking for the source of that nasty smell he brings into her house. But she hadn't said any of those things. She'd lied, promised she'd been at home all evening, and it's too late now for stories about shut-ins and supper trays. In answer to Mr. Herze's question, Malina nods but doesn't try to speak because her voice will crack and give her away. That's another one of the things that always gets her in trouble.

"Very well," Mr. Herze says, and throws the car into drive.

———

Mother came into Grace's bedroom an hour ago, threw open the heavy curtains and white sheers she had closed the night before, and told Grace it was high time to get up. You're feeling better, she said—a statement, not a question. No sense sleeping the day away. There's food to be made and men to be fed. After taking Grace's robe from the closet and laying it across Grace's lap, Mother disappeared into the bathroom where she rummaged through the drawers. When she returned, she sat on the bed's edge, dipped a small sponge into a heavy foundation, and dabbed at Grace's cheek. After a few moments, Mother leaned back and lifted her face as if to get the best light. There must have been a red mark or possibly a bruise, but it was covered now and Mother said again for Grace to hustle herself on downstairs. Company was coming and it wouldn't be fitting to sleep all day.

"Do you smell it?" Grace had said before Mother disappeared through the door.

Mother glanced at the open window but didn't answer.

"The tobacco. The factories. Don't you smell it?" Grace drew in a deep breath. "Do you remember them?"

The smell of damp tobacco, sweet and rich, floated across the city every morning of Grace's childhood. When the weather was nice, she would wake beneath an open window and inhale, knowing the thick scent would be there. Many such factories stood then. Now, only a few.

"Don't be silly," Mother had said. "It's the fireworks you smell. Time to get moving."

At the bottom of the stairs, Grace holds on to the banister with one hand and rests the other on her stomach. It's a habit, must be, because she doesn't realize it's there until a tiny foot, or maybe a knee, bumps her from the inside. All night, the baby was busy rolling and knocking about in Grace's stomach. Now that Grace is awake, the baby will quiet down. The movement of Grace's typical day—the comings and goings, hanging out the laundry, climbing the stairs, boarding the bus to Willingham—will calm the baby, soothe her. For the baby, all is unchanged and that's enough to keep Grace on her feet.

There are voices coming from the kitchen. Two voices. Men. One is James, no mistaking that. The other is strained, barely clear. Grace stretches forward but doesn't move her feet. Yes, that's Mr. Symanski. Mother is whisking eggs in Grace's frying pan and coffee bubbles up in the percolator. She is feeding Mr. Symanski. A pop. Toast popping up in the toaster. Two slices, slightly charred. They are always a bit overdone. Mother will scrape off the blackened crust with a serrated knife and dump the crumbs in the sink. Outside the house, car doors slam. A man shouts out to his wife, "Don't forget the batteries." It's a reminder the search will go into the night.

"They are not saying what it means," Mr. Symanski says. "They say it may be meaning nothing. They say only that she isn't being found yet."

A spatula scrapes the bottom of the skillet. Mother is dishing up the eggs. Forks clatter on the table. Chairs scoot across the tile. Grace leans on the banister, bracing herself. She knows Elizabeth is gone, even if the others don't. Elizabeth didn't wander off. He took her, that man, and she won't ever come home.

"If it was being the river," Mr. Symanski says and at this, his voice breaks. He starts again. "If she is being lost in the river, they may never be finding her."

"What more did they tell you?" It's James's voice.

"They are having little hope. If she made her way that far, the people who are living there, the people who might have been seeing something, will not be caring to offer help. They are asking me where she would go. That is the only place she knew. The only place Ewa would take her."

Water runs in the sink and the fresh scent of dish soap spills out of the kitchen into the living room, where Grace stands. Moving about as she sets the salt and pepper on the table, opens and closes the refrigerator, drops dirty dishes in the soapy water, Mother catches a glimpse of Grace.

"Come in here," she says, leaning into the living room and waving Grace toward her. She jabs a single finger at Grace and then at the kitchen. She did the same when Grace was a child.

Grace wears nothing on her feet, so no one hears her until she clears her throat. With a shallow bow, she greets Mr. Symanski. Both men lift out of their chairs.

"Sit," she says. "Please, sit. What can I get you, Charles?"

Mr. Symanski waves away the offer and Mother points at a chair so Grace will know to take a seat.

Glancing over her shoulder, Grace says, "I'm so very sorry. From in there, I overheard."

James stands, pours Grace a cup of coffee, adds one sugar and a splash of cream. "You feeling better?" With one finger, he raises her chin. "What's this?"

Grace touches the small cut on her upper lip. The swollen spot is smooth and tender. She lays her other hand over James's, squeezes it. Just as the relief of feeling her baby move made Grace cry, the warmth of James's hand lifts her tears to the surface. She blinks them away.

"We bumped heads," Mother says, sliding between Grace and James to place folded linens on the table. She finger-presses the fold in each as she positions it. "Last night. When I was pulling muffins from the oven. My fault really. You know how clumsy I can be."

"Got you good," James says.

"Please don't fuss. Charles, are you getting plenty to eat? Mother, do you have seconds for him?"

"Your fever gone?" James says, brushing aside Grace's hair and placing one hand on her forehead. "Feel cool. That's good. But you look tired. Are you tired?"

The ache in her neck and shoulders makes Grace want to slouch forward and rest her arms on the table. She stretches and straightens her back so no one will notice. The baby stretches too. She's settling in, getting comfortable. Grace draws her fingers across James's cheek. It's rough because he didn't take the time to shave. Mother places a plate of eggs before Grace. James slides the salt and pepper toward her.

"It's the heat," Grace says, not knowing how long since James last spoke. "It wears me down." She lifts one of the napkins Mother set out on the table, gives it a shake, and lets it float across James's knee. Next, she drapes one across her own knee.

Turning his attention to Mr. Symanski, James lights a cigarette and rests both elbows on the table. What can he and Grace do? Does the rest of the family know yet? James would be happy to make a few calls before he leaves for the church. Mr. Symanski says there is no other family. There is no one. Mother leans in and whispers in Grace's ear while the men talk.

"Start eating."

Grace lifts her fork, twists it from side to side, studying it.

"I brought some things," Mr. Symanski says. "You ladies are gathering clothes, yes?"

"For the thrift store," Grace says.

"We put them in the garage." James tilts his head back and blows out a stream of smoke. "Five or six bags, wouldn't you say, Charles?"

"There is being six."

"That's fine," Grace says. "I'll see to them. Thank you. Thank you so much."

Mr. Symanski exhales as if he feels lighter now. They must be Ewa's things, clothes that have hung in the closet as painful reminders.

"The police will be coming soon," Mr. Symanski says. "About the shoe."

Grace drops her fork. It topples off the edge of the plate and comes to rest on the table.

Mother frowns and returns it to the plate's rim. "They found a shoe," she says to Grace. "Near the river." Mother is letting Grace know it wasn't her shoe they found. It was another.

"Didn't intend to trouble you with it until you were feeling well," James says.

"A shoe?" Grace says.

"We thought you might remember. It's white with a soft rubber sole. Is that the type Elizabeth was wearing?"

"I am knowing I should remember," Mr. Symanski says. "A father should be knowing, but I don't know white shoes or black shoes or any other shoes. The police show me, but I am not knowing."

"I'm not certain," Grace says. "I would have to think about it."

James rubs his cigarette into a small glass dish. "It's not to concern yourself with now. The police will come. They'll show you what they found."

"What if my Elizabeth is being gone?" Mr. Symanski says, and chokes again. "Is that meaning she isn't alone, isn't frightened? Is that better?"

"Yes," Grace says, blurting it out before she can stop herself. She can't tolerate the thought of Elizabeth living in the aftermath of what those men, that man, surely did to her. "I mean, yes," she says again. "Elizabeth knows she's not alone, never alone."

The skin under Mr. Symanski's eyes hangs in deep crescent-shaped folds. He stares at Grace as if hoping she'll say more.

Picking up her fork, Grace spears a small bit of her scrambled egg. "Elizabeth liked white sneakers. Wore them often," she says, staring at the prongs of her fork. While the men came for Grace in her own home, they must have taken Elizabeth to the river and dumped her there. "As I remember, it troubled her when they got scuffed or dirty. Ewa would buy a new pair to make Elizabeth happy." She smiles and touches Mr. Symanski's hand. The loose skin is cold and dry. "Ewa would fuss as if those white sneakers were a bother, but she didn't really mind them. Elizabeth has many pairs, doesn't she?"

"You are thinking it was my Elizabeth's shoe?"

Grace places the cold eggs into her mouth. They lie on her tongue. She swallows so she won't gag.

"Yes," Grace says. "I think, perhaps, it was her shoe."

CHAPTER NINE

Julia and Bill pull into the church parking lot later than most. Bill shifts the car into park, turns off the ignition, and crosses his arms on the steering wheel. He leans forward, resting his head on his hands, and exhales loudly. Julia and the twins have barely seen him in the past few days. His cheeks look to have thinned out, though it hardly seems possible it's happened in such a short time, and dark circles hang under his eyes.

"Today," he says, rolling his head to the side so he can see Julia. "Today's the day we find her."

Directly in front of them, the rounded nose of an old gray Plymouth rolls up, and the driver's-side door opens. Mr. Symanski pushes himself up and out of the car. Wearing a shirt and tie and a dark jacket that sags on his narrow shoulders, he shuffles no more than a few yards before one of the ladies glides up alongside him, takes hold of his arm, and escorts him to the front of one of two lines that snakes through the parking lot.

The lines are new this morning. As the neighbors and parishioners of St. Alban's climb from their cars, they take their place at the end of one of them. Bill motions for Julia to do the same, while he joins the men gathered near the entrance to the church basement. Julia cradles in one arm the loaves of sweet bread she mixed up and baked this morning and takes her place at the back of the closest line.

All of the ladies, like Julia, are dressed in fitted jackets and tailored skirts. Already many are fanning themselves with old church bulletins and fussing about desserts that will spoil if forced to sit out in this rising heat. Julia glances at her watch. She promised the girls she would come home at lunchtime to grill them cheese sandwiches, but given the length of this line, she might still be waiting when noon rolls around, though for what, she isn't sure.

"Why the holdup?" Julia asks the gentleman standing in the line next to her. She recognizes him and his wife from services but can't remember their names.

"Taking names," the man says. Without looking in Julia's direction, he helps his wife slip off her peplum jacket.

"Who's taking names? And for what purpose?" Julia hugs her sweet bread in hopes of keeping it warm. When she goes home at lunchtime, she'll mix up four beef-and-corn casseroles to be baked at the church and served up for the men's supper. She'll definitely have to make a trip to the market tomorrow.

"Police," the man's wife says. A gold bobby pin has pulled loose at the nape of her neck and sparkles where it catches the light. "They're recording who is here and who isn't. They found her shoe, you know. Down by the river."

Julia starts to ask why the police would do such a thing, but even though she doesn't entirely understand, it's clear enough they think who is or isn't here might have some bearing on what did or did not happen to Elizabeth. It's clear enough that had Elizabeth simply wandered off, the police would have no interest in who is or is not participating in the search.

The line doesn't move as slowly as Julia had feared and when she reaches the front, Bill rejoins her. Two police officers sit behind a metal table, thick binders opened up before them. One asks questions of Bill and Julia; the other, of the man and his wife. Bill answers, giving their name, address, and the names of their neighbors on either side. He answers yes without even a glimpse of his surroundings when asked if he recognizes everyone he sees and answers no when asked if he has seen any strangers joining in the search. He also points out the two latter questions are, in fact, the same question asked two different ways.

"That's the point," the officer says.

Julia leans around Bill. "The point to what?" she asks.

The officer ignores her and says, "Have any neighbors, friends, or relatives failed to include themselves?"

Again, taking no time to consider his answer, Bill says, "No."

Next to Bill and Julia, the man and his wife scan the people who mill about before answering the same question.

"Jerry Lawson," the woman says, finally tucking in the loose-hanging pin.

The other officer nods as if she is not the first to mention that name.

"What of Jerry Lawson?" Bill says, resting both hands on the table. Even hunched over, Bill is taller than the man.

"He is not here," the woman says while her husband remains silent. "They asked who is not here, so we told them."

"Why on earth would you take it upon yourself to mention the Lawsons?" Julia says. "They're not neighbors of yours. If they were, you might recall they have only recently become parents." She smiles at the officer. "A few weeks ago. We would never expect them to be here with a new baby at home."

"Actually, they adopted," the woman says. "And we have every right to mention Jerry Lawson. Everyone here knows of his troubles."

"A new baby is a new baby," Julia says, more loudly than she had intended. Ladies toting casserole dishes and covered pots and pans and gentlemen escorting the ladies by the arm stop to listen. Julia frowns at them and waves them on their way. "It doesn't much matter where that sweet baby came from." And then, because news of Jerry Lawson standing in the middle of Alder wearing little more than his undergarments while arguing with Warren Herze has obviously made its way to St. Alban's, she turns to the officer and says, "This woman is spreading gossip, and it stinks so bad she might as well be spreading manure. She knows Jerry Lawson's troubles have nothing to do with Elizabeth Symanski or this search."

Before Julia can say anything more, Bill wraps one hand around her wrist and squeezes, a signal she need say no more. He gives her a wink.

"No one is unaccounted for among this group," he says to the officer. "Write that down. No one is unaccounted for."

When the officer has asked his last question, Julia follows Bill toward the church basement. She feels it as they pass among the others waiting in line and climbing from their cars. The early assumption that Elizabeth would be found walking aimlessly down Woodward first gave way to the worry she wandered all the way to the river and now, because the police are taking names and asking questions, these early theories have given way to fears of a violent end for Elizabeth.

———

Mother's pierogi. Walking into the kitchen, this is what Grace smells. Because James said so, Grace will stay home today while the other ladies work at the church. It's for the best, Mother had whispered as James gathered his things to leave for the day, and Grace had to agree even though she felt guilty for having nothing to contribute. With her back to Grace, Mother stands at the stove. Her elbow juts out to the side and moves in a small circle. She is stirring the pierogi so they don't stick. Already, Mother has made enough of the crescent-shaped noodles to cover two trays. Potato and onion. They were always Grace's favorite.

"Will you take them to the church?" Grace says.

Mother nods, pulls a cast-iron pot from the oven, and motions for Grace to take a seat. Wearing mitts on both hands, Mother carries the large pot to the table, sets it in front of Grace, lifts the lid, and lets the padded mitts drop from her hands. With her fingers, she plucks a damp towel from inside the large pot and tests that it's not too hot by tossing it from hand to hand. Once satisfied with its temperature, she rolls it up and presses it to Grace's neck and shoulders.

"He wanted to check in on you," Mother says, returning to her noodles. "Called three times while you were sleeping. I told him you were fine and spent the morning rolling out pierogi."

Grace grabs hold of the warm towel with both hands and draws it around her neck. "So he knew you were lying," she says with a laugh, but stops herself when the small slit on her upper lip tears open. Holding the towel in place with one hand, she flips open the newspaper left on the table since breakfast. A few days ago, she searched the paper for news of the dead woman on Willingham, mostly for Julia's benefit—something to talk about other than the baby in the corner. Today, she's looking for news of Elizabeth and of herself, though she won't find anything about what happened to her.

Mother walks back to the table, this time with a plate of warm pierogi. She places them in front of Grace, pours a glass of milk, and slides the salt within reach. "You'll want some of that nice pink lipstick today," she says. "It'll freshen you up." And then, waving a hand at the swell in Grace's belly, she says, "Go on and eat. You need to eat."

As Grace cuts her pierogi into thirds, the thing she has done since she was a child, Mother fishes half a dozen noodles from the potato water and taps them out on a sheet of waxed paper.

"Any sign?" Mother says, dropping the last few uncooked noodles in the pot. When Grace doesn't answer, Mother gives another wave in the direction of Grace's belly. "Having a man so close to the end can spur a baby on. Any sign she's thinking about coming early?"

Grace shakes her head.

"Drink that milk then, and let's go."

Grace follows Mother out the kitchen door, down the concrete stairs, and toward the back of the house. At the garage, Mother lifts its heavy door and throws it overhead.

"Can't be afraid in your own home," Mother says, stepping into the garage. She kicks at a small sliver of glass and motions for Grace to join her.

"I'm not afraid," Grace says. "In a day or two. I'll come out in a day or two."

"Today." Mother tucks under her skirt, sinks to her knees, and picks up glass Grace missed the night before. "Now. Or it'll sink in. It'll get the better of you."

Grace looks down the alley and then out toward the street.

"It's not yet noon on a Sunday," Mother says, tossing a few pieces of glass in the garbage can. "Damn fool like that isn't going to be out and about on a Sunday morning." She gives another nod, directing Grace inside. "You check over there. Won't do if this glass finds its way into one of James's tires."

Grace might have thought panic would swell up as she entered the garage. She might have thought her breathing would quicken, her heart would begin to pound, sweat would break out across her brow and upper lip. But all is quiet. She floats deep into the garage. The outside air had ruffled her skirt, but inside, the air stops. Her hair hangs down her back, held off her face by a white silk scarf. Her skin is cool and dry. She lowers herself onto hands and knees, lays one hand flat on the dirt floor, and moves it slowly and lightly from side to side, searching for bits of glass.

"Put that damn fool thing away."

It's Mother. She has left the garage and disappeared into the alley. Grace pushes herself to her knees. Now her chest begins to lift and lower. Her breathing does quicken. Her heart does pound.

"Good Lord in heaven." It's still Mother. "You are the damnedest old fool I ever laid eyes on."

Two faces pop around the corner of the garage. The twins. Their skin is tanned and freckles pepper the bridge of their noses and the rounds of their cheeks. Their long red hair has been woven into braids, two on each girl. One raises a hand. A wave. Julia is next to appear. Her red hair has been tightly wound and pinned on top of her head. Because she wears her nicer heels and her linen skirt, Grace knows she's been to the church already today. Grace walks over to one of the garbage cans, lifts its lid, and lets glass tumble from her hand.

"Your mother is about to clobber Orin Schofield," Julia says, a white porcelain casserole dish cradled in her hands. She must have gotten word Grace wasn't feeling well and she's brought food. "You better get out here."

Across the alley, Orin Schofield stands near his garage and holds the same piece of wood he carried the night Elizabeth disappeared.

"It was one of those two," he says, jabbing the board at the twins.

"Quit your fussing," Mother says. "And get yourself back inside."

"I saw them running." Orin stabs at the air again. "Running right there. One of them, anyway. Just last night. Right there. Broke my damn window, they did."

"A window was broken?" Grace asks. Once outside the garage, her pounding heart slows and the air is easier to inhale

"Third one in two nights," Orin says, dropping the board to his side, leaning on it and pulling a kerchief from his front pocket. He mops his eyes and neck. "And they set my garbage on fire. My garbage. Damn near burned down my house. Thought it was those colored boys from down the block. Thinking maybe I was wrong."

Julia shakes her head. "Orin, you think these two put a match to your garbage? They aren't even allowed out of the house. Bill has threatened to take a belt to their backsides if they disobey. And believe me, they won't risk that."

"We didn't break your old window." It's Izzy. Arms crossed, one hip thrust to the side, she faces Orin. "Or set fire to your stinky garbage."

"Manners, Izzy."

The other twin, Arie, stares at Grace. Her eyes seem to settle on Grace's split lip. When Grace glances her way, the girl lowers her eyes to the ground.

"Mr. Schofield, sir," Izzy says. "We did not break your window or burn up your garbage."

"What about that one?" Orin says, poking the board in Arie's direction. The collar of his white shirt is too big for his neck, as if he's shrunk over the years, and his pants pucker where he's pulled his belt too tight. "That one have anything to say?"

Arie slides backward, shaking her head.

"That's enough, Orin," Julia says, handing the casserole dish to Grace and taking a step toward Orin. "You're frightening the girls. You brought those broken windows on yourself. Running your mouth down at the Filmore. Brought it all on yourself. If you've anything else to say, you take it up with Bill."

"I said it before," Mother says, stretching overhead and pulling closed the garage door. "And I'll say it again. Get on inside, you old goat."

Orin hobbles to his garage, leaning on his board as he goes, then grabs a rusted metal folding chair from inside and pops it open at the alley's edge. "Don't let me catch the two of you poking around my house." Orin slaps the chair's canvas back and brushes off its seat. "See this chair? It and I will be here in this alley every day. I'll be keeping an eye out. Keeping an eye out for you two or whoever else is causing trouble. You know what's best," he says, lowering himself into the seat, "you won't let me catch you."

CHAPTER TEN

It's Monday morning and traffic is light along Woodward. It's as if everyone in the city has spent these past few days searching for Elizabeth and is exhausted by it. Pressing one hand against the seat back in front of her as the bus pulls away and letting the other rest on the swell in her stomach, Grace hopes none of the ladies will notice she has forgotten her white gloves. She must have overlooked them on her bedroom dresser or possibly on the table near the back door.

Before leaving to catch the bus this morning, Grace had touched Mother on the sleeve and said, "I think I should tell."

Setting aside the broom she had been pushing across the kitchen floor, Mother covered Grace's hand with one of her own. "It's Monday," she said. "Go to Willingham. Fill your cupboards. They'll be needing more food down at that church."

"It might help the police." Grace lingered in the doorway. "What if those men, that man, did the same to Elizabeth? What if he does it again? James's only concern will be for me. For the baby."

"Heaven help that child if those men got her," Mother said, holding open the door so Grace could pass. "But your telling won't change that." Then she smoothed Grace's blond hair, a reminder to keep her makeup fresh and her hair carefully combed, pinned, and sprayed. A pretty face will keep peace in the house.

"Don't think more of your husband than you should," Mother had said. "Don't make that mistake."

Continuing down Woodward, the bus gathers speed and the morning air, just beginning to warm, rushes through the open windows. Reaching up with one bare hand, Grace holds her pillbox hat in place. The other ladies don't bother with hats anymore. They don't care to ruin their new, higher hairstyles, but today Grace wears her gray pillbox with the velvet trim she normally wears only on Sundays. It covers the small gash on the back of her head she worries might be seen. She shifts her weight from one hip to the other to avoid the cross-breeze. Not meaning to, she lets out a soft groan. Mother said Grace's tailbone is only bruised and she shouldn't carry on about it.

"Grace," Malina Herze says, leaning across the aisle. "Are you okay, dear?" Malina cups the tight curl on the end of her dark bob.

Grace drops her bare hand to her lap. "I'm fine. It's just this heat."

Reaching out with her own white-gloved hand, Malina squeezes Grace's wrist. Grace flinches but doesn't pull away. Her wrists and arms are sore, still ache where one of them pinned her to the ground.

"Don't be fooled by the bake sale's new date, dear," Malina says. One of her carefully tweezed eyebrows, the right one, lifts, her forehead crinkling when she notices Grace's exposed hands. "You heard, didn't you? It's postponed only a few weeks. You know, of course, pierogi freeze quite nicely. No need to wait until the last minute."

While Saturday brought news of the white sneaker found along the river, Sunday passed with no news at all. And today, Monday, the search will continue even though the men should be returning to work. Others at the factory will work evening shifts and over the next weekend if they have to, over as many weekends as it takes, so the men from Alder and its neighboring streets can continue to look for Elizabeth. These workers have pledged their overtime to the families of those who search.

Monday also brought news that the bake sale has been officially postponed and that Malina Herze has taken up the job of organizing the ladies. Just as she had a schedule and a list for the bake sale, she now has a schedule and a list for the search. This morning, Malina gave the wives of Alder Avenue the morning off to tend to their families and run their errands. From this day on, they'll work in four-hour shifts, preparing food, cleaning up after the men, brewing fresh coffee. They must hope and pray every day brings news of Elizabeth's safe homecoming, but must also brace themselves for a new kind of life, one that may include never knowing what became of the girl and a search that may never end.

Just past the thrift store, the bus stops, its door opens, and Julia appears. She must have had Bill drop her at the store this morning. Usually, she and Grace do their volunteering together. Many times over the years, they've sorted donations at the small shop under Malina's watchful eye. Grace would scold Julia when she pulled the blouses inside out before slipping them on a hanger. Julia would hang them up anyway and when Malina asked why they were laughing, Grace would say it was nothing, just a silly joke she had told. Once Malina busied herself with another load of clothes, Grace would turn the next blouse inside out, slip it on a hanger, and give Julia a wink.

Knowing Julia will sit next to her, Grace slides toward the window to make room and rests her face against the glass. A sharp pain shoots through her cheek and up into her eye. She straightens in her seat and pulls a compact from her purse to check her lipstick. Across the aisle, two of the ladies smile at her with tilted heads. Grace, with her bulging stomach, is a reminder to them, to everyone who sees her, that life will go on. No matter how terrible the news of Elizabeth might be, those ladies see Grace and think she is sweet and beautiful and that she'll give birth to a child who is the same.

"Didn't expect to see you today," Grace says when Julia drops onto the seat next to her.

Julia doesn't answer and instead points toward the street. Two men walk out of the hardware store next to the thrift shop. One of the two carries a clipboard. He scribbles as they walk to the next store. Once there, he yanks on the door's handle and both disappear inside. They are men looking for Elizabeth. The busload of ladies has paused to allow the men to pass.

There is talk this morning of the women on Willingham. No one has thought much about that dead woman in the days since Elizabeth disappeared. There's been no news of the woman, no arrest. Now that they're traveling back to Willingham, thoughts of her work their way back to the surface. The ladies are worried, too, though no one wants to say it aloud, that maybe the dead woman sheds some light on what became of Elizabeth. All around Grace, the ladies have been talking about the police they'll most likely see on Willingham. It's possible there is no more work to be done in the alley where that woman was killed, but they'll definitely be searching the river because today is day four, the day the men say Elizabeth's body would surely float to the surface if she had drowned.

"Bill dropped me on his way to the church," Julia says once the bus has pulled away from the curb. "I've had the girls cleaning out closets. Gives them something to do while I'm gone." Then she whispers, "Too many bags to tote on the bus. It'll drive Malina wild to find out I dropped them off at the store myself."

Grace lets out a short laugh but tries not to smile. Every smile causes the small cut to split again. Julia is the only one of the ladies Grace laughs with. The others make her altogether too aware of the length of her skirt, the curls in her hair, or the shade of lipstick she has chosen. She worries her choices are all wrong and that the ladies will later whisper about her. Julia is the friend who would tell Grace if a lipstick shade was unbecoming, but only so she could snag the tube for her own use.

"Did you hear?" Julia says, leaning in to whisper. This is how it starts. She'll say something funny, something irresistible, even today, even knowing Elizabeth is still gone. Julia wants things to be normal again too. "About Malina's flowers?"

Grace shakes her head.

"Someone urinated on them. Walked right down the middle of the street and there in front of God and Alder Avenue, urinated on them. More than once, it would appear."

"That is not true."

"Told me herself. She's started spraying them at all hours. Poor things are already waterlogged. They'll be wilting before you know it. Probably won't last the month." Julia tells the rest from behind the cover of one hand. "She actually thought the twins had done it. Cornered me at the church and accused them. So, of course, I asked her to explain the logistics of that. She agreed it would be rather difficult. And rather conspicuous."

"Julia, stop," Grace says, trying not to smile so her lip won't swell up on her. "It's not right to carry on like this."

On past bus rides, Grace and Julia would sometimes laugh until Grace's cheeks and stomach ached. And when, later in the day, Grace would return to an empty house, she could never recall what had made her laugh, but the memory of it always made her smile. Later still in the day, Grace would call. What are you fixing for supper, one would ask the other. Coffee? I'll be right down. Usually Julia came to Grace's house. And then after supper, one last call asking how that beefsteak turned out or what's the best way to tackle a grease stain, to which Julia would reply . . . don't throw out the shirt, throw out the husband. And again, they would laugh.

Julia gives Grace one last nudge. "But it feels good, doesn't it, to laugh?"

The bus continues toward Willingham Avenue. The morning air, light and almost crisp, blows through the open windows. Outside the bus, cars drive past, most of them with their windows rolled down. The ladies in those cars hold the steering wheel at ten and two and wear sheer scarves—yellow, pink, or white—folded in half, draped over their hair and tied under their chins. At the stoplights, the men rest an elbow on the doorframe and hang their lit cigarettes out the window. As the bus nears downtown, the cars stack up deeper at each stoplight and the buildings rise higher on both sides of Woodward, narrowing the street. The smell of river water pushes aside the smell of freshly clipped grass and concrete just hosed down. At the intersection of Woodward and Willingham, the bus slows. The air settles.

"Come with me to the cleaners?" Julia says, standing once the bus has stopped.

Grace shakes her head and slides back down onto the seat. "I'm not feeling well. I have enough in my freezer to get by. I think I'll take the bus back home."

Julia stretches over the seat to lay a hand on Grace's forehead. "James mentioned you'd been feeling poorly. No fever." She straightens. "Get some rest. I'll call later, stop by before I go to the church."

Julia slips into the aisle behind Malina Herze and plugs her nose as if smelling the urine from Malina's flowerbeds. Again Grace resists the urge to smile. She lifts a hand to wave good-bye but quickly lowers it so no one will notice she forgot her gloves. Even before the bus has pulled away toward its last stop, where it will turn around to drive back up Woodward, Grace knows she'll not come on the morning bus again. She can't see the others because she is so changed. The other ladies are changed too, but not in a lasting way. Already they are easing back to a normal life, a life that won't include Elizabeth Symanski. But Grace won't ease back, and eventually they'll notice. Eventually, they'll want to know why.

Julia will be the first, maybe the only one, to raise questions with Grace. The others will be too polite, just as they're too polite to mention an unfortunate lipstick color. They'll assume it's a private matter, perhaps a problem in Grace's marriage or bad news regarding the baby, and they'll be caring but distant because they won't want Grace's troubles to rub off on them. Julia, however, won't concern herself with privacy or contagious problems. She'll ask questions, many questions. She'll be bold and persistent. She'll come to Grace's house, sweep the floors, wring the laundry, cook the meals. She'll want to do the things Grace did for Julia when her daughter died. She'll want to nurse Grace until she is well again. Julia will be a constant reminder that Grace's life will never again be as it once was.

"Is there an afternoon bus to Willingham?" Grace calls up to the driver after the door has closed.

The bus pops and hisses and continues down Woodward.

Speaking to Grace through the rearview mirror, the driver says, "Twelve fifteen at Alder. That your street?"

"Thank you," she says. "That'll be fine."

———

Aunt Julia won't be home for hours. She's off shopping with the other ladies, and that will keep her away all morning. Still, Izzy and Arie twice look up and down the street because it wouldn't do for one of Aunt Julia's friends to catch them outside. From somewhere north of Alder Avenue, a round of firecrackers explodes, one shooting off right on top of another. Grandma says they start earlier and earlier every year, and isn't that a shame. Those firecrackers are like a starting pistol, and clutching a cold, wet bottle against her stomach, Izzy gives a wave and she and Arie take off running through the side yard that cuts between the Turners' and Brandenbergs' houses. The girls hit the alley and their feet slip in the dry dirt and kick up clouds of dust. They keep running even though their throats are dry and they need to spit and their legs are tired from going all the way to Beersdorf's Grocery and back.

Izzy would have thought Arie would run all the way to Aunt Julia's because she's scared of the alley now, but something makes her shorten her stride, slow, and eventually stop. Straight ahead, a few yards past Mrs. Richardson's garage, Mr. Schofield's rusted old chair and sawed-off piece of wood sit in the middle of the alley. No sign of rusted old Mr. Schofield.

The girls had been halfway to Beersdorf's Grocery before Arie realized where they were going. Izzy told her no one was twisting her arm and she could go on back home if she wanted. She knew Arie wasn't brave enough for that, so they walked the rest of the way to Beersdorf's, one block west and three blocks south, all the while watching for men who might be searching for Elizabeth. Every time they saw a car coming, they ducked behind a clump of bushes or the trunk of an elm. "Why bother walking all the way to Beersdorf's when we don't have any money?" Arie had said when they were halfway there. But money wasn't the thing that kept Arie from wanting to go to Beersdorf's.

Besides being afraid of the back alley, which seemed to make

Arie afraid of everything, she didn't want to go to Beersdorf's because Aunt Julia didn't shop there anymore. Arie figured there must be a good reason. Grandma always says there's no moss growing under Aunt Julia and she wouldn't do something, or not do something, without a good reason. Not too long ago, Aunt Julia did shop at Beersdorf's and only took the bus to Willingham once or twice a week. Beersdorf's couldn't have turned into a bad place in such a short time. That's what Izzy thought. Arie thought it didn't take long at all for things to turn bad. Just look at a banana.

Slipping the Royal Crown under her shirt had been easy for Izzy. Mr. Beersdorf was more interested in the Negroes standing outside his shop than he was in keeping an eye on two girls. Loitering. That's what people called what those Negroes were doing. Arie was more interested in those Negroes too. She was even scared of them, keeping both eyes on them the whole time they were in the store. She didn't know a Royal Crown was tucked under Izzy's shirt until they were down the street and around the corner and headed toward home. Several times during the walk back, Arie said, "How are you going to open that stolen bottle of pop?" Standing now in the middle of the alley and seeing the Richardsons' garage door is wide open, and not wanting old Mr. Schofield to catch them breaking Aunt Julia's rules, Izzy knows exactly how she'll open this bottle of pop.

The Richardsons' house is quiet. No sign of Mrs. Richardson or anyone else. Even though none of the ladies of Alder are working at the church this morning because it's their turn to catch up on things around the house, they'll all be on the bus to Willingham with Aunt Julia or down in their basements running their laundry through a wringer. Across the alley at Mr. Schofield's house, a screen door squeals and slaps shut. The colored men have a schedule. That's what Aunt Julia and Uncle Bill said. Not that it's a dependable schedule, but worth knowing all the same. They like to catch the 10:00 a.m. bus, at least a few of them, as if they might have a job. They're back again for the 5:15. No telling what goes on in the middle of the night. But be mindful, that's what Uncle Bill said. Mr. Schofield must know about the schedule too.

Holding the wet bottle that isn't so cold anymore against her stomach, Izzy yanks Arie toward the open garage. She follows for a few steps and then pulls away.

"I'm not going in there," Arie says, keeping her voice low in case those are Mr. Schofield's footsteps.

"Would you rather get a whipping from him?" Izzy points at the rusted old folding chair and gives Arie another yank.

Once inside the garage, the air is instantly cooler. They stand motionless, both of them holding their breath so they can hear better. No one shouts at them for being where they don't belong. Izzy points toward the back of the garage, and once she's sure there is no piece of wood tapping across the gravel outside, she walks to the wooden bench straight ahead and flips open the lid on Mr. Richardson's toolbox. The musty smell and the gritty tools, which are mostly heavier than Izzy would have thought they would be, make her think about fathers and the things they keep and don't keep around the house. She doesn't know anything about fathers, but she does know the large tool that opens and closes wide enough to grab a bottle cap is called a pair of pliers. Yes, a pair of pliers should work real good.

"Have a seat," she whispers to Arie. "I'll have this open in no time."

The tangy smell of fireworks has followed them into the garage. It's growing stronger, as if someone close is shooting them off.

"I'm not drinking any of that stolen pop," Arie says. She slips far enough into the garage that no one will be able to see her, crosses her arms over her chest like she's hugging herself, and sinks into the rough wooden wall.

Izzy wrenches off the cap, takes a long drink, coughing because the bubbles swell up in her throat, and says, "Suit yourself." She takes another drink, holds up the bottle to check how much is left, and from the middle of the garage she points at the south wall. "Look there," she says. "We could use that."

Walking across the dirt floor, Izzy shivers, maybe from the cooler air or maybe from the stolen pop racing through her veins, and lifts a length of rope from the hook where it hangs. She can almost taste the smoke in the air now.

"Could be a leash for Patches," she says, starting to take another drink but stopping because her stomach doesn't feel so good.

"You stealing rope now too?" Arie asks, and smiles because she knows Izzy's stomach hurts. "Don't bother. That's way too big for a cat."

"Yeah," Izzy says, watching for any sign of Mr. Schofield. "You're probably right. Good jump rope, though."

"Now, this would make a good leash." Arie slides a few more feet into the garage and nudges whatever it is with her toe as though testing to see if it's alive.

Izzy tosses the rope over one shoulder and joins her. "What is it?" she says. The smell of something burning grows stronger as Izzy walks toward Arie. It's probably the boys who live a block past Tuttle Avenue. Aunt Julia says boys who grow up find trouble to stir up. Before Izzy and Arie climbed into Uncle Bill's car, their suitcases already stowed in the trunk, Grandma had pointed at Izzy and told her not to get any ideas about boys. She jabbed her finger twice, even poking Izzy in the chest the second time, and said it again. We won't have any accidents in this house, Grandma had said. And when she asked if Izzy understood, she nodded even though she hadn't.

"Looks like old clothes and things," Arie says. "Must be Mrs. Richardson's stuff."

Reaching into one of the bags, Arie pulls out a thin white belt. Tiny pink and white jewels cover the small round buckle. She threads one end of the belt through the buckle and pulls it until the belt is the size of a cat's neck. "It's perfect," she says in a loud voice.

Izzy leaps forward and slaps a hand over Arie's mouth. They stand still and listen. A few quiet moments pass. No sign of Mr. Schofield. Izzy drops her hand from Arie's mouth.

"Sorry," Arie whispers.

Izzy tilts her head and raises her brows at Arie. Usually, Arie is the one giving this look to Izzy. "How come it's okay for you to steal?" Izzy asks as she walks over to the six brown bags lined up against the wall, where Mr. Richardson won't hit them with his car. "But not okay for me?" She pulls out a blouse by its sleeve and lets it float back into the bag.

"It's not stealing. She's throwing all this out. It's with the trash."

Both girls stop talking and Izzy crosses a finger over her lips. On the other side of the garage, something creaks, like the old metal legs of an old rusted folding chair groaning under the weight of an old Mr. Schofield. Placing one foot directly in front of the other because that's the quietest way, Izzy walks toward the back of the garage and presses an ear to the cool wall. Hearing nothing more and forgetting her upset stomach, she takes another drink but the Royal Crown has turned warm. They'll have to peek outside to see if Mr. Schofield is sitting in his chair. If he is, they could be stuck here until suppertime.

"This must have fallen out of one of the bags." Izzy whispers loudly enough for only Arie to hear and stoops to pick up a lady's white dress shoe from the dirt floor. Letting it dangle from one finger, she holds it up to inspect it in better light and to give Arie a good look at it.

"That shoe is lots bigger than the ones in the bags." Arie moves closer, but not too close. "And it's almost new. It's Mrs. Richardson's."

"They're all Mrs. Richardson's," Izzy says, scanning the dirt floor for a spot to dump the rest of the pop.

"But this one is bigger. Pregnant women buy bigger shoes. This shoe isn't supposed to be garbage."

"What does pregnant have to do with anything?"

"Don't you remember Aunt Julia's feet? Remember how spongy they got?" Arie waves a hand in front of her face, obviously smelling the same nasty smoke Izzy smells. "Remember how we went to Hudson's and she bought big shoes? This is one of Mrs. Richardson's big pregnant shoes."

Izzy remembers going to Hudson's but shakes her head anyway. She doesn't like thinking about anything that has to do with Maryanne. They visited once and the baby was there, filling up Aunt Julia's house. When they visited again, she was gone, and the house has been empty ever since, hollow even.

"Well, we can't ask her if it's hers," Izzy says, being careful to whisper, but it's hard to do when she gets this annoyed with Arie. "Better put it back with the others." She rubs the shoe against her shirt, buffing off the dirt, and tosses it toward Arie.

Never one to easily catch a ball, Arie lunges, reaches out, but the shoe sails past her and she falls into one of Mr. Richardson's garbage cans. The lid topples off and a cloud of smoke erupts from the silver can and rolls up into the air.

Arie slaps a hand over her mouth, and Izzy drops her pop bottle.

"The lid," Izzy whispers, jabbing a finger at the lid lying on the ground, but then waves Arie off. "No, stop. It'll be hot." Grabbing a skirt from one of the bags, Izzy wraps it around her hand, picks up the lid by its edge, and tosses it toward the can. It misses, bouncing off the rim and landing near Arie's feet.

"You better come on out of there," a voice shouts.

It's Mr. Schofield. The girls flap their arms at the rising smoke and back away from the growing flame.

"Got myself a rifle out here," Mr. Schofield shouts.

Izzy grabs Arie. "It's us, Mr. Schofield," she says, hugging Arie to her. "Mr. Schofield, it's just us."

Even though Izzy can't see Mr. Schofield, can only hear him, she knows he'll be walking with a limp, almost dragging his right leg as if that side of his body is heavier than the other. One shoulder will be sagging forward and his jowls will be drooping. They wobble when he walks or talks. It's the polio he had as a child, Aunt Julia once told them. It never quite leaves a person and now it's eating him away from the inside out. She says Izzy and Arie are lucky they'll never have to worry about ending up like Mr. Schofield.

"Come on out," Mr. Schofield shouts again. "I smell your goddamned fire."

"No, Mr. Schofield. It's us. It's us."

"Goddamn you and your fire."

Izzy pulls Arie deeper into the garage, into the farthest, darkest corner. "It's us, Mr. Schofield. It's Arie and Izzy."

But Mr. Schofield doesn't hear.

"Come on out or I start firing."

CHAPTER ELEVEN

Once off the bus, Malina hurries across Willingham while the other ladies linger to stare at the warehouse. Positioned squarely at the T-junction where Willingham Avenue dead-ends into Chamberlin, the white stone building stands three stories high. Its windowsills are chipped and crumbling as if it's sinking into the footings, and the doorways are boarded over. This is where those Negro women gather to show themselves to the husbands. Some say the women strip themselves of their blouses and under-garments so the men will want them more.

The ladies stare only for a moment, their lips puckered and their arms crossed, and then they remember their real concern should be for Elizabeth and not the Negro women or what the hus-bands may be up to. Reminding themselves of the finer things in life, they tug at their gloves, check the clasps on their handbags, smooth their curls, and head off to the deli or the cleaners or the drugstore. In twenty minutes, they'll all meet at the bakery. On the bus ride over, the ladies agreed that if Mrs. Nowack insisted on keeping her doors open on payday, they'd be patrons no longer. Together, in twenty minutes' time, this is what they'll tell Mrs. Nowack.

Next door to the warehouse, the factory's parking lot is only half full. Most of the men, Mr. Herze included, have gathered again at the church. Once Malina is certain Mr. Herze's sedan is not among the cars parked there, she swivels on one heel and walks toward the river. For the next twenty minutes, the ladies will scurry from store to store. They'll not notice Malina's whereabouts. Twenty minutes is certainly enough time. If Mr. Herze's girl is still alive, a block or so down Chamberlin is where Malina will likely find her.

"I'm quite certain it's true," Doris Taylor had said after the ladies of Alder Avenue boarded the bus. She sat on the edge of her seat and spoke loudly so her voice would carry over the air rushing through the open windows. "Mrs. Nowack has no intention of closing her doors on payday. What are we to do?"

Though it was Doris who spoke, the ladies scooted about in their seats to look to Malina. It was a reminder she was one of the oldest among them.

"I really haven't any opinion," Malina had said.

The ladies, a few with their mouths dangling open, stared at Malina, waiting, obviously thinking she had spoken in jest. Again, resenting the ladies for thrusting her into a matronly position, Malina snapped her own mouth shut so the ladies might realize their rude behavior and flicked a hand at them, urging them to turn away.

"We should all go to Mrs. Nowack," Doris Taylor had said.

Doris brought cinnamon rolls to the bake sale every year even though they always sold poorly. She used too few pecans and consistently overcooked them. "All of us together. As one. We'll tell her we'll not shop in her store if she refuses to close her doors. One of our ladies might be tempted to go to Willingham on payday if the bakery remains open. It's for our own safety. Malina said so herself just the other day."

Again, the ladies looked to Malina. "Of course," she said, letting out a long sigh, and smiling. "It's a fine idea. You should listen to Doris."

Malina had worries of her own, more than enough, and no desire to take on the worries of others. Laying her head back so as to avoid any more gaping mouths, Malina had stared at Grace Richardson sitting across the aisle. Looking straight ahead, her eyes seemingly focused on nothing, Grace had rubbed her two bare hands in slow, steady circles over her round stomach. Every so often, her eyelids slowly closed and took so long in opening again, Malina wondered each time if Grace were asleep. She didn't wake from this stupor until Julia Wagner boarded the bus.

"Maybe those women will leave now that one of them is dead," a lady had said as the bus pulled away from its stop outside the thrift store. "And you know, don't you, that men have been fired. If there are no men left who will open a pocketbook, those women will all but vanish."

"We shouldn't be talking about this," said another. "Think of Elizabeth. It's all so unseemly. It's disrespectful to her, don't you think?"

And then the conversation turned to Jerry Lawson. By now,

everyone knew, even those who lived blocks from Alder, that Jerry had been fired. What a shame for poor Betty Lawson. What was she to do now that she knew such things about her husband? What was that poor child to do? What was her name? Cynthia, wasn't it? Poor Cynthia, all but abandoned. Jerry would be able to make no sort of living. The ladies next wondered aloud if it was only one woman for Jerry Lawson or if he took several. One would be worse than many, they all agreed, because if it were only one, that might mean he actually cared for her. My God, it might mean he actually cared.

"My Harry said the woman was killed with a hammer." The lady's name escaped Malina. She lived somewhere just north of Alder and rarely attended services. "Can you imagine? The police could tell, just by looking at the woman, that it was a hammer, or something much like it. How do you suppose they know such things? How does one look at a hole in the head and know what caused it?"

"What do you know of the dead woman?" Malina said, still watching Grace rub her hands lightly over her stomach as she chatted with Julia Wagner. The two were not listening to the ladies talk but were giggling among themselves.

"Why on earth would you ask?" several of the ladies said, one echoing another.

Malina gripped the seat in front of her, bracing herself as the bus neared its stop at Willingham. What must it look like when a person is hit in the head with a hammer? "Have you read anything? Have your husbands told you what she looked like?"

Doris Taylor pulled a tissue from her handbag, folded it, and blotted her fresh lipstick. "She was one of them. What more could possibly matter?"

There must have been a time when Mr. Herze's girl looked like Grace Richardson. The girl probably rubbed her hands over her stomach and stared at nothing, her thoughts filled with dreams of a healthy, happy baby and a man to love her. If Mr. Herze's girl were the dead one, what had become of the baby in the carriage? Malina had leafed through every newspaper that landed on her doorstep since the day that woman, some woman, was killed. She studied the papers until the ink stained her fingertips and the paper had torn at the fold, not certain why it mattered to her or why she craved any hint as to which woman had died. But every day the craving grew. Even if she knew, it wouldn't help her predicament. No matter who died or who killed her, Malina had still told a lie.

"It's no never mind," Malina had said as the bus slowed to its stop at Woodward and Willingham. "I'll see you ladies at the bakery in twenty minutes. What a fine idea you've had, Doris."

As Malina nears the alley where the woman was killed, she walks mostly on her toes so her red leather heels don't slap the concrete and give her away. At the alley's entrance, she stops and tugs on her three-quarter-length sleeves. The saleslady at Hudson's said not everyone could wear the new length but Malina, being as tiny as she is, would carry it beautifully.

For so much to have transpired since the woman was killed, the alley looks no different, except perhaps it appears smaller in the daylight, less foreboding. Seeing it again for the first time since that night, the alley isn't so long and dark, and what had seemed like quite a distance when she was following that woman and her carriage is really no more than a few steps. For an instant, Malina is tempted to travel those few steps and look for the hammer she dropped. It would be a relief to have the proper tool hanging on Mr. Herze's pegboard again, but that is foolish thinking. The police will have found that hammer, or possibly someone else found it, and whisked it away. Before temptation can again overwhelm her better judgment, Malina continues toward the river.

The colored women stand in a small group. A few of them sit on the curb, their long black legs stretched before them. Others sit cross-legged on the same curb, picking at blades of grass or their own unkempt nails. Still others stand in the middle of the street. There was a time, not so long ago, those women wouldn't dare show themselves on Willingham Avenue. But the highways have pushed them west and north, and now every day they inch closer. Often they are seen lounging, waiting, biding their time until the ladies finish their shopping and leave for the day. They'll all but take over on paydays, some of the ladies say, and that is likely the beginning of the end. Soon the ladies will be chased from Willingham just as they were chased from Beersdorf's Grocery. Already some of the ladies have begun traveling to Hamtramck to do their shopping.

Standing on the outskirts of the group, almost as if she is not one of them, is the girl. Malina worried that she might not recognize her, but even from this distance, almost a full block away, there is no doubt. The girl has a kind of grace about her, probably due to her slender limbs and long neck. Wondering if the girl has smooth skin, Malina takes a few more steps toward the group. Slowly, as if the girl senses someone staring at her, her head rolls to the side and she looks back at Malina. Other heads turn. A few of the women push themselves off the ground. Others cross arms over their chests.

A tall, round woman with heavy legs sticking out from a black skirt stands in the center of the group. She has narrow shoulders, flabby arms, and surprisingly large hips. Like the others, she turns to face Malina, but even as she turns, the large woman doesn't move the hand that clutches the handle of a baby carriage. This woman is much taller than the one who frightened Malina in the alley that night, though she does bear the same unfortunate shape. The woman takes a step toward Malina, and yet she doesn't let go of the carriage. She is protecting it, protecting the baby inside, from Malina.

There couldn't possibly be more than one such carriage. The one parked in the middle of the street has the same large metal wheels, the same black canopy, and if Malina could get close enough, it would have the same squeal as the one the girl pushed. This large woman, however, is built like someone who has birthed a baby—full roomy hips, soft sagging arms. It hadn't seemed possible Mr. Herze's girl could be the mother. Her hips were narrow; her legs, frail and lean. That night on Willingham, the girl must have been watching over the baby, doing a favor for the real mother. It makes sense she would be kind. Mr. Herze likes proper manners and polite conversation. He appreciates kindness. His girl is graceful and considerate. It shouldn't be a surprise. While Mr. Herze's girl is clearly not the dead one, there is no need to peek inside that carriage.

Back on Willingham, the ladies will be finishing their shopping. They'll gather now inside Nowack's Bakery, where they'll buy up all the apple cakes. It's the thing Mrs. Nowack bakes every Monday and probably what drew many of the ladies to Willingham today when they might otherwise have preferred to stay away. Malina will want to get to the bakery to buy one of the cakes for Mr. Herze before they're gone. He does like a slice, lightly dusted with confectioner's sugar, before bed. Once Doris Taylor and the others have had their say with Mrs. Nowack, no one will be buying anything.

Malina should feel some relief that the child is not Mr. Herze's doing, but there's still the matter of Jerry Lawson pointing at her and accusing her. He might storm across the street again, give Mr. Herze reason to doubt Malina. She really does wish she hadn't lied. After a few backward steps, those Negro women staring at her all the while, Malina swings around, no longer concerned if her heels slap loudly against the concrete, and walks back to Willingham and Nowack's Bakery as quickly as her slender skirt and three-quarter-sleeve jacket will allow.

————

Two weeks before Grace was to marry James, Mother said it was high time Grace learn to make pierogi. Mother stood at Grace's stove and shook her head. "Butter will scorch," she had said, and slid the pan of simmering onions to a cool burner. They tried again two days later. What else could Grace offer if not a warm supper every night? On the second day, Grace strained the cooked potatoes, pouring the water down the drain. Again, Mother shook her head. Her recipe said to retain the water from the cooked potatoes. Grace boiled a half-dozen more and Mother sighed at the waste.

Mother gave up after the third try, when Grace added too much filling to the pierogi. Grace crimped the edges with a knuckle as she had seen Mother do, but she had rolled the dough too thin, and each crescent-shaped dumpling split when she dropped it into the boiling pot. Cheesy potato filling clouded the water.

"What else have you to offer?"

Setting a bowl of pierogi dough on the kitchen table where she can lean over it and use her weight, Grace presses, folds and turns the dough, presses, folds and turns. Mother's dough is always smooth and elastic. Grace's sticks to her fingers in heavy white clumps. Stepping off the early-morning bus that returned her to Alder well ahead of the other ladies, Grace had thought the cooler, drier air of early day would help her dough. If this batch of pierogi turns out well, she'll send them to the church with James and then make and freeze more for the bake sale. She adds another spoonful of flour, and with the heel of her hand, begins again. Hearing a shout from the back alley, she straightens, nearly knocking the bowl to the floor.

"You better come on out of there." And then, "Got myself a rifle . . ."

With the back of one sticky hand, Grace first pushes aside the curtains in the back door, and even knowing he won't be there, she looks for James. There is more shouting, though this time, it isn't a man's voice. Grace wipes her hands on her apron as she sidesteps to the kitchen window, picking blobs of dough from between her fingers as she goes. Smoke rolls out of the garage in a thin plume. Now she considers the telephone, but there is no number to call for James. He'll be out on Woodward or down near the river, hoping not to find a body that has floated to the surface. She throws open the back door.

"It's us, Mr. Schofield." Again, a girl's voice. "It's only us."

In the alley near Grace's garage, Orin Schofield stands, a rifle of some sort braced against his shoulder. The rising smoke has changed from white to black.

"Orin," Grace shouts. "Put that away."

Walking in a wide arch that keeps her far from the open garage and clear of Orin's aim, Grace waves away the smell of the smoke. She used to close the garage door for James every morning. After he'd leave for work, she would finish washing the breakfast dishes and then wander through the backyard, maybe pulling a weed or two, watering her bushes, snapping off her marigolds' brown, withered blossoms, and eventually close the garage door. She didn't follow him this morning, might never follow him again.

"Who is it?" Grace shouts into the garage. "Who's in there?"

The girls appear, one dragging the other by the arm. That's Izzy in front and Arie trailing behind.

"We didn't do it," Izzy says, moving away from the black smoke.

The rising column has thinned. Orange sparks flutter into the air and die out.

"It's the trash can," Izzy says. "It's a fire in the trash can."

"Orin," Grace shouts again, waving the girls toward her. "Put that gun away. Girls, here. Come here. Orin, it's Izzy and Arie."

Orin stands on the other side of the smoky cloud. He taps the side of the garage with the barrel of his rifle. "Come on out," he shouts. "Come out of that goddamned garage."

"Orin, please." Grace gathers the twins under the maple. She runs her hands over their arms, cups the face of each and scans them for any sign they've been hurt. "Stay here," she says, pushing away Arie's hand when she tries to grab Grace by the arm.

The crack of the rifle makes Grace stumble. She grabs for the baby. An instinct. Next she reaches for the girls. They run to her, together scooping Grace, one on each side. Another shot. Grace is back on her feet. She corrals the girls, pulls them close. They huddle together under the hard maple, all three inhaling what the others exhale. As the silence widens, Grace straightens to her full height. She brushes back the girls hair, checks them over again. One of the girls, Izzy because Arie wouldn't be so bold, hugs Grace's stomach and presses an ear over the baby.

On the other side of the alley, Mr. Williamson stomps out his side door and across his backyard but slows when he sees Orin, a gun to his shoulder, his cheek resting against the wooden handle. Though he no longer has a job to go to, Mr. Williamson dresses every morning in a shirt and tie, belted trousers, and his calfskin wingtips. His silver hair is as thick as the day Grace met him and is smoothed back and held in place by a hair dressing. Probably Top Brass, the same as James uses. Mrs. Williamson follows her husband, but stops near her clothesline. As always, a blue scarf covers her thinning white hair, and the bib apron hanging loosely from her neck has been left untied at the waist. Mr. Williamson stops short of reaching Orin and doesn't move any closer until the gun's barrel begins to sink.

"What are you shooting at there, Orin?" Mr. Williamson says.

"Someone's in there." Orin waves the gun's narrow tip at the garage. He stumbles as if he's dizzy. His eyes settle on Grace and the twins, all three still standing in a cluster, their arms inter-twined. His cheeks and nose are red. He brushes away sweat that drips down his temples. "Look at that right there." He stabs the gun toward the garage, stumbles again. "I told you, didn't I? Those two started a fire."

The smoke coming from the garage has thinned to little more than a trickle. Mr. Williamson takes another few steps toward Orin.

"Think whoever stirred up this trouble is long gone by now," Mr. Williamson says. "How about you let me have that gun of yours?"

"I heard them. Heard them tossing things about." Orin swings around to face Grace and the twins. The rifle swings around too. "You done this," he says. "You two girls."

Izzy starts to say something, but Grace gives her a squeeze, si-lencing her.

"I seen it with my own eyes," Orin says, shaking his head as if clearing his thoughts.

"Say, why not let me take a look at this for you," Mr. Williamson says as he edges up next to Orin, then lays one flat palm on the gun's barrel and slowly forces it toward the ground. "You know I clean all my own guns." When the barrel's tip points directly at the ground, Mr. Williamson eases the gun from Orin. "I'll give it a good once-over and get it back to you lickety-split. Even bring one of Martha's cobblers when I return it."

Orin stares at the gun as it passes into Mr. Williamson's hands.

When the gun is safely with Mr. Williamson, Izzy shakes loose of Grace and looks her straight in the eye. "We didn't do anything.

We didn't start that fire. I promise. Please, you can't tell Aunt Julia. We didn't, I promise."

"You two set that fire at my place. Broke my goddamned windows, too."

"No, that's not true," Izzy says. "None of that's true. We wanted to hide, that's all. We saw Mr. Schofield's chair in the alley and didn't want him to catch us. Right, Arie? Isn't that true? Please, Mrs. Richardson. Don't tell."

"It's the coloreds, then," Orin says, pushing Mr. Williamson aside so he can see down the alley. "Every day, they're coming through here. Coloreds starting fires and breaking windows."

Grace grabs one of the twins, takes no time to decide which one. "Did you see them?" she says.

The girl's eyes shine and she tries to pull away, but Grace squeezes tighter. Arie. The other twin, Izzy, grabs at Grace's arm to drag her away.

"Did you see those men?" Grace shouts.

With both hands, Izzy pulls at Grace's arm. "We didn't see anyone, Mrs. Richardson. We didn't see anyone and we didn't start any fire."

"I suppose it's best we all calm ourselves," Mr. Williamson says. "Let's not look to stir up trouble we don't need. How about we get you home, Orin?"

"By God, I'm not going anywhere," Orin says. "My chair. Sit me down right there."

"Why don't you ladies go on inside," Mr. Williamson says. He winks in Grace's direction and tugs at his tie though it doesn't need straightening. "I'll see that the fire is out. Doesn't appear any harm's been done."

Grace loosens her grip on Arie. "I'm so sorry," she says, rubbing the red spot on Arie's slender shoulder. "Come, girls." She wraps an arm around each, nods her thanks to Mr. and Mrs. Williamson, and walks the twins to the side of the house. She'll take them inside, wash their faces with a cool cloth, call Julia to come fetch them. She should probably feed them something, a peanut-butter sandwich, and give them milk to drink. Someone may call the police. They may come and look inside her garage.

"We're fine, Mrs. Richardson," Izzy says, reaching for Arie's hand and yanking her away from the stairs leading into Grace's kitchen. "We'll go home now, straight home."

"We should wait for your aunt. I can't let you go alone."

Izzy continues to pull Arie down the driveway toward the street.

"She's out shopping. We're fine. We'll go straight home. We didn't start that fire, Mrs. Richardson. I promise we didn't."

"I'll walk with you," Grace says.

"No," Izzy says, holding up one hand to stop Grace from following. "Straight home, I promise."

Arie says nothing and every time Grace looks her way, she drops her eyes or looks off to the side. While Izzy is clearly afraid of what Julia will have to say should she find out the twins disobeyed her, Arie is frightened of something else. It's almost as if she is frightened of Grace.

"Please," Izzy says one more time. "Please don't tell."

Grace lifts a hand and points. "Straight home, you two. And until Elizabeth is found, please stay there."

CHAPTER TWELVE

A rie and Izzy run all the way to Aunt Julia's house, not once looking back at Mrs. Richardson. They drop the length of rope on the front porch, flip off their sneakers at the back door, and run through the kitchen and up the stairs, even though running is not allowed in the house. They toss the slender, jeweled belt in their bedroom closet, change into clean blouses that won't smell of smoke, and return to the living room. While Izzy acts as lookout for Aunt Julia, Arie sinks into the sofa, hugs one of Aunt Julia's ruffled throw pillows to her chest, and takes deep breaths until her heart begins to slow. The pillow smells like the cologne Uncle Bill wears to church, and it makes her feel even worse for having done something she knows will scare him and Aunt Julia. They'll worry Izzy and Arie are going to end up like Elizabeth because they won't stay inside and do as they're told.

"Do you see her?" Arie says for the third time in twenty minutes.

Izzy lifts a finger, signaling Arie should wait. Alder Avenue has been quiet since a group of ladies marched down the street almost half an hour ago, their arms full of groceries. Aunt Julia was not among them.

"No," Izzy says, "But there's men at Mrs. Herze's house now. Looks like police."

Arie jumps from the sofa and joins Izzy at the window. Across the street, two men in dark suits stand on Mrs. Herze's porch and a police car is parked in her driveway.

"Is that about the fire?" Arie says. "Are they here because of us?"

"Uh-oh," Izzy says, letting the drape fall closed and pushing Arie back to her seat.

Uncle Bill never uses the driveway. He always circles the block, drives up the alley, and parks in the garage. But that's his car pulling into the driveway and that's Aunt Julia sitting next to him. An engine rattles and falls silent. Two doors slam. Footsteps, one light set, one heavy set, cross the front porch. Izzy and Arie sit side by side on the sofa, hands in their laps, feet dangling near the floor. Keys rattle in the front lock. The door swings open.

Aunt Julia is the first inside. Her hair has frizzed since she left the house this morning. Later in the day, when she tires of trying to tame it with pins and hairspray and it becomes a tangle of wild red hair, she'll tie a scarf over it. She holds one bag of groceries that she tosses on the entry table before rushing into the living room. Behind her, Uncle Bill carries a few more bags, but he doesn't toss his aside.

"You were shot at?" Aunt Julia says, first grabbing Arie and then Izzy. Like Mrs. Richardson did, she pushes the hair off their faces to check for cuts or bruises, trails her fingers along their arms, rolls their hands from front to back. "You're not hurt?"

"He didn't really shoot at . . ."

"Stop," Aunt Julia says. "Not another word. You were forbidden . . . forbidden to leave this house." She stands and paces the length of the sofa. Whenever Aunt Julia gets angry, her voice slips back to where it's most comfortable. Her Southern twang, Uncle Bill likes to call it. "I told you, didn't I? Didn't I make it clear? Didn't I make it crystal clear? My God, that bowed-up fool shot at you?"

Arie waits for Izzy to answer, but even she must have decided it best to keep quiet.

"Well," Aunt Julia says. "Are you going to tell me what happened?"

"We were only looking for Patches," Izzy says. "We'll never find her if we can't go outside."

"Don't you dare get smart with me."

Uncle Bill walks to the entry, sets his groceries next to the bag Aunt Julia dropped, and returns. He rests his hands on Aunt Julia's shoulders. His dark eyes always have a way of looking sad. Grandma says those dark, sad eyes are what snagged Aunt Julia. Grandma says women, all ages and all types, have a softness for sad eyes.

"Why don't you two go out front for a few minutes," Uncle Bill says, leaning around Aunt Julia. He is the only one who makes Aunt Julia look small. "Let me and your aunt talk in private."

Arie waits for Izzy to stand first, then follows her to the front door.

"Do not even think about leaving that yard," Aunt Julia says, swatting away Uncle Bill's hands and flopping down on the center of the sofa. "Am I understood?"

"Yes, ma'am," Izzy says.

"Yes, ma'am," Arie says.

Izzy gives an extra tug on the front door to make sure it's closed and lets the screen door slam, something she knows will upset Aunt Julia. The men and the police car are no longer at Mrs. Herze's house. Arie exhales, thinking that is a good sign, then drops down on the first stair and slides over to make room for Izzy. But instead of joining Arie, Izzy grabs the rope she found in Mrs. Richardson's garage and marches across the porch. Mrs. Richardson had been too worried about the fire and gunshots at her house to notice the rope Izzy had carried from the garage or the thin belt that had been wrapped like a bandage around Arie's hand. Once down the stairs, Izzy walks to the very end of the sidewalk. She stands there, hands on hips, and even though she doesn't say it, she's thinking about stepping from their yard onto Alder and disobeying Aunt Julia all over again. Aunt Julia would say Izzy is chugged-full of angry, though Arie isn't exactly sure about what.

Taking one end of the rope in each hand, Izzy lets it hang to the ground and, with a single swing, begins to skip. She twirls the rope faster and faster, slapping it against the hot concrete, probably thinking the noise will make Aunt Julia mad too, except it really isn't all that loud.

Across the street at Mr. and Mrs. Herze's house, a big blue car pulls into their drive. One of the car's doors swings open and a black shoe appears. The rest of Mr. Herze follows. Without closing his door, he walks down the driveway using long strides, crosses the street, and marches directly up to Arie and Izzy. They've never been so close to Mr. Herze. He smells like Uncle Bill's Sunday cologne, except much stronger, and his stomach pushes against his white shirt, making it look like his buttons might pop right off if he were to take a deep breath. He examines the girls just as Mrs. Richardson and Aunt Julia did, except when his hands run over their arms, they're rough and dry and cold even though it's hot outside.

"Your uncle is home, girls?" he says, brushing aside Izzy's hair and then Arie's. "You're unharmed?"

"Yes, sir," Izzy says.

Arie says nothing but slides one foot away and drags the other to meet it.

"Warren," Mrs. Herze calls out from her side of the street. "What's brought you home so early?" She waves one hand overhead and teeters on the edge of the curb. Her dark hair makes her white skin look plastic. Everything about Mrs. Herze shines like it's store-bought.

Mr. Herze doesn't answer. His eyes dart back and forth between Izzy and Arie. "Don't let that Orin Schofield frighten you," he says, his eyes landing on Izzy and sticking there. "He actually take a shot at you?"

"Not at us, sir," Izzy says. "At the garage. In the dirt. Don't think he meant to hurt anyone."

"Shall I fix you something, Warren?" Mrs. Herze shouts, louder this time. She takes one step into the street. "A sandwich?" She continues to wave a hand overhead. "Are you at all hungry?"

"You tell your uncle to stay home with you girls for the rest of the day," Mr. Herze says, his eyes still stuck on Izzy. "Tell him Mr. Herze said so."

"Yes, sir."

"And if you two find yourselves in any more trouble, you let me know."

Again, "Yes, sir."

"Warren, will you want dinner? A change of clothes?"

"All right, then." Mr. Herze takes each of them by the hand, gives a squeeze, drops Arie's, still holds Izzy's. "You two take care."

Arie pulls Izzy by the arm. Mr. Herze's hand drops away.

"Anything at all," he says, reaching out to grab Izzy's fingers but unable to reach them. "You call on me."

"Thank you, Mr. Herze," Izzy says, stumbling as Arie drags her toward the front door.

"We'll tell Uncle Bill you were here," Arie says, not sure why she says it or why she is suddenly happy Uncle Bill is much stronger and much bigger than Mr. Herze.

———

Grace leans against her kitchen counter, six slices of white bread laid out before her like playing cards, and wonders again if she made a mistake letting the twins go home to an empty house. This is usually the busiest part of Grace's day. She likes to get her chores done before the lunch hour and save her afternoons to tidy the house and touch up her makeup before James comes home. Puttering, Mother always called it. Grace likes to leave her puttering to the afternoons. At this earlier hour, there would normally be laundry to hang out, groceries to put away, a supper to begin planning. But today, she forgot to start any laundry and didn't bother with the market. Nearby, the stand mixer runs on low. Grace pours a stream of oil into the bowl and as the mixer churns, she begins to count to thirty. Her thoughts drift. She loses track and begins again. Give it thirty seconds, Mother always says.

Grace didn't call James after Orin Schofield fired his rifle into their garage, but she knew someone would find him and send him home. It's just as well. He promised to take Grace's tuna salad back to the church so the men could have a quick sandwich for lunch. It's one of those dishes Grace can always count on to turn out well. Warm air rushes into the kitchen when the back door swings open. James follows, nearly falling as he rushes across the threshold. Four long strides carry him to Grace, his footsteps clicking on the gray tile floor. He's picked up a speck of gravel or a stone in the sole of his shoe.

James says nothing at first, but as Grace did with the girls, he cups her cheeks, looks her over from head to toe, smooths damp strands of hair from her face.

"You're all right?"

She touches his square jaw. It's rough because he didn't bother to shave this morning.

"I'm fine," she says, and rests one hand on the baby. "We're fine." She watches as oil blends with the eggs and lemon juice.

Knowing James would come home to check on her, Grace had run a brush through her hair and freshened her lipstick and powder. She knew the glow of her hair when it's newly brushed and the shine on her cheeks that comes with a dab of rouge would reassure him.

"It was a silly misunderstanding," she says, drawing one finger through the mayonnaise and touching it to James's lips.

He's angry; of course he's angry. He storms about the kitchen, nearly knocking over a chair, stopping several times to stare out the window over the sink, hoping, just hoping, to catch sight of Orin Schofield. He's outraged. Gunfire at his own home. The police should come and have a word with Orin, but Grace says no. Orin shot into the dirt. He was really quite deliberate. He meant no harm. And a good scare might be just what those girls need. The real danger is how they disobey Julia and Bill.

"And the fire?" James says, wrapping his arms around Grace's full belly. "What happened with the fire?" He has exhausted himself, stomping and ranting. He leans into Grace, lets his face sink into her hair, and breathes in. With each movement, the stone wedged in his shoe still taps.

Grace shuts off her mixer and pulls a warm hardboiled egg from the pot on the stove. She taps it lightly on the edge of the sink, giving herself time to think.

"The girls," she says, scratching at the cracked shell with one fingernail and peeling it back. The white of the egg tears away with the thin shell. She should have cooled them first. "I think the girls were playing with fireworks." The lie comes quickly, easily. "It really only simmered. Burned itself out. I promised them I wouldn't tell Julia." With a paring knife, she slices through the firm, slippery egg white and pops the sliver in James's mouth. "You're sweet to worry so. Mr. Williamson took the gun. It won't happen again."

James slides around Grace so he can stand at the window. He doesn't notice the clicking sound his shoe continues to make or he would dig out the gravel with a nail or one of Grace's steak knives. He is watching out that window for Orin or maybe for the colored men who walk down the alley. He'll be wondering if those men are really the ones who started the fire. If Grace thinks it, James will think it too.

"What is that?" Grace says, pointing at James's back pocket.

"Found it in the garage." He pulls out a white shoe.

It's a woman's shoe. Two-inch heel. Everyday wear. It's crushed and marred with black smudges. It's Grace's.

"Sorry," he says. "Must have run it over."

Grace takes the shoe by its cracked heel. After the men had gone, leaving her alone in the garage, she limped back to the house. She had walked on the toe of her bare foot, her nylon surely snagging, because on the other, she wore a heel. Always so forgetful. She should have remembered the shoe and thrown it away with the glass she and Mother picked up from the garage floor.

"It must have been in with the things Mr. Symanski brought," she says. Another lie, quickly, easily. "Ewa's, I suppose."

"Probably right."

James holds a can of tuna beneath the opener hung from the underside of a cabinet. "I don't want you going out back anymore. Definitely don't want you near Orin Schofield." Then he locks the can in place and cranks the silver handle. "No reason for you even to go into the garage."

Grace drops three diced eggs into her largest bowl but is unsure how much relish to add. She's never made such a large batch. James dumps the tuna into the same bowl, sets the empty can on the counter, and leads Grace to the table, where he helps her to sit.

"I talked to a fellow today," he says, pacing between the sink and table. His shoe clicks, though not as loudly, as if the stone has worked its way up into the tread. "He was down at the church, speaking with a lot of folks. I talked to him about selling the house. He says plenty of folks are ready to sell since Elizabeth disappeared. Says he's had a dozen calls. Felt bad talking to him, what with Elizabeth still out there."

The last time Grace heard tapping on her kitchen floor, she had been afraid it would wake Betty Lawson's baby. She had been sleeping in the far corner while the ladies of the St. Alban's Charitable Ventures Committee chatted in Grace's living room.

"We can't be the last to give it serious thought." James drops into a seat and scoots his chair under the table. "Gracie, you listening?"

"We can't leave Mr. Symanski," Grace says. "Not now. What if Elizabeth comes home and we're gone?"

Grace wants to believe the words, tries to speak them with the soft tenderness she thinks her voice should have, but they come out flat and hollow, each word too deep, too loud. She knows Elizabeth will never come home.

"I'm sorry to say it," James says. "And I won't say it to Charles, but I can't have you living here. It's not safe anymore."

Grace shifts in her seat. Though her inner thighs still ache and her tailbone is yet tender, the small cut on her lip has almost healed over. It's little more than a red blemish that might be mistaken for a smudge of lipstick. James doesn't ask about it anymore.

"The agent says he's bound to sell a lot of houses around here," James continues. "Says folks will eventually start to worry. Can't wait around, he says. Nobody wants to be the last to get out. Says those folks moving in at the Filmore are a sure sign of what's to come. He'll swing by in a few days. Give the place a once-over."

James opens five more cans of tuna and Grace makes two dozen sandwiches, cuts them on the diagonal, and covers them with plastic wrap. As she works, James talks about where they might move. Well north of Eight Mile. Lots of folks are moving out there. It'll be a three-bedroom ranch with wall-to-wall carpet and a double sink in the kitchen. Can be expensive, though, so he can't make any promises. Drive won't be so bad, not since the highway went in. He'll give Grace everything she wants, everything she needs. A lawn, bigger than this one. Nice neighbors, too, with kids, lots of kids. And the buses run up north, so no need for Grace to worry. Or maybe it's high time she take another stab at learning to drive.

"I won't stop looking for Elizabeth," he says, and lifts her face to his. "No matter where we go, I won't stop looking until we find her." Then he places both hands on either side of Grace's large stomach and slides them up to her face and again tilts it to his. His eyelids are heavy. No doubt, he's thinking about the day Grace isn't pregnant anymore and he can be with her as only a husband is allowed.

"Will the agent put a sign in our yard, bring strangers through the house?" Grace pulls away slowly and begins to put clean dishes in her cupboards.

"If he likes this old girl enough, if the house is solid, he might buy her himself," James says, walking toward the back door. His shoe continues to click. "Be best that way. No need to get the neighbors worried. He'd give us a nice price too. We'd be out of here before you know it. Even before the baby is born." He opens the door, tugs on his hat, pulls it low over his eyes. "But I won't stop until we find something."

"She wasn't wearing those sneakers," Grace says.

James pushes the door closed. "Who?"

"She was tapping," Grace says, pointing at James's black steel-toed boots. "Like you are now. Tapping because she wore her black leather shoes. Elizabeth always wore them with her lavender dress, with any of her nicer dresses. That wasn't her shoe they found."

"It's something," James says. "We'll tell them, tell the police. But I don't think they ever made much of a single shoe. It could have belonged to anyone."

"I don't think Elizabeth wandered away, James," Grace says. "I think something bad, very bad, happened to her. I think she'll never come home."

"Don't you worry," James says. "We'll find her. You trust me, don't you?"

"Most definitely," she says, sliding a foot to the right so the light shining through the front window catches her hair. If it glows and her lips shine, James will feel better.

Because he's so very glad Grace is unharmed, James smiles. The whole drive home he probably imagined what his life would be like without Grace and his baby. The thought surely frightened him, but seeing Grace now, he is reassured life works out for the best. Mother is right. James doesn't want to hear the truth and Grace can never tell.

CHAPTER THIRTEEN

The moment the twins have left the house and Bill has closed the front door behind them, Julia kicks off her shoes, hikes her skirt over her knees, and runs up the steps two at a time, not caring that she'll snag her nylons. Once upstairs, she throws open the girls' bedroom door, yanks Arie's suitcase from under her bed, and flings it into the center of her mattress.

"Don't say a word," she says when Bill enters the room. She pulls open the dresser's top drawer, scoops an armful of undergarments and socks and flings them into the open suitcase. "They're going back to my mother's."

Bill moves in front of the dresser, not allowing Julia to open the next drawer. "Your mother is not there, remember?"

Dropping one shoulder, Julia rams it into Bill's side, trying to move him. He crosses his arms. "I'm not budging, and the girls are not leaving," he says, and once Julia begins to simmer down, he rests his hands on her shoulders.

"Can you imagine what might have happened?" Julia says.

Edging away from Bill, she flips the suitcase closed and drops onto the bed. Her skirt hugs her thighs well above her knees from her trek up the stairs. She tugs and wiggles until she has yanked it back into place. "Who on God's green earth fires a rifle at two young girls?"

"You know he wasn't firing at them." Bill sits next to Julia but not so close as to let their legs touch. He always knows when best to keep his distance.

"I know no such thing," Julia says. "You didn't hear him caterwauling the other day."

"I'll speak to the girls," Bill says, patting Julia's hand. "We should make sure they keep clear of Orin for a while. But I'd guess the fright they got will do the best job of keeping them close to home."

Julia slides off the bed, drops to her knees in front of Bill, and takes his hands in hers. "That's not enough," she says. "They're going to be our responsibility one day. You know they're getting to be too much for my mother. If not now, then soon enough."

"Yes," Bill says. "And I'll be happy to have them."

"We need to move," she says. "Right now. Sell this house and move. Our own neighbors are firing on us."

Bill shakes his head. "You're overreacting."

"Why shouldn't we move?" Julia lifts up and rests her hands on Bill's chest. "We'll never be comfortable having a family here. And what about a baby? I know you wouldn't want to bring a baby into this neighborhood. It's not the same as it used to be. Even after Elizabeth finds her way back . . ."

"This is no time to think about a baby."

"It's the perfect time," Julia says "Our baby and Grace's, growing up together. Perfect. No matter where we live, it'll be wonderful. We could adopt like Jerry and Betty. She's not admitting it, but I know that's what they did. We could go to Kansas City. The train, it'll take us straight into Union Station. You were a good father to Maryanne. Why don't you want that again? Did you not love her?"

"What did you say to me?"

Bill doesn't make a motion toward her, doesn't lift a hand or make a fist, but something in the room shifts and it feels as if he wants to slap her.

"There has to be some reason," Julia says, leaning back and resting on her knees again. "Is that it? Did you not love Maryanne?"

"You think I didn't love our daughter?"

"Is it me? Do you think I wouldn't be a good mother? Do you think I'm to blame for what's happened to Elizabeth too? That I'm unfit?"

"I think Elizabeth Symanski won't ever come home," he says. "Everybody knows it and nobody's saying it. I've been up and down Woodward, me and others, more times than I can count. We've been through every neighborhood within five miles. We've talked to every employee in every store, in every restaurant, in every bar. We've been through every park and talked to every neighbor. We've asked them all, Julia, and not a single person remembers seeing her that day."

"Stop," Julia says. "You stop saying that."

"You know how Elizabeth walks. She'd run into folks, people would notice. But no one, Julia. No one even thought they might have seen her. We have list after list of every person we've talked to. And not a single one. She didn't wander away. She didn't walk down the streets on her own. Someone took her, Julia. Took her away, and that's why no one has seen her. Probably swept her up in a car and drove off. If not right here on Alder, then somewhere close. If she'd have wandered off like before, someone would have seen her. Someone would remember. But one thing's for damned sure. Bringing a baby into this house won't bring her back."

"Of course she'll come home. She'll find her way. You'll keep looking and you'll find her."

Bill shakes his head. "She's gone, Julia. And I hate to think what became of her."

"Don't you say that. Don't you dare say that."

"Nobody is blaming you, Julia. You're doing that to yourself. But now is the time to be thinking about the girls. Time we think about keeping them safe."

"And you think I don't want that?"

"They're most important now. Those girls and you too." Bill pushes away Julia's hands and stands. "It's no time to think about bringing a baby into this house. Not my own, and damned sure not one born of another man."

———

Malina waves a hand overhead and walks toward Mr. Herze's car as he climbs inside. Across the street, the twins are backing up the sidewalk leading to Julia's porch. It doesn't seem possible that, even from this distance, Malina can smell Mr. Herze's girl. The odor must have leaked from inside his car when he opened the door. Whether or not it's Malina's imagination, eventually the smell will come home again with Mr. Herze because his girl is not the dead one.

"Won't you come inside for a bite to eat?" she calls out yet again.

Mr. Herze's large blue sedan backs down the driveway and into the street. One long arm reaches out the driver's-side window and waves at the girls. Malina steps over her hedge of snapdragons, all of them wilting with the heavy watering she gave them this morning. She teeters on one heel, nearly twisting an ankle before she marches off the curb and into the street.

"Hurry home," she shouts. "I'm planning a lovely roast tonight. Hurry home."

Standing in the middle of the street, Mr. Herze's sedan having reached the end of Alder Avenue, where it will idle at the stop sign before turning right, Malina stares at Julia's house and at the twins standing in the front yard. Such a thin line between girls and young women. Malina has seen it before, the subtle pleasantries that morph so slowly into something else that others don't recognize it, won't recognize it. They think Mr. Herze is a kind man, giving, thoughtful—charming, even. The other girls, women, didn't have the twins' good fortune. These girls will leave in a few short weeks, possibly sooner. By now, they've already been here several days. Soon they'll be gone. It's nothing to worry about.

"You girls," Malina shouts.

Together, the girls look Malina's way.

"Do you see these flowers?"

"Yes, ma'am," they say together, one speaking over the other.

"I have to plant more. Several dozen more. And do you two know why I must plant more?"

"Yes, ma'am," one of the twins says. "Aunt Julia told us someone peed on your flowers."

"Watch your tongue, young lady. And these are snapdragons, not just any old flowers."

"Sorry. Aunt Julia told us someone peed on your snapdragons."

"And you've trampled them too."

"No, ma'am." It's the one who's fresh most days, not as polite as the other one. "We didn't do either. You can't blame us for that."

Malina squints to get a good look at them. She doubles up both fists, plants them at her waist, and leans forward so the girls will know she's quite serious. "See to it you stay away from my flowers," she says. "Do you understand? Stay away from my yard." The girls nod and have the good sense to say nothing more. And then, because it certainly couldn't hurt, she says, "And stay away from Mr. Herze."

The girls nod and one drags the other onto the porch. "Yes, ma'am," one of them says while the other pulls open the screen door.

"Hold on there," Malina says. "Did you two see those men here at my house?"

One of the girls drops the screen door, letting it slam shut, and they both nod.

"That's none of your business," Malina says. "Do you understand me? They were here mistakenly. Don't you go spreading rumors. Do you understand?"

Another nod and the girls run inside, again letting the screen slap shut.

After returning from her morning shopping on Willingham

Avenue, Malina had unpacked her groceries and set to work on her carrot cakes. Because the bake sale was postponed, she had time for more baking, but really, it's the icing that takes so long. Her carrot cakes always bring a hefty price and people expect a lovely scalloped edge when they are paying good money. She was in the middle of grating her third carrot when she heard a knock at the front door.

"How may I help you?" Malina had said, brushing her hands together. A few orange carrot slivers fluttered to the ground.

Two men, each wearing a dark gray suit and a necktie that was entirely too wide, stood on the porch. At the sight of Malina, they removed their hats. Both were rather short, and if it weren't for their handsome dark suits, a person might have considered them scrawny.

"Detective Warren," the fair-haired officer said, and dipped his chin. Perspiration stained the tips of his yellow hair. He tossed his head in the direction of the taller man standing next to him. "And this is Detective Burrows. Like to ask a few questions, ma'am."

"Certainly," she said. "Though I don't know how much more I can tell you. The other officers, the dark-haired officers, I told them all that I know." Pulling a handkerchief from her skirt pocket, Malina tapped it to her chest and neck. The bodice was a rather snug fit, but it did create a lovely silhouette. "Not that I knew much, mind you. My husband knows Charles, Mr. Symanski, much better than I. They worked together, you know, before Charles retired. I was a new bride then." She smiled and winked at the man with the silky blond hair. "It's been more than twenty-five years. I married quite young."

The eyes of the sweet blond detective followed the tissue as Malina tapped it against her moist skin.

"And what of the Lawsons?" the taller officer said. His hair was an ordinary brown color, straight and cropped in a harsh line that fell just above his eyes.

"The Lawsons?" Malina said, tucking her chin.

"Yes, ma'am. On the evening of June fourth, a Wednesday evening, Mr. Lawson reports that he saw you on the street, rather late at night. And that you saw him, as well. Do you recall that evening?"

"Well, that's ridiculous. Why on earth would I be out late at night? That's simply not true."

The ordinary detective placed his hat on his head and tugged it low. "So you weren't driving toward Woodward between ten thirty and eleven o'clock on the evening of June fourth?"

"I don't drive at night. The glare, it troubles me. It has for years."

"He is out often, we understand, this Mr. Lawson," the yellow-haired officer said. "Other neighbors have reported that he is often on the street late at night, keeping watch while his wife walks their child."

"The baby only recently came to live with them," Malina said. And then she whispered, "Adopted."

"And in the time since the baby's arrival, you have known Mrs. Lawson to walk the child at night and Mr. Lawson to watch over from the end of his drive?" The yellow-haired detective pointed across the street toward the end of the Lawsons' driveway. "From there?"

"I'm sure I wouldn't know the first thing about the nightly routines of the Lawsons."

"It's odd, don't you think?" the yellow-haired officer said, speaking more to his partner than to Malina.

"What's that?"

The yellow-haired officer tilted his head to one side and studied the front of the Lawsons' house. "Why do you suppose Mr. Lawson doesn't walk along?" he said. "With his wife? Why not join her? If his intent is to ensure her and the child's safety, why not walk along?"

Malina laughed. "I've an easy answer for that. He is never dressed in more than shorts and an undershirt. I'm quite certain the neighborhood wouldn't stand for his gallivanting around in such attire. He's really quite ridiculous."

"So you have seen him?" the ordinary detective said. "Mr. Lawson on the street? Wearing his ridiculous shorts and undershirt?"

Malina pinched her brow before realizing the unsightly creases she was causing. "I don't know what you expect me to say."

"We don't expect anything, ma'am. But think for a moment. You may have seen him but are not certain of the date. Is that possible?"

"As I said before, I don't drive after dark. It's the glare."

The man with the ordinary brown hair closed his notebook and slid his pencil in a front pocket. "Thank you for your time, ma'am."

"That's all?" Malina said. "Aren't you here about Elizabeth Symanski? Are you doing nothing to find the child?"

At the bottom of the stairs, the ordinary detective said, "There are many fine officers working to find Miss Symanski."

"Do you mean to question me about that Negro woman, the one who was killed? That happened on a Wednesday night. Is that what you mean to question me about?"

"Thank you for your time, ma'am," the sweet detective said, and removed his hat again.

"You understand, don't you?" Malina called out again as the officers neared their car.

Leaning over the porch railing, Malina lifted one foot off the ground and pointed her toe to create a lovely, long line so they'd remember her kindly.

"I don't drive at night. I can't, you see."

The car began to back out of the driveway.

"It's the glare. I didn't see Jerry Lawson that night or any other."

The officer who was driving rolled the steering wheel one direction and then the other.

"You'll not say otherwise, will you? You'll not tell my husband I was out that evening? He'll be terribly upset if you tell him such a thing."

And then the car was gone and Malina whispered.

"He'll be terribly upset if you tell him I've lied."

CHAPTER FOURTEEN

The next morning, Grace stays home, keeping herself busy in the kitchen as the other ladies travel to Willingham to do their shopping. While the quiet of an empty house gives her too much time to think, it's easier to tolerate than the fear of boarding the morning bus and sitting next to one of the ladies, most likely Julia. As she scrubs her sink and cleans out her nearly empty refrigerator, Grace listens for the twins. The other children in the neighborhood are too old to run through the back alley or play in the front yards. They are teenagers with cars and jobs, too old to be shooed off the street by the likes of Grace. When ten o'clock draws near, she hears the squeal of a rusted chair being unfolded in the alley, but no sign of the girls. Perhaps the threat of Orin Schofield scared them inside, or perhaps it's the heavy drizzle after so many dry, hot days that has kept them behind closed doors. By the time Grace combs out her hair, dresses for the day, and boards the midday bus bound for Willingham, Julia will have finished her shopping and returned home. It's the best Grace can do to keep the girls safe.

No ladies rode the bus at the later hour, and on Willingham, none scurry from store to store. They will be at the church, where they'll stay all afternoon and evening, ignoring the shifts Malina assigned. And so Willingham Avenue is quiet except for the sounds of the factory—the pounding and drumming as the men stamp out the parts, metal on metal, and sharp edges being rounded off and made smooth. The gray sky hangs low, and rain drips off Grace's pillbox hat and down her cheeks and nose.

"You are being soaked to the bone," Mrs. Nowack says when Grace walks through the bakery's door. As she normally does, Mrs. Nowack wears a full gray skirt that skims the floor and a bib apron tied around her thick waist. She squints at Grace through small, round glasses and frowns, which causes her wrinkled cheeks to plump up and her thin lips to draw in on themselves. "Come, child, get out of that weather."

Inside the small shop, the air is gritty. It's flour, and sugar, too, that cloud the air. While Mrs. Nowack calls out for someone to bring a dry towel, Grace removes the pins that secure her hat and adjusts the hair on the crown of her head so she's sure that spot won't show. From behind a black curtain that separates the back room from the front of the shop, a young colored woman appears, a white towel hung from one arm. She wears slim red pants that nip in at her ankles and a white sleeveless blouse with a slender lapel. Her dark hair is round and thick, too wide for her narrow face. The girl gives Mrs. Nowack the towel and glances in Grace's direction before slipping behind the curtain.

"You are coming late today, yes?" After handing Grace the towel, Mrs. Nowack removes her glasses, rubs the lenses with an apron corner, and puts them on again. She dips her head and studies Grace over the tops of the lenses. "What is it I can be getting for you?"

"I'd like to make pierogi," Grace says, patting her face and neck with the soft towel. No matter how upset James might be with her for leaving the house, Mother always says idle hands are troubled hands. "For the bake sale. I'm preparing them this year and have never had much luck on my own. I was hoping you might teach me."

Mrs. Nowack slips behind her counter, her gray skirt swinging from side to side and making her appear to float. "You are seeing I have little else to do, yes?" She lays both hands on top of the glass shelves that run the length of the store. "The others, they are not shopping here anymore. This is what they are telling me."

Tattered signs, some written in English, others in Polish, hang from shelves that are empty except for a few trays of braided bread. The wide loaves, knotted and golden brown, glisten where they were brushed with egg whites. While James has told Grace little of the search for Elizabeth and nothing of the dead woman from the alley, he was willing to share the ladies' plan to boycott Mrs. Nowack.

"I'm sorry," Grace says. "I only heard. I wasn't here that day."

Mrs. Nowack waves away the unpleasantness with one plump hand. "Come," she says, holding open the black curtain that leads to the back of the shop. "You are having lunch with us and then we will be making pierogi."

This is where Mrs. Nowack does her baking. Her double-stacked oven shines and the burners on the stovetop have been freshly lined with aluminum foil. Large bags of flour sit on the bottom rung of the wooden shelves pushed along the far wall, and on the higher rungs, square jars of spices sit side by side, their black-and-white labels perfectly aligned. Near the back door, silver pots and pans have been stacked and left to dry on the counter. Grace follows Mrs. Nowack through the small room, out the back door, and onto a narrow concrete patio. The rain has stopped, and for now the air is cool and light, though probably not for long.

"You can be sitting here," Mrs. Nowack says, nudging Grace toward a wooden picnic table. "Go ahead. There is being plenty of room. I will be having lunch out soon."

While Mrs. Nowack returns to the bakery to fetch lunch, Grace stands in the center of the concrete patio, wraps her arms around her chest so that they rest on her large stomach, and stares straight ahead. Three colored women already sit at the picnic table. One of them sits backward on a damp bench, her legs extended, one ankle crossed over the other. A strong brow shades her wide-set eyes and balances her square jaw. Long, thin braids hang over her shoulders and down her back. A small colored bead is threaded on the end of each, so that when she moves they must knock against one another and sound much like a wind chime. A second woman sits on the bench opposite the first, her legs tucked under the table in a more proper fashion. Plump brown rolls pop out of the deep, rounded neckline of her red blouse. Whereas the face of the first woman is defined by sharp angles, the second woman has round cheeks and a small dimple in the center of her chin. The last woman at the table is standing, one foot propped up on the bench. She is the one who brought Grace a dry towel. Her face is shaped like a perfect heart—large brown eyes, prominent cheekbones, and a tapered chin. Mrs. Nowack had called her Cassia. She is slender like a girl, but she's not a girl. A black baby carriage, covered with a yellow quilt, stands next to her.

———

Steady thumping echoes up and down Alder Avenue, disrupting the typically quiet lunch hour. With the break in the rain, someone has decided to pound her rugs. Malina wraps both hands around the water spigot's red handle, gives two turns, and grabs the end of the hose. Cold water spills from the brass coupling and splashes on her nylons. Tiny droplets dribble down her legs and into her shoes. Now, she'll have to change her clothes before going to the church. Had they gotten a better dose of rain, she'd have skipped the watering, but it was scarcely enough to discolor her concrete walk. She drags the hose to the front yard and folds one thumb over the coupling so the water squirts in a narrow fan, soaking her snapdragons. Three of the towering plants, all of them pink, have been crushed as if by a large boot or perhaps two pairs of small white sneakers.

Near the street, the thumping is louder. It's Betty Lawson. Standing on her porch, she swings a broom as if it were a baseball bat and pounds the dust from her rugs. Across Alder Avenue, those twins stand outside Julia's house, both of them twirling ridiculous hoops around their waists. One of the twins is quite good at it, her hips moving smoothly, the large hoop swinging freely around her waist. The other moves with jerky motions and her hoop sags, dropping first to her knees and then to her feet. Tossing aside the hose, Malina shouts out that the twins should get themselves back inside and keep their grubby feet away from her flowers. After all that nonsense with Orin Schofield, they should know better. Then she stomps her soggy white shoes and hurries toward Betty's house.

"Hello, Betty," Malina shouts. "Did you see the twins? What will these kids think of next?"

Betty leans on her corn-bristled broom, one hand on her hip, her elbow cocked out to the side. She has yet to comb out her pin curls from her dull brown hair and is still dressed in a lavender duster. Three small rugs, all of them multicolored and braided, hang over the porch's railing. Without answering Malina's greeting, Betty lifts the broom by its wooden handle and slaps it against the rug hanging closest to Malina. A cloud of dust flies into the air.

"I'll be leaving for the church shortly," Malina says. "Can I run any errands for you? Maybe you need something for the little one."

"What is it that you want, Malina?" Betty says.

"Very well," Malina says, backing down the sidewalk in case Betty should take another swipe at the rugs. A few doors down, the twins still twirl their hoops. Every so often, one of them falls and rattles on the concrete. When next she gets a good look at those twins, she'll check the bottom of their white sneakers for pink stains. "It's your husband."

"Yes."

"I'd rather prefer he not drag me into his troubles."

"And I'd rather prefer my husband not go to jail." Betty lifts her broom overhead and smacks the next rug.

"Don't be silly," Malina says. "No one is going to jail. I'd simply prefer he not insist he saw me driving about after dark."

Betty walks to the edge of her porch so her feet hang over the first stair. "Do you have any idea the trouble you have caused? Do you have any idea what people are saying?"

"I hardly think I'm to blame for your husband's troubles."

"Why won't you tell the truth? You saw Jerry that night, standing right here. You saw him, even waved at him."

"I can't say something that isn't true. It's really quite important Jerry make clear to Mr. Herze that he was mistaken. You're both mistaken. It's quite important Jerry tell Mr. Herze I was not the one he saw on the street."

Betty hugs the broom handle to her chest and angles her head off to one side. "You're afraid, aren't you?" she says, dropping the bristled end of the broom to the first stair and in one motion sweeping it clean. "You're afraid of your own husband."

"That's ridiculous," Malina says. "I've every reason to ask that Jerry stop spreading lies about me."

"Go home, Malina," Betty says, dropping her broom to the next stair.

Malina backs farther down the sidewalk. The clouds have thinned and in some spots, given way to clear sky. The sun breaks through and warms her face and arms. The bright light does her no justice. Her skin has thinned in recent years. It used to sparkle like the skin on those two girls. Almond-colored freckles sparkle on the girls' smooth skin and their blue eyes shine. Malina has always wished for blue eyes. Hers are a rather ordinary brown. In her younger days, people often complimented her perfect skin. Like silk, they would sometimes say, or satin. Which is more lovely? She was careless in those early days. She knows better now. It was a silly lie. After so many years, she knows better. At the sound of a car engine, Malina whirls around, but it's not Mr. Herze. Two houses down, those twins still twirl their hoops. One of them counts out loud and doesn't stop until the hoop falls to her feet. When Malina turns back, Betty Lawson is leaning on the broom and slowly shaking her head.

"My husband might have a weak character," Betty says, "but he's never given me cause to fear him. Other people saw my Jerry that night, and they've been good enough to tell the truth. I guess it's only right I warn you. The police said you lacked credibility. That's what they said of your account. That means they know you were lying. That means your Warren knows too."

―――――

"You just going to stand there?" the Negro woman with the rounded red neckline says to Grace. The others call her Sylvie. She has wide shoulders, almost like a man's, and if she were to stand she'd be a full head taller than Grace. "Come. Sit."

Clutching her handbag to her side, Grace tiptoes through the thin layer of mud left by the rain and slides onto the end of the nearest bench. She places her bag in her lap and crosses her hands on the tabletop, which is rough where long slivers of it have torn or rotted away. Sitting opposite Grace, the woman who wears the plunging red blouse picks at the soft wood and flicks bits of it onto the ground.

"Bet that keeps breaking open on you, doesn't it?" The large woman stops picking at the wood, brushes her hands together, and points at Grace's lip. The woman has painted tiny white crescents over the root of each fingernail. They glitter like rhinestones on the tips of her dark fingers.

Grace lifts a hand to cover her lip. Studying Grace's face and pregnant stomach, the woman—Sylvie—leans back when Mrs. Nowack reappears with a plate and sets it in front of her. With her fork, Sylvie pokes at the hollowed-out pepper stuffed with ground beef and stares at Grace while Mrs. Nowack delivers three more plates.

The woman sitting next to Grace finally swings her feet around and tucks her legs under the table. Just as Grace thought they would, the small beads on the ends of the woman's braids clatter like a chime when she moves. Mrs. Nowack calls her Lucille. She leans forward to get a look at Grace's split lip but says nothing.

"Your man do it to you?" It's Cassia, the one who brought Grace the towel. She bends over the carriage, peeks under the thin quilt. "Shhh, shhh, shhh," she says, looking again at Grace. Thick black lashes frame the girl's brown eyes.

"We bumped heads," Grace says. "Mother and I."

Cassia lowers the corner of the quilt but continues to rest one hand on the carriage's handle. "I know a lip that's been split by the back of a hand," she says.

Lucille leans forward again, squints as if trying to get a better look, and then nods.

"It's all right," Sylvie says, laying aside her fork, tilting her face toward the sky, and stretching her broad shoulders. The rolls of her chest rise out of her rounded neckline. "Ain't nothing we don't already know about."

Cassia slides her fingers off the carriage's handle, reaches across the table and, with one hand, cups Grace's chin. With the other, she touches the tender spot on Grace's upper lip.

"Not so bad," she says.

Trailing two fingers up the side of Grace's face, Cassia brushes back Grace's bangs as if inspecting her for hidden cuts and bruises. The tiny hands are like a child's, frail and delicate, Grace barely able to feel them. Finding nothing, Cassia smooths Grace's hair into place. Grace leans back until her chin slips from the tender hand.

"Yep," Cassia says, lowering herself onto the bench. "Not so bad." After another quick peek under the quilt, she settles into her seat and, with one hand, continues rocking the carriage.

"Why won't you ladies come to the bakery anymore?" It's Lucille, the one with the braids. Her eyes are dark brown, almost black.

"Pardon?" Grace glances overhead, thinking if it were to rain, she would have reason to excuse herself.

"You and the other ladies," Sylvie says, smiling as if to make up for Lucille's harsh tone. "Mrs. Nowack says you all won't come anymore and she won't have so much baking to do."

"We're frightened, I suppose," Grace says.

"Because you all are afraid of being here when they pull that girl out of the river?" Lucille says. As she waits for an answer, she taps her fork on the edge of her plate. The muscles along her jawline pulse as if she's grinding her teeth. "Will you all come back after they find her?"

"I don't think I can answer that."

"Maybe they're afraid of ending up like Tyla," Lucille says.

"Hush about that," Sylvie says, wagging her finger in the same fashion Grace's own mother did when Grace was a child. "No one said nothing about Tyla." She nods in Cassia's direction and presses a finger to her lips. "No one said nothing."

"Don't matter why they stopped coming," Lucille says. "Still a pity for Mrs. Nowack."

Across the table, Cassia nods along with Lucille and dips her fork into the baked pepper. At first she takes small bites, chewing each a good long time, but she must decide she likes it because she eats faster. Between bites, she grabs hold of the carriage's handle, gives it a gentle shake, and makes that shhhing noise. The handle is speckled with rust and the black canopy is frayed at its edges. When Cassia seems content the baby is asleep, she settles into her seat, one hand in her lap, the other scooping out the last of the ground beef. Lucille and Sylvie begin to eat as well, and the table falls silent. As they eat, the women look at one another without turning their heads, but instead by flicking their eyes this way and that as if hoping Grace won't notice. The silence continues to build, interrupted only by quiet chewing and the sound of forks tapping against the glossy, white plates.

"Is she yours?" Grace says to Cassia because she can think of nothing else to say and no other way to break the silence. "What's her name?"

Cassia drops her fork. It bounces off the side of her plate and tumbles onto the table and then onto the ground. She grabs on to the carriage's handle and yanks it toward her, the wheels letting off a high-pitched squeal.

"Uh-oh," Lucille says. "Now you gone and done it."

"Yeah, she's my baby," Cassia says, still rocking, the wheels squealing louder as she pushes and pulls the carriage. "Why? You think she shouldn't be?"

"No, I thought she was . . ." Grace glances at Sylvie but doesn't say her name. Cassia is so young. Her hips are narrow and her waist scarcely tapered, still like a girl's. Sylvie has curves like a woman who has given birth to a baby. "I guess I only meant . . ."

"Something wrong with her being mine?" Cassia says. She rocks the carriage back and forth. The metal frame squeaks and whines. The tattered yellow blanket slips from the carriage's handle and flutters toward the ground. As if the carriage's handle has suddenly become too hot, Cassia jerks her hand away.

Struggling to stand, her large stomach slowing her, Grace reaches to catch the quilt before it falls. She snags one corner and raises it up so the end doesn't drag in the mud. She starts to hand it back to Cassia, but she has lowered her head and is staring at the tabletop. The other two women are attending her, talking to her in quiet whispers and touching her lightly on the shoulder and back. Looking around for Mrs. Nowack but not finding her, Grace swings her legs off the end of the bench and stands. She shakes out the quilt like a sheet, snaps it, and lets it flutter down over the carriage, but before it has settled, she jerks it back. The bassinet is empty. It's tattered and in places the fabric is worn away entirely, exposing the metal frame beneath. She looks from the empty stroller to Cassia to the other women at the table. A hand presses down on her shoulder. It's Lucille. She yanks the quilt from Grace and forces her back into her seat.

Slipping around the end of the table, Lucille snaps the quilt just as Grace had done, and lets it float down over the carriage. "Well," she says to Grace once the quilt is in place. "Something wrong with that baby? Something wrong with Cassia being that baby's mama?"

Sylvie fixes her elbows on the table, but instead of Grace, she looks at the woman with the braids. "Don't you be getting on this girl like that."

"I'll be getting on who I damn well want." Lucille flips her braids over her shoulders, crosses her arms, and presses her chest up and out as if trying to make herself as large as Sylvie.

Sylvie stands. "Girl didn't do nothing to you."

"She asking about Cassia's baby," Lucille says, moving behind Grace so Grace can hear her but cannot see her. "That's something."

"She sure is my baby," Cassia says.

"Yes, of course." Grace clutches her bag to her chest and edges away from the sound of Lucille's voice. "She's lovely, I'm sure."

"See there, Cassia," Sylvie says, motioning for Lucille to sit. When Lucille doesn't move, Sylvie jabs her finger at her and then at the bench, again reminding Grace of her own mother, albeit a taller, rounder, broader version. "Your baby girl is lovely. No need to get upset."

Lucille lowers herself onto the bench, choosing to sit as far away from Grace as possible, and begins to eat. Across the table, Sylvie does the same. Cassia watches the two of them for a few moments and then picks up her fork from the ground and wipes it on her napkin, all the while keeping a firm grip on the carriage's rusted handle. Sylvie waves her fork at Grace, a signal she should start eating too. Instead, Grace stands, drops her napkin in her plate, and to no one in particular, she says, "Thank you for having me to lunch."

"You'll come tomorrow," Sylvie says. A light drizzle has started up again. The tiny drops sparkle on her dark skin. "Got to stay later if you want to make pierogi. We always roll it out after lunch. 'Course, you know we cook up all that pierogi." She winks at Grace with her warm brown eyes. "We help you, will you bring those ladies back for Mrs. Nowack? Bring them back so she'll have customers."

"I'll do my best," Grace says. "I'll do what I can."

Sylvie waves her fingers in the air. "You want us teaching you. Not Mrs. Nowack. She got arthritis real bad. You don't want Mrs. Nowack making your noodles. That's for damn sure."

CHAPTER FIFTEEN

G race only meant to rest her eyes for a few minutes after her trip to the bakery, but she slept several hours because here it is, suppertime. She walks down the stairs toward muted voices coming from the front room. The oven clicks and the soothing smell of one of the chicken casseroles Mother left in the freezer before going home fills the house. James must have come home while Grace slept and popped it in the oven. He would have woken her if there were news. Instead, the doorbell woke her. Friends and neighbors use the side door off the kitchen. They tap lightly on the glass or on the doorframe. The doorbell means company.

Pausing at the bottom of the stairs, Grace leans out to see who has come to visit. A draft blows across the living room and stirs her hair and the hem of her dress. James stands at the front door with his back to her. He leans against the jamb, one foot resting on the opposite ankle. He turns when a floorboard creaks under Grace's feet.

"Didn't mean to wake you," he says. Only the middle two buttons on his shirt are buttoned and he didn't bother to comb his hair after having washed it. It curls on the ends when he brushes it with his fingers and not a proper brush. Now that his days are spent searching, he comes home every night to have supper with Grace. He always freshens up, usually after they eat. He slaps cool water on his face, washes his hands and forearms with a good dose of soap—all meant to give him a second wind before rejoining the search.

A man wearing a dark blue shirt stands in the doorway. He tips his hat at her. A second man, dressed in the same blue shirt and wearing the same blue hat, stands next to him.

"Mrs. Richardson?" the first man says.

He's a police officer, the same one who sat at Mr. Symanski's kitchen table after Elizabeth first disappeared. He had rubbed his temples that night, not quite certain he understood how a grown woman was really no more than a child. He is the same age as Grace, but even late in the day when he should have a shadow on his lower jaw and chin, his face is smooth. His dark hair flips up in tight curls.

"She can't tell you any more than I have," James says. He rubs the bridge of his nose between two fingers.

"Do you mind?" The other officer, taller with light brown hair, leans into the house so he can speak directly to Grace.

"James, you should invite them in," Grace says, not moving from her spot at the bottom of the stairs.

The men have shifted about in the threshold and have blocked the breeze. The oven still clicks, throwing off heat.

"May we?" the taller officer says to James.

James steps aside, allowing the officers to pass, and waves at Grace to join them. The officers remove their hats and tuck them under an arm.

"I remember you," Grace says to the officer with the smooth face and dark curls. His hair is dented where he wore his hat. "Please have a seat. May I get you something to drink?"

"No, ma'am," he says. "I'm Officer Warinski." He nudges the gentleman standing at his side. "Officer Thompson."

"Do you have word of Elizabeth?" Grace says.

"They wonder if something has happened here, Grace," James says, gesturing for her to take a seat.

She sits on the edge of the skirted sofa, gathers her crochet work from the coffee table, and spreads it across her lap. The tweed sofa, even through the fabric of her cotton skirt, is rough against the backs of her legs.

"Wonder if what has happened?"

"We've questioned a man," the taller officer says, "in connection with a crime in the area."

Grace clears her throat, smiles for the two officers, and scoots back, settling into the cushions. When she started crocheting the baby's blanket two months ago, she chose a bulky white yarn suitable for a boy or girl. Placing her fingers to the hook's flat grip, she pokes the head through the bottom loop. As she begins her first stitch, James walks around the back of the sofa and rests his hands on her shoulders. She grabs his fingers and kisses the back of one wrist.

"Is it to do with Elizabeth?" she asks. Yarn over, draw through, yarn over, release.

"This man," Officer Warinski says, ignoring Grace's question, "has given us information about a crime at this location."

The door is closed behind the two men and the breeze is gone. The house is dark because Grace never drew open the drapes. She begins another single crochet. That was her twelfth stitch. She must remember to count. So often she forgets and has to pull out her work and start again.

"A crime?" she says. The tightness begins in her stomach and rises into her throat. Again, "A crime?" She hears her own voice as if it's someone else's.

"I told them they were mistaken," James says, kneading her shoulders with his fingers. "No mischief around here."

"None," Grace says, she thinks she says. She loses her stitch. "No mischief around here."

Both officers stare at her, only at her.

"Could we speak in private, ma'am?" Officer Warinski says.

"Our supper is growing cold." Grace's neck is damp under James's hands. "I haven't anything to add."

"Wrong house, I suppose," James says, and pulls his hands from Grace's shoulders. "Though I can't say I've heard of any trouble for the neighbors, either." He walks past the men and opens the door. "Other than the Symanskis."

He doesn't tell them about Orin Schofield firing his rifle or the fire in the garbage can or the broken windows more and more neighbors are waking up to. Protecting the street, Grace supposes. Like parents protect a child. Since Elizabeth disappeared, all the neighbors are beginning to do the same. No one wants to admit what is becoming, what has become, of Alder Avenue.

Officer Thompson steps outside. The officer with the curls, Officer Warinski, makes no move to leave and continues to study Grace. He is young, too young really.

"This man, he says a woman was hurt here," the young officer says. "At this address. Quite badly, we believe."

Grace lifts her chin. Her face must be red, but she could blame it on the heat. She touches her top lip with the end of her tongue. The sore spot has nearly healed over.

"I'm sorry," she says. "If someone was hurt, I'm terribly sorry. Please tell her. If you find her. Tell her I'm so very sorry."

Waiting for the second officer to leave, James holds open the door. Fresh air rushes through the house again, chilling the damp spots James left on Grace's neck and shoulders.

"If you think of anything," Officer Warinski says. Again, his eyes are only on Grace. "Any information would be helpful." He dips his head, watches her. "It might be our only chance."

"To find Elizabeth?" James says. "Is that what you mean? Did this man take her? Is that what happened?"

"I'm afraid we can't discuss the particulars," Officer Thompson says from the front porch.

"Can't," James says, "or won't? This is our neighborhood. We've a right to know."

Officer Thompson shakes his head but offers nothing more. The other officer continues to stare at Grace, waiting and watching for a clue that she has lied to them.

"Mind if we have a look out back?" the curly-haired Warinski says. "Give your garage a once-over."

James leans against the doorjamb, crosses one foot over the

other again. "Don't see the need," he says. "It'll only get the neighbors to talking, and I don't see the sense in that."

"Ma'am," Officer Warinski says. "Do you see the need?"

Grace shakes her head and runs her fingers across the many rows she has crocheted over the last few months. Mother says the stitches are too tight, too simple.

"I'm sorry, but I don't," she says. "It would be a waste of your valuable time."

James dips his head as if he were wearing a hat. "Gentlemen," he says, signaling the men should leave. "We'll let you know if we hear anything."

Officer Warinski crosses in front of James and follows the other officer outside.

"One moment," Grace says from her seat on the sofa.

The men reappear in the doorway, remove their hats again.

"What is it you would have liked to hear me say?"

"Ma'am?"

"You've arrested a man?"

"He's in our custody," the taller officer says.

"What can I say to you, here and now, that will keep him from our streets? Tell me about this crime and I'll say yes. I'll say it happened. Even though it'll be a lie, wouldn't that help you?"

The officer with the dark curls and smooth skin steps forward. "Sir," he says to James. "Will you leave us?"

"I damn sure will not," James says, and drops down on one knee in front of Grace. "What are you talking about, Gracie? Did something happen?"

Grace stretches out one hand, touches James's rough jaw. He

only shaves every few days now. All of the men look the same—tired, drawn, their belts cinched a little tighter because even though the ladies feed them every day, they seem to have lost weight. Or maybe it's the way they carry themselves, walking with short strides and hunched backs as if burdened by a heavy load, that makes them look like less than they were before Elizabeth disappeared.

"No, James. Nothing's happened. But maybe I could say something that would help these men. Something that would help Elizabeth, help keep our streets safe."

It's too late to protect Elizabeth, but Grace can still save the twins or possibly another one of the ladies. She can get that man off of Alder Avenue before he tries again to set things right. If the one they've arrested knows what happened to Grace and that it happened here at this address, he must be one of the three. It's probably the one who slipped out into the alley because he couldn't bear the sight. He can give the police a name, direct them toward the man who did this terrible thing to her and to Elizabeth. But if there was no crime, the police will have no need of a name.

"Tell me," Grace says. "I'll say whatever I must to help Elizabeth."

"Would you say a woman was attacked in your garage?" Again, it's the officer with the dark curls. "Would you say three men threw her to the ground, that one of those men violated her while another held her down? Would you say those things?"

James pushes off the ground and lunges at the man. The second officer stops him with a stiff arm to his chest.

"Tell me, Mrs. Richardson," the curly-haired officer says,

ignoring James and keeping his eyes firmly on Grace. He drops his gaze to the small cut on her upper lip and lets his eyes roam over her face as if searching for more scratches and bruises. "Did these things happen? Did they happen to you?"

James stands at a distance, the other officer's hand pressed to the middle of his chest. All three wait for Grace's answer. She can feel the small hand of the girl, Cassia was her name, lifting Grace's face, telling her the cut didn't look so bad. The girl had seen worse, far worse. Nothing that won't heal.

"Gracie?"

Grace shakes her head. "Well, of course those things aren't true," she says. "At least, not as far as I know. And I think I would know if someone were attacked in my own garage. I simply thought I could help."

James holds up both hands and backs away from the officers.

"What will happen now?" Grace says. "Because there was no one harmed here, what will happen to the man?"

The curly-haired officer with the smooth skin pulls on his hat, meets Grace's eyes as if preparing to answer, but turns away instead.

One more time, James makes a sweeping gesture intended to invite the officers to leave. They walk across the porch and down the sidewalk, and when they have neared the driveway, James slams the door.

"Smells like supper's ready," he says, walking past Grace toward the kitchen.

The legs of a chair scoot across the tile. Silverware clatters on the laminate tabletop.

"Strange, huh?" he calls back to Grace. His voice is flat when he speaks. He's angry but won't want Grace to see it in his face. "Why would some fellow say that about our place? About you?"

Grace walks over to the window and pushes aside the drapes. The officers have reached the end of the driveway. One of them, the curly-haired one, walks around the black-and-white patrol car, and from the driver's side, he tips his hat at Grace.

"They probably got the wrong address, don't you think?" she says. The officers' car rolls away from the front of the house. Across the street, a few neighbors shield their eyes as they watch. "It was silly, what I did. I'm sorry."

She's now certain it's the third man they've arrested. All she remembers are his eyes. They were a deep brown and his lids drooped, making him look sorry for what was about to happen. He's the only one who would tell. Those men, all three of them, probably live at the Filmore. She has seen other colored men passing down the street at the usual times, but she hasn't seen any one of the three, not since the night they came for her. The man, the one with sorrowful eyes, must have confessed to the police. He must have described Grace, told them the woman was pregnant and had long blond hair and lived at 721 Alder. That's why the officer with the dark curls and smooth young face had looked at Grace like he knew everything. He knew about the sore spot on the back of her head and why her lip was split. Grace is the only pregnant wife on the block. Maybe the only one on the street. The officers want Grace to tell the truth because Elizabeth can't. They are thinking it's a shame when people won't speak up. They are thinking Grace is their only hope. They are thinking there's hope to be had.

James's body is warm when he steps up behind Grace. He wraps his arms around her, and she leans into him.

"Don't know what I'd do if something happened to you," he says.

Resting her head on James's chest, Grace closes her eyes, holds his hands, and wonders if he loves her enough to stay should he find out the truth. Mother thinks not. "Nothing bad will ever happen to us."

"Promise me," James says, burying his face in her hair.

"I promise."

———

Before climbing into bed, Malina scrubs her face, dabs night cream on the delicate skin beneath her eyes, and tucks her hair into a sleep net. From the drawer in her nightstand, she pulls out her white pills and sets the bottle where Mr. Herze is sure to see it. He knows how heavily Malina sleeps when she's taken one. Dr. Cannon had said they'd calm her, minimize the stresses of her day. Mr. Herze doesn't approve of them, never has, and most days she is able to refrain by doing her counting and breathing.

The first weeks after she stopped taking the medication were the most difficult. The pills tugged at her all day from the kitchen cabinet where she normally kept them. Mr. Herze had insisted she stop. He said they made her eyes foggy and her habits lazy. Time and his insistence lessened the pills' charm. Even as she swallows two of them while waiting for Mr. Herze, she doesn't swallow them because she craves the relief they will bring to the tense muscle running from her neck to her shoulders or the order they will bring to the worries tumbling around her head. She swallows them because Mr. Herze, as angry as he might be at the sight of that small brown bottle, will know better than to try to wake her.

Even if Betty Lawson was telling the truth and Mr. Herze knows for certain Malina lied to him, he won't be able to question her about it tonight. He won't be able to rage about his hatred of Malina's silly lies, a rage that always leads him to strike her. A rage that has led to blackened eyes, bruised cheeks, sore ribs, and a broken collarbone—or, more precisely, a fractured clavicle. She will sleep soundly and peacefully tonight, and tomorrow or the next day she'll conjure a story to explain why she lied about driving the night that colored woman was killed. It was a trip to the shut-ins. She's so sorry she lied. She thought he'd be cross at her for putting herself in danger by driving so late at night. Or she was delivering fresh linens to the church that were needed early the next morning. Or she was afraid Mr. Herze had had car trouble, a flat tire, perhaps. She didn't see anything that happened on Willingham. She didn't see anything at all.

Thirty minutes after washing down the pills with a glass of lukewarm water, Malina slides beneath the cool sheets, switches off the lamp at her bedside, and stares at the white sheers fluttering in her window. The light, flimsy fabric dances in the breeze, and as it flutters and flaps, a thin fog settles in behind her eyes. Downstairs, the back door opens and closes. Mr. Herze's footsteps cross the kitchen. The floorboards in the hallway creak as he passes through to the foyer, and then silence. He is standing at the bottom of the stairs, probably looking up toward the closed bedroom door, probably wondering what he is to do with Malina. One footstep and then a second and then a third as he climbs the stairs.

It's been another day and night spent searching for Elizabeth. Mr. Herze will be tired and sore. Normally Malina would rub his shoulders and fix him a sandwich. The bedroom door opens and light from the hallway spills into the room and across Malina's face. Her eyelids are closed. Don't let them flinch in the light. Those are the sounds of Mr. Herze pulling off his shirt and unbuckling his belt. Water runs in the bathroom sink and flows through the pipes that travel down the walls. He sits on the edge of the mattress, his weight causing Malina to roll from one side to the other because isn't that what one would do in her sleep? He smells crisp and clean, like Malina's French-milled soap. She buys the pink bars special-order through the Sears catalog. Her jaw loosens and her shoulders soften as the pills melt and soak in. A few feet away, air rushes in through Mr. Herze's nose and out through his mouth.

"Malina?"

It's a deep whisper. Malina can't stop the shiver that travels up her spine and into her neck. The word seems to echo in the dark room.

"Malina?" Again, no louder.

When Malina wakes in the morning, she hopes he'll be gone.

CHAPTER SIXTEEN

It's long past dark and Grace should be sleeping. Instead, she is listening. The colored men have already come and gone. Every night around ten they pass, although now, because Orin Schofield sits in the back alley, the men walk down the middle of Alder Avenue. She's glad Orin's there. She even finds herself hoping, wishing he would find those men out on the street. Something is different since she told the police no woman was attacked in her garage. Saying it never happened is different from not telling. It's worse. It means those men—that man—can come back.

The year Grace turned eleven, she again stood in line on the Fourth of July to board the *Ste. Claire*, but rather than entertaining worries over soiled brass railings, she had thought of the boy, young man, with the easy laugh and dark hair. Or she likes to believe she thought of him, that she remembered him from the year before. The ladies' shoulders were still fortified by pleats and pads, their waists still sculpted, their frames tall and proud. But when the ship's horn called out, Mother said nothing about it being no time for sorrow.

It was a different girl in James's arms that year. Grace stood on the edge of the open-air dance floor, holding her hair at the nape of her neck, and she heard him before she saw him. He spun by, holding a dark-haired girl this time, spinning, twirling, faster with each pass. Grace had watched him, imagining how happy the girl in his arms must have been. She must have felt safe in his hands. Mother and Father danced that year too. It was the only year Father took Mother in his arms.

The floor pulsed underfoot as Grace watched the dancers. James says he remembers a little blond girl standing alone, the wind pulling at her hair. He says he spun by and ruffled that head of hair because even then, he knew she was special. Grace doesn't remember him ever catching her eye or giving her a wink or a nod. But she smiles when he remembers and says she remembers too.

That was the last year Father would board the *Ste. Claire*. He, like others, like James, went to war in the months that followed. This is why the whole country had been bracing itself. This is why the ladies loosened their hair and wore stout shoulders in their suits. Wives and mothers rode streetcars to Michigan Central, waved good-bye to their husbands and sons as they boarded outbound trains, so many of them never to be seen again. By the next Fourth of July, Grace knew Father would never come home.

Downstairs, James bangs about in the kitchen. He came home an hour ago and will have made coffee and read the newspaper. It's what he does every night. Grace has told him he's drinking too much coffee and smoking too many cigarettes. There's all that food, she says, knowing the ladies are filling the church tables every day and night. Eat. You're wasting away. He'll watch a ball game if there's one showing. More and more of the games are airing on the television. Hardly any reason to go to the ballpark anymore. Grace blinks when the bedroom door opens and light from the hallway brightens the room. She slides into a sitting position, her back resting against the headboard.

"Didn't mean to wake you," James says, yanking out his shirttail and unbuttoning his shirt.

Grace doesn't have to ask. She need only inhale as if she's about to speak.

"Nope, nothing," James says, and lays a hand on Grace's stomach. "How's my little guy tonight?"

"She's fine," Grace says. Her smile comes easily and for a moment, things feel as they are meant to.

Pulling his black leather belt from his trousers, James hangs it from a hook on the back of the bedroom door and sits on the edge of the bed. Propping one foot on the opposite knee, he pulls at the laces on his boot.

"Did you have a good evening?" he says, not mentioning the police who visited at suppertime.

"I wish I could do more. It's so quiet here on the street. Everyone's helping but me." Because she'll go again another day and doesn't want James to forbid it, she doesn't tell him about the trip to Willingham or the pierogi or the women.

After taking off his first boot, James removes the second, bends to the closet floor, and hooks both on the shoe rack—right boot on the right side, left boot on the left. When he rises, a white leather shoe dangles from one finger.

"It was yours?" he says. "That shoe in the garage was yours. Here's the mate."

Grace doesn't remember returning the single shoe to the closet. It should have been thrown away with the other clothes. It must have been there, hanging from the shoe rack since the night the man came for her.

"How about that?" Grace says. "I guess it was." She smiles and shrugs because she is always the one to misplace the keys or her favorite hairbrush or one of Mother's recipes.

It seems that it happened so long ago, that several weeks and months have passed since the men came. But it's only days. Grace can count them on one hand. She wakes every morning, thinking so much time has passed. Things she should remember, memories that should be clear and sharp, have faded, even disappeared, as if many months separate then from now. It must feel this way because time is supposed to heal her. That's what Mother said, so Grace's mind is speeding it up, tricking her into thinking weeks and months have ticked by. But the slipping away isn't because of the healing. That moment and those men seem far away, distant, because Grace is so changed. Not in a small way. Not in a passing way that happens over a day or a week. She is entirely changed. She is changed in a way so large it would usually take months and years to emerge. Surely something so huge must show through. Mother said not to tell, but surely James will see it.

The shoe dangles from James's finger. He rotates it from side to side, inspecting it from all angles. He's thinking, perhaps wondering about the police who said something terrible happened in the garage, perhaps remembering what the officer with the soft curls said about a woman suffering a horrific attack. Without saying anything else, James lowers himself to one knee and slides the shoe onto the round wire that will hold its shape.

"Shame," he says. "We'll buy you a new pair."

Grace scoots down between the sheets, and James slides in next to her. Tomorrow, she'll go to Willingham Avenue again. If the women ask, she might tell them what really happened. They would look at her a moment, maybe sigh, and then say it's not so bad. Seen worse. Resting one hand on James's chest where she can feel it rise and fall, Grace nestles against him in such a way that her head fits perfectly on his shoulder, and she thinks of Orin Schofield sitting in his chair in the back alley, waiting, maybe even hoping, the colored men pass. Earlier this evening, after Mrs. Williamson would have washed up her supper dishes and Mr. Williamson would have fallen asleep listening to the radio, Mrs. Williamson tied a blue scarf around her thinning hair, walked out her back door, across the alley, up to Orin Schofield's house, and returned to him his rifle.

———

The twins have been asleep for a few hours and still Bill isn't home. Since the search for Elizabeth first began, all of the husbands have been coming home late, but tonight Bill is later than the rest. Well over an hour ago, Julia heard the thud of car doors, footsteps on concrete, front doors slamming and locking as the other husbands came home. Still, no sign of Bill.

A new kind of worry settled over the ladies cooking and serving at the church today. All day they whispered about visions of a colored man wrapping a large hand around Elizabeth's thin wrist, dragging her into a car, leaving her somewhere to die. With word of the arrest, the ladies could no longer assume, even pretend to assume, Elizabeth wandered away. It wasn't a tragic accident. Whatever happened to Elizabeth could happen to any one of them.

The dining-room window has been fully dark for at least two hours when a stream of light flashes across the small window in the front door. Julia only guesses at the time. She never checks the clock. Better not to know. Overhead, the girls' room has been quiet for some time. A car engine rattles in the driveway and falls silent. The light disappears. Keys jingle in the lock. The front door swings open.

During the year following Maryanne's death, Julia learned to leave supper in the oven while she waited for Bill to come home at night. Those were the months he was drinking and everyone knew it. Too often, his food would grow cold and he wouldn't bother to eat. She learned it was always best he eat a little something, if only a few bites.

"Sorry," Bill says, stumbling through the front door.

It's as if the last two years, the better years, never existed.

"Sorry I'm late."

Julia pushes back her chair and rushes to catch him before he falls. He throws his arms around her shoulders. She braces herself to carry his weight and pushes against his chest to steady him. It all comes back to her as if no time has passed.

"Come eat," she says, wrapping an arm around his waist after he has regained his balance. "Supper's hot. Fresh out of the oven. Made those biscuits you love. Any word of Elizabeth?"

When Julia first met Bill, she was two inches taller than he, but that didn't last long. Her family had only just moved from Kentucky. She had a slow, thick drawl that she worked to be rid of every day. She knew Bill before his beard came in, when his shoulders were narrow and frail, when acne glowed red on his cheeks and forehead. He was a boy when they fell in love.

"Shouldn't be staying out so late," he says, then drops into a seat at the table and picks up the closest glass.

"Let me fill that." The more water she can get down him, the better. "Is there news? I heard they arrested someone."

Talking is good. She learned this in the early months after Maryanne died too. The more she talks, the longer he'll stay awake, the better chance he'll eat a decent meal.

"Kansas City is too damn far." Not seeming to hear Julia, Bill sips from the glass and sets it down, sloshing water on the white tablecloth. "Too damn far."

Julia soaks up the water spot with a linen napkin and holds the glass out to Bill. "Don't you worry about that. Take another drink."

"Too damn far," Bill says, crossing his arms on the table and laying his head on them.

Julia shakes his shoulder so he won't fall asleep. "Sit tight. I'll fix you a plate." She stands to fetch supper from the kitchen. "I boiled fresh corn," she says. "Your favorite, and the girls and I made a banana pudding." She stops when Bill says something. Because his face is buried in his arms, she can't understand him.

"What's that?" she says.

"Remember how much she cried?"

"Who?"

"The baby. You remember?"

"Colic. The doctor called it colic."

"Goddamn, she cried. All the damn time."

"Babies cry."

Julia stares down on Bill, his head lying on the table so she can see only one side of his face. A dark shadow covers his jaw and upper lip.

It started when Maryanne was two weeks old. At first she cried for only thirty minutes or so after her bottle. Julia would swaddle her and pace the upstairs hallway, gently bouncing her. When that didn't work, and the crying stretched to more than an hour, she tried removing the blanket and sitting motionless in the rocking chair with Maryanne cradled in her arms. By the time the baby was four weeks old, she cried every night for two hours, a hard cry that made her cough and sometimes choke. "Colic," the doctor had said. "Burp her good. She'll outgrow it in a month or so."

So Julia burped her baby and walked with her, rocked her, sang to her, left her alone in her room, drove with her in the car. By six weeks, Maryanne cried every waking minute, her body growing stiff, like a block of wood or cement, not even living, not like a baby at all. She screamed. Her face glistened and red splotches covered her cheeks and neck. Bill and Julia never slept. Bill's eyes swelled. His hair grew too long. He lost weight. The joints in Julia's fingers and arms burned. Pain pounded constantly behind both eyes. Tufts of her hair fell out in the bristles of her brush.

"Why are you saying this?" Julia asks.

Bill doesn't answer.

She shakes his shoulder. "Tell me."

"Christ but she cried. Didn't you get tired of all the crying?"

"Stop saying that."

"I did," he mumbles into the crook of his arm. "Got damned tired of it."

Julia begins to back toward the stairs that will lead her away from Bill. "These are horrible things to say."

"Had my fill," Bill says, his head lying on one arm while the other hangs limp at his side. "Damn sure had my fill."

At the base of the staircase, Julia stops. "Is this why you don't want another baby?"

No answer. Bill might be asleep. Julia stares at him, thinking she doesn't know him at all.

"Is that all you remember of her?" she asks again. "The crying?"

He mumbles something.

"You're never going to want another baby, are you?"

His eyes are open now, but his head hasn't moved. He stares across the dining room into a blank wall. Julia starts up the stairs, slowly, one at a time.

"Julia."

She stops.

"I sure am sorry," he says.

Now she turns, looks down on him slumped over the table.

"Sorry about what? What do you mean by that?"

"Sure am sorry," he says. "Sure am."

Clinging to the banister, Julia walks down two stairs. "What did you do, Bill?"

His eyes are closed again. He doesn't answer.

She walks down two more stairs. "Bill. What is it? Tell me."

For days, there has been talk of Jerry Lawson's troubles. Many of the ladies have wondered aloud if Jerry Lawson was fired because he killed that colored woman down on Willingham. Studying her own husband now, Julia wonders if the rumors will next begin to swirl about him.

"What did you do, Bill?"

She waits for an answer. The house is still. The girls are sleeping. The neighbors have settled in for the night. Somewhere nearby, a radio rolls over static and stops on an announcer calling a baseball game. Traffic on Woodward hums even at this late hour. Bill's breathing becomes rhythmic and shallow. He's fallen asleep. Julia walks slowly up the stairs.

"I damn sure had my fill," she hears when she reaches the landing and can no longer see Bill.

The night Maryanne died was the only night of her short life she didn't cry.

Day 6

CHAPTER SEVENTEEN

Izzy squints into the morning sunlight that bounces off the bathroom mirror and after counting out one hundred strokes of her hair, she sets aside the brush. Her cheeks and chin are red from her having scrubbed her face with a soapy washcloth, and her hair falls smoothly over her shoulders. Next she brushes her teeth, tucks in the white cotton blouse that had the least wrinkles when she pulled it from her drawer, and slips on a blue headband to keep the hair out of her face. No wonder Arie spends so much time in the bathroom every morning.

From out in the hallway, Arie bangs on the door for the third time because if Izzy doesn't hurry up, Arie won't be ready to leave for the church on time. Aunt Julia insisted both girls take a bath even though they took one last night because they spent all morning scraping paint off Uncle Bill's garage. After Izzy complained at the breakfast table that the television was nothing but gray fuzz and the house was hot and they knew every single record by heart and why couldn't someone take them to Jefferson Beach, Aunt Julia had handed Arie a three-inch putty knife and Izzy a wire brush and said if they were so bored, she would be happy to give them something to fill their time. Taking one last glimpse in the mirror, Izzy throws open the bathroom door, lowers her head, and rushes down the hall before Arie has a chance to notice Izzy has made herself up to look just like her twin sister.

Downstairs in the entryway, the front door stands open. A car trunk slams and Aunt Julia marches up the sidewalk and onto the porch. Though Izzy knows it isn't possible, Aunt Julia's chest looks bigger today than it was yesterday. Every day, Aunt Julia's curves appear to grow, making Izzy certain hers never will. Ducking her chin to her chest, Izzy digs at the linoleum floor with the tip of one toe because that's what Arie would do if she got caught staring at the gap in Aunt Julia's blouse.

"Would you tell Izzy to get a move on?" Aunt Julia says, walking through the door and toward the kitchen, a sweet, perfumed smell following her inside. "We're going to be late if that child doesn't get going."

Izzy continues to stare at the floor and tries not to smile. "Aunt Julia," she says, pitching her voice the slightest bit higher so she'll sound like Arie. "Could Izzy and I stay home today?"

Aunt Julia stops and crosses her arms over her chest. She thinks Izzy is Arie because Izzy has brushed her hair with one hundred strokes, scrubbed her face until it burned, and wears a tucked-in blouse that isn't wrinkled.

"I promise to make Izzy behave," Izzy says. "But I'd rather not go to the church. It scares me to be there."

"What do you mean?" Aunt Julia runs a hand over Izzy's glossy hair, thinking it's Arie's glossy hair.

"It makes me think about Elizabeth all the time," Izzy says, "and that scares me."

"I don't know," Aunt Julia says, looking overhead to where Arie is in the bathroom, brushing her hair and scrubbing her face. "It's not that I worry so much about you, but Izzy isn't one to mind me these days."

"I'll make her listen," Izzy says. "I promise I won't let Izzy out of my sight."

Once Aunt Julia's red taillights have disappeared around the corner at Alder and Woodward and while the water still runs in the upstairs bathroom, Izzy yanks at her crisp white cotton blouse so it hangs loose at her waist, pulls off her headband, and runs out the back door, across the yard, and into the alley. She would have brought Arie, but she is all of a sudden afraid of the alley and wouldn't have approved anyway. Izzy runs until she reaches the Turners' house, and once there, she squats behind the overgrown bushes Mr. Turner never trims. From this end of the block, Izzy can see the top floor of Aunt Julia's house. She squints and maybe sees Arie standing in their bedroom window. Just in case, she gives Arie a big wave so she'll know everything is all right. Then Izzy drops back behind the bush and watches for approaching cars.

After waiting for a good long time and hearing and seeing nothing, Izzy peeks out from behind the bush. Across the intersection, just outside Mr. Symanski's house, a group of three men huddles around a clipboard. Two of the men carry walking sticks, the third holds the clipboard. After talking for a few minutes, the three men walk toward the Filmore and disappear around back, where they must be heading down into the poplar trees. They'll poke at the shrubs and mushy piles of leaves back there in hopes one of them will finally poke Elizabeth. When Izzy is sure the men are gone, she jumps up from behind Mr. Turner's shaggy bushes, gives one last wave in case Arie can see her, and runs toward Beersdorf's Grocery.

———

A small bell overhead rings when Grace pushes open the bakery door. As it was yesterday, the air inside the small shop is thick and warm. The glass cabinets and the wire shelves are still empty. It's payday on Willingham Avenue, usually the busiest day of the week, but today, all the other shops have closed. Soft voices drift out of the back room. That's Cassia's voice, the young mother with the black carriage, light and sweet, calling for more flour. And Sylvie, the largest of the women Grace met yesterday, telling Cassia no more, you'll ruin the dough. Setting her handbag on Mrs. Nowack's counter, Grace pulls off her gloves one finger at a time.

Outside the shop, two police cars drive by, stop at the intersection of Willingham and Chamberlin, and turn left. They are probably headed to the river, where they'll search for Elizabeth. Grace draws in a deep breath. It's easier to breathe here on Willingham. Everything is easier here on Willingham. The baby doesn't ride quite as low and heavy and the ache in her tailbone is gone. This is what a good night's sleep does for a person. This is what Orin Schofield, sitting watch in the alley, a rifle resting in his lap, has done for Grace.

"You are coming just in time," Mrs. Nowack says, walking from behind the black curtain. Her gray skirt brushes the floor and her small black loafers peek out from under the hem of her skirt. Her spongy, wide feet spill over the tops of her shoes. From under the counter, she pulls four large silver trays. "Hurry before they are rolling out the dough. We have many hands today and will be finishing in no time. You are wanting to learn, yes?"

Behind Mrs. Nowack, near the register, the baby carriage Grace saw the day before is pushed against the wall. It's covered with the same tattered yellow quilt.

"They'll keep nicely in the freezer?" Grace whispers as if there were a baby sleeping in the carriage. "The bake sale has been postponed, you know." She turns at the sound of another engine idling outside the shop. Somewhere nearby, a car carrier rolls toward the docks, its heavy load shaking the floor beneath Grace's feet. Soon enough, the carrier, or one much like it, will return north, empty of its load. Its loose chains and weathered straps will rattle as it passes through the streets.

"They will be keeping in the freezer as long as you need," Mrs. Nowack says, also looking out the store's front window.

That's Julia's car sitting at the stop sign, and that's Julia sitting behind the wheel, unmistakable with her tangle of red hair. She stares straight ahead at the warehouse, looking almost as if she's lost.

On her way to catch the afternoon bus to Willingham, Grace had stopped at Julia's for coffee and a visit. Already Grace was feeling guilty for avoiding Julia. Grace had ignored a ringing phone that she knew was Julia and had hidden from a few knocks on her back door. A short visit would set things right.

Even from the front porch, Grace could smell the sweetness of ripened bananas—Julia's homemade banana bread.

"I'm making pierogi today," Grace had said, taking a seat at Julia's kitchen table and stirring a sugar cube into her coffee. "Mrs. Nowack is going to help me."

Standing at her stove, Julia poured a cup of milk into a small saucepan, then added a half stick of butter and a packed cup of brown sugar. Once her butter melted, she would add powdered sugar, beat it until it was smooth, and lastly drizzle the icing over her banana bread. Only glancing at Grace, Julia turned up the heat on her burner and beat the mixture with a wire whisk. Her lids drooped and her eyes were red as if she'd been crying, not recently, but during the night, perhaps all night. And her red hair, though never quite restrained, hung over her shoulders in loose, matted strands. It was the same look Julia had had in the weeks and months after Maryanne died.

"And how does that figure with James? I'm sure he can't be happy about it, intent as he is on keeping you in that house."

The sounds of metal scraping against wood floated into the kitchen through an open window. In the backyard, the twins were scraping loose paint off the garage. When the sounds fell silent for more than a moment, Julia leaned toward the open window and shouted, "There's still meat on that bone."

"I'm not telling him, and neither are you," Grace said, sipping her coffee and shaking off Julia's offer of a cigarette.

Before putting the milk back in the refrigerator, Julia poured herself a glass and offered one to Grace. It was Wednesday—diet day for Julia. Monday, Wednesday, Friday . . . one spoonful of the Swedish Milk Diet whisked into a glass of milk four times a day.

"Maybe you should eat something of a bit more substance," Grace said.

Over the stove, a small timer pinged. Julia drank the milk, shook her head at the gritty texture she often complained about, and pulled two loaves of banana bread from the oven. She shook the oven mitts from her hands, arched her back, and cocked one hip to the side. "Girl's got to keep her figure." She bounced that hip and tried to laugh as she shook her large chest in Grace's direction. Normally, Grace would blush and swat a hand at Julia, maybe tell her to put those things away, but today, before Grace could do either, Julia dropped her hip back where it belonged and let her shoulders sag.

"Where have you been, Grace?" Julia said, wiping the back of her hand across her mouth. "You haven't been on the bus. I've called, stopped at the house."

"I haven't been well, I guess." It's true enough. "Is everything all right? Did something happen?" Grace began to stand so she could reach out and touch Julia's arm, but Julia pulled away.

"It's nothing," Julia said, and busied herself rinsing out the dirty dishes.

"You should stay home today," Grace said. "Take a break from going to the church. Spend some time with the girls."

Julia waved away Grace's suggestion and pushed aside the ruffled café curtains to watch the twins through the window. The sound of metal chipping away at loose paint still echoed through the backyard. "I wonder," she had said, "if things will ever be good again."

Holding four large silver trays, Mrs. Nowack shoulders her way through the black curtain separating the back of the bakery from the front, and holds it open for Grace.

"You're sure it's no bother?" Grace says.

Out on the street, Julia's car finally rolls through the intersection, turns right, and disappears. Grace should have stayed with Julia, should have asked again what was really troubling her. But there was a bus to catch and Grace was eager to leave Alder and all the things that reminded her of how much was lost. The thing that troubled Julia was most likely the thing that troubled everyone on Alder Avenue. Six days and Elizabeth is still missing. Julia will be fighting her imagination, trying to escape the visions of Elizabeth alone, frightened, or dying or dead. Grace fights the same visions, but they don't spring from her imagination. They spring from the memory of the night those men, that man, came for her.

"You are seeing I have no customers," Mrs. Nowack says. "Come, we are having plenty of time for pierogi."

"Do we leave the baby here?" Grace asks. "Unattended?"

Mrs. Nowack lets the curtain fall closed and sets the trays on the counter. Through the round glasses perched on the end of her nose, she squints at Grace. "You know there is being no baby, yes?"

Grace nods. "Was there ever?"

"You are seeing only a mother who wishes her baby had lived. One child giving birth to another. Too much sadness I am thinking, and this is what happens."

Grace slides her feet across the gritty tile, slowly so she makes no noise, and at the carriage, she pinches a corner of the quilt and pulls. The quilt falls away from the empty bassinet. She wonders, if the women knew what happened to her, would they coo to her and touch her softly on the shoulders and back as they had done for Cassia.

"It is being like Elizabeth, yes?" Mrs. Nowack says. "Who knows what all this sadness will be doing to us."

Grace shakes out the quilt and drapes it over the carriage.

"Coming," Mrs. Nowack says, picking up her trays. "We are having much work. Busy is good. Busy is very good."

Outside on Willingham, two more police cars drive past. This time, their lights flash, their sirens whine. They don't stop at the intersection like the other two police cars but drive straight through the stop sign and head toward the river.

Letting the black curtain fall closed, Mrs. Nowack sets her trays back on the counter and walks across the black-and-white tile to the front window. Yet another police car drives past.

"Or perhaps today is not being the day for our work." She shakes her head and makes a clicking sound with her tongue. "I am afraid we are having bad news. It is being best you go home."

————

Julia should have said no to Arie and insisted she and Izzy come with her to the church. If she weren't thinking only of herself, she would have, but as Arie stood before Julia with her freshly scrubbed face and neatly combed hair, begging for a chance to stay home, Julia thought it might be easier if she left the house by herself. She could have never explained to the girls why she wanted to drive by the factory on the way to the church or what she was hoping to find there.

All of Willingham Avenue's shops are closed today, their windows dark, except for the bakery. Julia stares straight ahead at the factory's parking lot. It's only half full of cars, all of them owned by men Julia doesn't know. They'll be cars that belong to men who never met Elizabeth, men who live east of Woodward or north of Eight Mile. They'll be cars that belong to men who work two shifts to make up for men who search. Where Willingham dead-ends into Chamberlin, Julia rests her foot on the brake and lets the car idle. No women stand in the warehouse next to the factory. The ladies said the women come on payday, tempt the men, put themselves on display in the windows. But the warehouse door is boarded up and every window is empty and black. The glass is broken out of a few and plywood has been nailed at all angles to keep out the trespassers.

Julia didn't really expect to find Bill's car here. She'll find it at the church, or he'll be out driving through one of the neighborhoods Grace's husband marked off on the map. She should have never let her mind wander to the dead woman on Willingham when Bill sat at the dining-room table, his head buried in his arms, and said that he was so very sorry. But what else was she to think? What else could torment a man? What other than guilt and remorse? She flips on her right blinker, turns off Willingham onto Chamberlin, and her mind wanders to what became of Elizabeth Symanski.

In the church basement, Julia circles the room, raving about the splendid smell that met her the moment she climbed out of her car. Making her way to the end of the rectangular table draped with a freshly washed and ironed white linen, Julia unwraps her banana bread, apologizing all the while that she didn't go to nearly the trouble of the others. She thinks to ask one of the ladies if Bill has been through for lunch yet, but because the casserole dishes are full and the coffee cups sit in perfect rows on the square card table she knows none of the men have arrived. She also doesn't ask because she's afraid the ladies will hear doubt in her voice, or fear, or panic.

Today, there is talk of a funeral. Julia hears this in snippets of conversation that flow about the room. With the arrest of the colored man from the Filmore, the ladies assume Elizabeth will soon be found. Julia isn't certain anymore if she saw Elizabeth walk through that gate. What does she remember because it actually happened and what does she remember because she wants so badly for it to be true? When the police asked her, which they did three times, they said they wanted only to establish a timeline. They weren't trying to place blame. This is how life works, they said. Sometimes it's a messy thing to behold. Relax. Close your eyes if it helps. What do you know to be true?

After Julia has unwrapped her banana bread, sliced the first loaf, and set out the butter to soften, she fills two pitchers to freshen the water in the percolators. As she moves about the room, stacking the coffee cups and filling the creamers, the ladies follow her with their eyes. They shift their gaze when Julia smiles at them, but look back the moment they think she has turned away. They know something but don't want to tell Julia. Or maybe they are blaming Julia for what has happened, maybe worrying about what will become of her, or perhaps they can see in Julia's face or in her eyes or in the way she walks that she is slowly sinking into the fear of what her own husband may have done.

CHAPTER EIGHTEEN

After Izzy gives one last wave in case Arie can see her from the bedroom window, she runs out of the alley and onto Alder Avenue. When she sees a second group of searchers, she squats behind another bush. One block later, she spots a third group and hides on the far side of an elm that hasn't been chopped down yet. Elms used to grow along both sides of Alder Avenue. The trees formed an arch in summer when their leaves were thick, and in the winter, their bare branches were like claws trapping the houses below. Most of the elms are gone now, from Alder and all the other streets too.

While hiding from the most recent set of searchers and watching as the three men walk up to a door, tap lightly, and step back to wait for the lady of the house to appear, it occurs to Izzy she recognizes none of them, and if she doesn't recognize them, they won't recognize her. Even if they do catch sight of her and wonder why she is running about a neighborhood no one considers safe anymore, they won't know to tell Aunt Julia because they won't know where Izzy belongs. She runs the rest of the way without worrying about who might see her until she spots Mr. Herze's giant blue sedan on the corner just past Beersdorf's Grocery. The car's fins run half its length and the chrome front end glitters where it catches the sun—definitely Mr. Herze's car.

The fans hit Izzy full in the face when she pulls open Beersdorf's heavy door. The small store smells of sour milk and bleach. Behind the front counter, Mr. Beersdorf stands, one hand resting on his register, the other on his large belly. When the girls used to shop here with Aunt Julia—before the neighborhood turned like a bad banana—Mr. Beersdorf's apron was crisp and white and his belly was even bigger. Now the apron is gray and his belly has deflated because Mrs. Beersdorf died and he doesn't have anyone to do his cooking and cleaning anymore. He flicks his eyes in Izzy's direction but quickly turns his attention back to the large Negro woman standing at the display cases that run along the far side of the store. The plump woman wears a pink-and-white calico dress belted at her thick waist. With one hand, she holds a young girl by the wrist and is picking through Mr. Beersdorf's tomatoes with the other. Izzy scans the rest of the shop. No sign of Mr. Herze. He must be among those searching the neighborhood, probably one of the men who carries a clipboard.

"Don't you bruise my wares," Mr. Beersdorf calls out.

As if to get Mr. Beersdorf's goat, something Grandma likes to say, the woman is taking her own sweet time picking through every single tomato. The woman pays no mind to Mr. Beersdorf and continues picking and sorting. While Mr. Beersdorf is busy frowning at the woman, Izzy makes her way to the far side of the shop, her sneakers sliding easily across the black-and-gray checkered floor. She walks with a straight back and lets her arms hang naturally at her sides. The trick is to move with a normal stride and not glance about to see who's watching. Behind her, where the tall windows let in the only light, the shop's door opens. A blast of warm air rushes inside, blowing strands of Izzy's red hair across her face. That same blast causes Mr. Beersdorf to stand to his full height and stick out his belly. Izzy turns to see what has caused Mr. Beersdorf to double in size.

Three colored men walk into the shop. One of them leans against the doorframe while the other two walk inside. One of the men is much taller and wider than the others and a tuft of hair grows from his chin. As the two men stroll past Mr. Beersdorf, paying him no attention, Izzy continues across the store, back straight, arms loose, no glancing about.

At the end of aisle one, red and green pennants hang overhead, their narrow tips fluttering from the gust of air the men let in, and a large cardboard cutout of a boy wearing a cowboy hat points toward a bin of canned peas and corn. His cheeks and the end of his round nose are red as if he's had too much sun, and a blue kerchief is tied around his cardboard neck. The same cardboard boy stood over that bin when Izzy and Arie used to come to the store with Aunt Julia. They were younger then and Mrs. Beersdorf would say the cowboy was glad to see the girls and that he had been waiting all year for them to return. Izzy dashes past the display, fearing the boy is watching her and knows exactly what she's up to.

Izzy tried to find a can of tuna in Aunt Julia's cupboards, even mentioned one afternoon that some tuna sure would taste good.

Aunt Julia said she had used up the last of it for the men down at the church and she'd put more on her shopping list, but after two trips to Willingham, Aunt Julia still hadn't brought any home. There was only one way Izzy was going to get tuna.

She first spotted the cans the last time she and Arie were at Beersdorf's, shortly before Izzy slipped the stolen pop under her shirt. If they were going to ever find their cat, tuna would be the perfect bait, and finding Patches is about the only way Izzy can think of to get Arie feeling better. For months, Arie worried and fussed about that dog the Russians shot up into space. She would stare into a black sky, hoping she might see that spaceship with the dog inside, as if her seeing it would have meant that dog was safe. About the time Arie stopped looking for that dog, their cat disappeared and then Arie started being afraid of the alley and just about everything else, it seemed. If it's not one thing with Arie, it's another.

Keeping her head down, Izzy passes behind the little girl and the woman sorting through the tomatoes, continues to the far end of the aisle, and squats to the lowest shelf. Checking both ways to make sure Mr. Beersdorf hasn't appeared, she palms a can of tuna and tucks it into her elastic waistband. Behind her, the little girl lets out a squeal.

"Hush up," the girl's mother says, rolling another tomato from side to side as she inspects it. "Mind yourself."

Izzy twists up her face the same way Arie does when she's angry and points it at the girl, who promptly wraps both arms around her mother's wide legs and hides her face in her mother's thighs. With the girl no longer watching, Izzy stands slowly so the tuna won't break free of her waistband. Half a dozen long strides will take her to the end of the aisle and back to the front of the store. When Izzy reaches her full height, the can tucked securely in place, the little Negro girl peeks out from behind her mother's thighs. Izzy holds a finger to her lips. The little girl lets go of her mother's legs, jumps into the center of the aisle, and shapes her face into the same scowl Izzy made. Two pigtails stick out from the girl's head like fuzzy black handles. She jumps up and down and tugs at her mother's blouse. Looking first at Izzy and then down at her daughter, the mother sets aside her tomato and reaches out to scoop up the girl, but she bounces out of reach and begins flapping her arms and pointing at Izzy.

"Stealer, stealer," the girl chants. *"Stealer, stealer."*

The mother fends off the small flailing arms and manages to wrap one hand around the girl's shoulder. In the wake of the flapping and floundering, a few tomatoes tumble out of the display case. Izzy dashes toward the cardboard cowboy at the end of the aisle. The girl squeals and yanks away from her mother. As the woman lunges for her daughter, managing only to grab the girl's small wrist, her foot lands in the center of a fallen tomato. The woman slips, losing her grip on the girl, and the girl flies across the aisle and into Izzy's path.

Throwing out both hands like she does when she flies over her bike's handlebars, Izzy sails past the little girl and falls face-first toward the checkered floor. The can of tuna breaks loose of her elastic waistband, drops out the leg of her shorts, bounces up, and hits the little girl in the head. The can continues to bounce across the black-and-gray tile and comes to rest a few feet beyond Izzy's reach.

"Hey there," Mr. Beersdorf shouts.

At the end of the aisle, Mr. Beersdorf appears. He stops under the pennants that now hang motionless. To the left of him stands the cardboard cutout, but from where she lies, facedown, Izzy can see only the boy's brown paper backing and the wooden slats that hold him in place.

"What's happening here?" Mr. Beersdorf says. "You there." He points down at Izzy. "What's your name? Do I know your parents?"

Izzy scrambles to her knees. Behind her, the little girl is crying and the mother is trying to pick her up.

"You'll pay for that produce," Mr. Beersdorf shouts, jabbing a finger at the woman struggling with her crying child.

On hands and knees, Izzy snatches up the can, jumps to her feet, darts between Mr. Beersdorf and the cardboard cowboy, and runs toward the door.

"Stop there," Mr. Beersdorf shouts over the screaming little girl. "Bring back that can."

At the front of the store, the colored man who waited while the other two walked into the shop pushes open the door and ushers Izzy outside with a one-handed sweeping gesture. "That's twice I saved you, huh?" he says as she runs past. He smiles down on Izzy, his teeth bright and white against his warm, brown skin. He has soft, lazy eyes like Uncle Bill and stands with a strong, straight back. Izzy smiles, though she isn't sure what the man means to say, and holding the tuna in one hand she runs out of the store and through the empty parking lot. Knowing Mr. Beersdorf won't follow her because he'll be too worried about all those Negroes, Izzy slows to a walk when she reaches the street, tosses the can into the air, and catches it. Tosses it and catches it.

"I'm guessing your aunt doesn't know you're out and about, does she? And I'm guessing you didn't buy that can of tuna."

Izzy wraps both hands around the small can, hiding it as best she can. Three men walk toward her. Two carry long sticks meant for poking through bushes. The men wear hats, white cotton work shirts rolled up at the sleeves, faded blue pants that have no crease, and black boots. They stand on either side of the third man. Izzy knows the third man. Just as she thought, Mr. Herze carries the clipboard.

———

The ladies have set up fewer tables at the church today than they did a few days ago. Fewer and fewer men are joining in the search. Some say they are troubled by taking charity from the men who work double shifts. Today is payday, the start of a new pay period. It's time they get back to work. Others say now that a man has been arrested, there's no need to continue looking. That Negro will talk soon enough, the men say. Give the police some time. That Negro'll talk.

It had been nearly noon when Malina finally woke, and Mr. Herze had already left for the day. His cologne no longer lingered and the air in the hallway was cool and dry, no leftover steam from the hot water he would have run to bathe himself before leaving. The pills had worked. He never tried to wake her. But they also muddied Malina's thoughts and caused her to sleep late. Once out of bed, she had slipped on the first wrinkle-resistant dress she came across in her closet, and on her way out of the house she fished her yellow rubber gloves from beneath the sink, and once through the back door she shook the cornstarch from them. Across the street and a few doors down, a moving truck was parked outside Betty Lawson's house. Yes, it was a moving truck. That was Jerry Lawson holding open his front door as two Negro men carried a blue tweed sofa from the house. Soon enough, one of Malina's troubles would be gone. Mr. Herze would never again sit at the Lawsons' kitchen table and listen to a police officer call Malina a liar, because the Lawsons would no longer live on Alder Avenue.

At the bottom of the stairs leading into the church basement, Malina bids hello to Sara Washburn, coordinator for today's luncheon. With a clipboard in hand, Sara checks off Malina's name and makes note of the stuffed-pepper meatloaf Malina has brought and smiles because she has remembered to do exactly as Malina instructed. Sara's brown hair flips up in tight curls that ride just above her shoulders and the plaid dress she wears is too heavy for such a warm day. Malina gives Sara a wink and a pat on the shoulder, not because Malina is fond of the woman, but because the relief of having seen the moving van outside the Lawsons' house has lifted her spirits. She might even call herself giddy. Setting her casserole with the other homemade dishes, she trails a finger along the table and inspects what all the other ladies have brought. Card tables have been set up and covered with linens, place settings have been put out, and the coffee bubbles up at a small table near the back of the room. Behind the table stands Julia Wagner.

"I didn't expect to see you here," Malina says. "I rather thought you'd be home with the twins."

Julia glances up from a sheet of limp paper she holds in her hands. Because of the small dark print and thin worn edges, it's probably something cut from a newspaper. She smiles but says nothing.

"I see you brought your banana bread," Malina says, drawing a cup of coffee from one of the percolators. "Mr. Herze does love it so. You should think about bringing it to the bake sale this year."

A pale yellow scarf is tied over Julia's hair, which has yet to see a brush today, and as is usually the case, her blouse is too snug through the chest. The strain has caused a gap to open up between two buttons—a gap Julia has tried to remedy with a safety pin.

"Pardon?" Julia says, folding the paper and setting it on the table. She looks about the room as if she's forgotten where she is.

"The bake sale," Malina says. "I should think your banana bread would prove quite popular."

"No," Julia says. "What did you say about the girls?"

"Nothing," Malina says. "But I did see them out and about today before I left the house, or I should say I saw one of them. I guess I assumed you were home. I didn't expect to find you here."

"You saw the girls outside?"

Malina nods and tries not to stare at the pin woven into Julia's blouse. Each time she inhales, that silver prong catches the overhead light and sparkles.

"Only one of them," Malina says. "She was walking down the street. Not causing any trouble, though I do suspect they are the culprits who have trampled my flowers on occasion."

"Would you mind the coffee?" Julia asks, slipping from behind the table. "I think I'd better run home."

At the bottom of the stairs leading into the dining hall, one of the husbands appears, his hat in hand, fingering the brim as he stretches his neck to scan the room. "Doris," he calls out, brushing aside the ladies who approach him. "Where's my Doris?"

"Very well," Malina says, taking Julia's place behind the table while keeping watch over the commotion going on across the room. Not even this extra duty will dampen Malina's mood. Julia has always been an odd sort of neighbor, and Malina's found it difficult to converse with her ever since her baby died. It's such a lot of sadness to contend with. "Don't forget this." Malina picks up the tattered, worn slip of paper and stretches across the table to hand it to Julia.

Julia takes the clipping between two fingers and opens it.

"Did you ever consider this?" she says, lifting the article and pressing it toward Malina for a closer look.

"What ever do you mean?"

The ladies continue to congregate near the stairwell. "I'm here." It's Doris Taylor's voice, rising above the rest. "My goodness, I'm right here."

"A place like this," Julia says, paying the ladies no mind. "The Willows. Have you heard of it?"

Malina walks from behind the table, crosses her arms, and leans forward so she can see what Julia holds in her hands. "What on earth? I haven't the faintest notion what this is. The twins, Julia. You're supposed to be tending to the twins."

"You and Warren, you've never had children. You must have considered it. Adoption. Did you ever consider adoption?"

"I am quite sure that is none of your business, Julia Wagner."

"Let us pass." It's Doris's husband. "Step away, all of you. Let us pass."

All around the room, the ladies begin scurrying about, collecting their bags and wraps. Some of them fuss with their casseroles and cover them with foil while others gather the plates, saucers, and flatware and stack them on the back credenza. Still others rip linens from the tables and stuff them in cloth laundry bags.

"How dare you broach such a personal question?" Malina says. "You should concern yourself with those girls and stop all this foolishness."

"You think I don't concern myself with the girls?" Julia says.

Julia's perfume, something cheap and sweet, snags in Malina's throat. She coughs into her fist. Julia throws back her shoulders, lifts her chin, and the gap in her blouse widens, straining the safety pin's thin-coiled wire.

"I think adoption is a private thing not to be discussed in this manner, and you should concern yourself with the two children you already have." Malina clears her throat as much to give herself time to think as to soothe the irritation from Julia's perfume. "I think maybe you're not well. It's no wonder. What with all the stress of Elizabeth disappearing, I can't imagine the guilt you're feeling. I only meant to suggest you bring your banana bread to the sale. You're such a fine cook. Nothing more. Really, nothing more."

"Ladies, ladies, you two hurry along." It's Sara Washburn, calling out from across the room. When Julia and Malina make no move to leave, Sara walks toward them, a white cotton sweater slung over one arm and both hands wrapped around her clipboard. "Leave these things," she says. "Switch off that coffee and go home."

"You think I can't care for Izzy and Arie?" Julia says, ignoring Sara.

"I said no such thing." Malina pauses, reaches out to touch Julia's arm.

Julia jerks away, nearly stumbling. "It's what you all think, isn't it? That I'm unfit."

"Ladies," Sara says, clutching the clipboard to her chest as if to protect herself. "Leave this to another time. I'd like to lock up."

"Please, Julia. I said nothing about you being unfit. For goodness sake, what has gotten into you? The girls stay only a few weeks. How much trouble could they or you possibly get into? They really are of no concern to me."

"Ladies, let's move along," Sara says.

"And what if they were to stay? Would you worry then? Am I only fit to care for them a few weeks at a time?"

"Is that true?" Malina says, her giddy mood slipping away. Looking from Sara Washburn in her bold plaid dress to Julia, who is bursting through her white cotton blouse, Malina tries to draw in another deep breath to clear her head, but the air is too heavy with Julia's perfume. "They'll stay on? The girls will stay?"

"Ladies," Sara shouts.

Julia drops the tattered sheet of paper on the table. Her round, full chest rises and falls. More of her red hair has pulled loose of the scarf that held it from her face, and wiry strands stick out from her head. Both she and Malina turn to Sara.

"It's Elizabeth," Sara says, her shoulders sinking. "They've found her. They've found our Elizabeth. Please, it's time to go home."

CHAPTER NINETEEN

G race agrees with Mrs. Nowack when she suggests it might be best that Grace go straight home, and after the fifth police car has raced past the bakery and turned toward the river, she boards the bus that will carry her back to Alder Avenue. But rather than stopping at her own house, she walks directly to Mr. Symanski's, opens the iron gate, climbs the three stairs leading onto his porch, and knocks lightly. The door opens. Mr. Symanski wears a wrinkled shirt and a tie that falls too short. His pants hang loose on his waist and bag at his ankles. A pair of men's shoes cut from soft kidskin leather sit to the side of the door. The tip of his big toe pokes through a small hole in his right sock.

"I thought to check on you," Grace says. "I was down on Willingham. . . ."

She lets her words trail off into silence, afraid to mention the many police cars and blaring sirens. Tugging off her white gloves one finger at a time, she checks the street for any sign of an officer who might be coming to deliver bad news.

Mr. Symanski blinks twice and squints again, as if not certain who Grace is, and then he smiles. "Come in," he says. "Before the heat is getting you."

Outside Mr. Symanski's, tufts of crabgrass have grown up through the cracks in the sidewalk. The yard has become shabby in the short time since Elizabeth disappeared. It must have started when Ewa died, the slow, steady falling apart, but Grace hadn't noticed until now.

In the living room, Grace tucks her gloves into her handbag. The air is heavy and stale, making it difficult to breathe. So often in the days since Elizabeth disappeared, it's been difficult for Grace to breathe.

"The baby is well?" Mr. Symanski says.

Grace nods and pushes aside the heavy drapes in the front room. Light spills into the house, and the dust in the air sparkles. Across the street, the Filmore Apartments are quiet. They're always quiet. In the evenings, when the people come home from work, they must park their cars and disappear inside straightaway. Everyone says some of the families living there are Negroes, but Grace has never seen them coming or going through the glass doors. She's only seen the men who roam the alley and now the street. The one who came for her hasn't been among them since the night of the attack. Grace excuses herself and, in the kitchen, pulls a bottle of diluted vinegar from under the sink, grabs a few pages from yesterday's newspaper, and walks back to the living room.

"The police came to see you?" Mr. Symanski says.

"They did." She sets aside the bottle so she can use both hands to wad up the newspaper.

A half dozen times since the officers questioned James and Grace, their patrol car has rolled down Alder Avenue. Each time, the car drove slowly as it crept past her house, giving her a chance to rush outside and admit to them she lied. They could find Elizabeth if only Grace would tell the truth.

"Yesterday," she says. "They came yesterday."

Sprinkling the diluted vinegar on the crumpled ball of newspaper, Grace rubs small circles on the living room's cloudy window.

"They are asking you more questions?" Mr. Symanski says.

Another deep breath so her voice won't quiver.

"I wish I could have told them something," she says, and rubs her nose.

Ewa's vinegar water is stronger than the mixture Grace has at home. But stronger is better. The glass glistens and squeals as Grace scrubs.

"I wish I could have told them something that would help. But they arrested a man. Does it give you any peace to know that?"

Maybe there is some comfort in knowing. Maybe not knowing is the thing that tortures a father, keeps him up at night, turns his hair to straw, makes his shoulders cave and his spine bow. The street must surely be safer with one of them arrested. This must bring some peace.

Mr. Symanski sits on the sofa. He used to sit in the brown recliner pushed against the wall, and Ewa would sit next to him in her chair. With his hands in his lap, he smiles at the bright window.

"They have no one," he says.

"But they arrested a man."

"They are telling me it was unrelated," Mr. Symanski says. "I don't understand unrelated. I am thinking Elizabeth doesn't matter as much as another might."

"I don't understand, either," Grace says. "They let him go? How can they do that?"

Mr. Symanski shakes his head. "They say they can be holding a man only so long. That is all they are telling me."

"Did he live there?" Grace says, pointing at the Filmore. She squints into the freshly cleaned window just as Mr. Symanski had squinted when she first opened the door. As she stares across Alder Avenue, she wipes down the marble sill with her soggy newspaper. "Is he here on this street? Have you ever seen him?"

"I am never looking."

"I wish I could have helped you," she says, knowing the man is back on the street because she was too afraid to tell the truth. "I wish I could have said something to the police, told them something that would have stopped all this."

From his seat on the sofa, Mr. Symanski stares down at the sliver of toe poking through his sock. "You are helping me now," he says. "You are being a good neighbor. And always so good to my Elizabeth. Always so good. You'll be having your own soon and knowing how wonderful a daughter is to love."

After scrubbing the kitchen window, wiping down the counters, and promising to deliver a roast in a few days to fill Mr. Symanski's empty refrigerator—or possibly a stuffed chicken if he has tired of a roast every week—Grace walks with Mr. Symanski to the front gate. Once there, she hugs him lightly and pushes on the gate's latch. It sticks, so she gives it a second jostle. Down the street, near her own house, one of the twins walks toward her. From this distance, she can't tell which one.

"The police came to see me today," Mr. Symanski says. "Just before you are here, they came."

Grace lets the gate fall closed and whirls around to face Mr. Symanski. "Oh, no."

The twin is a half block closer. Because her head jerks from side to side as if she's afraid of her surroundings and because her shoulders droop, Grace knows it's Arie.

"Yes," Mr. Symanski says. "It was being the river. That is all they are telling me. Today they are finding her. It is being the other men who tell them it is my Elizabeth."

Grace reaches out, squeezes Mr. Symanski's wrist, pulls him into her arms. "What can I say? It's my fault. All of this. My fault."

Mr. Symanski, hunched over at an awkward angle because of Grace's large stomach, rests his head on her shoulder. "This is not being true," he says. "My Elizabeth, she is being at peace?"

Grace dabs at her eyes. She wants to ask how it happened, what the police found, but Arie is only a house away and she shouldn't see this or hear this.

"Can I help you inside?" Grace says, glancing back at Arie. She has walked a few yards closer and stopped. She stands at the sidewalk that leads to the Archers', who live next door, and has wrapped herself in both arms. Even from this distance, Grace can see Arie is crying.

"Go," Mr. Symanski says. "Go and see to the child." Halfway up the sidewalk, he stops and turns back. "It is being hardest to be the only one left."

Grace watches until Mr. Symanski reaches his porch, then she bangs on the latch again and once through the gate, she rushes toward Arie.

"Arie, dear. What is it? What's wrong?"

Arie's lips roll in on themselves and she backs away. She shakes her head but doesn't speak.

"Honey, please. Why are you crying?" Grace takes another few steps closer, but this time, she moves slowly.

Arie must know about Elizabeth's death. Grace should be crying too, but she's known all along things would come to this end.

"It's Izzy," Arie says, still cradling herself with her own arms. "I'm afraid what happened to you is going to happen to her."

———

When Mrs. Richardson reaches out to cup Arie's shoulder, Arie stumbles away. It's rude, and Aunt Julia would be disappointed, but something bad happened to Mrs. Richardson in that alley, something so bad she hasn't even told Aunt Julia, and Arie doesn't want to be touched by it.

Again, Arie says in little more than a whisper, "I'm afraid what happened to you is going to happen to Izzy." She sniffles and drags her hand across her nose.

Mrs. Richardson doesn't try to come any closer. Her white hair glows in the bright sun. None of it breaks free of the band holding it from her face or frizzes at her temples like Arie's hair always does. In the street, a car drives by. Mrs. Richardson doesn't smile or wave even though it's the neighborly thing to do. Now she is the one afraid to get too near.

"What do you mean by that, Arie? What do you think hap-pened to me?"

After Arie had finished cleaning up to go to church with Aunt Julia, she had run downstairs, her sneakers in hand. Sock-footed, she skated into the kitchen. Empty. She shouted into the backyard. Nothing. Lastly, she looked out the front window. The driveway was empty. Aunt Julia was gone, and so was Izzy. She ran back up-stairs, and from her bedroom window, she scanned Alder Avenue. Every door along the street was closed. Most of the driveways were empty. She crawled over Izzy's bed, a rumpled mess because she never makes hospital corners or smooths her quilt, and looked out the side window. She looked past the roofs and antennae and over-head lines, and at the far end of the alley, she saw a person. She couldn't say she saw Izzy because the person was too far away, and yet, she knew it was Izzy because an arm stretched into the air and waved in broad strokes.

Arie watched the alley for half an hour. It was early, she told herself. Not until five o'clock would Mr. Schofield set up his chair again. Like everyone on Alder Avenue, Mr. Schofield knew the col-ored men came at ten and five, or thereabouts. Surely Izzy would be home long before that. But then one o'clock passed, and two o'clock and soon, Aunt Julia would be home. Arie had to go looking.

The street had jumped to life while Arie was upstairs watching the alley. Cars drove past, whipped into driveways, and ladies scurried to their front doors. Arie had clung to the banister with both hands as she walked down the stairs to the sidewalk and she waited for one of the ladies to shout out to her and tell her to get back inside. But no one noticed her or scolded her. Three times Arie walked up and down Alder. Cars continued to drive down the street, but instead of more ladies, it was their husbands, home at an odd hour, and because they, too, hurried inside without tending to their trash cans or setting out the sprinkler or using the daylight to mow the lawn, and because time was slipping away and five o'clock would eventually come, fear welled up in Arie and she couldn't stop that fear from spilling out as tears when she saw Mrs. Richardson a half block away.

"I asked you a question," Mrs. Richardson says, grabbing Arie's arm. It's the same spot she grabbed when she thought Izzy and Arie started the fire. "What do you mean? What do you know about what happened to me?"

Arie stares down on Mrs. Richardson's hand. Her fingers pinch but Arie doesn't pull away.

"The bad thing that happened to you," Arie says. "The bad thing that happened in the garage." She lifts her eyes. "I can't find Izzy and I'm afraid the same will happen to her."

Mrs. Richardson's hand softens and drops from Arie's arm. "Come," she says, taking Arie's hand, gently this time. "That looks like your aunt's car. Let's get you home and then we'll find Izzy."

Mrs. Richardson smiles at Arie and talks with a smooth, steady voice. She is trying to sound like she's not scared, but red patches grow where her white collar rests on her neck and sweat collects on the soft hairs above her top lip and on the tender skin under her eyes. And instead of walking toward Aunt Julia, Mrs. Richardson almost runs, dragging Arie along behind.

Up ahead, Aunt Julia's car rolls into the driveway. Uncle Bill doesn't like for her to drive it because he says it's on its last leg, but Aunt Julia said first leg or last leg, she had to drive it today because the bus wouldn't do. She parks the car where the back bumper is left to stick out into the street, and without closing the door behind her, she walks toward Arie and Mrs. Richardson, slowly at first and then more quickly when she sees Mrs. Richardson is in a hurry.

Across the street, Mrs. Herze pulls into her driveway too. Mr. Herze's big blue car is already parked there. He must have been one of the husbands who came home early. Arie's been thinking only about the bad thing that might have happened to Izzy, but because Aunt Julia walks with long, quick steps and her makeup is smeared and because the husbands are home early and because every house is closed up tight, something else bad is happening right here on Alder Avenue.

Like Aunt Julia did, Mrs. Herze doesn't bother to park her car properly and she runs over a patch of her snapdragons with one tire. They're all dying anyway because she hoses them down several times during the day in case someone peed on them. Mrs. Herze throws open her door and waves across the street at Aunt Julia.

"Julia, stop," Mrs. Herze calls out, waving something in the air.

Aunt Julia pauses but doesn't look back. "Leave me be, Malina."

"Please stop," Mrs. Herze shouts again. Making her way down her driveway, she teeters on tall heels and a white handbag swings from her wrist. "Please, hear me out."

Aunt Julia doesn't wait for Mrs. Herze but continues toward Arie. Once close enough to see Arie has been crying, Aunt Julia draws her into a hug and says, "What's wrong, sugar?" Aunt Julia smells like ripe bananas and brown-sugar frosting.

Mrs. Herze continues to wobble across the street on her narrow heels, all the while waving something in the air and begging Aunt Julia to listen and understand.

Saying nothing more to Mrs. Herze, Aunt Julia stoops before Arie and holds her by both shoulders. "Why are you crying? What's all this fuss?" Aunt Julia smiles and talks with a hushed voice. Her speech becomes sluggish and she punches the beginning of each word. Uncle Bill says tough times, happy times, any sort of times can draw out Aunt Julia's Southern drawl.

"Julia, I saved your clipping." Mrs. Herze stumbles to a stop behind Aunt Julia. Clumps of her short black hair stick to her forehead where she has sweated, except she would call it perspiration, and her red lipstick bleeds into the thin lines that cut into her top lip. "Look here, I brought it back to you."

Aunt Julia takes a deep breath. A silver safety pin meant to keep a gap in her blouse closed has popped open. Its sharp end points at Arie. Aunt Julia brushes her fingers across Arie's brow.

"Now, tell me," Aunt Julia says, "what's all the fuss?" Then she turns to Mrs. Richardson. "Did she hear about Elizabeth?"

Mrs. Herze stomps one white shoe, grabs Aunt Julia's shoulder, and gives a yank. Aunt Julia, still squatted in front of Arie, falls backward and lands on her hind end. Mrs. Richardson lunges but can't stop Aunt Julia from toppling over.

"What on earth has gotten into you, Malina?" Mrs. Richardson says, her large belly making it difficult for her to stretch out a helping hand to Aunt Julia.

"I only meant to help, Julia," Mrs. Herze says, gazing down on Aunt Julia and ignoring Mrs. Richardson's question. A gray streak cuts through the part in Mrs. Herze's black hair. "You're being entirely unreasonable."

"Malina."

The loud, deep voice silences everyone. There, across the street, standing near the back of his car, his hand resting on the peak of one of its tall blue fins, is Mr. Herze.

"What on earth are you doing there?" he shouts. "Leave those people be."

Mrs. Herze crosses her arms over her chest, tips forward at the waist so she is hovering over Aunt Julia, and drops her voice to a whisper. "Please, listen to me," she says. Her eyes are stretched wide open and her thin, black brows ride higher than they normally do. Tiny stray hairs pepper her lids. Grandma would say Mrs. Herze needs to reacquaint herself with a pair of tweezers. "Please. Send those girls back to your mother."

"Good Lord, Malina," Aunt Julia says, snatching the sheet of paper from Mrs. Herze. "What kind of crazy has gotten its claws in you? Is this about those flowers of yours? Is that what has you in such a state?" Aunt Julia brushes away Mrs. Herze and reaches for Mrs. Richardson's hand and the tissue she has pulled from her pocketbook. Once standing, Aunt Julia dabs at the stains under her eyes and says, "I suppose you'd better listen to your husband and leave us be."

Aunt Julia continues to pat her face and chest until Mrs. Herze has backed into the middle of the street. Then Aunt Julia drops her eyes to Arie and lets them drift right, left, and right again.

"Where's Izzy?" she says, the wadded-up tissue dangling from her fingers. The words crawl out of her mouth.

Mrs. Herze stops backing away. Behind her, Mr. Herze stands in the driveway.

"Where is your sister?"

CHAPTER TWENTY

Malina lingers in the middle of the street until a car forces her to move. She gives a kindly wave to the driver and steps onto the curb outside her house. Mr. Herze stands near his sedan. He rubs the top of the car's fin as if it were Malina's thigh. Her cheeks burn. Certainly, they've turned red. Across the street, Julia kneels before the twin and stares up at her. Grace stands at the girl's side, one hand resting on her shoulder.

"Arie, you promised me you two would stay inside," Julia says. "You crossed your heart and promised me." One of Julia's nylons is torn and a hole has opened up in her skirt's side seam.

The girl shakes her head. "No," she says.

Malina braves the street again and presses her ear toward the threesome.

"What do you mean, no? You stood right there in that entry and gave me your word. You gave me your word, Arie. You said you'd watch over your sister."

The girl shakes her head. Malina takes another step.

"I didn't make that promise," the girl says. "It was Izzy. She was pretending to be me."

They talk some more, the girl pointing toward the Filmore Apartments, Grace patting the girl's shoulder and shaking her head, Julia looking up and down Alder Avenue. How long has she been gone? When did you last see her? Where would she go? Did you know she was going? Did you know she had gone?

"You said you saw one of the girls today," Julia shouts when she notices Malina standing nearby. "Was it Izzy? Did she say where she was going?"

Malina shakes her head and can't stop herself from glancing back at Mr. Herze.

Grace wraps an arm around the girl and walks her up Julia's driveway. "I'll get her inside," she says. "And then I'll check with the neighbors."

"I'll get my keys," Mr. Herze calls out. "She won't be far. I'll drive around a few blocks."

The screen door slams once when Mr. Herze goes inside and again when he returns. Another car comes along to force Malina and Julia from the street. It's Grace Richardson's husband. He pulls over, climbs out of his car, and jumps back in after Julia tells him of the missing child.

"Move this car," Mr. Herze shouts at Malina. "I can't very well get out with you blocking me in."

Malina fumbles with the clasp on her purse and digs one hand inside, searching for her keys.

"How about you, Warren?" Julia says, after James Richardson has driven away. "Did you happen to see one of the girls while you were out today? It would have been Izzy."

Walking out of Julia's house, Grace's skin is white except for the red glow that creeps up her neck. She has taken the other twin inside and now that twin sits in the front window, her face pressed to the glass, and looks as if she's watching Mr. Herze.

Standing at the side of his car, his keys in hand, Mr. Herze stares across the street at Julia but doesn't answer.

"Warren," Julia says again. "Did you see her?"

He looks down at his keys, jostles them, pulls open the car door.

"Warren?"

"Well, good Lord in heaven," Mr. Herze says. He tosses his keys into the air, catches them, and slams the door shut. "Unless you've got a third one running around, that must be the one you're looking for."

Down the block, James Richardson pulls into his drive. He has seen the same as Mr. Herze. Walking on the side of the street, where the last few elms throw a spot of shade, is the other twin. James Richardson walks to the street and makes a motion with his thumb, signaling to the girl she'd better hurry on home. She hugs something to her chest and begins a lazy jog. As she gets closer and sees Julia standing on the curb, arms crossed, the girl slows her pace. Malina walks toward her for a closer look. The girl definitely holds something in her arms. It's a stack of paper—white, glossy paper—one sheet the exact size of the next. A stack at least a half-inch thick. Malina leans close as the girl passes. LOST CAT, it reads across the top in large black letters.

The girl continues the long, slow walk toward home. Without saying a word, Julia stretches out one arm and points a single finger at her house. The girl walks past Julia, head bowed. At the stairs leading to the front door, Grace, still pale, ruffles the top of the girl's head with one hand. The girl ducks, pulls away from Grace's touch, disappears inside, and the door closes. Leaning heavily on the banister, Grace makes her way down the last few stairs and walks up the sidewalk toward the street. Not until she hears the front door close does Julia drop her arm. She looks past Malina and turns to face Grace.

A few days ago, Malina saw a stack of paper exactly like the one clutched in the girl's arms. It came home with Mr. Herze. The girls at the office made them—flyers for Elizabeth Symanski that the men taped in windows along Woodward. The paper was glossy, smooth, not like regular writing paper. A machine at the factory churned out one sheet exactly like the next. The girls knew how to make it work. Mr. Herze would never bother with such a chore. One flyer after another, each sheet exactly like the last and the next. Now the twin who is bold enough to walk right past Malina without even a hello carries a stack of those same flyers. LOST CAT, the top one read. All the rest will be exactly the same.

———

There is something final about the sound of Julia's screen door slamming behind Izzy. First there is the squeal as the door opens, the creak when its springs are stretched as far as they'll go, the momentary silence as it falls closed, and then the slap. The afternoon breeze is cool on Julia's shin and knee where her torn nylon bares her skin. She tucks in the loose tail of her white blouse, straightens her skirt's waistband, and pulls the bent safety pin from her blouse. Across the street, Malina has followed her husband inside. No sign of James Richardson, either. He must not have seen Grace here at Julia's house and he's gone inside his own house to look for her. Julia will send Grace straight home so James doesn't worry. As Grace waddles toward her, this is what Julia intends to do. News of Elizabeth will weigh heavily on everyone and Grace is in no condition to abide all this sadness. Even though most had stopped expecting Elizabeth would come home, expecting a thing is a wide world away from knowing a thing.

"You heard, then?" Grace says. She stops beside Julia, clasps her hands together under her large stomach, and clears her throat as if preparing to say something bigger.

Julia nods. "Do you know how?" she says and then starts again. "Do you know what happened to her?"

"The river," Grace says. "That's all Mr. Symanski told me."

"It all stops now, doesn't it?" Julia says. "No more lunches? No more desserts and coffee? No more searching?"

"People think those men took her." Grace dips her head in the direction of the Filmore Apartments. She doesn't have to say more. "Do you know? Even the police think it. They arrested one of them but had to let him go. You know that, right? You know that's happened?"

"Yes, I know that."

It's not the words that warn Julia what's to come, it's how Grace says them. Her tone is flat, as if she's reading from a typed sheet of paper.

"Then, why?" Grace says.

"Why what?"

"Why do you leave the girls to their own devices? It's not safe. They're not safe."

"I know it's my burden, Grace. No need to make me wallow in it."

"I don't think anything is your fault, but I don't think you realize how our street has changed." Grace's skin is pale and her lips are dry, cracked. "I think you need to mind those girls," she says, "before something terrible happens."

"Mind them like I didn't mind Elizabeth? You're as bad as Malina."

"Julia, stop." Grace reaches for Julia's hands, but Julia pulls them away. "What happened to Elizabeth wasn't your fault, and I wish you'd stop saying it was."

"Why do you wish that, Grace?"

Julia is going to make Grace say it. She is going to stare at Grace, hold her eyes firm, not move an inch until Grace says it right out loud.

"Because if you think it was your fault, you must think it was my fault too."

Everything did change with that slamming door. Elizabeth will never come home and this is Julia's fault. Her own daughter will never come home and this is Julia's fault too. Julia doesn't know how to be a mother. She failed Maryanne and she will fail the twins. Julia's own daughter died because Julia was a careless, hapless mother, and now there will never be another baby and Elizabeth will never come home.

"It was your fault, Grace," Julia says. "Yours as much as mine."

———

It's five o'clock, must be because that's the time the colored men always pass. From her bedroom window, Grace sees him. Yes, that's him. That's the one. She recognizes him even from this distance. It's the way he walks, with a rounded back and a swagger. That's what she'd call it. A swagger. And then he lifts his left hand. One other time she's seen him and it was his left hand. He draws it down over his chin, his beard. This is how he trains it. Over and over, stroking the short, dark beard, drawing those fingers together, drawing them to a point.

James is gone and Grace is glad for it. A few minutes ago, he left the house. Go to Julia's, Grace had said to him after he reported to her what she already knew. While he sat at the kitchen table, telling her Elizabeth was gone for good, Grace stood beside her ironing board, her new steam iron in hand, one of James's Sunday shirts laid out before her. She worked the iron back and forth over the shirt's yoke, every so often pressing a button to release a stream of water. It was supposed to make life easier, more manageable. No more sprinkling from a bottle or pre-dampening in the sink. The iron sizzled and hissed and she inhaled the light steam. James thought she was pale and that her eyes were red and swollen because Elizabeth was gone and because the ironing was too much work. It was the moment she should have told him about the man who came for her and for Elizabeth and that she worried he hadn't set things right yet, so he'd come again for the twins or someone else. But she said nothing.

Julia was right. It was Grace's fault Elizabeth died. She would bear the weight of that truth for the rest of her life. And because she didn't tell James in that quiet moment sitting in the kitchen as he stroked the back of her hand and brushed his fingers across her cheeks, she was dooming herself to carry the weight of what was yet to come. Saying none of these things to James, she asked him to check on Julia and the girls. Bill's not yet home. She'll need your help. She'll have to tell the twins about Elizabeth and she shouldn't do that alone. Sit with her awhile, make sure she and the girls are well, and then hurry home for supper. Grace owed Julia something—an apology, an admission, some sign of regret—but her husband was all she had to offer. She also knew the men would soon pass by her house, every day at five o'clock, and that today, the one who had come for her would be among them. Elizabeth was never a danger to him. Only Grace. But she lied to the police. She said it never happened. She made it safe for him to return, and so she sent James away.

With her hands clasped under her belly, Grace crosses the bedroom and stands at the back window. She rests her fingertips on the cool marble sill. In the alley below, Orin Schofield sits in his chair just as she knew he would. He's hunched over, maybe asleep. His rifle will be propped against his garage within easy reach but where the other neighbors won't see it and take it away from him again. Go to Julia's, Grace had told James, and now she's happy for it.

There are four of them today. They walk with a slow, lazy pace and are only just past the house when Grace pushes open the kitchen door.

"Orin," she calls out toward the alley. "I need you, Orin."

She waits, listens. The chair will creak when he stands. Hearing nothing, she calls out again, louder this time, but not so loud that the men walking down the street will hear.

"Orin, up here. I need you up here at the house."

The metal chair whines. In a few moments, he'll appear around the side of the garage. She wonders if he knows Elizabeth is gone and that the man walking down their street took her and killed her and whatever else he did, Grace cannot let herself imagine.

"You there."

Now Grace shouts so the men will hear and so Orin will know there's trouble and bring his rifle. She walks to the end of the drive-way, slowly at first, but then more quickly. She doesn't want them to get too near Julia's house, where James might see them.

"You there. You stop."

The street is quiet for this time of day. Having received word Elizabeth was pulled from the river, the husbands are already home. Garage doors are closed, curtains are drawn, even windows, it seems, have been shut because the usual sounds of supper being served—glasses knocking against one another, a stray piece of sil-verware being dropped, someone shuffling a stack of everyday china—have been silenced. Even though Grace can't hear them, she knows her neighbors are sitting down to the table, all of them whispering about the funeral that will come and wondering what will follow. Will Alder Avenue ever be the same, or has it changed—have their lives changed—in a lasting way? Grace glances behind her. Still no sign of Orin.

Only two of the men hear her and turn. The man with the beard continues his slow pace. Across the street, Mrs. Wallace,

246

who had been sweeping her porch, props her broom against her house, walks inside, and closes the door. The two men look at Grace and then at each other. The first jabs the second in the side, shrugs, and they hurry down the street to catch up to the other men.

"Yes, you," Grace shouts. "I mean you."

The baby hangs heavy today, heavier always at the end of the day. That'll mean a boy, Mother likes to say. But Grace thinks it means only a strong, healthy baby.

"How can you walk here?" she says.

Behind her, two footsteps and a tap, two footsteps and a tap. Orin is using his gun like a cane, just as he did the three-foot length of wood. He must see her and the men, too, because the steps and the tap quicken. Soon she'll hear him breathing. He'll cough because the walking is a strain. If she could turn toward him, she'd see his face flushed, sweat dripping from his temples, a white button-down shirt wilted and clinging to his soft midsection. Only one man pays her attention this time. He looks at Grace and then to each side as if wondering whom she means to question.

"Ma'am?"

He's the one who couldn't watch. Grace's memory of him is correct. His lids droop over his large brown eyes in a way that makes him appear kinder and more thoughtful than the others. He let it happen but couldn't bring himself to watch.

"I know what he did," Grace shouts. "I know it was him."

Two others turn, but the bearded man stands with his back to Grace. The footsteps and the tapping have stopped. Grace points so Orin will know which one. She points at the tallest man. His wide shoulders roll forward. Thick veins run like cords from his wrists to his elbows. Grace can't see them from such a distance, but she knows they're there because that night, he hovered over her, those arms flanking her, trapping her. Like the other three, he turns. He looks past her at first, past both her and Orin as if they're not worth noticing, and then his eyes focus. They settle on Grace.

"Did you know, Orin? They found our Elizabeth today. Pulled her from the river." Grace lifts her hand again. Points. "That's the one who took her and dumped her like garbage."

Orin must be tired. Every morning, every evening, and late every night he waits in the alley. He must have wondered why the men stopped coming, or maybe he thought he kept them at bay. Maybe he has felt pride these days since Elizabeth disappeared. For the first time in many years, he must have felt useful, powerful even. But now he sees the men are here on the street. He hasn't frightened them away, and it's Grace who has stripped him of his pride.

"Orin," she says again because he doesn't move. "That one there. That one."

"Thought for sure you'd tell."

The sound of his voice, pitched so much deeper than James's, knocks Grace backward. She's remembering the smell of this man—spicy cologne sprayed on much earlier in the day and the sour patch under each arm. He knows the police came to see her. He knows the officers questioned her and that she lied. This is why he's back. It's safe for him now. Someone was arrested, someone stronger and less selfish than Grace. It may have been the man with the soft, kind eyes. Whoever it was, he was strong enough to try to stop it from happening again. He told the police a woman was hurt at 721 Alder. A pregnant woman, badly injured. But Grace lied. Because she wanted to protect her marriage and the life she had planned for her daughter, she had smiled for the officers, hid the ache in her tailbone and the stiffness in her neck, and now the man is back, walking down Alder Avenue, caring so little about what he did that he is scarcely able to recognize Grace.

"I know you did it," she says.

It's a whisper now. At her side, Orin shuffles forward. Standing, when normally he sits, he struggles with the gun's weight.

"What'd I do?" the one says, looking to the others who stand at his side. "Any of you all know?"

The men shake their heads. The man with the lids that droop kicks at the ground and crosses his arms. It's not only Elizabeth whom Grace has harmed, it's this kinder man too. She wants to lay a hand on his shoulder to calm him. Stop your fidgeting, that's what Mother would have said. As if knowing Grace's thoughts, the man with the beard trained by three fingers wraps a hand around the kinder man's shoulder, presses, probably squeezes, and the kinder man stands still.

"You must be mistaken, ma'am," the man with the beard says. "If nobody tells, then nothing happened. Ain't that the way it goes?"

From the corner of her eye, Grace sees a flash. It's the late-day sun reflecting off dark metal. A thin barrel rises and levels off. Orin coughs. Each breath is a struggle for him. It wasn't always so bad. Every year, the breathing, the walking, the standing, all of it becomes harder for him. The doctors give shots now that burn and pinch and what happened to Orin won't happen to the rest of them. He nods in the direction of the men, confirming which is his target. The man knows Grace didn't tell. He knows she never will and he knows the kinder man betrayed him.

"No, Orin," Grace says. She rests her palm on the thin barrel and pushes it toward the ground. It's the way Mr. Williamson lowered it the day Orin shot into her garage. "No."

With his large hand wrapped around the kinder man's shoulder, the man who ruined Grace and killed Elizabeth takes a shallow bow. He knew she wouldn't do it, and he turns and they all walk away. But because Grace is too weak, they'll come again.

CHAPTER TWENTY-ONE

Julia stands in front of her refrigerator, staring inside. She should be getting supper on the table for the twins and Bill. From the top shelf, she grabs a loaf of banana bread tightly wrapped in aluminum foil. Some of her bananas were too ripe for pudding, so she used them to make bread because waste not, want not. She squeezes the tightly wrapped loaf until the ends pop open and then tosses it across the kitchen toward the trash can sitting at the back door. She grabs three more foil-wrapped loaves, all of them meant to feed the searchers tomorrow, but the search is over and all this food will go to waste after all. Like the first loaf, she throws all three across the kitchen. Next she slides out a pale blue casserole dish trimmed in a white Butterprint pattern. It's her banana pudding with a three-inch meringue, also meant to go to the church tomorrow. Her meringues never bleed or weep, and this one, like all the others, is perfect. Sliding her palm under the cool dish, she holds it near her shoulder and launches it at the trash can, where it shatters against the wall. Next, the baby lima beans in cream sauce. They've always been Bill's favorite. They sail across the room in a lemon-colored casserole dish and splatter on contact—the flat, pasty beans first sticking to the wall and then falling away to the floor.

"Aunt Julia."

Julia swings around.

"Is something bad happening?" Izzy says. She stands in the kitchen entry, one hand on Arie's shoulder, the other hanging limp at her side. Both girls' feet are bare and their hair is damp from their bath.

"No," Julia says. "It's nothing. You two get on back upstairs."

Arie steps away, but Izzy doesn't move.

"Is it Elizabeth? Did they find her?"

"Not now, Izzy. Later, when Uncle Bill gets home."

"I wasn't doing anything bad," Izzy says. "I was only looking for Patches. You never let us look."

Arie has continued to back down the hallway, but Izzy stands firm.

"I'm sorry I pretended. Arie didn't know. I was only—"

"I said, upstairs now."

"But Aunt Julia, we—"

"You'll never find that cat."

Julia reaches into the refrigerator and pulls out the last loaf of banana bread, rears back, and throws it. The small, tightly bound package hits the wall with a thud.

"That cat is at your grandmother's house, way across town, and it's probably dead by now."

Izzy's bottom lip pokes out. "That's not true. There's no reason to think she's dead."

Turning her back on Izzy, Julia says, "Upstairs. Now."

Julia stares at the mess she has made until the girls' bedroom door slams shut. Once she is certain they have settled in, she walks over to the foyer and takes a quick look out the front of the house. No sign of Bill, even though the other husbands are home for the evening. She drops the curtain and at the entryway table picks up the tattered, yellowing article about the Willows that Malina returned. Julia's unfolded and refolded it so many times, it has begun to tear along the creases. Back in the kitchen, she stands alongside the trash can splattered with yellow pudding, banana slivers, and slippery beans, and lets the flimsy sheet drop.

Julia used to tell herself she kept the article because she loved the house pictured in it. A crisply painted balustrade wraps around the front porch and rounded arches stretch between the squared-off columns that support the second-story patio. Looking at the picture now, a greasy stain ballooning in its center, she imagines the unwed girls sit on that top patio when the weather is nice. They must be lonely, shipped off to Kansas City to quietly give birth to their babies. The girls come from all over the country because every railroad leads directly to Kansas City and eventually to 2929 Main Street, the Willows. Julia pulls the article from the trash, wipes it on her apron, and holds it close. There might be someone sitting on the small, private porch. In the grainy print, she can't be certain, but if she went there in person, she could see for herself.

Uncertain how long she has stood in the kitchen and stared at the faded picture, it's a knock that rouses her. When she opens the door, James stands there, one hand propped against the side of the house. His sleeves are rolled up and his shirttail is untucked. It's the same double-stitched chambray work shirt Bill wears on weekends. The same navy twill pants. The same black leather work boots with the steel-tipped toes. When Bill used to come home at the end of the day, he would always do the same—yank out his shirttail. Sometimes, after he walked through the door, Julia would unbutton his shirt for him and slip it off his shoulders, leaving him in his undershirt. Before Maryanne was born, he would help Julia out of her shirt too, and they would make love on the living-room floor.

"Everything all right down here?" James says, pushing off the side of the house and glancing down the street. "Grace asked me to check in."

Julia pushes open the screen door and invites him inside. As he passes, she inhales the warm air he brings with him. He smells the same as Bill always did. Is it grease? Oil? Metal shavings? Even though he didn't work at the factory today, James carries that smell. She feels his footsteps through the floorboards. He fills up the entry, blocks the light shining through the sheers in the dining room.

"Julia?" James says, staring into the kitchen. "What's happened?"

Julia tucks the article back in the drawer where she has kept it for the last year. "Bill won't have another baby with me," she says.

She can only say it because James isn't looking at her. He's looking at the pudding dripping down her wall and the browning slivers of banana stuck to the side of her trash can.

"Won't even touch me."

Unable to face him, she talks to the floor. The black boots come toward her. Warm hands grip her shoulders.

"I used to be the one who couldn't take care of her own baby," Julia says, her cheek resting on James's chest. "Now I'm the one who couldn't take care of Elizabeth. Caught the same trout twice, I suppose."

With her eyes closed, it could be Bill before everything went wrong. The hands are sturdy. He's broad like Bill, and tall. Makes her feel small. She's usually the tallest woman. They called her lanky as a child. All arms and legs. Mother said she'd outgrow the awkward stage, said Julia would stop growing up and start filling out. Now it's James standing in front of her, smelling like oil or grease or metal shavings. When she reaches out to touch his chest, it feels like Bill's. Stiff fabric, small reinforced buttons, warm. She leans into him. The hands that cupped her arms slip over her shoulders and down where they wrap around her waist and draw her in.

————

Making her way across the garage, Malina tiptoes around the many bags of clothes she has accumulated for the thrift drive. Upstairs, Mr. Herze is napping, so she'll work quickly and quietly. He hasn't made use of his tools since he took down the storm windows this past spring, and he won't make use of them during the hot summer months. By the time autumn arrives and he takes it upon himself to repair a fence railing or replace a windowsill, he'll have long since forgotten he once owned a red-handled hammer. He'll have no reason to wonder what became of it or why a brown-handled hammer hangs in its place.

Now that Elizabeth has been found, things will return to normal. The men will go back to work, and the ladies will continue their plans for the bake sale. When she reaches Mr. Herze's workbench, Malina stretches across the smooth wooden slab, grabs the brown-handled hammer, and lifts it from the pegboard. It's brand-new, the cleanest of all the tools. No sense getting herself dirty when she'll have to get supper on the table shortly.

Outside the garage, Malina rests her arms on the top rail of the cedar fence surrounding her backyard. The fence offers plenty of privacy, and the gates on either side of the house are secured by a slide-bolt latch. Alternating yellow, white, pink, and red flowers line the yard's outer limits. The plants are happier here in the backyard, taller than in the front, probably because of the shade thrown by the Petersons' elm, one of the few left standing on the street. Its branches dip over her fence. No telling what kind of sickness that tree will dump in her yard. Feeling the seam on her right nylon is not quite straight, she yanks it into place, and seeing no one out and about because they've all been frightened indoors by news of Elizabeth's death, she slips through the gate. She'll start here. It's definitely the spot those twins would first come upon were they to sneak into Malina's backyard.

The sweet officer with the smooth blond hair hadn't helped Malina. After the twin was safely home, Malina had followed Mr. Herze inside and from her front window she watched Julia and Grace argue on the street. When Mr. Herze called down the stairs that he would be bathing and taking a nap before supper, Malina shuffled through her papers until she found the number that the young blond officer gave to her. She telephoned the officer and told him someone had urinated on her flowers. She told him those twin girls living across the street were most probably the culprits. They run amok, trespass on private property, stay out past suppertime. They don't even belong on this street. They have a perfectly good grandmother living somewhere east of Woodward. Consider what happened to poor Elizabeth Symanski. How much more tragedy could a neighborhood suffer? Could it bear the same happening to two young, innocent children? Couldn't the officer see to it that those twins went home? But the officer, who wasn't so sweet over the telephone where Malina couldn't see his silky blond hair and thin red lips, told her kids would be kids and there wasn't anything he could or would do.

Cupping the telephone's mouthpiece to stifle the sound of her voice, Malina went so far as to beg. She wanted to make the officer understand that the gift of those flyers meant Mr. Herze's interests had festered. And now she's been told those girls might stay on, might stay on forever. She wanted the officer to understand this was always the way and Malina knew better than Mr. Herze what came next. There have been others for Mr. Herze, mostly women. But like the girl from Willingham, it can be difficult to tell. Could be a girl. Could be a woman. Such a thin line between the two. When it happens, Malina will see it in the twin's eyes, whichever one Mr. Herze chooses. It will be an expression others might mistake for shock and then sadness and finally resignation. They'll wonder why the girl's eyes are suddenly hollowed out and darker than before. All the signs, Malina ignored them. The girls were supposed to go home in a few weeks. Every other year, they stayed only a few weeks. But Malina said nothing of Mr. Herze's gift to the girls or all the other things she knew. Unless the twins cause you or your property damage, the sweet officer had said, there really is nothing I can or will do.

Because Arie is scared, because Arie is always scared, Izzy has to drag her down the stairs toward the front door. But Izzy is wrong. Arie isn't scared, she's worried. Aunt Julia doesn't usually yell and throw food and say things like a cat is dead when probably it isn't. Izzy keeps tugging, getting angrier with every stair. They tug back and forth, silently, making twisted-up angry faces at each other, all the way across the entry and out the door. It's not fair Izzy always has to be the brave one and the strong one and the only one who will fight back. Arie tugs the other way because sometimes it's best to stop and think and Grandma always says calmer heads prevail. Before Aunt Julia or Mr. Richardson, who both stand inside the kitchen, can notice the girls sneaking from the house, they have run outside, off the porch, and across the lawn.

On Izzy's way back from Beersdorf's, she said she tried to put out the stolen tuna, but when she couldn't get it open, she threw it away and hung up some of the flyers Mr. Herze gave her. As he handed her the stack of flyers and a roll of gray tape, he said she had to keep them a secret, not tell anyone where she got them or he'd be in trouble. He made her promise not to go off on her own to do the searching, but she did. She also taped a bunch of flyers to poles and on the sides of houses and buildings. Now she wanted

Arie to go with her so they could take them all down before Aunt Julia found them and Izzy got in trouble all over again.

When they reach the middle of Alder, they stop running and check behind them. No sign of Aunt Julia or Mr. Richardson. Every house on the block is locked up tight. Across the street, Mrs. Herze walks out of her garage and that's a hammer in her hand. Arie tugs on Izzy's shirt so she'll see Mrs. Herze too. Standing between the garage and the side of her house, Mrs. Herze checks both ways like she's crossing a street, but since there isn't any traffic, she must be checking for who might catch her doing whatever it is she is doing. Now, instead of tugging back and forth, the girls link up hands and when Mrs. Herze opens the gate and disappears around the back of her house, they follow.

A wooden fence runs around Mrs. Herze's backyard, but it's easy enough for the twins to look through the slats and see what's going on back there. No longer concerned with who might be watching, Mrs. Herze drops the hammer into the grass, tucks her skirt around her knees, and lowers herself to the ground. Picking up the hammer again, she lifts it overhead with both hands and brings it down in the center of a tower of pink blossoms. The petals spray up as the hammer hits the ground with a soft thud. She lifts the hammer again, takes another swing. This time, white petals and green leaves scatter and a sweet smell oozes from the crushed and broken stems. Reaching out as far as she can in both directions along the fence line, Mrs. Herze beats those flowers. For several minutes, she pounds left then right, like two little feet marching through her snapdragons. When she can reach no farther, even by bracing herself with one hand, she sits back and tosses the hammer to her side. It bounces off the gate, rattling the slide bolt.

"You're going to blame that on us," Izzy says, "aren't you?"

Using her forearm, carefully like she's afraid to touch her face with dirty fingers, Mrs. Herze wipes the hair from her eyes. Her chest pumps and sweat bubbles hang on her upper lip.

"You two have no business in my yard," she says. "No business at all."

Arie tucks her chin, sorry that she dragged Izzy over here because now they're going to get in trouble, and Aunt Julia is going to know they snuck out of the house when they were supposed to be upstairs in their room.

"We think there might be a dead cat around here," Izzy says, lifting her chin to make up for Arie's drooping one. "Have you seen it?"

"Yes, that cat is dead and I did see it with my very own eyes. Dead as could be. Now you two can go away, back to that grandmother of yours, and stop running around this neighborhood in search of that godforsaken animal. You stop or you'll end up just like Elizabeth Symanski."

"You ruined these flowers and you're going to blame us." Izzy pokes Arie in the side so she'll agree.

Mrs. Herze presses both palms flat on the ground, pushes herself off her knees, and brushes pink and white blossoms from her skirt.

"I'm doing no such thing," Mrs. Herze says. "I imagine you two will have some explaining to do. I suspect your aunt will be ever so interested to see this mess. And I know she'll believe me because you two have been nothing but trouble for that woman since you arrived."

"You're a liar." Again, Izzy is the one to speak up.

Mrs. Herze smooths the apron that hangs at her waist. "My word against yours," she says.

"Not quite," Arie says, then reaches over the fence, flips the slide-bolt latch, and scoops up the hammer lying in the grass. Finally, she is the brave one, the quick-thinking one, the one who will make everything better.

Izzy lets out a cheer, claps her hands, and the two run away, leaving the gate hanging wide open.

CHAPTER TWENTY-TWO

Standing in her entryway, her cheek resting on James's chest, Julia inhales. The air around Grace's husband is warm. He's thick and solid, what a man should be. This could be her life before. Before Maryanne died. Before Elizabeth Symanski died. Before Bill drifted away. Before.

She draws up her hands to James's neck, weaves her fingers into the ends of his hair where it curls, tilts her face, and pulls him toward her. The clock over the stove ticks. A fan in the front room squeals as it rolls from side to side. In the distance, a car door slams. Julia presses against him. Raising one hand to the back of her head, James rests the other on her waist. He makes a sound as if clearing his throat, pulls back before their lips touch, drops both hands, lifts them out to the side, and stumbles away. They stand, neither of them moving. The doorknob rattles, and the front door swings open.

Wearing the same double-stitched work shirt as James, Bill walks into the house. No one would notice the way his steps are just off center, but Julia does. Soon enough, his face will swell again from the drinking, and his skin will take on a yellow cast. He's later than all the other husbands but has made it home in time for supper. He doesn't notice James and Julia as he fumbles with the lock on the door. His keys rattle and he steadies himself by holding on to the doorknob. With one good tug, his key comes loose. He straightens and turns. Saying nothing, he crosses his arms and his eyes come to rest on James, who has dropped his hands back to his sides.

"Didn't expect to find you here," Bill says.

James is almost ten years older than Bill and holds a higher-grade job at the factory. He was Bill's first supervisor and helped him keep his job during that difficult year after Maryanne died.

"James came to check in on the girls," Julia says. "He wanted to see to it that they were all right. That we were all right."

With the back of her hand, Julia wipes her mouth even though her lips never touched James's. The pulse of her beating heart carries to her eardrums, making it difficult to hear. She hugs herself with both arms.

"Can see to those girls myself," Bill says.

"Grace asked that I check in on them," James says. "Will be on my way now that you're home."

Bill takes a small backward step, giving way to James.

"Good enough," Bill says.

The men stand face-to-face, filling up the small entry.

"Good enough," James says after a long silence, and reaches for the doorknob. "I'm sure Grace will be checking in real soon, Julia."

Julia looks up from the floor at the sound of small feet running up the stairs and across the porch. The twins stop short, one bumping into the other, both of them stumbling across the threshold. One of them, Arie, lifts a hammer with both hands as if it's a trophy. She lowers it at the sight of Bill and James staring at each other.

"Leave that outside," Julia says, and waves at the girls to hurry past and go straight to their room.

Outside the door, Arie sets the hammer on the porch, wipes her hands on her shirt, and follows Izzy upstairs.

"All right, then," James says, reaching out to pat Bill on the shoulder. "You all have a nice evening."

———

The walk back home is slow for Grace and Orin. When the colored men have reached the intersection of Alder Avenue and Woodward, Grace hurries Orin along because James will stay only a short time at Julia's house and no good will come from him finding the twosome out on the street. After walking a few yards, Grace has to carry the rifle for Orin. With the barrel pointed down, she hugs it to her side where a passerby won't notice what is cradled in her arms. When they have neared the house, Grace hears the twins. They are out and about again even though Grace tried to warn Julia to keep a closer eye. The street is otherwise silent. Grace stops every few yards to give Orin a chance to rest and to look over her shoulder for any sign of James. Orin says his shoes are pinching his feet and Grace says they'll soak them when he gets home. At Grace's house, they step onto her driveway and continue to shuffle toward the alley. Once there, Orin points at his chair. Still holding the rifle, Grace steadies the rusted seat, but before Orin can lower himself, James appears at her side, reaches for the rifle, and yanks it from her.

"What in God's name?" he says, holding the gun in one hand and grabbing Orin by the arm with the other. "How did you get this back? Good Lord in heaven, what are you doing?"

Orin drops into his chair, pulls a yellowed kerchief from his pocket, and mops his forehead. "Taking care," he says between breaths. "Taking goddamn care."

"James, please," Grace says. "Don't fuss. There's been no trouble."

"I see trouble written all over this gun. You get inside. I'll see to Orin."

From her bedroom window, Grace again looks down on the alley as James helps Orin home. When they have disappeared, she slides open her closet door to hang up James's freshly ironed shirts. She is always precise as to how she hangs them. White ones first, because he wears those on Sundays, and then his darker shirts for evenings at home and weekend projects. The tip of every collar is pressed to a sharp point and the cuffs hang down stiff. On weekends, when James tinkers with his car or mows the lawn, he rolls his sleeves, ruining the sharply pressed cuffs. After a few moments, the kitchen door opens. Footsteps on the stairs.

"Gracie?"

In one hand, James carries his work boots. He rests the other on Grace's shoulder, leans in, and kisses her cheek. She covers his hand with hers, squeezes.

"Orin told me something happened," he says. "You were talking to some colored men? He says you wanted him to shoot one of them? Is that true, Gracie? I told him that couldn't be true."

"Do I seem at all different to you?"

James lets out a long breath, probably tired of nothing going as it should, tired of something always being troublesome. "Well, sure," James says. "You're bigger."

"But I'm different," she says, letting her gaze float from the lifeless shirts to James. "Don't I seem it?"

James squats in the open closet and slips his boots onto the shoe rack. He stands and unbuttons his shirt. Since this heat settled in, he stopped wearing an undershirt. Dark, wiry hair forms a long triangle on his chest that disappears below his brown leather belt. He turns toward the closet as if looking for something, pulls off his shirt, lets it slip first off one shoulder and then the other. He tosses it behind him so it lands on the bed and bends down again. When he stands, Grace's white shoe dangles from one finger as it did the day he first discovered it in the closet.

"You're fine, Gracie," he says, staring at the shoe and not Grace. Something will be gnawing at him, though he might not be certain what it is. Maybe he'll be wondering how one shoe found its way into the garage, where he crushed it with his car, while the other found its way safely to the rack in his closet. "You're beautiful. Now, tell me what happened out there? Orin said one of them spoke to you. What did he say?"

"It's no never mind," Grace says, backing away from James to sit on the edge of the bed. She rests her hands in her lap.

"Orin told me. The man said you didn't tell. What did he mean?"

Grace folds her hands together. "When will the funeral be? Do you know?"

"Not yet." The shoe still dangles from one finger. "Don't you worry about that. Please, Gracie. What aren't you telling me?"

"The fire," she says. "It was the fire in the garage. I told you it was probably just the girls playing with fireworks."

"And?"

"I didn't really think that. I only told you it was the girls so you wouldn't worry, so you'd think it was a harmless accident. I think it was the men from the alley, the ones who leave the broken glass. I thought you'd be angry, maybe get into an argument."

James nods as if he understands but his brow sits low over his eyes and he chews on the inside of his cheek the same way he does when he reads in the newspaper about another factory closing its doors. He slips the shoe over the rack and walks up to Grace.

"Do you know what happened to Elizabeth, Gracie? Was it one of those men? Was it the one you pointed out to Orin?"

Grace fingers the narrow lace that trims the hem of her full blouse.

"Someone killed Elizabeth, Gracie. It wasn't an accident."

Grace shakes her head and continues to run her fingers along the rough lace edging.

"They shot her in the back of the head," James says and points to a spot above his ear. "Here, they shot her right here. If you know something, you have to tell me."

"James, stop," Grace says. "Stop saying these terrible things."

"What do you know, Gracie? Tell me now."

"Orin is confused," she says, sliding a few feet toward the end of the bed so she can stand and walk past James to the bedroom door. "Orin's confused, is all." She walks into the hallway. "I have supper for Mr. Symanski. You'll run it down to him? This is all so awful. Who would do such a thing to Elizabeth?"

"Gracie?"

"Wash up," she says. "Supper in fifteen minutes."

Day 7

CHAPTER TWENTY-THREE

The first two times Julia tries to wake Bill, he doesn't stir. Now he will definitely be late to work. All the men will be returning to the factory today, and Bill should be among them. Behind her, the twins' door is closed; their room, quiet. She checks her watch.

After James left the house yesterday, Bill had stood in the entry and stared at Julia. He didn't speak, didn't ask her to explain, didn't notice the mess in the kitchen. Just stared. What had happened between James and Julia left something tangible in the room, something concrete enough that it filled up the entry and pushed Bill and Julia apart. By the time Bill left, slamming the front door behind him, he knew the truth even though Julia hadn't uttered a word. She had waited up for him, but at some point during the night, she fell asleep on the sofa and didn't wake when he came in.

"Bill," Julia says, pushing open the bedroom door. She kneads her neck with one hand where it's tightened up from sleeping without a pillow. "You're late to work." She leans into the room but doesn't cross inside. "You need to get up."

The bed creaks and Bill throws back the top cover. He is fully dressed in the clothes he wore the day before and still wears his black boots. Both are untied. Black laces dangle across the white sheets. Pushing himself into a sitting position, he swings his legs over the side of the bed. Even from across the room, Julia smells the liquor. Black-and-white scotch. He drinks it over ice.

"Figure I'd better get my house in order first," he says, his voice rough from cigar smoke.

"What do you mean by that?"

Julia crosses into the room but stops at the foot of the bed. She leans over and tugs on the quilt, straightening Bill's side.

"What did he do?" Bill says.

"What did who do?"

"James Richardson. In this house. What did he do to you?"

Feeling as if she's naked from the waist up, Julia folds her arms over her chest. "Don't be ridiculous. Why aren't you going to work?"

"Asked you a question. Plain and simple."

"And I'm telling you, it's a silly question."

Bill groans as he stands from the bed. He often comes home from the factory rubbing his lower back or the thick muscles at the base of his neck. He walks over to the window that overlooks the street.

"He touch you?"

"Keep your voice down. You'll wake the girls."

"Answer me, then. He touch you?"

Julia backs into the doorway and leans there. "Why aren't you going to work, Bill?"

"You going to tell me what I walked in on last night?"

"You didn't walk in on anything. James was . . . he was comforting me. He was being kind."

"He was comforting my wife?" Bill says slowly, thinking about each word as if not quite certain what they mean.

"Yes, he was."

Julia stares at him. His rounded shoulders hang, his hair is mussed on top, his jawline droops. He has lost more of himself than Julia has in the years since Maryanne died. Studying him now, she realizes how weak he's become. So weak that all he remembers of their daughter is that she cried. All he remembers is her small red face and the tiny, rigid body. All he did during those few short months she lived was complain. He needed more sleep. Couldn't be expected to work a full day if he couldn't get a decent night's sleep. No one else's baby cried so much. Why theirs?

Bill unfastens the small buttons on the front of his shirt. Next, he unbuckles his belt, pulls it from his waistband, and tosses it on the bed.

"He lay his hands on you?"

Maybe Bill got so tired of all the crying he decided to stop it himself. Maybe that's what has weighed so heavily on him all these years. When he mumbled about being sorry, he wasn't talking about some woman down on Willingham or Elizabeth Symanski. Julia hadn't considered it before. Never. Now it's so obvious. The doctor was wrong. Babies don't die for no reason. It's not the grief that has made Bill so weak. It's the guilt.

"I asked you a question. Did he lay his hands on you?"

"Only after I laid mine on him."

Peeling off his shirt and tossing it on the bed, too, Bill lifts his eyes. "Excuse me? You want to repeat that?"

Though she's gone too far, Julia can't stop. She swallows and lifts her chin. She knows it now. Bill did something to Maryanne the night she died. He must have gone to the nursery while Julia slept. He must have decided he couldn't live with it another day. All those nights after Maryanne died, he walked through this house as if Julia weren't living in it alongside him. He looked past her, around her, through her. He was numb. He must have forgotten his guilt in these recent years, forgotten Maryanne. He became playful again, almost seemed to love Julia as he did in the beginning. But then came Grace's baby, Betty Lawson's baby, Elizabeth's disappearance—one of them reminded him, drew his guilt to the surface. She knows he did it, knows that's why he can't live with the thought of another child.

She had overslept the morning it happened. When she woke, startled by the silence, she threw back the covers. She stood on the cool oak floors, curled under her toes, and as she rubbed her feet together to warm them, she listened. Inside the nursery, the weight of the air lifted. The temperature dropped. It was as if a window opened. Or someone shook a blanket. She walked across the wooden floor, slowly, hoping it wouldn't squeak underfoot. At the crib, she placed one hand on the top rail, reached inside with the other. Maryanne's tiny leg was cool.

The pain of it took two weeks settling in and then it stayed. The doctor rubbed his thick gray eyebrows and said it happens sometimes. No good reason why. Don't go thinking you'll find one. Then he patted Bill on the back.

"After a time, she'll be ready again," the doctor had said.

In the beginning, people offered privacy. A soft touch on the shoulder. A hug. They brought casseroles and lemon squares. Grace came every day, slipping silently through the front door to do the laundry, push a broom, scrub the pots and pans. She was the only one brave enough to wade through it day after day. James worked outside. He raked leaves and cleaned gutters. When a few weeks had passed, Bill thanked Grace and James, sent them away with a handshake and a hug, and closed the door to Maryanne's room.

"Got to put it behind us," he had said.

When a few more months passed, people began to talk about time. They said it would heal Julia and Bill. Not to worry, it always healed. But the pain continued to sink in, deeper one day than it was the last.

She'd asked Bill, "Do you feel it's easier now?"

She needed to remember Maryanne, to talk about her. Julia needed to feel like she had been a good mother. Needed to feel like it wouldn't happen again.

"All the talk in the world won't bring her back," Bill had said, and slowly he came home from work later and later. He would drive himself down Alder Avenue, stagger through the door. Other nights, someone from the bar would bring him home and help him up the stairs. Strangers stumbling through her house, dropping her husband on her bed.

And finally, signaling the grief should be over, when almost a year had passed, people began to say Julia and Bill should try to have another baby. Such a shame that a lovely girl and a good man shouldn't have a child. Julia held out her arms to Bill, told him they ached. It started after Maryanne died, her shoulders and forearms and joints aching because she couldn't hold her baby.

"You want to say that to me again?" Bill says. His chest swells. He squeezes both hands into fists.

"It's been a long time since a man's touched me," Julia says. "James is as good as any other."

Bill crosses the room in two long strides and, grabbing Julia's upper arm, he slams her against the wall. Her head bounces off the doorframe. With one forearm across her chest, Bill holds her there. Standing over her, he smells like smoke from Harris's Bar. He seems larger again, like he was before Maryanne died. His chest pumps up and down as he breathes through his nose, his mouth closed tight.

Barely able to speak because of the weight of Bill's arm on her chest, Julia says, "Get. Out."

———

Today is the first day the men have gone back to work and Mr. Herze and the others will resume a normal schedule. Within the half hour, Mr. Herze will come home and Malina has yet to set supper on the table, mix his Vernors, or deal with the trampled flowers in the backyard. Perhaps she'll yank those snapdragons out entirely. Perhaps that would be best. But not until Julia has seen them. All day, Malina has kept watch for Julia, even knocked on her door a few times. Not even those twins have shown themselves. Checking the street for any sign of Mr. Herze's car and knowing she'll need to get home soon, Malina knocks one last time on Grace's door. From inside the house comes the sound of footsteps and the front door finally swings open.

"Thank goodness," Malina says, fingering the string of pearls at her neck. "You are home. I hope I didn't interrupt your supper."

Grace wipes her hands on a dish towel. "Not at all. James isn't home yet. Please, come in."

"No time, really," Malina says, crossing over the threshold. "Are you ill? It's so dreadfully dark and dreary in here."

"How may I help you, Malina?"

"A hammer," Malina says. "I'm in need of a hammer."

"A hammer?" Grace says.

"I've been all over the neighborhood. Perhaps James has one?"

"In the garage, I imagine."

No bulb hangs from the ceiling of the Richardsons' garage to light Malina's way. She pauses until her eyes adjust to the dim light and then she sees it—a large green metal toolbox pushed up against the back wall, where James won't accidentally run it over with his car. Next to the toolbox, several bags of clothing, shoes, purses, and belts have also been stored against the wall and out of the way. With one finger, Malina flips up the latch on the toolbox and opens the lid. Two hammers lie on top. Each has a rounded head and no clawed end. They are a different kind of hammer, not at all what she needs.

"What are these clothes here?" Malina shouts from the back of the garage. "Are they meant for the clothing drive?"

"Mr. Symanski brought them," Grace shouts back. "Mostly Ewa's things, I imagine. He asked that I get them to you, to the thrift store."

"Let me take them off your hands," Malina says. She gathers the three bags filled with clothing and leaves the belts, purses, and shoes for another time because they won't need to be laundered. Stepping back into the sunlight, the three bags cradled in her arms, she smiles at Grace. "I'll see that these get to the thrift store. You shouldn't be bothered with them. The news of Elizabeth must be especially difficult for you."

Grace lingers inside the shadow thrown by the house and smiles in lieu of proper thanks. "Did you find what you need?"

"It really isn't important," Malina says, tired of constantly concerning herself with Mr. Herze's hammer. He'll have no reason to take notice of his tools during these hot months. Before he sets about winterizing the house this autumn, she'll buy yet another hammer to replace what the twins stole from her, one with a red handle. "Why, Grace," Malina says, noticing how Grace's eyes flick from side to side and how she clings to the railing with both hands. "Are you frightened? Has something frightened you, dear?"

Grace shakes her head, but Malina knows fear when she sees it.

"You'll come to supper one night soon," Malina says, bracing the bags against her hips. "You and James. I'll spoil you before your little one comes along. That would be nice, don't you think?"

Grace really is a lovely person. A little young for a man like James, but that isn't for Malina to judge. She is, after all, much younger than Mr. Herze. She likes to tell people she was seventeen when she married, but really she was fifteen. Only thirteen when they first met. Perhaps this fear is something else Grace and Malina share in common.

"You'd like that, wouldn't you?" Malina says. "A warm supper served up by someone else for a change."

But before Grace can answer, Malina notices the cars driving past the house, more than normal for a lazy afternoon, and the sound of engines shutting off and doors slamming. For the first time in several days, husbands are coming home from work. A commotion rises up in the back alley—rocks spraying across a wooden fence. A black sedan slows behind Grace's house and rolls into the dark garage—James Richardson already home from work.

"I've got to run," Malina says, hurrying past Grace toward the street. "Very soon you'll come to supper. You and James. Won't that be lovely?"

CHAPTER TWENTY-FOUR

I t's nearly suppertime. Izzy and Arie are especially hungry because Aunt Julia never made lunch and they had to fend for themselves. Izzy stands at the end of her bed and yanks the bottom two corners of her bedspread, but because she never bothered to straighten the sheets beneath, it won't ever look as tidy as Arie's. Izzy crosses both hands over her rumbling stomach and takes a good long look at her work. For the second time, Arie says that she would like to help but can't because it's against the rules, but do a good job and Aunt Julia might fry up some chicken for supper. Izzy says she can fix her own bed, thank you very much and now she wishes Arie hadn't mentioned fried chicken because her stomach hurts even worse.

Arie always makes her bed first thing in the morning. She will tug at her sheets until they are taut, tuck sharp hospital corners, and snap her bedspread so it floats smoothly, perfectly down over the bed. Deciding she doesn't care about a smooth quilt even if it means no supper, Izzy flops down on her mattress, folds her arms behind her head, and wonders why Aunt Julia would throw food against the kitchen wall and if Uncle Bill will ever come home again or if he, like Izzy's mom, is gone for good.

Sitting on her own perfectly made bed, Arie shakes her head at Izzy and continues to work the tip of a steak knife through the belt they found in Mrs. Richardson's garage. Before starting, Arie had measured out the size of Patches' neck as best she could remember so when she eventually works the knife through, they'll be able to buckle the belt to create a loop that is the perfect size.

"Girls?" It's Aunt Julia tapping on the door. "May I come in?"

The door opens and Aunt Julia walks into the room. Her face and neck are red and her hair is mussed on top. If she had been downstairs frying chicken, she'd be wearing her white cotton bib apron, but she's not. Izzy sure was hoping for fried chicken.

"Do you girls need to talk about Elizabeth?" Aunt Julia says. "Do you have questions?"

Both shake their heads. They saw Elizabeth only a few times a year. Sometimes they would sit with her while Aunt Julia talked with Mr. and Mrs. Symanski, but she never spoke.

"Then I think we need to have a conversation about stealing?" Aunt Julia says.

Izzy and Arie had hoped Aunt Julia was going to tell them not to worry, that Uncle Bill would be home soon and that the argument was just a silly thing between grown-ups. That's what they had hoped for. That, and a plate of chicken.

"I would have thought you knew better," Aunt Julia says.

"Izzy did it," Arie says, holding the knife in one hand and the belt in the other. The clear jewels on the small buckle shine because she cleaned them with a cotton ball and rubbing alcohol. Arie points the knife at Izzy. "I wasn't even there." And then she lowers the knife when she remembers she's not supposed to ever point one. "Sorry," she says, even though Aunt Julia didn't see.

Aunt Julia exhales and blinks slowly like she's tired of teaching the two of them a lesson. She waves Izzy off her bed, pulls back the bedspread, and begins straightening and smoothing her sheets.

"You didn't have any," Izzy says. "I checked all the cupboards. We needed it for Patches. I'll pay him back."

"I'll help earn the money," Arie says, already feeling bad for telling on Izzy.

Aunt Julia tucks two perfect hospital corners on Izzy's bed, shakes out the blue spread, and lets it fall into place. "You'll pay who back?" she says, then sits and cradles Izzy's pillow in her arms.

"Mr. Beersdorf."

"The hammer belongs to Mr. Beersdorf?" Aunt Julia fluffs the pillow and, holding it by two corners, gives it a good shake and props it against the center of the headboard. "You know you aren't supposed to go that far."

"No," Izzy says. "That's Mrs. Herze's hammer."

"Why do you have Malina's hammer, of all things?"

Arie scoots to the edge of her mattress and lets her legs hang over the edge. She sets the knife on the dresser between their two beds and lays the belt over her lap. "We saw her pounding her flowers with it and she was going to blame us. She tries to blame everything on us. We didn't do anything. We caught her and I took it so we could show you. We weren't stealing."

"So the hammer belongs to Malina?" she says. "Why, then, do you owe Mr. Beersdorf money?"

"I stole a can of tuna from him," Izzy says.

Instead of whirling around to face Izzy, Aunt Julia stares at the belt spread across Arie's lap. The buckle glitters where it catches the sunlight.

"I wanted to put out tuna for Patches because she loves it. It was my idea. All my idea. Arie didn't even know. I tricked you into thinking I was Arie and I went to Beersdorf's by myself."

Aunt Julia says nothing.

Arie glances at Izzy and then at Aunt Julia. Arie wants Izzy to tell her what's wrong with Aunt Julia, but Izzy doesn't know. Aunt Julia stands and lifts the thin belt from Arie's lap.

"Where did you get this?" Aunt Julia asks, pulling the belt through a loose fist. When she reaches the buckle, she runs her pointer finger over the tiny, clear jewels.

Arie is frightened because Izzy can feel it deep in her chest. Izzy can hear her own heartbeat too, and the inside of her mouth swells until it feels too small for her tongue. That means Arie is feeling the same.

"Mrs. Richardson was going to throw it away," Arie says.

"It was with her trash," Izzy says. "We only took it because it was trash. It's going to be a leash for Patches."

Izzy stands so she can show Aunt Julia where Arie was making a new hole in the thin piece of leather, but Aunt Julia jerks the belt away.

"This is not Mrs. Richardson's belt. This is Elizabeth Symanski's." She waves the belt in Arie's face. "Where did you get it?"

"That's not right," Izzy says, slipping around Aunt Julia to sit next to Arie. She takes Arie's hand. "It was trash in Mrs. Richardson's garage."

"You stole this from Mr. Symanski?" Aunt Julia shakes her head as she says it. "I can't imagine you would do such a thing. How could you?"

"No," Izzy says.

Arie's eyes are closed and she is shaking her head so she doesn't have to look at the belt. "We'd never steal from Elizabeth, never steal from Mr. Symanski."

Aunt Julia hugs the belt to her chest. "How will I ever explain this to him? His daughter isn't even buried yet and you're stealing from her."

"We didn't, Aunt Julia," Izzy says. "We didn't."

"Let me make one thing perfectly clear. You are forbidden, and I mean forbidden, to leave this house. And I assume that hammer belongs to Mr. Herze, not Mrs. Herze. He's just come home, so you'll return it now. See that you apologize and then straight back here with you both. I imagine Uncle Bill will treat you to a whipping and then give you chores to earn money so you can repay Mr. Beersdorf." Holding the belt against her chest with both hands, Aunt Julia walks from the room.

"We didn't steal it," Izzy shouts after her. "I promise, we didn't steal."

"In this house," Aunt Julia says, pausing in the doorway, "your promises amount to nothing."

———

Taking tiny steps so as to not trip over the curb, Malina walks faster, almost runs from Grace's house to hers, ignoring the cars that drive past, all of them carrying husbands home to supper. Though her hair falls into her eyes, she can't stop to brush it away because in her arms she carries three bags of clothes. By the time she reaches the sidewalk leading to her house, she knows she's too late. Mr. Herze's blue sedan sits in the driveway and on the porch—her porch—stand those twins.

Mr. Herze leans in the doorway like a younger man might do, his body loose, one leg crossed over the other. In his hands, he holds something and shakes his head.

"What are you two doing here?" Malina says. "You shouldn't be bothering Mr. Herze."

"Aunt Julia made us," the one twin says. "She said we stole and we have to apologize to both of you."

Malina walks up the stairs and positions herself between the twins, forcing them to stumble as they move aside.

"What on earth have you done?" she says, and drops the bags. Flimsy blouses and rumpled skirts scatter at Mr. Herze's feet.

"Malina?" Mr. Herze says.

A shiny silver hammer with a brown handle lies in Mr. Herze's open palm. It's clean again, as if Julia scrubbed and dried it before sending the girls to return it.

"These girls say they took this from our backyard," Mr. Herze says, holding the hammer out for Malina to inspect.

She touches the smooth brown handle. "Is it yours?"

"Not mine," Mr. Herze says.

"She was pounding down her flowers," the one twin says. It's the loud one who is entirely too full of herself. "We saw her and she was going to blame us. She told us our cat was dead and that we ruined those flowers. She says we trampled them and peed on them. That's why we took the hammer."

Mr. Herze shoves the tool at Malina. "Is this true?"

"How can it be true if we don't own such a hammer? They're telling tales. I shouldn't venture to guess why."

The timid twin backs down the stairs.

"We have to give it back," the mouthy twin says. "We took it and we're sorry. It's yours." And she jumps from the porch, grabs the other one's hand, and together they run across the lawn, leap Malina's hedge of wilted snapdragons, and sprint across the street.

"I went looking for my hammer," Mr. Herze says. "Wanted to assure those two this wasn't mine." He wraps his hand around the handle and taps the flat head in his palm. "Couldn't find it."

Malina tucks under her skirt and kneels to the clothes spilled across her porch. These must be Elizabeth Symanski's things. So much lavender and pink. She did love her pastels, even though they washed her out. As Malina shoves the clothes back into the bags, she says, "I'm sure I don't know anything about hammers and such."

Shoving the last of the clothes into the bags, Malina gathers them, but before she can stand, Mr. Herze's hand strikes her left cheek. She stumbles across the porch, falls into the banister, and the bags of clothes fly into the front yard. The railing knocks the wind out of her. Her diaphragm contracts like a fist opening and closing. She gasps for air, trying to fill her lungs, and presses both hands over her cheek. Beneath this cover, the sting fades to a burn. She sucks in one good breath and glances at the neighbors on either side.

"Was it you?" Mr. Herze says. Sweat trickles down the sides of his face and disappears into his jowls. "You're best served to tell me now. Did you kill her?"

Malina drops her hands from her face. It's the strangest of feelings, when a person has the wind knocked out of her. The body wanting so badly to draw in a breath and yet it can't. Staring at Mr. Herze, this is how her body struggles yet again. Slowly, she shakes her head.

Mr. Herze will go into the kitchen now and mix his own drink while he waits for the television set to warm up. This used to happen more often. When Malina was younger, she was careless and would lie without thinking. Maybe she would forget to cook the spareribs in the refrigerator and when they spoiled she would throw them out and lie about the smell coming from the garbage can. With age, she learned to be more careful, to not give herself reason to lie. Pride. That's what made her lie about the driving and the hammer. No woman wants the others to see her driveway standing empty long after her husband should be home.

"This will not end well," Mr. Herze says. He also looks up and down Alder Avenue as if he, too, is concerned about the neighbors, then walks inside and slams the door.

Day 8

CHAPTER TWENTY-FIVE

A ll of the ladies were out and about this morning after spending a quiet day yesterday to reflect on the loss of Elizabeth
and the state of their own neighborhood. Because most of them
traveled to Willingham for their regular shopping trip, news will
have spread and everyone will know about Grace and Orin and the
colored men. They will have watched Grace and the men from behind the cover of heavy drapes, but they won't have heard enough.
They'll want to know more but won't dare ask. Malina is one to ask.
No longer able to ignore Malina's shouts, Grace finally stops on the
sidewalk.

"I'm running late," Grace says, tugging at her white gloves as
she walks toward Malina. Julia's house is directly across the street.
Another morning has passed with no phone call or bus ride. Maybe
on her way home, Grace will be able to stop in for a visit. She'll feel
better after spending some time on Willingham, stronger again.
Mrs. Nowack and the women will help her make pierogi and they
won't ask about the colored men or wonder what terrible things

Grace has done. They'll mix up dough, roll it, boil it, and send Grace home with a box full of pierogi. It'll be easier to breathe as soon as she gets to Willingham, and when she returns, she'll stop to see Julia. "I'm afraid I haven't time to visit."

"I didn't realize how much mending there was to do with those clothes I took from your garage," Malina says.

Inside her own garage, Malina is bent over one of the several boxes and bags that cover the floor. Old clothes, sheets, and towels spill out of each one. She lifts a delicate yellow blouse, holds it up by the shoulders, shakes it, and folds it over her arm.

"I'm afraid I didn't realize either." Grace checks her watch. The bus will be along shortly. She resists glancing back at Julia's house. James said Grace should pop in for a visit because Julia was having a tough time of it. The bus will be along shortly and Grace can't miss it. She'll have to visit Julia later. "If you'll point out which bag," she says. "I'll get right to it."

Malina scans the garage floor. Beyond her, Warren Herze's tools hang from a pegboard. More and more of the neighborhood men have taken up the same idea, all of them so worried about their tools. Folks can't be trusted anymore, some of them say. Not like it used to be. Got to keep track as best we can. All the tools fit perfectly, as if they are part of a child's puzzle. The hammer is the one missing piece.

"There," Malina says. "Right near your feet. That whole bag needs to be mended. I hate to ask it of you. Perhaps one of the other ladies can help."

"I'll get busy on them today."

There is a pause while Malina digs into another bag and Grace braces for the questions. What ever were you doing talking with a Negro, and why would you have Orin shoot the man? What is it that you know, Grace Richardson, that the rest of us don't? With Elizabeth lying in a box, won't you tell us what you know?

"You're a dear," Malina says, and continues her sorting and folding.

The pause ends. No questions. Not even a mention of Elizabeth or her funeral or what could be done for poor Mr. Symanski.

"I'll get some help with these," Grace says, groaning as she bends to lift the brown bag.

"Thank you ever so much," Malina says, staring at the peg-board. "Feel free to drop them at the thrift store when you're finished."

———

Julia should get up. Every other morning, she's out of bed by six thirty. Breakfast for Bill, dishes, and then breakfast for the twins. They usually want pancakes. But Bill is gone, and the girls, even if they are awake, make no noise. They don't need her yet, but before the day is over, they will. Soon enough, if not already, everyone will know Bill is gone. It's as if Maryanne has died a second time. As if Julia knowing the truth brought back her baby and killed her again. As if Julia knowing is as bad as what Bill did. The pain of it sits on her chest, pressing down so she struggles for every breath. Her legs are heavy. Her arms ache.

She must have dozed off, because when she wakes again, the room is hot. Swinging both legs off the edge of the bed, she rests her feet on the floor and pushes herself into a sitting position. At first she welcomes the stillness. Near the door, her packed suitcase waits for her. She had planned to leave the girls with Bill, but that was before. Now that he is gone, they can come with her. They'll make a vacation of it. The girls need some time away. All this acting out can be cured with a little extra time spent together. They'll ride on the train, stay in a nice hotel, eat supper at a fine restaurant. The nurses and doctors at the Willows will see how good Julia is to the girls, how much they love one another, and they'll give her a baby even though she has no husband. Even though Elizabeth Symanski will never come home. Even though Julia's own baby died.

In the kitchen, Julia scrambles eggs instead of frying pancakes, but then she notices the time. It's past noon, too late really for breakfast. She listens for the girls in their room overhead. She waits for footsteps pounding down the hallway or the sound of one of them bouncing off her mattress, the springs creaking under her weight. Nothing. She leans over the sink so she can see into the backyard. During this time of day, they like to sit in the shade thrown by Bill's shed. Using white sticks of chalk, they draw on the concrete slab there. Sometimes tic-tac-toe boxes, other times line figures. The slab is empty and the latest drawings have been worn away to a few white slashes. At the bottom of the stairs, she shouts overhead, "Izzy, Arie, come on down."

She waits but hears nothing.

The girls need to bathe so their hair will have time to dry before they leave for the station. There must be several trains to choose from. The newspaper article said every line in the country leads straight into the heart of Kansas City. They probably leave at all hours. She slides the eggs to a cool burner, sits, and flips through the phonebook, not entirely certain what she is searching for.

It's nearly one o'clock when she thinks of the girls again. Most of the year, she is alone in the house while Bill is off to work. She is accustomed to the quiet, to the creak of the fan, the hum of the refrigerator when it clicks on. She forgets sometimes that it should be otherwise when the girls are visiting. She looks out the back window again and then out the front door. So she can get a better view, she walks to the end of the driveway, the bright sunlight making her squint. She calls for the girls up and down the street. No sign of them. Back inside, she climbs the stairs and opens their bedroom door.

The walls are white because the girls couldn't agree on a color two years ago when Bill painted it. And when Julia bought each a new bedspread for her bed, they still couldn't agree. It was blue popcorn chenille for Izzy and yellow for Arie. Arie makes her bed every morning without being asked. She tucks her hospital corners, straightens her bedspread, and fluffs her pillow. Izzy is careless with her bed, leaving the wrinkled sheets and the bedspread to hang unevenly. Julia can't bear to see one half of the room tidy and the other disheveled, so she always fixes Izzy's bed. Arie should complain, has a right to, but she never does. Some days, Arie tries to do the work for her sister, but Julia won't allow it. Izzy might break the rules. Arie never does.

This morning, this afternoon, like always, Arie's yellow bedspread lies smoothly across her bed and her pillow is centered on the headboard. Izzy's should be untidy. Her spread should be crumpled, her pillow flat where she slept on it. But Izzy's bed is as well made as Arie's. It looks like it did yesterday after Julia fixed it. She had scolded the girls for stealing from Mr. Symanski. She had told them their promises meant nothing. Izzy's bed looks as if it hasn't been slept in and the rosary that usually hangs from Arie's headboard is gone.

Stumbling backward, Julia grabs for the doorknob to steady herself. They were here last night. After Julia made a mess of the kitchen. After James came. No, that was Wednesday. They were home Wednesday. And then Thursday. Bill and she argued that morning. She told him to keep his voice down. The girls were sleeping. Bill trapped Julia against the wall and she ordered him to go. And then the stolen tuna and the hammer and Elizabeth's belt. That was last night. Did she fix them supper? Surely she fed them. But what did she prepare? And didn't she see them to bed before falling asleep herself?

She runs down the stairs and into the kitchen. Food overflows the trash can. The sour smell spills out into the living room and the foyer. There are only a few dirty dishes in the sink and dried-out strips of crust peeled from bread and slivers of SPAM—the girls' favorite. Sandwiches they made for themselves.

Back in the foyer, Julia fumbles through her address book until she finds the number, dials, and waits. She had not asked where Bill was going when he left, but he had no choice other than his brother's house. Catherine answers. No, Bill isn't here. No, she doesn't know where he is, at work most likely, and yes, she'll pass on the message when she hears from him. Call back as soon as there's news. Julia hangs up the phone. The house is empty. Like Elizabeth Symanski, the twins are gone.

———

Malina stands in her garage, surrounded by the donations she has gathered from the ladies. She really should have done a better job sorting and delivering them as they arrived on her doorstep. Across the street, Julia Wagner walks out of her house, and from the end of her driveway, she shouts for those twins. She must be calling them home to lunch. Malina tosses aside the gentleman's shirt she had been folding and steps out of the garage into the sunlight.

Julia disappears inside and the street is quiet for a short while. She reappears, this time stumbling out the front door and down the drive. Her red hair hangs in her face and she wears a white cotton gown—her nightclothes. She begins to shout at the girls to come home. Over and over, she calls for them, her words stretching out to make room for her accent. Most days, Julia stands on her front porch and shouts at those girls as if calling home a dog. But something is different about her voice today. It's strained, like she is nearly out of breath, and it's pitched a bit higher, each word a bit rounder. That's a scream. Yes, a person would call that a scream. Watching until Julia has disappeared back into her house, Malina runs inside, grabs her driving gloves and the car keys, and throws open the front door.

Slowing the car as she reaches the intersection of Woodward and Willingham, Malina turns right and parks in front of Wilson's Cleaners. The street is empty because it's past lunchtime. All of the ladies have come and gone. In a few weeks, at this very hour on a Saturday afternoon, the street will fill with folding tables and chairs. People from all over the city will come to buy homemade baked goods. They will have only Malina to thank for it. How many hours has she spent planning where each table will sit, following up to make certain every lady has done her baking, even brewing and serving the fresh coffee herself?

Once past Wilson's Cleaners, Malina crosses Willingham and walks toward the factory. The men are back to work and the lot is full, but from the far side of the street, she'll be able to see through all the cars, and among them, she'll find Mr. Herze's. It will be there. She's certain of it. After those twins left the house yesterday, Malina had gathered up the clothing scattered across her lawn and followed Mr. Herze into the house. She promised him she had seen nothing, done nothing. He pushed her away, pulled on his hat, and left without another word. All night, he was gone, never came home to breakfast, and even when Malina left the house at well past noon, he had not yet come home. Surely he's not the reason Julia stood at the end of her driveway, screaming and wearing her nightclothes.

Malina hasn't been to Nowack's Bakery in several days. None of the ladies are shopping there anymore because she won't close on payday. It's odd, then, that the door stands open and the strong smell of sautéed onions seeps outside. With no customers, who would Mrs. Nowack be baking for? The fans are running, too. Another sign that Mrs. Nowack is baking. Malina intended to walk past without even glancing at the shop. She intended to slip around the corner and from there, watch the parking lot. She certainly never intended to go inside the bakery, but that carriage stood in the center of the store, where a person walking past couldn't help but see it.

She walks up the stairs that lead to the door and crosses inside. A small bell chimes. Straight ahead, the carriage's black canopy is raised, and a yellow quilt lies across the bassinet. The canopy's frame is twisted and the handle rusted. She moves closer, first sliding one foot across a white square tile and then another across a black tile.

"You are coming to buy bread?" Mrs. Nowack says, walking out from the back room. Her gray skirt is dusted with flour and her cheeks are red and shiny.

"I'm doing no such thing."

Malina inches closer to the carriage.

Mrs. Nowack pushes aside the black curtain that leads to the back of the store. "Cassia," she calls. "You are to be coming here to fetch this baby."

A girl—*the* girl—walks out from behind the curtain. Her black hands are coated with flour up to her wrists and she wears a small white apron around her waist. She stops when she sees Malina.

"It's too hot out back," the girl says, staring at Malina. "You said my baby shouldn't be back there."

"You are to be taking her," Mrs. Nowack says. "And you, if you are not buying, you are leaving."

Malina takes another step toward the carriage, the narrow heel of her shoe tapping the floor. "I'll do no such thing," she says.

The girl is smaller even than she appeared the other night walking down a dark street. She rests her tiny hands on the carriage's handle and pulls it toward her. Her face is like a doll's; her shoulders and hips, slight. There must be an odor to her, like the one Malina washes from Mr. Herze's shirts, but Malina can't smell it over the onions and butter. With the carriage in hand, the girl backs toward the curtain, her feet so small and light they move silently. This girl wasn't supposed to be the mother. The other woman—the

larger one with rounded, full hips and thick legs—she was supposed to be the mother. But here is this girl, Mr. Herze's girl, pulling on a carriage that carries Mr. Herze's baby.

As if she belongs in this place, Grace Richardson walks out
from the back room, a large white pastry box in hand.

"We have a good start, Mrs. Nowack." She stops when she sees
Malina and sets the box on the counter as if hoping Malina didn't
see her carrying it.

"I want to see inside that carriage," Malina says.

Grace reaches out with one bare hand and touches the girl's
arm. She touches that girl as if they know each other. She touches
that girl as if they care for each other.

"We're nearly done back there," Grace says to the girl. "It's not
so hot anymore."

"I want to see under that quilt," Malina says.

The girl tilts her small face and studies Malina. She is probably
remembering Malina from a picture, perhaps the one on Mr.
Herze's desk. The girl shakes her head.

"I gave it back," the girl says. "I already gave it back."

"Stop talking your gibberish." Malina stomps one white heel.
"I've a right to look in that carriage."

"I already gave that hammer back," the girl says again.

Grace crosses in front of the girl and pushes the carriage behind
her. "This is of no interest to you, Malina," she says. And then,
leaning forward so she can whisper, Grace says, "I promise you, it's
of no concern to you."

"Of course it's of no concern to me," Malina says, and backs
toward the door, but she stops when she notices the white box

sitting on the counter. "Those are not pierogi, are they, Grace Richardson? I couldn't imagine you'd let these women prepare food we are to eat. You have them do your cooking, and you leave your mending to me? It's shameful."

Grace was going to be Malina's friend. She and James were going to come to supper and then she would call Malina for coffee and they might spend afternoons chatting together while the baby slept. Malina would bring sweet baby clothes as gifts and Grace would be her friend.

"You, Grace Richardson, are shameful."

CHAPTER TWENTY-SIX

At the picnic table behind the bakery, Grace sits and, with white thread and a needle, reattaches a button to one of the dresses Mr. Symanski left in her garage. It's the perfect excuse to stay a bit longer. She sits quietly, has for several minutes, so the baby has woken and is kicking and rolling. In between stitches, Grace rests a hand on her stomach to feel a small foot or knee. Each time she does, Cassia reaches out and lays her hand alongside Grace's.

After Malina stomped out of the bakery, Cassia and the other women had worked silently to clean up from the pierogi, and because Mrs. Nowack had no more cooking or baking for them to do, they set to work on Grace's mending. Sitting opposite Grace, Sylvie and Lucille each hold a dress close to their noses, squinting as they poke a needle through the fabric and pull it out the other side. Every so often, they hold up their dresses by the shoulders, swing them from side to side, and show off their work. Sitting next to Grace, Cassia rocks her carriage. Her motion carries through the wooden seat. Julia once said, before Maryanne died, that a woman rocks a baby in time to her own heart. That's what Grace feels— Cassia's heartbeat.

"Who these dresses belong to?" Sylvie asks.

Grace runs her fingers across the buttons on the bodice of the dress resting in her lap.

"Elizabeth," she says.

"If you're giving them away," Cassia says, still rocking, "why you fixing them?"

"It's the right thing to do."

Cassia shrugs and Sylvie and Lucille carry on with their mending. Sylvie works a needle as quickly and smoothly as Grace's own mother. Lucille struggles to reattach the buttons, shouting out every so often when she pokes herself.

"Do you know Malina Herze?" Grace asks, tugging on the cuff of one of Elizabeth's dresses. She doesn't look at any of them as she asks the question. "Before she came here today, did you know her?"

Sylvie sets aside her needle and thread, folds the dress over one arm. "Yeah, we know her. Know she causes trouble for Mrs. Nowack."

"Does she cause any other trouble?"

"Person causes one kind of trouble," Lucille says, biting through a strand of thread, "they bound to cause another."

"You should stay away from her, Cassia."

Cassia squirms on her seat. "I gave it back," she says. "No one should be giving me any trouble. I kept it with me at first, but I gave it back."

"The hammer?" Grace says. "Are you talking about a hammer?" She pauses, waiting for an answer. "Why did you have Malina's hammer? Who did you give it to?"

"I found it," Cassia says. "And I returned it."

"She didn't do no such thing," Lucille says. She flicks her eyes toward the carriage and winks at Grace. "Cassia is confused, is all. She didn't have no hammer. She just gets herself confused." Having finished her work, Lucille passes the lavender dress to Grace and reaches into the brown bag for another. The beads on her thin braids rattle as she moves. "Will the ladies come back now? Will they come shopping here again?"

"I'm sorry," Grace says, holding the dress by its shoulders so she can inspect it. "But I don't think so."

She gives the dress a shake, irons it flat with her hands, and fingers the lace collar. Elizabeth used to scratch and tug at her neckline whenever she wore the dress, but she never asked to take it off. Birthdays and Easter. It was always her favorite. And every year, twice a year, Ewa would bend and straighten her fingers and complain about the dress's tiny buttons and stiff lace. Lifting the dress to her face, Grace inhales. It smells of Elizabeth, a light, sweet scent, the same as Ewa.

"The first day I came here, you mentioned a woman. I think her name was Tyla." Grace hugs Elizabeth's dress. "She was the woman who was killed here, wasn't she?"

The women look among themselves but say nothing.

"You must have known her. You must miss her."

"Ain't no one missing Tyla," Cassia says.

Sylvie lays a hand on Cassia's shoulder. "She was mean as a snake, that's for sure."

"Both of you, hush." It's Lucille. With one eye closed, she is trying to thread a needle with blue thread. "No one needs to talk about that." The thread finds its way through the eye of the needle and Lucille looks at Grace. "No need to talk about that," she says again.

Grace folds Elizabeth's dress in half and then in half again. "Stay away from Malina," Grace says to Cassia.

Grace will have to return to Alder Avenue soon. She'll stop at Julia's and apologize for having not visited earlier. It's time to go home.

"As best you can, stay away."

———

Standing in Julia's kitchen, tugging on their thick belts and tapping their heavy boots, the police don't understand. How could they? No, Bill isn't here. He's been gone since yesterday morning. Julia doesn't know where. She called his brother's house. They'll tell him when they see him. He wasn't at work, either. When did she last see the girls? She can't remember. They don't understand why she can't remember. Julia must have cooked the girls something for supper. The mess in the kitchen is nothing. It was an accident. She tipped over the garbage. Yes, Julia must have cooked them supper, must have seen them to bed after they took a bath and washed their hair, but she can't remember.

The officer with brown hair scribbles with a yellow pencil. His name is Thompson. He's the man who counted out eight houses and told Julia she probably didn't see quite as much as she thought she saw the day Elizabeth disappeared. He was the first to know it was Julia's fault Elizabeth would never come home.

"Their bedroom?" he asks, and both men follow Julia upstairs.

This is where they sleep. Arie in the yellow. Izzy in the blue. Julia always tidies up for Izzy. She isn't so handy making a bed. But not today. It was already done so nicely. Julia begins to cry. She tells them that yesterday Izzy tricked her and snuck away to Beersdorf's. The officers already know this. They'll keep checking the streets between here and there, but so far, no sign of either girl.

Walking down the stairs, one of the officers holds Julia by the elbow so she won't stumble. At the landing, she looks through the front door that stands open. Out on Alder Avenue, people are coming and going. No one bothers to close the door.

There was a belt and stolen tuna and the hammer. The girls came home with a hammer. They stole it from a neighbor's yard. Malina Herze's yard. Julia scolded them. She ordered them to return it and apologize. She must have insisted, because why wouldn't she? Yes, now she remembers. They did try to take it back. They came home a few minutes later and said Mr. Herze didn't want the hammer. He said it wasn't his and a man would know his own hammer, but he took it anyway. If Warren Herze was home, it must have been after five. Five thirty or so. That's it. She last saw them shortly after five o'clock. Yesterday. No, Bill wasn't home. Yes, he was gone all night.

Soon enough, porch lights will glow up and down the street

and stray beams of light, cast off from flashlights, will dart around side yards and throw their glare on picture windows. Everyone is remembering Elizabeth Symanski and hoping this doesn't turn out the same.

———

When the two officers have made their way down Julia's sidewalk and it's apparent they are headed to Malina's house, she walks back into the dining room and picks a carrot from the bunch lying on the table. Its leafy greens are a beautiful deep shade, not yet drooping or turning brown. The orange color is uniform from top to bottom. Suitable for one of her cakes. Behind her, in the kitchen, the side door creaks. Mr. Herze must have left it ajar. So odd he would go directly into the garage when arriving home early from work. Malina had watched him through the kitchen window. Wearing a shirt and tie and his best leather shoes, he walked from his car in through the garage's side door. When he reappeared seconds later, Malina hurried back into the living room. He entered the house through the door off the kitchen, rushed past Malina, and as he climbed the stairs two at a time, he called out that he'd be taking up with the search party. When he came back down the stairs, red faced and panting and moving slower than he had on the way up, he wore brown slacks, a weekend shirt, and the shoes he normally wore when mowing the lawn. He left the house through the front door.

Shifting her attention back to the carrot, Malina rolls it from side to side, grabs the grater with her left hand, and begins to scrub the carrot over its tiny blades. Through her front window, she has been watching the ladies gather at the ends of their driveways. There is no reason for anyone to suspect Mr. Herze, no reason Malina should. Had she bothered to walk a few yards past the bakery, she would have seen his sedan parked in its usual spot. But in the end, she hadn't seen the need. She left the bakery, marched to her car, and drove straight home.

It meant nothing to see that girl with the carriage. Any one of a dozen men could be the father of that child. Any one of a dozen women could be its mother. But there was the look the girl and Grace Richardson gave Malina. They both looked kindly upon Malina, their eyelids heavy, their lips slightly parted. They inhaled as if preparing to speak but not quite knowing the best words to use. They had looked at Malina with pity. With pity, for goodness sake.

Outside, the men and ladies continue to shout up and down the street. They leave their groups and spread out, disappearing around houses and down the block. It will do no good. If the twins were anywhere near, they would have heard the first call, and while their manners are atrocious, they generally come running when Julia calls. Still, from far away, and somewhat closer and as close as the next yard over, people shout out to those twins. Malina hears their calls through the mesh screen in her open dining-room window. Arie. Izzy. Or Arabelle. Isabelle. At the sound of a knock, Malina sets down the carrot, wipes her hands on her apron, and opens the door.

"Mrs. Herze?" the officer asks.

It's the officer with the dark curls. He asks Malina's name as if he doesn't remember her. She was hoping for the sweet blond detective with the red lips.

"Certainly," Malina says.

"We've a few questions for you," the one with the straight brown hair says. "You are familiar with the girls who live across the street?"

"They don't live there," Malina says. "They are only visiting."

"And you are aware they're missing?"

"My husband is among the men searching."

"Yes, ma'am," the officer with dark curls says. "We understand they came to see you yesterday."

"You make it sound as if they were visiting for pleasure."

The straight-haired officer flips open a small notebook and taps on it with a pencil. He is hurrying Malina along.

"They are a menace, those two," she says. "They were sent to deliver an apology." Malina unties the apron at her waist and folds it over one arm. "Would you like to see what they did to my flowerbeds?"

"Do you recall the time of their visit, ma'am?"

"I certainly do. Five forty-five. Precisely. Mr. Herze had arrived home, and he is always quite precise."

"And they had stolen something from you, ma'am?"

Malina smooths the apron that lies over her arm. She line dries them every Saturday morning, sprinkles warm water on them, and presses each with a hot iron. Behind her, the side door creaks, drawn open by the breeze that whips past the two officers and through the house. If they would ask, Malina would tell them. She knows she would. If only they would ask her. . . . Do you think your husband is a bad man? Has he done bad things? Why would those girls steal a hammer? Such an odd thing for two girls to do. She would tell the truth, wouldn't she, if only they would ask.

"Those two stole the fruits of my labor," she says. "Ruined my lovely flowers."

"A hammer?" one officer says, glancing at the small notebook he holds in his hand. "Yes, a hammer. They were here to return the tool?"

"Why on earth would I know about such a thing?"

"They didn't return a hammer to Mr. Herze?"

"In order to return something, one must have first borrowed it."

"But the girls were here?"

"To deliver an apology, yes."

"And have you seen them since? Today, have you seen them today?" the curly-haired officer asks. "Or your husband? Is he available? Perhaps he has seen them."

"He is most certainly not available. I already told you he is searching with the others. And no, I haven't seen them. They're wild, you know. It's no wonder. Can the police really do nothing to help this neighborhood? First Elizabeth Symanski and now this."

The officer with the cropped brown hair flips his small notebook closed but does not answer.

"Do you mean to imply they have been gone since last evening?" Malina says. "Do you mean to imply they've been gone all this time?"

The officer with the curls nods and pulls a sheet of folded paper from his back pocket. "Is this familiar to you?"

Malina leans over the crumpled flyer. LOST CAT, it reads.

"They were taped up in a nearby neighborhood. Mrs. Wagner

thought your husband may have given them to the girls. She said he'd made other similar flyers."

Malina touches the glossy paper. "I'm sure I wouldn't know. What difference does that make to the matter at hand?"

"Only trying to determine their comings and goings." The officer pulls on his hat, tips his head, says thank you, and asks Malina to contact them should she remember anything else.

Once the officers are gone, Malina walks back into the dining room to continue her work. When she has grated the first carrot down to a nub, she picks another from her pile and gives it the same inspection. Outside on Alder, men begin climbing into cars two at a time. Like Malina, they have received word the girls have been gone for hours, have been gone since coming to see Mr. Herze. The men are spreading out. A few of them will likely drive to the river where they found Elizabeth Symanski.

Rolling the carrot from side to side, Malina decides it, too, is good enough for one of her cakes. She begins to scrub it over the grater but stops when blood trickles down the knuckles of her first and second finger. She wipes them on her apron, making a mental note to scrub the stain with a toothbrush and dollop of baking soda, and starts on the next carrot.

Soon enough, the pile of carrots grows too large and falls over on itself, spraying orange slivers across the white tablecloth. Two cups per cake and she must have at least six cups by now. Everyone who comes to the bake sale hopes for one of Malina's cakes. It's a shame to disappoint any of them. Three more cakes means three more happy people. With both hands, she scoops up a pile of carrots and walks from the dining room toward the kitchen. A few of the orange slivers float down, spinning, tumbling onto the floor. As she passes the side door, she stops. Outside, voices continue to call out. Holding the carrots in her upturned palms, she kicks open the door and walks across the driveway.

Mr. Herze keeps his garage just so. He sweeps the concrete floor every Saturday and stores his nails and screws in wide-mouthed mason jars, each topped with a gold lid. Malina has ruined his tidy space with her bags and boxes. As if presenting the carrots to someone, Malina walks into the garage, stepping this way and that and lifting her knees when need be. Once near Mr. Herze's workbench, she stops. Straight ahead, every outline on the pegboard is full. The hammer—Mr. Herze's hammer—fits perfectly inside its black outline. The red-handled hammer, second tool from the left, hangs exactly as it should. Exactly as it had been the night Malina took it from the wall, tucked it in her handbag, and drove to Willingham Avenue. Exactly as it had been when that woman startled Malina and then said such terrible things. Things like what happens when a white man fathers a Negro child, how that baby will be the spitting image of the white man and everyone will know who fathered that child. And the girl, Mr. Herze's girl, shouted at the woman to shut her mouth. Told the woman to never say one thing bad about the baby in the carriage or she'd be sorry. Goddamn it, she'd be sorry. The woman laughed at the girl. You're crazy as a loon, the woman had said, and Malina ran away, leaving her hammer behind. That hammer, that same hammer, hangs exactly as it should in its spot on Mr. Herze's pegboard.

———

Grace gets off the bus at Alder, and the moment she starts down the street toward home she notices something is familiar. Not familiar in a way that makes her happy to be home. It's familiar in a way that makes her breath quicken, her skin turn cold, and her mouth go dry.

Balancing the pastry box on her large stomach and cradling the bag of mended clothes in one arm, she walks straight ahead, trying not to notice all of the ladies standing in their front yards, a few poking about behind bushes. She doesn't take notice when cars drive up from behind and men who should be at work climb out. She doesn't even look when James's black sedan rolls past. A block ahead, he pulls into the driveway, doesn't bother driving around to the garage, and runs back to Grace. He takes the box and bag from her.

"Anything?" he asks.

James's hair is slicked back from his face where he's combed it out of the way with his fingers, and smears of black grease cover his forearms where he didn't take the time to wash up. A dull pain rolls around Grace's baby. She doesn't answer.

"Anything?" he says again. "Has Julia heard anything?"

Grace backs away.

"The twins?" she says.

Next, James will sketch a map of the neighborhood on the back of an envelope. He'll draw boxes around each block and assign men two at a time. When it begins to get dark, all of the ladies will switch on their porch lights and they'll bring hot coffee. They'll check under porches and behind shrubs. A few men will walk around the Filmore, waiting, almost hoping someone from inside will come out. But they won't. The police have already arrived, probably the same two officers, but this time they park at Julia's house rather than Mr. Symanski's. Only Grace knows what has happened. Only she knows how the men have grabbed the girls by their thin arms, made them cry out. The twins are both stronger than Grace, if not in size, then in spirit. They would cry loudly, as loudly as they could, but the men would silence them. Only Grace knows.

"Grace," James says, bending to see into her face. "Are you well?"

The elms used to shade the front of their house and their lawn. Grace could leave the drapes open on the living-room windows year-round, but now the late-day sun would fade her sofa and carpeting. She holds up one hand to shield her eyes. James looks small, smaller than he ever has in all their married years.

"Did you check in the garage?" Grace says.

"The garage? You mean for the girls?"

Grace stares straight ahead at their own garage, its door open because she never closed it. Orin Schofield's empty chair leans against the far corner where James must have placed it. Orin hasn't come back outside since Grace called him to the street and showed him where the colored men now walk. She should have told Orin to pull the trigger. He'd have done it, if only she'd have let him.

Out on Alder Avenue, more cars pull into driveways and more husbands disappear inside before reappearing in their white undershirts and soft-soled shoes. Mr. Symanski comes too. He stands on the sidewalk outside Grace's house. He wears gray slacks, a pair Grace hasn't taken to the cleaners in several weeks. His white shirt is wrinkled and his tie hangs loose around his neck. His skin is fading to gray as if the life is draining out of him little by little. He won't really die. Instead, he'll continue to fade until eventually all of him is gone.

"Check every garage," Grace says, and walks past James onto the street.

CHAPTER TWENTY-SEVEN

At the sound of a car door slamming, the officer with dark curly hair stands from his chair at the kitchen table and walks into the entry. Julia remains seated, her hands flat on the red tabletop. She leans back and fingers a small chip in the Formica. This is the spot where Izzy usually sits. Grace must have already cleaned the table because its chrome edging shines, no fingerprints or water spots. Julia is never able to get such a shine when she cleans. It's the vinegar water Grace uses. Much stronger than Julia's.

The slamming car door is followed by footsteps on the porch. It'll be an officer or another man from the neighborhood asking for directions on where to search. Julia doesn't bother to check who it might be. At the kitchen sink, Grace wrings out a dishrag. She hasn't spoken since she arrived but promptly set about sweeping and mopping and scrubbing every surface with her strong vinegar water. Just as it was when Maryanne died. Grace is the one strong enough to tackle the inside of Julia's house.

"They told me it happens sometimes," Julia says.

Grace leans over the counter and continues to scrub the stains in the bottom of the sink, stains that have been there for years, stains Grace will get out that Julia never could.

"When Maryanne died, that's what the doctor said. Did I ever tell you?"

Pushing off the counter, Grace takes a clean towel from the drawer to her left and dries her hands. Her blond hair is swept back and held off her face by a white band. It's pure, lovely.

"Never seemed right to me. A baby dying for no good reason at all. Does that figure right to you?"

"No," Grace says. "No, it never did."

Julia should care this will upset Grace, make her worry after her own baby's safety, but she doesn't. She can't.

"He killed her."

A few feet shuffle, a reminder there are others in the room.

"Bill," Julia says. "That's why he's gone. He killed Maryanne, and he's seeing that I suffer for it. He's seeing to it I never have another baby."

Grace looks at someone beyond Julia's shoulder, but she doesn't care anymore what people know.

"Bill wouldn't," Grace says. "He'd never do such a thing."

"He couldn't stand the crying. That's what he said. Couldn't sleep, couldn't eat, couldn't work. Couldn't be bothered with her crying."

"Did he tell you this, ma'am?"

The voice comes from behind her. It's the officer with the dark curls, the same one who couldn't understand why Julia didn't remember when the girls disappeared.

"I kissed James," Julia says. The lie is like the crack of a whip in the quiet room. "There." She points to the entry. "I kissed him right there, and I'm not one bit sorry for it."

Grace glances at the officer as if he can explain. He shakes his head.

"Pardon?" Grace says.

"There," Julia says. "In the entry. Because he came and you didn't."

The officer approaches the table, where he stands over Julia.

"Everything is pitch-perfect for you, isn't it?" Julia says, staring at Grace and ignoring the officer.

"Ma'am, who is Maryanne?"

"You have your fine husband, and soon, a baby of your own," Julia says. "Your house. Your friends. People think highly of you and James. They don't even realize Elizabeth was your fault too. Your fault as much as mine." Julia pauses, inhales, smelling the soap Grace squeezed into the bucket of water she used to mop up the food Julia threw across the room. "And now the twins are gone just like Elizabeth. No one will blame you for them, either. Only me."

"Ma'am, do you believe your husband has killed someone?"

"It won't always be this way, Grace," Julia says. "Your baby could die too."

It's the worst thing Julia could say to Grace, worse even than the kiss. It's the most hurtful thing. She's not brave enough or good enough to shoulder this pain alone.

Grace unties the apron around her waist and lays it over the back of a chair. While the heat causes Julia's hair to frizz, it smooths Grace's, makes it shine, even under the kitchen's poor lighting. Her cheeks are flushed and damp from the washing and scrubbing, but her eyes are dry and clear. She tugs on the blouse that hangs over her large stomach and clears her throat as if to say something. But instead she walks past Julia, past the officer waiting for Julia to give him an answer, and out the door.

———

Up and down Alder, porch lights shine as they did the night Elizabeth disappeared. But tonight, the air is cooler and easier to take in, even with the weight of the baby pulling at Grace's lower back. The ladies stand outside their screen doors, some of them wearing aprons even though they won't be serving supper tonight. A block and a half down Alder Avenue, the street is bright with porch lights and streetlights. Mr. Symanski stands under the nearest one, its glow hemming him in. As with Elizabeth's search, he has been left behind by the other men. When Grace reaches her own driveway, she stands near the back bumper of James's car. He didn't take the time to drive it around to the alley and pull it into the garage. He leaves it in the driveway whenever he thinks he might need it again soon.

There are three of them this time. They are silhouettes walking up the street. Mr. Symanski must see them too. They pass the Filmore, where the windows are mostly dark and the parking lot half full. When the three shadows reach the streetlight outside Mr. Symanski's house, they transform into three men. Grace walks into the center of the street. Still more than a block away, one of the men stops while the other two continue on. Even from this distance, Grace can feel him staring at her. He lifts a hand. She knows he is stroking his chin, petting it. She turns and walks back to her driveway.

These men don't bother with the alley anymore—haven't since Elizabeth disappeared, haven't since they took her and killed her. In the beginning, long before the neighbors began talking about the Filmore and the coloreds, they passed only in the night when the neighborhood was sleeping. They would leave their green glass scattered through the alley so someone would know they had been there, so someone would know they were coming. But they have gotten away with what they did to Elizabeth and to Grace and now they've taken the twins. They are proud. He is proud, and he flaunts it by walking where good people walk.

The car keys lie in the center of the front seat. James knows he should stop being so careless, knows the neighborhood is a changed place and he can't leave his keys lying about anymore. But there they are. Grace opens the door and picks them up, wraps her fingers around them, squeezes until the metal warms. She knows the house key because she has the same one in her handbag. The other key is too small. She tries the silver one. First one way, and then the other. It slides in. It turns.

———

With one clean hand, Malina reaches behind herself and catches the white ribbon that cascades down her back, descending from a delicate bow attached at her wide embossed collar. A back bow, the saleswoman called it. It's Malina's loveliest dress—a red-and-white floral print with an empire waist most perfectly suited to accentuate her slender figure. She does wish she had spent more time in the sun. A person might call her skin sallow, gray even. She could dab more color on her cheeks. That would certainly help. Yet her waistline is no larger than the day she walked down the aisle to join hands with Mr. Herze. For that, she is thankful and proud. But she does so wish she had soaked up more sun. Letting the ribbon slip through her fingers, she brushes her hands together and picks up the decorator's bag.

She begins by cupping the white triangular bag in one hand so the large end stands open and the narrow end hangs toward the table. Next, she scoops up a spoonful of icing and drops it inside. Another few scoops and she folds over the wide end of the bag, squeezing it slowly until icing drips from the tip. She licks her fingers, wraps one hand around the small end, and places the other above the bulge of icing. Already, ten cakes have been iced and a scalloped edge drawn on each. Because it's so hot in the house, the trim has slid off a few of them and is melting down the cakes' sides.

It will be payday again. Eventually. It comes quicker than any other day. Even before Mr. Herze comes home, Malina can smell it. She smells it every day now, so maybe payday doesn't matter anymore. That sweet musky smell will stick to Mr. Herze's collar. She'll fill the kitchen sink and soak the shirt overnight. A year of paydays has passed since she first smelled it. She didn't know what it was in those early days. Only that it was a sour, unforgiving smell that seeped into her house and she could never quite scrub it away.

She squeezes the white bag and icing drips onto the cake. Too warm. A scallop won't hold its shape if the icing is too warm. The consistency is so important, the most important thing, really. Not quite as stiff as the icing she uses to sculpt leaves and rose petals, but thicker and drier than what she uses to ice the top and sides. Hold the bag horizontal to the cake. Give it one short burst of pressure to lay down the wide end of the shell, then let up. Slowly draw the tip forward and tap it to the cake to cut off the flow. A single perfect scallop. She had thought the weather was cool enough, but the house is too warm. She should have opened more windows. Her scallop droops and melts over the edge. She straightens the bag and begins again.

Another cake is done. It's all Malina can do today. The bake sale would normally have taken place in a few short weeks but they changed the date because Elizabeth Symanski disappeared and now they know she is dead. Now the cakes will have to set another few weeks. Shame Malina didn't think of that earlier.

Malina lays the icing bag on the table, unties the apron from around her waist, wipes her fingers on it, and tosses it on the dining room table. In the foyer, she slips off her sensible two-inch heels and steps into the white stilettos with the slender toes. They are more suited to the red-and-white dress she wears. Admiring the curve of her delicate ankle, she rolls her foot in a slow circle. First one and then the other. Her calves, so perfectly formed, haven't changed in all these years. So lovely. Taking a deep breath that makes her chest lift up and her lungs fill, she grabs the ribbon that flows down her back and walks toward the side door.

Eventually the child will outgrow that carriage. Eventually it will walk down Willingham, doughy and soft like Mr. Herze. It will be a creamy brown color and will tuck its small fist in its mother's dark-brown hand. Eventually it will be tall and walk with a gait like

Mr. Herze, shoulders rounded, hump at the base of its neck, always seeming tired, worn-out. Eventually everyone will know.

Eventually, someone will begin to suspect Mr. Herze killed that woman. They'll discover that the woman, before she died, spoke poorly of the child in the carriage, and Mr. Herze, like any man, would protect his own. It's the only reason a good man would kill. But then, someone, eventually everyone, will tap their heads and purse their lips and think a wife would do the same. Mistakenly, accidentally, she would do the same. She would lash out with the only thing she had in hand if suddenly she realized her husband was father to another woman's baby. And lastly, they'll realize as they should have in the first place, that it was the mother. Wouldn't the mother—the girl—kill to protect her child? Wouldn't that be most likely of all? And the man who loves the mother—the girl—would protect her because he is good. He would bring home the hammer that did the killing and put it back as if that night, that terrible night, never happened.

A man who would do these things doesn't covet the baby's mother because she is thin and slight. He protects her and so he must love her. Nor does he covet the twins across the street who skip through sprinklers and trample lovely snapdragons. He watches those twins with a longing, missing the children he could never have with his wife. He watches those twins and imagines the day his child by another woman does the running and skipping and laughing. He loves the baby and he loves its mother. Eventually, someone, everyone, will know.

Within hours, the men will end their search, if not because the twins are found, then because they must rest and prepare to begin again tomorrow, and Mr. Herze will come home. The police will realize Mr. Herze and Malina saw the twins last. If Malina is wrong, and Mr. Herze looks upon the twins with a foul sort of longing, the police will discover it. They will wonder why Mr. Herze would make a gift of those flyers and they'll discover the truth. Surely the police will discover it. If they don't, Mr. Herze will in due course remarry. This new wife won't tolerate a house tainted by Malina. This new wife will be thin and slight and she'll insist they move north, where the yards stretch out and the homes are newly built. The twins will be safe because Malina is gone.

Letting the screen door slam shut behind her, Malina crosses the drive and walks into the garage, where she makes her way through the bags and boxes, sidestepping them, trying not to damage the dangling hems and cuffs. The last of the clothes are ready to be delivered to the thrift store. Clean and folded, properly mended. Someone will see to them. The key to Mr. Herze's storage cabinet hangs on the pegboard inside a carefully drawn line right next to the hammer. Both of them, a perfect fit. Outside, voices shout—Izzy, Arie and Isabelle, Arabelle. Engines rattle to a start, screen doors slam shut, dogs bark at strangers in their yards. Surely, someone will see to all these clothes.

CHAPTER TWENTY-EIGHT

J ames tried a few times to teach Grace. When they were first married, she practiced in the parking lot at St. Alban's on a Saturday afternoon. He had placed her hands on the steering wheel and kept one of his own on it to guide her. "Like this," he had said. The car sprung forward when Grace jammed her foot into the gas pedal. And when she pressed too hard on the brake, James fell, both hands reaching for the dash. He laughed, pulled Grace to him, and kissed her hard on the mouth. "Eyes forward and straight ahead."

Father never taught Grace to drive because he died before she was old enough to learn. Several summers passed before she and Mother boarded the *Ste. Claire* again. Mother taught herself to drive during those years after Father died and took a job as a receptionist for Ford. In the summer of 1946, she pulled on a linen jacket and her best Sunday hat and said it was time to get on with it.

Grace had no urge to run ahead of the crowd that year and felt no tingle when her feet hit the wooden gangplank. She was one of the ladies now, tall as any other. Her waist was narrow, her neck slender, her frame strong and straight. As it had been every other year, she heard him before she saw him. The musicians paused and there was that burst of laughter. When the music began again, he spun past, another girl whose hair color Grace doesn't remember in his arms. He had thinned out during his years away. Many of the men had that look, as if they had been forced to go without. He had noticed her and smiled. He remembers this smile but says it wasn't the first. He says the first was when Grace was a child. That's romance talking, not reason.

First she lowers the gearshift into reverse. Then she taps on the gas. The car lunges backward. Again, another tap. It rolls and jumps past the sidewalk and bounces off the edge of the curb. In the middle of the street, Grace pulls the gearshift down, and with her eyes forward and straight ahead, she rolls the steering wheel, one hand over the other like she has seen James do so many times.

The one won't move out of the way. Grace knows this. Because she didn't tell the police. Because he knows her as he does. Because he took Elizabeth and now the twins. Because she wouldn't let Orin fire. Because he feels he belongs, the one won't move. The others will, and they do. As Grace starts down Alder Avenue, stomping on the gas so the car gains speed, the other two scatter. One of them is probably the kinder man with the tired eyes. One dives to the left, one to the right, where Mr. Symanski stands. Only one stays his course, not moving from the middle of the road. He's daring her, wanting to make a fool of her, wanting to prove she can't change what has happened and that some part of him will always live inside her. She jams her toe to the floorboard. Had James been in the seat next to her, he would have braced himself. There is a loud thump. The silhouette flies up and away. It's gone.

The car is still now. Inside, the air is warm and thin as if she has used it all up and there is nothing left. The only voices are muted but slowly they become louder. There is yelling, screaming. She lies across the seat, one hand on her baby, waiting. She closes her eyes.

———

One of the officers stares down on Julia, his shoulders square, his black shoes planted wide. Another stands behind her, a hand on her chair as if afraid she might try to run from the house. He has written down the name Maryanne in his small notebook. A third stands in the front room, occasionally speaking into a radio that crackles and hums. Grace must have closed the door as she left, because a burst of air blows through the house and out the kitchen window when someone opens it again. Small feet run across the linoleum entry into the kitchen. Julia lifts her head. The twins rush in, bringing with them the smell of outside—sweat-stained shirts, dirt under their nails, unwashed hair. They run to Julia, throwing their slender arms around her neck, smothering her with their warm bodies.

"Aunt Julia."

She can't tell which one is which because they've buried their faces in her hair. She wraps an arm around each. Bill stands behind them. He wears a white shirt buttoned at the collar and cuffs. He waits there, making sure they are well and then turns to leave.

"What did you do?" Julia says, the girls' slender bodies pressed to her cheeks, one on either side.

An officer holds out a hand, signaling Julia should stay in her seat and Bill should not move.

"What did you do to them?" she says again.

The two girls back away from Julia. "He found us, Aunt Julia. Don't be angry."

"Your mother's place," Bill says, and then he faces the officer, talking to him and not Julia. "Few miles north on Woodward and east a couple blocks."

"You're lying," Julia says, standing though the officer behind grabs her shoulder.

"No, Aunt Julia."

One of the girls hangs from Julia's wrist, but Julia yanks it away and the twin stumbles.

"It's him," Julia says, pushing back from the table and standing. Her chair topples. "Tell them, Bill. Tell them you killed Maryanne."

"Mrs. Herze said we'd never find Patches," one of the girls says. "She said our cat was dead and that we ruined her flowers. We didn't. We didn't ruin those flowers. We went to find Patches. We went to Grandma's to put out our flyers. Mr. Herze made them. Every one exactly the same. But we didn't know which street to take. We couldn't find her house."

"Tell me, Bill," Julia shouts.

Hair hangs in the girls' faces in stringy clumps because they never took that bath. One is crying. It must be Arie. The other has red cheeks and her fists are clenched. Izzy.

"Stop it, Aunt Julia." It's Izzy. Arie is crying too hard to speak. "Uncle Bill found us. He was there at Grandma's. He knew he'd find us there."

There are more officers in the kitchen now. Too many. It smells like vinegar and the black leather shoes they wear. The stiff soles click across the floor, probably will leave black scars. And those blue uniforms. They are too heavy in this heat. The officers sweat in them and their sour odors fill the house.

"I was glad," Bill says.

He lifts his eyes to Julia.

"God help me, Julia, but that morning, when you found Mary-anne. For an instant, I was relieved."

Julia falls back into her chair.

"It exhausted me. All those nights. All that crying." Bill turns from Julia to the officer at his right. Talking one man to another, he says, "I couldn't stop myself, couldn't stop feeling that way. God, for an instant, I was relieved." He coughs into a closed fist. His voice breaks. "What man feels that? What father? What kind of a father feels such a thing?"

The curly-haired officer stands at Bill's side. Outside, the shouts for Izzy and Arie have stopped. No more footsteps on the front porch. Upstairs, a door shuts and water begins to run. The twins are gone.

"I didn't hurt her, Julia," Bill says. "But I think it's worse, what I did. What I felt, the relief, I think it's worse."

The officer with the brown hair pulls on his hat, tucks his pad of paper under one arm, and walks from the kitchen. Bill stands alone, his arms hanging heavy at his sides. His hair is matted and his neck is speckled with red spots where he's scratched at bug bites.

"How did you know to find them there?" Julia asks, staring at the small chip in her red tabletop.

"Didn't know for sure. Figured it was that damn cat of theirs."

"I felt it too, Bill."

"No, you didn't. That's a lie. Don't you tell me that lie."

Julia shakes her head. "I did. It was as if I hadn't exhaled since she was born, and then I did. It was that quick. Every day, I think about the things I didn't know, about the things I could have done to help her."

He is crying now. Softly, like sometimes a man does. His eyes red and wet, his face streaked with the sheen.

"I'm no kind of father."

"You're as good a father as I was a mother."

"That's not true."

"It is, Bill. We're peas in a pod. No different."

"I can't do it again."

Julia stands on her toes and wraps her arms around his neck. The night air is tinted with smoke. Fireworks or perhaps somewhere a neighbor is burning yard waste. The shirt Bill wears must be his brother's. The soft cotton smells of a day drying on the clothesline. Outside, a crash rings out. There are shouts again and running feet. There is a loud pop, as if a car has backfired, and the police run from the house. Izzy and Arie appear at the bottom of the stairs, or maybe they've been there all along. And then Arie says, which is surprising because Julia would have thought Izzy would be the one to say it, "Sounded like a gunshot."

CHAPTER TWENTY-NINE

On hands and knees, Julia dips her sponge in a bucket of warm, soapy water and squeezes with both hands until it runs dry. She crawls a few feet, presses the clean sponge to the baseboard, and begins again. Leaning on her left hand, she scrubs with her right until her shoulder burns. She straightens, dips the sponge in the water again, which is quickly becoming cold, squeezes and wrings it, and rests it on the side of the bucket.

The baseboards haven't been cleaned in three years. The oak wood shines, almost looks yellow where she has scrubbed away the haze of dust and dirt. She pulls off her rubber gloves, turning each inside out as she tosses them to the floor. The crib is the only thing left in the room, and Grace is the only person who might have use of it. Many of the ladies have given Grace things over the past several months—clothes, quilts, diapers—but Julia never offered. Even though the crib was used only a short time, what mother would want to lay her child in such a bed—one where another baby died? Or would the kiss be the thing that stopped Grace from accepting the crib? That's what Julia thought during the three days Grace was in the hospital. But then she was released, still pregnant with a healthy baby, and came to see Julia.

There was silence when Grace entered Julia's house. They stood together in the foyer, where Julia had said she kissed Grace's husband.

"I've come to apologize," Grace had said.

"You should sit," Julia said. "Put your feet up."

Grace shook her head. "I've worried about the girls all summer, you know."

"Yes," Julia said. "But you have nothing to apologize for, Grace. Nothing. I'm the one who should be apologizing. What I said about James, about the kiss, it was a lie. Such a terrible lie."

And then Grace told Julia. She told Julia about three men—two of them faceless and one whose face and hands and smell Grace knows better than her own. One man who Grace knows so well he must live inside her even now. Julia looked at Grace's stomach and nearly tripped as she stumbled away. Grace shook her head. No, the baby belongs to James. The men came only a few weeks ago, the night Elizabeth's shoe was found. And as soon as Grace said it, Julia knew they were the ones.

"Elizabeth," Julia whispered.

It was true, after all. Elizabeth didn't wander off down Willingham to the river and find trouble far from home. Those men took her from Alder Avenue, from right outside her own house. They spared Grace, but they killed Elizabeth.

"No," Grace said.

But Grace only said that because it was Julia's fault Elizabeth was there for those men, Julia's fault Elizabeth was such easy prey, Julia's fault they could take Elizabeth from her own front yard.

"I know what you're thinking, Julia. But I promise you, it wasn't your doing."

Again, Julia offered Grace a seat. Grace shook her head, walked toward the door, and placed one hand on the knob.

"The one who is dead," she said, "the one I hit, I knew it was him. I wasn't hoping to find the twins when I got in that car." Her voice broke. She swallowed and continued. "I thought the girls were already gone. I thought it for certain. It wasn't an accident. I wanted that man dead. I thought he'd killed Elizabeth and taken the twins. I was wrong. So now I have to say I killed him because of what he did to me." She paused and looked at Julia for the first time since she began talking. "What he did to me, is that reason enough?"

Upstairs, the girls were quiet. They were in their room, or maybe listening at the landing.

"James?" Julia said.

Grace shook her head, knowing what Julia meant to ask. She meant to ask if Grace would ever tell James about the men.

"He'd never forgive himself," Grace said. "Mother thought he wouldn't want me after it happened, but she was wrong. It's the guilt that would destroy him. I think he knows that too. Deep down, I think he knows that too. I can't do it to him, to us."

When Grace said it was time to get home, Julia asked her to wait a moment and rummaged through the coat closet's top shelf until she found the belt the twins had stolen. She couldn't repair the hole Arie dug in the thin leather, but returning it was the right thing to do.

"Could you give this back to Mr. Symanski?" Julia had said. "The girls, they stole it. Tried to tell me it was yours, that it was trash from your garage. I can't imagine what they were thinking." She ran a finger across the small buckle that sparkled where Arie had scrubbed it clean. "I remember Elizabeth wearing it. One of her favorites. Do you remember?" She stretched out her arm, handed the belt to Grace. "I know I'm a coward for it, but I can't bring myself to face him."

Grace stood at the front door, one hand resting on the silver doorknob. "I suspect they did find it in my garage," she said, shaking her head and pushing away the belt. "You let them keep it. And talk to Arie, would you? Tell her I'm going to be all right." She pulled open the door and paused on the porch as if enjoying the feel of the sun on her face. "Promise you'll believe me. Promise because you are my dearest friend and I wouldn't lie to you. What happened to Elizabeth . . . it wasn't your fault."

Regardless of whether Grace will want the crib or not, Julia can't take it apart without Bill's help. She was able to lug the small dresser downstairs by packing up all the tiny clothes, removing the drawers, and carting them down, one by one. She'll ask Bill what he thinks when he comes in from outside. He's been out back for forty-five minutes, struggling to tighten rusted screws and bolts so Julia's clothesline won't droop. But she doesn't really need to ask. She knows Bill will say to save Grace the heartache and give the crib to the church. Give it to them and don't tell them to whom it once belonged.

"What are you doing, Aunt Julia?"

Huddled together in the nursery doorway, the girls lean into the room but don't cross over the threshold. Both have wet hair. They took their baths without being asked, a sign they are trying to make up for running off.

"You'll both need a trim soon," Julia says, pushing off the floor. "A nice haircut before school starts."

"Where did everything go?" Izzy's voice bounces off the walls, almost echoes in the nearly empty room.

The girls must have peeked into the nursery at some point over the last three years. What child wouldn't? A mysterious door that is always closed. Of course they peeked. Julia motions with her head for the girls to come inside.

Izzy is the first to move because she isn't afraid. She is never afraid. She marches across the small room, opens and closes the closet door, and then walks over to the window, where she waves at Arie to join her. The air is light and crisp this morning. Izzy draws a deep breath in through her nose. Across the street, the windows in Warren Herze's house are dark, the driveway empty. He'll likely move soon and eventually he'll remarry. He could never stay in that house. He could never walk into that garage again.

"I owe you two an apology," Julia says, and motions for Arie to join her inside the room. "I should have known you were gone. I left you both alone, and I'm sorry as I can be."

"We thought you'd come the first night," Arie says as she walks up next to Julia and leans into her until their bodies touch. Arie is warm and smells of soap and shampoo. She stares at the crib sitting alone in the corner of the room. "When it got dark," she says, "we thought you'd miss us and that you'd come looking. We walked all night."

"Will we lose privileges?" Izzy asks, resting her head against Julia's arm. Her damp hair leaves a wet stain on Julia's sleeve.

"You two should stay," Julia says. "Stay here with Uncle Bill and me. Not live at Grandma's anymore. Go to school here and live here. Izzy, this could be your room to have all to yourself."

"What about that?" Izzy says, pointing at the crib.

"We'll give it to someone with a baby," Julia says. "Would you girls like to stay? To have your own rooms? Here with Uncle Bill and me. We'd like it very much if you'd stay."

"Can we paint the room blue?" Izzy asks.

"Yes," Julia says. "Blue would be a fine choice."

———

It's a perfect day for rolling dough, cooler, drier. This may have been Grace's problem all along. But the heat hadn't caused trouble for the women of Willingham. Their pierogi had turned out perfectly and are tucked safely in Grace's freezer. If she had gone back to Nowack's Bakery, if she would ever go back, the women would make more, but there won't be a bake sale this year. Without Malina, there may never be another. Grace pushes her wooden pin over the smooth dough, her large belly only allowing her to reach halfway across the table. She straightens, stretches, and the baby rolls, settling on a more comfortable position.

When the water boils, Grace drops in her first pierogi. She stands back, but not so far that she can't see inside the pot. White foam trims the small crescent-shaped dumpling, but the seal holds. No leaks, no swollen, waterlogged center. Soon, it floats, bouncing along the rolling boil. Grace sets her timer for two minutes. When it dings, she reaches in with a wire ladle, scoops up the noodle, and taps it out on a sheet of waxed paper. After she fishes two perfect pierogi from the pot, she adds them three at a time, gently stirring so they don't stick. Soon enough, two dozen are done. When they are cool to the touch, she lays them in even rows in a casserole dish, each layer separated by a sheet of waxed paper, and covers the entire dish with aluminum foil. At the back door, she pulls on her gloves and hat, grabs the casserole dish and a paper bag full of Elizabeth's clothes, and walks from the house.

Grace doesn't go to Willingham anymore. She and James will move soon, and she'll have to find a new place to do her shopping. By the time they settle in their new house, she'll be a mother. She may not want to shop every day anymore. She might go only once or twice a week. Julia sometimes calls to see if Grace needs anything from the deli or the bakery. She always says no, thank you, but stop in for coffee when you get home. Julia and Bill won't move now, but maybe someday.

The door to Mr. Symanski's house opens.

"I am knowing that smell," he says.

"They won't be as good as Ewa's."

"Yes," he says, taking the brown bag from Grace. "I am thinking they will be very close."

Grace pauses inside the house, adjusts to the emptiness, and then follows Mr. Symanski into the kitchen. She sets the casserole dish on the stove and removes her gloves and hat. Mr. Symanski reaches into the brown paper bag he set on the counter and slowly, by its lavender sleeve, pulls out the dress lying on top. To afford Mr. Symanski his privacy, Grace turns toward the sink.

"I thought you'd want to keep some of her things," she says.

She can't bring herself to look, but probably Mr. Symanski is touching the dress's tiny white buttons the women reattached.

"It was always being her favorite," he says.

Grace pushes off the counter and turns. "She was wearing it the last time I saw her, Charles."

He sits at the kitchen table, letting the dress lie across his lap. His silver hair has gotten too long and it brushes against his white-collared shirt. Ewa would have never let it grow so long.

"I am not being able to sleep with her things in the house," Mr. Symanski says. "That is why I am giving them away. The police, they scolded me for doing it, but I am not being able to sleep."

"Yes," Grace says.

"It was being afternoon, you know. The river, it's one of the only places I am remembering anymore. So many years working down there. I am thinking the river would take her away and it would be seeming as if it never happened. Such a big river. Wouldn't you be thinking the same?"

Grace pulls out a chair and sits opposite Mr. Symanski.

"Charles?"

"It is being a horrible thing to be the last one," he says. "You are knowing this, yes?"

"Yes."

"I am not wanting Elizabeth to be last. Not wanting her to be alone. They are saying she would never be so long with us. I am trying to outlive her, but it is too difficult. What would have become of her if she is being the last one left? I am just too tired to carry the thought."

Grace reaches across the table, but Mr. Symanski doesn't take her hands.

"I am thinking someone would hear the noise." His eyes drift off to the right as if he can see Warren Herze's house, but he can't. "The shot. No one heard. No one came. I am not wanting her to die in her favorite dress," he says. "So many people looking for my Elizabeth. That was being most painful. I am knowing maybe I was wrong. Maybe she wouldn't have been alone. And then I am wanting her back so badly I am hoping the men will find her. I am believing they might and that she will be coming home. I am sitting with all of you ladies, hoping they are finding her."

Grace stands, walks around the kitchen table, and sits in the chair nearest Mr. Symanski.

"I am not wanting her to be the last one left," he says. "But I am thinking I was wrong. This is being why the river didn't take her away."

Grace stays with Mr. Symanski until she knows James will be home soon. She won't leave him to wonder where she is. He worries so much after all that has happened. He worries these bad things will seep into his own home and taint what is good. He worries like Grace used to.

"You'll be telling who you must," Mr. Symanski says at the front door. "I am not caring for myself. You are knowing this, yes?" He blinks slowly. "If you cannot be telling them while I am alive, tell them when I'm gone. It will be soon. Every day, I am feeling closer to my Ewa, and Elizabeth, too. They are being together. No one is being alone but me."

Grace pulls Mr. Symanski's hands together, lifts them to her lips, and then lowers them to her stomach. He smiles at the kicks and rolls he feels there. A few cars drive past. There are three For Sale signs in the neighborhood now. A fourth sign will soon go up at Orin Schofield's house. He'll move south to live with his daughter and her family. Others in the neighborhood, those without the money to move, will stay and do what they can to keep a nice yard and well-tended house.

No one talks to one another like they once did. People say two of the Negro families have moved away, but Grace never saw them come or go. She never saw them living alongside her. Green glass still litters the back alley some mornings. Though James fusses at her, Grace continues to clean it up. Some of the other neighbors leave it, only kicking aside the larger pieces and shards that might flatten a tire.

James and Grace won't sail on the *Ste. Claire* this year because the baby is so close to coming. But they have already agreed. On July 4, they'll drive to the foot of Woodward and watch as the passengers gather on the gangplank, and after everyone has boarded, the ship will pull away, drawing a lazy wake behind her. Steam will flow from her stacks, and the hollow horn will blast, echoing through the streets of downtown Detroit. It'll be a lonely sound and, for a time, Grace will feel something has been lost. But then she'll remember the shine on the brass railings and the glossy dance floor where she first fell in love with her husband. She and James will watch and listen until the boat disappears down the Detroit River, leaving behind an empty stretch of water. They'll take their own daughter one day and they'll always arrive early to secure a spot in the front of the line so the railings and the fittings will shine as if never before touched.

At the end of Mr. Symanski's sidewalk, Grace pushes open his iron gate. The latch is broken. Tonight, over supper, she'll ask James to fix it. She and James, together, will come this weekend to trim Mr. Symanski's lawn and invite him for Sunday supper. Grace will make a roast and potatoes and Mr. Symanski and James will watch baseball on the television. Bill and Julia and the girls will come for dessert. The girls like to sprinkle salt on the ice when James makes ice cream. Then they'll sit outdoors until long past dark. On the other side of the gate, Grace pulls it closed and walks toward home.

ACKNOWLEDGMENTS

It has been my great fortune to again work with the wonderful Denise Roy. My deepest thanks to you, Denise, for your suggestions, observations, and insights and for knowing my characters better than I know them. My thanks, also, to Brian Tart and the entire team at Dutton and Plume for their support of my work.

Over the past few years, during which I have had the privilege to work with Jenny Bent of the Bent Agency, I have learned that perseverance is a most important quality in an agent. Jenny is a shining example of this trait. My thanks to you, Jenny, for never giving up, for your honesty, and for your guidance.

I would again like to thank Karina Berg Johansson and Adam Smith for their friendship and for wielding those red pens with abandon. Thank you to Stacy Brandenburg for the laughs and to Kim Turner for the ongoing support.

My thanks to Orville and Evelyn Roy, Suzanne Lanza, and Michele Moons for sharing their memories of the great city of Detroit. My thanks to my mother, Jeanette, for inspiring dedication and to my father, Norm, for being the first storyteller in my life. Supper continues to be late at my house and the laundry is never caught up, so, once again, thanks to Bill, Andrew, and Savanna for always understanding.

And finally, as I once worked in the corporate world, I know there are a great many people laboring on behalf of my books who I never get a chance to work with directly or to thank. So my thanks to all of you in sales, publicity, design, editing, distribution, inventory control, IT, HR, legal, finance, tax, manufacturing, and all other Penguin divisions I may have forgotten. And because I once was one . . . thank you to the accountants.

ABOUT THE AUTHOR

Lori Roy was born and raised in Manhattan, Kansas, where she graduated from Kansas State University. Her debut novel, *Bent Road*, was awarded the Edgar Allan Poe Award for Best First Novel by an American Author, named a 2011 *New York Times* Notable Crime Book, and chosen as a 2012 Notable Book by the state of Kansas. *Until She Comes Home* is her second novel. Lori currently lives with her family in west central Florida.